PEARL HARBOR

PEARL HARBOR

TRAGEDY TO TRIUMPH

GERRY FELD

OTHER TITLES BY GERRY FELD

A Journey into War
Published in 2017

A Soldiers *Final Journey*
Published in 2019

Vietnam Honor and Sacrifice
Published in 2020

Sarah Rosenbaum's Dachau Redemption
Published in 2021

PT Boats; Terrors of the Pacific
Published in 2021

Sister Dominique's Incredible War
Published in 2023

PREFACE

On September 23, 1970, the epic movie *Tora, Tora, Tora* came to the big screen. It's considered to be the most factual film ever produced about the attack on Pearl Harbor. The movie was derived from the story "Tora, Tora, Tora" that was written by Dr. Gordon W. Prange in 1963 for the November and December issues of *Readers Digest*. The material was then transferred to book form under the title of, *At Dawn we Slept*, which was published in 1981. Doctor Prange added two more books about the attack titled *December 7, 1941, The day Japan attacked Pearl Harbor*, and *Pearl Harbor: The verdict of History*. Today, many historians consider these three books to be the most accurate trilogy of Pearl Harbor ever written. They are superb reading.

And yes, for all you skeptics, I have read all the works published by John Toland and Henry C. Claussen that have attempted to rewrite the history of the attack, but none of their writings have ever changed my mind as to the official facts.

Although this is my seventh book, it is the book I always wanted to write, but was not sure how to make it happen. My first try was purely factual, but would have been no different than any other historical account. Then I tried a pure fictional story, but it left me wanting, so both books were relegated to the back waters of my computer.

Eventually, I decided to write a historical account while placing my fictional characters into the overall larger story. It took some time to work out all the details, but eventually it came together.

I did a tremendous amount of research from a variety of sources, to assure the accuracy of my details, and delve into some of the smaller aspects of the attack many people have never known about, but make the story much more interesting.

This manuscript was actually started nearly four years ago. As I worked on my other books, I continued doing new research on Pearl Harbor. I read hundreds of historical documents, dating back to 1921, some I had seen before and others that were new to me. I took stacks of notes and tried to make sure each document was accurate and could be substantiated.

Finally, I decided I was ready to write my story about Pearl Harbor. The longer I worked on the first manuscript, the more I disliked it. So, with nearly 150 completed pages, I shelved it. As I was finishing *PT Boats; Terrors of the Pacific*, I decided to start over with my Pearl Harbor story, but from a different angle. That effort seemed awkward and I just could never make it work, so with nearly 125 completed pages, I shelved that as well.

As I finished *Sister Dominique's Incredible War*, I decided to start again. There were parts from both books that I really liked, so I began the task of cutting and pasting the material around a new base story.

This book contains a tremendous amount of historical information that is needed to tell the true story of the attack. But what we will never know is what took place behind all those closed doors as world leaders fought over tough decisions. After nearly fifty years of reading and studying the attack from both perspectives, I have come to know many of the major players on both sides of the Pacific quite well. I know their quirks, their fears, and how they agonized about their own decisions, and how they felt about other government officials involved in this difficult decision-making process. Due to my extensive study, I feel comfortable taking literary license, in an attempt to add examples of possible conversations that took place in those top-secret meetings in both Washington and Tokyo. I think having some idea of what took place behind those closed doors adds intrigue and drama to the overall story.

I hope you enjoy this account of the attack that changed the world forever and moved the United States into the atomic era.

****

All of the actual historical characters and each of the ships that were involved in the attack in one way or another have an asterisk by their names. That notation is used only once for each ship or individual. Times noted throughout the story are local times.

DEDICATION

There is no way a book about Pearl Harbor could be written without dedicating it to all the brave men that were caught up in the attack on December 7, 1941. Many of those that were killed so suddenly died without knowing what was happening or why. Those that survived the opening salvo went on to fight back, becoming the backbone of the United States Navy as it rebuilt. They trained new men, and helped devise new equipment that would be needed as the war progressed. Most never received any medals or awards, they just did what they knew had to be done.

Such a book should also be dedicated to all the families, friends, and relatives now gone, that waited for months to receive word of the fate of their loved ones that were stationed at Pearl Harbor that morning in December. Sadly, many men could not be identified, or even found, as in the case of the *USS Arizona, USS Utah* and *USS Oklahoma,* so many family members never knew the true fate of the loved one they cherished.

As always, I also dedicate this book to my wife JoAnn, who spent countless hours talking with me about how the book should be put together, and offered me many ideas and suggestions for consideration.

CONTENTS

Preface...i

Dedication iv

Rape of Nanking vii

The Rainbow Plan xii

Chapter One – The Bronx, New York City.................... 1

Chapter Two – Preparation.................................. 10

Chapter Three – The Orphanage 15

Chapter Four – Montana 20

Chapter Five – Tokyo, Japan 29

Chapter Six – San Diego, California......................... 39

Chapter Seven – Fears of war Deepen....................... 47

Chapter Eight – 1940 The War Expands 53

Chapter Nine - The USS *Honolulu* meets Honolulu 58

Chapter Ten – The Threat Grows 72

Chapter Eleven – The Akagi 81

Chapter Twelve - The Plan is Set 87

Chapter Thirteen – Things are Heating Up 92

Chapter Fourteen – Alerts and Confusion 99

Chapter Fifteen – Final Message............................ 105

Chapter Sixteen – Where to assign planes.................. 109

Chapter Seventeen – *Tora Tora Tora* 118

Chapter Eighteen - The Morning of Glory 128

Chapter Nineteen – The Wives 144

Chapter Twenty – Second Attack 159

Chapter Twenty-One – Fighting Back 171

Chapter Twenty-Two – Aftermath 197

Chapter Twenty-Three – Lady Lex... 207

Chapter Twenty-Four – Battle of the Coral Sea 217

Chapter Twenty-Five –Battle of Midway 253

Chapter Twenty-Six – The Return 308

Addenda.. 324

Epilogue – America 364

Epilogue – Japanese.. 371

Government Inquiries 375

Final Comment... 380

RAPE OF NANKING,
the first unprovoked attack
against America by Japan 12-12-1937

Many of history's greatest minds have agreed that World War Two began when Japan invaded China on July 7, 1937. As usual, they attacked without provocation, waging a war of utter destruction without any regard for human life. By August of 1937, they had run into heavier resistance than was expected as fighting continued around the city of Shanghai. The fighting was brutal and bloody with many instances of hand-to-hand combat, but that did not deter the Japanese commanders who had their eyes set on the city of Nanking. It was China's Capital city at the time, and was the site of America's oil assets in the far east.

As the Chinese forces began moving out of the metropolitan area, Japanese forces destroyed what was left of the city and killed an unknown number of civilians. As the Chinese Army continued retreating south, Japanese forces followed close behind, destroying everything in their path. On December 12, 1937, as Japanese General Matsui Iwane,* commander of Japan's Central China Front, approached Nanking with a force of nearly 100,000 soldiers, he decided the people involved in resistance needed to be taught a lesson that would break their spirit and will to continue fighting. He ordered his men to destroy the city, doing whatever they felt was necessary.

Over the next six weeks, his men looted and burned buildings, committed mass executions, and committed countless rapes of women and girls. When the army left the city, they had killed 150,000 Chinese soldiers that had surrendered, 50,000 civilian males, and had raped and murdered 20,000 females of all ages. It did not take long for the world to refer to it as the, "Rape of Nanking."

President Roosevelt was stunned when the British Embassy called the White House around midnight on December 12, to inform him of the Japanese attack on American forces near Nanking. The ambassador told Harry Hopkins,* the president's chief aide, that the information had been verified through the British Consulate in Singapore. During the attack on Nanking on December 12 at 1330 hours, the American gunboat Panay* and three American Oil Company tankers were anchored in the Yangtze River near the American Oil Company Terminal. The Panay had two assignments, first to provide protection for the tankers as they moved up river, and secondly, to help evacuate the balance of American Embassy workers and journalists from Nanking. Most of the rescued Americans were already on the Panay, when at 1337 hours, a lookout on the stern of the boat reported Japanese bombers approaching from the south. As the first two planes began strafing the ships, the third plane dropped a hundred-pound bomb that crashed through the roof of the Panay's Control House, seriously wounding Lt. Commander Hughes*, the skipper of the Panay. Several more bombs struck the vessel as machine gun bullets ripped into the thin hull. It was impossible for the crew of the Panay to return fire at the aircraft, since all their guns were positioned in place to strictly fire at shore batteries. Immediately, the call to abandon ship was given by the Panay's executive officer, Lt. Arthur Anders.* However, that made no difference to the pilots of the aircraft that then dove in low, strafing the survivors in the water.

During the air attack, a small Japanese gunboat arrived on scene, adding machine gun fire to the already chaotic situation. With the Panay sunk and the oil tankers burning, the only safe place for the survivors to take refuge was back on land in the oil terminal.

Several days before moving up river to the oil terminal at Nanking, the crew of the Panay had taken extra time to paint large American flags on the top deck and sides of the boat. Additionally, Lt. Anders, XO of the gunboat, stated emphatically that he had notified the Japanese command of what their mission was, and where they would be anchoring near the oil terminal.

Colin McDonald,* a New York Times reporter, was aboard the Panay during the attack. He stated that he watched a Japanese patrol boat continue strafing people in the water, as the damaged Panay sank into the river. He stated the American flag on the hull of the boat was clearly visible to the crew of the Japanese patrol boat.

Two days later, three rescue gunboats arrived. One was the USS Oahu,* the other two were British boats, the HMS Ladybird* and HMS Bee*. All three boats had sustained moderate damage from Japanese shore batteries as they sailed up the Yangtze, but were still in operable condition.

All the embassy workers and journalists were spread out among the two British boats, as the Oahu took on the wounded and dead. In all, three American sailors and eleven civilians were killed, while forty-three sailors were wounded, along with five civilians. All of the wounded were taken to the closest hospitals in Shanghai. There is no way of knowing how many other civilians were killed by machine gun fire and sank into the depths of Yangtze.

After inquiring a second time to make sure all the details had been confirmed, President Roosevelt looked coldly at Harry Hopkins and said, "Set up a meeting for 0900 hours with my war council."

At 0900 hours, the president was wheeled into his second-floor office where Secretary of War Henry Stimson,* Secretary of State Cordell Hull,* Chief of the Army Gen. George C. Marshall,* Secretary of the Navy Frank Knox,* and Chief of Naval Operations Admiral William Leahy,* stood patiently waiting.

After positioning himself near the fireplace, the president began. "Well gentlemen, you have all been briefed on the Panay incident, what the hell are we going to do!"

Henry Stimson shook his head. "This is bad, Mr. President, but we are not ready to go to war with Japan. It would be a drastic mistake for us to attack over this incident. We must find another way out."

Cordell Hull nodded his head in agreement. "Sir, we need to send an immediate cable to the Japanese, telling them this kind of behavior must stop, or military action will be required!"

General Marshall scoffed at Hull's statement. "What military action would we take, Mr. Secretary? We don't have the planes to bomb Japan, nor do we have the forces to attack the Japanese in China. Tell me, sir, what kind of action do we take?"

Before Secretary Hull could respond, Admiral Leahy spoke up. "General Marshall is right. There is no place we can militarily go after Japan, without creating an international incident larger than the Panay issue. We need to be careful here."

Walking closer to the president, Frank Knox said, "Mr. President, I think we should send the Japanese a stern message. The news is already out on the street, and people in New York are protesting in favor of military action. We need to let the Japanese know we will not allow this incident to go unpunished. You must get a message to them today!"

After several more rounds of discussion, the president raised his hand. "Alright, gentlemen. I can see everyone wants some sort of message be sent to Tokyo, and I concur. But I do not think bringing up military action right now would be the proper thing to do. I believe the Japanese might look at that as a declaration of war, and we would have a larger mess on our hands than we are prepared for. I will have Harry write up a message and get all of you copies before I send it. If you do not agree, let me know immediately."

About 1300hours on December 13, FDR send a stern message to Tokyo regarding the attack and loss of American lives. Now it would be a waiting game to see how they would react.

December 14, at 1000 hours, a message arrived at the State Department from Tokyo. The Japanese Government apologized for the incident, stating things had gotten out of hand, and they were not fully aware of what was taking place. They added that neither the pilots or the crew of the gunboat had seen the American flags before starting their attacks. Tokyo promised the United States slightly over two million dollars in reparations, which they did pay. Most newspapers in the United States felt nothing more could be done over the issue, and published stories that the Panay issue was properly dealt with and closed.

Although the issue over the Panay was closed, it gave the Japanese war council a good indication as to how unprepared the United States was for a war that was lurking over the horizon.

THE RAINBOW PLAN

In 1890, the United States first decided to construct a series of war plans they could have on file, for any nation that decided to attack. It was called the Rainbow Plan, as every nation they thought might be belligerent toward the United States was given a color to identify the specific plan.

Japan was given the color orange, so the battle plans for a war against Japan was labeled War Plan Orange. The original planners felt the United States would need to pull back from any islands they held in the far Pacific, while pulling all warships into their respective ports from which they could be directed to go out to sea and defeat Japan.

The plans provided intricate details on how each phase of the war was to proceed. Over the years the plan was changed and modified, becoming more complex until 1906, a year after the devastating defeat of Russia in the Russo-Japanese War. Everything now needed to be re-examined.

Immediately, the United States began planning for an all-out war with Japan, which required a complete rewrite of the entire plan of organization. After World War One, Japan became more prominent on the world stage, and had the desire to build a large navy, such as those of the United States and the European victors. Additionally, the League of Nations confirmed Japan's right to hold the islands they had taken from Germany during World War One. It was becoming more obvious that Japan was planning to be a major player on the world stage, despite what anyone wanted because of their militaristic background.

In 1920, the United States began to realize they could be caught up in a two-ocean war and changes to the plan were essential. By 1924, the United

States decided Japan would be a probable enemy, attacking the Panama Canal, Hawaii and possibly the west coast. The revised plan took the position that any war with Japan would be limited mostly to an all-naval affair, as planners felt there was no chance Japan could attack, seize and occupy these targets without full naval support. In order to have American sea power in the western Pacific, it would be essential for the United States to have a large naval base in the region. It was decided the base would be at Manila Bay in the Philippine Islands. The new Orange Plan now had a contingency to hold and reinforce the Philippine Islands as soon as possible, in the event of a war with Japan.

Planners decided it might even be necessary to invade Japan to bring the war to an end, but no further action was written into the Orange Plan on that matter.

By 1938, the plan had been changed and rewritten nearly a dozen times, giving both the Army and the Navy their own set of Orange directives. The final plan in 1938 removed the possibility of invading the Japanese homeland. The plan stated if Plan Orange could not bring Japan to its knees, they would have to take, "Such further action as may be required to win the war."

As Japan's war with China was going well, and they were expanding their island holdings, once again the plan was rewritten. Now the United States wrote specifically which islands they would seize to form a secure line of communications to the western Pacific.

By 1940, planners decided Japan would send a force of 100,000 men to capture Manila and its harbors, severing its line of communications with the United States. The plan also stated Japan might move forward with this plan before a declaration of war was made. Planners felt it would happen in either December or January, after the rice crop was harvested, and that there would be multiple landings.

Every effort would be made to fight off the Japanese ground forces before withdrawing to the Bataan Peninsula. This new plan stated that within six months, the American Fleet would be able to resupply the forces on Bataan while taking control of the western Pacific.

However by April of 1941, most American war planners were convinced such a battle would never take place, but if it actually did, most likely it would take the United States navy two years to fight its way back to the Philippines. Army leaders woefully stated all supplies on Luzon would be exhausted within six months, and the garrison would go down to defeat.

Plan Orange always maintained that attacks would come in the western Pacific, especially in the Philippines before Hawaii would be attacked. Planners felt if Japan attacked Hawaii, it would be on a weekend, most likely on an early Sunday morning, and without a declaration of war. That was the one piece of Plan Orange that turned out to be accurate.

Right up to Dec7, 1941, military leaders in the War Planning Department still held as fact that if war broke out in the Pacific, America would be prepared.

When you arrive at the WAR WARNINGS section of the book, you will notice Chief of Naval Operations Admiral Harold Stark refers to the Orange Plan as WPL46 (War Plans) section 46, while Chief of Staff George C. Marshal refers to Rainbow 5, which was Japan's color section in the Rainbow Plan.

CHAPTER ONE –
THE BRONX, NEW YORK CITY

From the late 1800s through 1940, many Italian immigrants settled into a community known as Little Italy in the Bronx. They were hard working people that took care of each other and attempted to handle their problems without intervention by the police or outsiders.

Because of the skills they brought with them from Italy, many people opened small shops, restaurants, and other facilities any normal town would need to function.

Frederico Santucci and his wife Maria were no different than any other Italian immigrants when they arrived at Ellis Island. They were sponsored by Maria's aunt and uncle that had arrived in the United States five years earlier. Maria was a well-qualified seamstress that actually owned her own sewing machine, and Frederico was a machinist by trade. It did not take long for either of them to find jobs in businesses owned by Italian entrepreneurs.

With a modest income, they soon moved out of Maria's aunt and uncles apartment into a small but adequate apartment of their own. To fulfill their dream, Maria soon became pregnant with their first child. They were proud parents when their daughter Dierdra was born. She was a healthy happy baby that Maria could take to work, ensuring the families income would continue to pay the bills. Eighteen months later, Maria delivered a strong healthy boy named Carmine. After his birth Maria quit her job, and began offering custom sewing out of their apartment.

Although Dierdra was rather quiet and reserved, Carmine was a rough and tumble boy with olive skin and a bushy crop of dark curly hair, that appeared to need cutting all too often. He was a likable lad and quickly made friends with a group of Italian boys from the neighborhood with similar families to his own. Carmine's favorite part of the week was Saturday's, when his mother took the children to the theater to watch Gary Cooper Westerns. The rest of the week Carmine would play out the movies with his friends, and reenacting many shootouts on Belmont Ave. Sometimes the boys would draw an audience of older people, just to see who was going to survive the shootout. But bedtime came early on Saturday nights as Carmine was always expected to be an altar boy at St. Raymond's Church on Sunday morning, just a few blocks from their home.

Father Vincent loved having Carmine as an altar boy, as he never left without making sure everything was put away properly after mass, while chastising the other boys for being lazy and trying to skip out without finishing their tasks.

Both Carmine and Dierdra were good students and enjoyed going to school. At night they would work with their parents, teaching them English, as neither of them had a very good grasp of their new adopted language.

Attending high school was hard on the children of Little Italy, as they had to travel by bus to a school several miles away that was mostly attended by white children. Fights often broke out among the boys, especially if an Italian boy gave special attention to a white girl. It did not take long for Carmine to learn the art of street fighting, and he was very good at it, partly because of his size.

When Carmine turned fourteen, Maria became very sick. She could no longer work so Frederico needed to work extra hours to assure the family was well taken care of. Frederico took Maria to several doctors in Little Italy, but none of them could figure out what the problem was. After Maria collapsed one evening and could not be revived, she was taken to a hospital in the lower Bronx. Three days later the doctors told Frederico she had some sort of brain tumor. No one knew much about her condition, they simply told Frederico she was going to die, and two days later she passed.

Frederico and the children had an extremely hard time with the loss of Maria. Now Frederico began spending time in bars and coming home drunk.

He became abusive to the children and began missing work because he was too drunk to do his job.

After being fired from the machine shop, Frederico took a low paying job as a street sweeper. Although he was making much less money, he was able to get handouts from market owners that felt sorry for his plight. Nevertheless, after showing up drunk one morning and hitting another worker, he was fired once again.

Unable to find a job because of his drinking, Frederico decided it was time to move away from Little Italy and start fresh. Years earlier he had met a young man that had come to New York to sell livestock from his father's ranch in Montana. After Frederico repaired his trailer, the man told him if he ever needed a job, he should come work on the ranch in Montana, as there was always repair work to be done.

So, Frederico decided to take Carmine on a road trip to Montana to find a job and begin a new life. He took Dierdra back to Maria's aunt and uncle, telling her when he found a place to live, he would send for her. Although Dierdra was upset about not going along on the trip with her father and brother, she was happy so see Federico happy and excited about life again.

With a small loan from Maria's aunt and uncle, Frederico packed all he could into the family station wagon, then headed west with Carmine. All was going well until the car broke down in Madison, Wisconsin. A mechanic was able to get it back on the road again, but the repair bill sucked up a tremendous amount of money. By the time they reached St. Cloud, Minnesota, there was not a penny left for gas or food. Sitting in a park along the Mississippi river, Frederico pondered the idea of getting a job. But he knew by the time they would have enough money to continue their journey, the winter snows would be blowing across the great plains and it would be too dangerous to cross the Rocky Mountains.

That night as they slept in the car, Frederico gave serious consideration to robbing a bank and heading west immediately so they would never get caught. When he had enough money saved up, he could send it back to the bank to repay them. The more he thought about the idea, the more sense it made.

The following morning Frederico drove around St. Cloud looking for a bank that appeared to be an easy target. Finally, he decided the Granite Bank on the east side of town was exactly the right place as there was little traffic in the area.

Turning off the car in the parking lot, Frederico looked at Carmine. "Son, I'm going into this bank to get some money. You stay right here unless the police show up, then run as fast as you can."

Feeling scared, Carmine looked at his father. "Is there no other way to get some money? I don't want anything to happen to you. We also must think of Dierdra."

Patting his son on the head, Frederico replied. "Everything will be alright, son. We will be on our way in just a few minutes, and soon you will be riding horses on the ranch."

Carmine nodded his head. "I will do as you say. Be careful."

Entering the bank, Frederico placed his hand in his jacket pocket and took hold of a pistol Carmine knew nothing about. Walking up to a teller, he pointed the gun at the young woman saying, "Please do not cause me any trouble. Just fill that green bag with money from your drawer, then everything will be fine and I will leave."

The terrified woman immediately cleaned out her cash drawer, filling the bag as she had been directed. Handing the bag to Frederico, she said. "That is all I have, please do not shoot me."

Nodding his head, Frederico began backing away from the counter, turning toward the door. A tall man with a long beard yelled out at him. "Drop the bag and your gun. No body will get hurt, and you can go free."

Turning around, Frederico looked at the pistol in the man's hand. "I have a child to feed, and I need gas to get to my new job. Please do not cause me any problems."

The man did not reply, he simply pulled back the hammer on his pistol, glaring at Frederico.

"You won't shoot me," Frederico said, as he turned once more toward the door.

A second later the old man pulled the trigger, sending a bullet across the lobby of the bank, striking Frederico in the left side. Instantly, Frederico spun around and returned fire, striking the old man twice. As the man fell to the floor, Frederico stumbled out the door toward the car where Carmine screamed in horror as he saw the blood on his father's jacket. One of the tellers ran toward the door getting a good description of the car as it sped from the parking lot.

Frederico fully understood that he was about to die, leaving his son all alone in a strange city where he knew not a soul, but there was nothing he could do now to change the situation. Driving into a wooded area, Frederico turned off the car. Handing the green bag to Carmine, he said, "You must run now. Keep thinking about Montana, you can get there if you try. Get a job and send for your sister as we planned. She needs to be with family."

As blood ran out of his father's mouth, Carmine said, "No Papa, you cannot leave me like this. I do not want to go on without you, I need you!"

Coughing up more blood, Frederico said. "This is all my fault, son, your mother would never have wanted me to rob a bank. This country has been good to us, go now and be proud you are an American. Make a good life, Carmine."

Just as Carmine was going to respond, his father took his last breath. For nearly half an hour, Carmine sat in the car as his mind swirled in several directions. Part of him wanted to return to Little Italy, as it was all he ever knew. Part of him wanted to forge on to Montana, as his father asked him to, but it was so far away and he was all alone. He was only fifteen years old, and now the world was against him.

Finally, Carmine removed the billfold from his pants and stuffed it into the green bag along with the money. After kissing his father on the cheek one more time, Carmine slid out of the car, removed the license plates, and ran deeper into the wooded area. Picking up a sharp stick, Carmine dug a hole in the ground big enough for the green bag and the New York license plates. After removing fifteen dollars, he placed the bag in the hole, covered it with dirt and tamped it down with his foot. After spreading leaves and grass over the area, he pitched the stick into a pond several yards away.

Now he had to come up with a plan to get to Montana. As he sat on a log, he heard a train whistle in the distance. He had read stories about men jumping on freight trains and riding cross country. Listening to the wail of the far-off whistle, Carmine decided that was the perfect way to get to Montana, no matter how long it took him.

He had walked about a mile when he heard sirens heading east out of town. He knew that somebody had found the car and now the police were heavily involved. Coming to a railroad track, Carmine followed it across a large bridge over the Mississippi river. Minutes later he was walking through a large rail yard where switch engines were building trains from cars that were parked on several side tracks.

Knowing he had found the place to find a train heading west, Carmine knew it would be a good idea to stay away from the woods until the next day before going back after his money. Having had nothing to eat in nearly two days, Carmine was starved. Seeing a small hotel with a restaurant near the rail yard, Carmine walked in and sat down at a booth. What he did not see, was the bank teller that had run to the door of the bank. She was seated at a table on the far side of the restaurant with her parents.

Standing up slowly, the bank teller walked over to a phone booth, turned her back toward Carmine and called the police. Just after Carmine ordered a hamburger, mashed potatoes and a glass of milk, three officers came into the restaurant and walked over to where he was seated.

An officer wearing sergeant stripes looked down at Carmine. "Stand up young man, you need to come with us."

Carmine looked up at the officers. "I just ordered a meal, I haven't eaten in two days. Honestly, I haven't done anything wrong!"

The sergeant shook his head. "Son, we know who you are. Your Pa robbed a bank today and shot a man. Someone saw you in the car as your Pa drove off. Please don't make this any harder, just get up and come with us."

Knowing there was no way out, Carmine stood up and closed his eyes as an officer placed hand cuffs on his wrists. Arriving at the police station, Carmine was placed in an interrogation room that had a long table, three worn out chairs and a dim light bulb overhead.

Moments later, a large man wearing captain's bars came into the room sitting down across from him. "Your father got you into a bit of trouble today, son. Tell me what your name is?"

Carmine was quiet for a moment before responding, "Cooper."

The captain nodded his head, "Cooper what? What is your last name?"

Carmine sat quietly, not saying a word. After several moments, Captain O' Conner said, "You were not in the bank, so we can't charge you with that. But we can charge you as an accessory. Your car doesn't have plates on it, are you from another state, what are you doing in Minnesota? Where were you going?"

Once again, Cooper sat quietly without saying another word. Leaning back in his chair, Captain O' Conner said. "You were ordering food when my men arrested you. Are you hungry?"

Carmine just looked at the table refusing to talk.

"Fine!" Captain O' Conner said. "We'll place you in a holding cell over night and see if you want to talk in the morning. What happens next is totally up to you."

After laying on the bunk for about an hour, an officer opened the cell door. He handed Carmine a white bag that smelled pretty good. "The captain had a chicken dinner brought over for you, and I brought a magazine you might want to look through."

After the cell door was closed, Carmine tore open the bag, devouring the food faster than he had ever eaten a meal before. Laying back on his bunk, he paged through the magazine slowly until he came to an advertisement for Dodge cars. Smiling, he decided the next day he would tell the captain his name was Cooper Dodge. After repeating the name several times, Carmine smiled. He thought it was a proper name for an old west gun fighter. A name even Gary Cooper would be proud of.

The following morning a social worker named Gus Admore was assigned to talk to Carmine. "So, how did you like your chicken last night?"

Carmine replied, "I've had better."

"Someone went to a lot of work to get you that meal last night, you know. You should be grateful," Mr. Admore replied.

"Not my problem," Carmine replied, looking down toward the floor.

Gus Admore nodded his head. "So, tell me, what's your last name? They told me your first name is Cooper, is that accurate?"

Looking directly at Gus, Carmine replied, "To be honest, I never really had a name, at least one I really liked."

Shaking his head, Admore said, "Everyone has a name, son. It won't kill you to tell me who you are. My name is Gus Admore. So tell me, who might you be?"

Carmine laughed. "Your name sounds phony, like you just made it up. Am I supposed to be excited that I'm sitting with the great Gus Admore, advocate for the poor and wretched? Because if that's the case, I'm not."

When Carmine had finished speaking, Admore slapped him across the face and pulled his dark hair. "Look punk, that is not how you treat an adult. Now, let's try this one more time!"

Carmine glared at Gus Admore and said, "So, that's how you were taught to treat another human being? Is this how you get your kicks? Bang around some poor defenseless kid, pull his hair and yell at him. Now I'm supposed to have respect for you, is that how this works?"

Captain O'Conner opened the door to the interrogation room, looking sternly at the angry social worker. "Put him back in his cell and let him cool off a bit. We'll talk with him later. Maybe by then he'll decide that cooperating with us might be the best thing to do."

Two hours later, Carmine was walked into the interrogation room once more. Looking at the captain he said. "If I tell you my name, what happens next"

Captain O'Conner smiled. "Well, I can't make a deal with a boy with no name. So, if you work with us, there is quite a bit I can do for you. It's all in your hands. In fact the guard at the bank will pull through alright from his wounds, so you have that in your favor.

Looking frustrated, Carmine stared up at the ceiling for a moment. "Cooper Dodge is my name, and no I don't know what my real name is. I was living on the streets of the Bronx when those people took me in. They thought I should be called Cooper, so I figured that would be a good name for me. The people that took me in had the last name of Dodge, so I just started using their name. I have been Cooper Dodge most of my life. Where I came from, I have no idea. I lived with a lot of people when I was a little kid, so I don't know who my parents were.

Nodding his head, the captain looked compassionately at Cooper. "How old are you, son?"

Cooper laughed and slapped the table. "Cut me in half and see if I have rings like a tree, then you and I will both have an answer to that question."

Captain O' Conner chuckled as he sat back in his chair. "So, the man you were with is not your father?"

"He and his wife took good care of me for a few years, so I kind of adopted them. He was an alright guy, and he generally treated me well."

Looking sternly at Cooper, the captain asked. "Now son, where is the money he took from the bank? You were in the car, so where is it?"

Cooper laughed, "How the hell should I know? We were speeding down one street after another and he tossed the bag out the window. Someone must have picked it up when they saw what was inside."

Slamming his fist on the table, Captain O'Conner yelled. "Cooper, or whatever your damn name is, you are nothing but a damn liar and a juvenile delinquent. I'm tired as hell of dealing with you, and I know you know where that money is. So here is my best deal. You tell us your real name, your father's real name, and where the money is, or I'm going to send you to the orphanage here in town and have them hold you until you are ready to cooperate. If you think you can snowball me you are sorrily mistaken, boy. And if in one month you aren't ready to cooperate, I'm going to have a judge send you to the reform school in Sauk Centre. Maybe then you'll wish you had been straight with me."

Cooper sat quiet, wishing he was back in New York and they had never started out on this trip. Now he was alone and in the biggest mess of his life, and he could see no way out of it.

CHAPTER TWO –
PREPARATION

As a child, Keisuke Mori loved standing on a hill overlooking the gravel airstrip west of Tottori Japan watching the colorful bi-planes. His heart would almost skip a beat every time he watched the pilots do wild turns and then zoom toward the earth at an incredible speed before once more reaching for the sky. When he was in middle school, he made a deal with the owner of the airfield to do maintenance work in exchange for flying hours. Soon Keisuke mastered the owners bi-plane and was able to attain his license. Now he began seeking out a career where he could fly and get paid for it, and he knew his answer was at the new navy airbase at Kyoto.

The staff at the base were impressed with Keisuke's flying skills but informed him he would need to attend Etajima Military Academy* if he wanted to be a pilot in the Imperial Japanese Navy.

With the blessing of his parents Keisuke applied for a position in the upcoming class. He studied relentlessly for the entrance exam, scoring the highest grade of the three hundred men that applied.

In order to not disgrace his parents, Keisuke studied tremendously hard, overlooking many social events that otherwise could have occupied his time. Like many young men, he was not out searching for a woman to be his wife, as his father had already arranged a wedding with a young woman that lived nearby. They would be married when he graduated from the academy.

Since entering the academy and spending time at several naval bases, Keisuke dreamed of nothing else but flying a carrier-based fighter or bomber. The day after graduation with his diploma and pilots license in hand, Keisuke applied for the naval air wing of the rapidly growing Japanese Navy.

This was the hurdle that worried Keisuke the most. He would have to sit in a room filled with high-ranking Japanese naval officers and experienced pilots and sell himself to them. He had to prove to these men that he had the intestinal fortitude to fly one of Japan's specialized attack aircraft. In all reality, this was the toughest part of the selection process, as it had been decided long ago that Imperial Japan was to be known worldwide for high-quality and daring combat pilots.

After his acceptance into the program and a short leave to be married, Keisuke reported for three months of pilot training at the large naval airbase at Hiroshima. With all the experience he had gathered flying the old bi-plane back in middle school, he became the top pilot in his training squadron. That assured him placement in a new attack wing that was being formed. What kind of plane he would fly did not matter, as that would be decided by the wing group leader, Commander Kimura, a hard charging and daring pilot who accepted no excuses.

Two days after moving over to the far side of the airfield where the new attack wing was being assembled, Lieutenant Keisuke Mori smiled brilliantly as he walked around the Aichi dive bomber he had just been issued.

As he stood looking up at the powerful radial engine that would take him and his two-man crew up to the heavens and out over the vast expanses of the Pacific Ocean, he felt humbled. He smiled when he saw his name stenciled below the canopy cockpit. From now on, dive bomber 1165 would be his aircraft. His only desire now was to master this aircraft, and be looked upon by his superiors as an outstanding aviator that could be trusted to handle any assignment.

Before the rest of his crew arrived, Keisuke took several photos of his aircraft that he could send back to his wife Etsuko. She still lived in Tokyo with her parents. As soon as he completed his flight training, Etsuko would move to the airbase he was assigned to. Keisuke could not wait for that to happen, as his young wife wrote that she was already pregnant with their first child.

Several minutes later, Petty Officer Inoue walked onto the warm tarmac with two other men in tow. Shaking hands with Keisuke, the Petty Officer began. "I have brought your new crew. First is Ensign Masashi Kaneko, he will be your bombardier, and is qualified to be your co-pilot if you should be unable to operate the aircraft. This crazy man with the shaved head is Warrant Officer Haruto Ishii. He will be your spotter and rear gunner. They will begin their final training tomorrow, so they will be ready to take to the skies with you."

The following morning Keisuke climbed into the cockpit of a Mitsubishi training plane with a stern looking warrant officer in the back seat. Once the ground crew had approved the aircraft ready for takeoff, the warrant officer said, "Let's see if you can get this piece of equipment off the ground without killing both of us."

Keisuke nodded his head as he turned over the speedy engine. In mere seconds, the engine rumbled to life and settled down nicely. Once the engine was up to operational temperature, Keisuke radioed the tower for permission to taxi and takeoff.

Minutes later, the wheels of the trainer left the tarmac as Keisuke poured fuel to the engine. Following directions from the Warrant Officer, Keisuke put the plane through a series of tight turns and quick dives. Finally, the instructor gave him permission to head out over the Sea of Japan at an altitude of two thousand feet. The sky was a brilliant blue with only a few light clouds to the west. Keisuke had never seen the ocean from this altitude before, and was amazed by the many different shades of blue and turquoise, signifying the different depths of the water and the coral reefs.

The warrant officer smiled slightly at the way Keisuke was handling the aircraft in the updrafts coming off the surface of the ocean. "Now, put on your oxygen mask, climb to thirteen thousand feet, and follow the coordinates you have on your knee pad for Liancourt Rocks. If you can follow directions, we should be there in under ten minutes."

After checking out the coordinates and looking at his compass, Keisuke made a sharp turn to the port side and pushed the throttles forward to reach the recommended flying speed. Eight minutes later, the rocks came into view. Looking down at his knee board, the directions told him to circle the islands from the west, and then to begin his dive when ordered by the warrant officer.

Keisuke was about a quarter way around the rocks when his passenger yelled out, "Dive!"

Without hesitation, Keisuke dropped the nose of his aircraft into a steep dive, keeping his eye glued to a spot in the water, directly in the middle of the rock group. The plane screamed as it hurled to earth at an incredible rate of speed. Reaching 3,000 feet, Keisuke pulled back the fake red bomb lever and called out, "Bomb away!"

Grabbing the stick tightly, while operating the foot pedals that felt like hunks of lead, the plane quickly began to level off as it went into a wide turn back toward the west. It had been an exhilarating experience for Keisuke, especially when he realized he was only about two hundred feet above the water as he began his turn.

Clapping his hands, the warrant officer called out, "Brilliant, brilliant! You never showed a moment of hesitation or lack of judgment. You shall go far as a dive bomber. The history of our sacred kingdom has not yet been written, I can assure you that men with your talent will write our new history across the skies of the Pacific. Now, take us home, for we shall be out again tomorrow and the next day and the next, dropping sand bombs on moving targets from your dive bomber. You shall learn much."

The following day as Keisuke flew his Aichi bomber, he looked down from 13,000 feet at an old naval transport being towed behind a destroyer. The thought of diving on the ship appeared very daunting. His hands shook and his breathing was erratic when the warrant officer yelled out, "Dive!"

The heavy bomber he was piloting now, was much smoother in the dive, but it also had a tendency to gain speed much faster than the trainer had, but Keisuke was quickly able to adjust. The old ship now began to look enormous as the distance between ship and plane narrowed rapidly. Closing in on the aiming point on the bow of the ship, he placed his hand on the bomb release lever. Reaching 3,000 feet, Keisuke released the hundred-pound sand bag. As he screamed past the old vessel, he knew his bag had missed the port side by about five yards. It would have been a wasted bomb during a battle, but he still had the two sixty-pound sand bags under each wing to partially redeem himself. Pouring fuel to the radial engine, Keisuke quickly climbed to 3,000 feet, made a sharp turn to the starboard side and dropped over into a shallower dive. Releasing the bags at 1000 feet, they smashed into the steel deck, sending a puff of dust skyward.

Once again, the warrant officer clapped his hands. "Two sixty-pound bombs can create a lot of damage and kill many sailors when used well. Lieutenant Keisuke, you recovered from your miss and still damaged that vessel. You are amazing, and someday you will be a lead pilot on a carrier."

CHAPTER THREE –
THE ORPHANAGE

The Children's Home in St. Cloud, Minnesota was a nicely constructed brown brick campus staffed with sisters from a local convent, along with a very well-trained group of local residents. The grounds were meticulously mowed and the flower gardens always filled with bright colorful plants.

But what made this orphanage the same as any other around the country were the cries of the children. Cries for the mothers and fathers that had to give up their children in order to survive in the worst depression the United States had ever seen. No amount of human contact could ever replace the feeling of true comfort of being held by your own mother. Every night the cries of the lonely and frightened children filled the corridors and social rooms.

No matter how much nursing and care giving could be administered by the staff, there were always occasions when small children would simply just will themselves to die out of pain and sorrow. It was always a heartbreaking experience for the staff, and a tragedy that repeated itself all too often.

Rain poured down in sheets, as rivers of water flowed down the steep driveway leading away from the entrance to the Children's Home in St. Cloud, Minnesota. Slowly, a squad car from the Stearns County Sheriff's Department rolled to a stop under the large entrance canopy. As the gusting winds nearly ripped the back door off the patrol car, the deputy held onto his hat as he assisted Cooper Dodge from the back seat.

Seconds later, a flood of light from the large fixture above the door broke through the darkness of the storm. As the heavy wooden door creaked open, a Catholic sister of about forty years, pushed open the screen door taking hold of Cooper's arm. "Good evening, Deputy. We weren't expecting you for another half hour, yet. So, who is this young man?"

Looking angrily at the boy, the deputy responded, "Totally uncooperative, that's who. But he says his name is Cooper Dodge, so that's what the judge wrote on the documents."

After walking a short distance toward a large office, the deputy removed the hand cuffs from Cooper's wrists.

"Please sit," Sister Rosetta said, as she pointed to a chair near her desk.

"I would prefer to stand if it's all the same to you, sister," Cooper replied with a smile.

Sister Rosetta nodded her head as she smiled at Cooper. "No need to play the tough game with me, son. I am not here to judge you, question you, or punish you. You are strictly here to live with us until the county decides what they want to do with you. That may take a week, it may take a month or more. Now, please have a seat so we can talk."

Nodding his head, Cooper sat down without saying a word.

After looking over the paperwork the deputy gave her, Sister Rosetta asked. "So, you wish to be called Cooper Dodge, is that correct?"

Cooper nodded his head and replied. "It's the only name I can really remember."

"Well then, that shall be your name while you are here. We are going to be holding you in our secure ward for the time being at the request of the judge. It is not like jail, and you will still have an open ward, but there is screen mesh over the windows. There will be a book of rules on your bed that we expect you to follow, and you will have some type of work detail you must accomplish every day. Every child here has some type of job to do. Do you think that will work for you, Cooper?"

Once again nodding his head, Cooper replied. "Yes, sister, that will not be a problem."

After being escorted to his room by one of the orderlies, Cooper laid down and closed his eyes. No matter how hard he fought to hold back the tears, they gushed out and he sobbed as he thought about his father sitting dead in the car, his sister so far away in New York, and his mother who had held the family together like glue, no matter what the problem. Why had it all changed? What happened to the love he had grown up with? Slowly, he drifted off to sleep as the rain splashed against the windows.

The following morning around 7:30am, a woman named Charlotte Epstein walked into Cooper's room and woke him up. Good morning, Cooper. Breakfast will be served in about twenty minutes. We sure would like you to come out and join us. Still feeling totally starved, Cooper had no problem joining the other residents in the security ward for a hot breakfast.

Walking into the room, Cooper saw another boy about his age sitting by himself on the left side of one of the tables. Walking up to the boy, Cooper said, "Mind if I join you?"

Shaking his head, the boy stuck out his hand. "I'm Paul, Paul Darnell."

After Cooper introduced himself, the boys began to eat breakfast. However, Cooper quickly picked up the feeling that Paul Darnell was not his name, and that he was likely holding back his personal information.

That evening, with all the daily chores completed, Cooper sat down on his bed to read a magazine. Seconds later, Paul walked in and sat down by the small writing desk each room had.

"So, are you in trouble with the law?"

Cooper shook his head. "No, my Pa was, but he's dead now. The police are angry with me because I won't answer their questions or give them my true name. So, what's your beef, Paul?"

Laughing, he shook his head. "Some people adopted me so I could work on their farm. I guess I was supposed to be their legal slave laborer. One day the old man came after me with a baseball bat for refusing to load cow manure for the third straight night, while his real kid did nothing. Well, I took the bat away from him and smashed every window in the barn. Then I jumped on one of the horses and rode out of there, never to return. One of the damn neighbors saw me sleeping down by the river and called the sheriff. The people don't want me back, so the judge is revoking the adoption. I fought with the deputy when they brought me back, so here I am in lock up. Cooper, I can't stay here. Before I was adopted out to that farmer, I spent six years here. I need to find peace somewhere."

Laying the magazine down, Cooper looked seriously at Paul. "My Pa and I were headed to a job in Montana, and Pa asked me to get there before he died, so I'm going there, hell or high water. I know where the money is my Pa stole. If we can get out of here, we can dig up the money, hitch a train to Montana and go to work on a real ranch. What do you think about that idea?"

Paul looked dead serious at Cooper. "Is this for real? I mean, are you seriously planning to go to Montana and start a new life? If you are, I would like nothing better, so you can count me in."

Over the next few days, the boys began looking for a way out of the building, but could not find anything that would work. On the fourth day, Cooper and Paul were cleaning floors near the back entrance when the delivery truck drove up to drop off groceries. They noticed the driver unlocked the door, but didn't re-lock it as he rolled the cart full of boxes into the kitchen. Instantly, the boys were out the back door running full speed down the hill toward the Mississippi River.

As they approached a beef packing plant to the north of the orphanage, they made a quick turn through the employee parking lot. Finding an old pickup with the keys hanging in the ignition, Cooper jumped in behind the wheel and started the engine. Moments later, they were driving across the tenth street bridge, heading for the wooded area where Cooper had hidden the money.

With the bag in his hand, Cooper raced back to the truck and spun the vehicle around. He drove to a parking lot near a lumber yard that was just a few blocks from the railyard. From there they ducked down several alleys until they were safely hiding under a box car. They waited a short time to see if anyone was following them before they went searching for a west bound freight train.

After the delivery driver left the security building, Charlotte Epstein observed the mops and buckets sitting in the corner of the registration office. She quickly did a search of the building before reporting that Cooper and Paul were missing.

Both Sister Rosetta and Sister Evangeline stood quietly for a moment as they tried to make sense of what had just happened. After a moment of silence, Sister Rosetta spoke.

"Sister, I think it's your turn to call the Sheriff and tell them Darnell and Dodge have escaped. They are not going to be happy about an escape from the security ward, and those boys could be a real problem."

About three in the afternoon a train rolled out of the yard heading west with about forty box cars and a few tankers. The boys made a run for the fifth car, and were on board in a matter of minutes. They found some cardboard sheeting in the car, allowing them to make up a rather comfortable seat for the ride. They were nervous about what would happen with the train when it reached Fargo. However, all their fears were put to rest, as the train crew dropped off several cars from the back of the train, added several more tankers, and left their car intact.

They rolled on throughout the night until they were halfway across the state at Bismark. The train pulled into the yard and uncoupled all the cars from the engines. It took about two hours for a new train to be assembled, and the engineer once again began heading west. The boys quickly jumped on a car filled with new Chevrolet's that were all unlocked. It was a lucky break, as the night turned cold as rain fell for several hours. They stayed inside the Chevrolet's through the yard at Williston, North Dakota and on into Missoula, Montana.

CHAPTER FOUR – MONTANA

As the train pulled into the massive rail yard in Missoula, Montana, the boys jumped from the transport and walked into town. They stopped by a charity shop where they were able to get some clean clothes and a heavy jacket.

Cooper was dismayed when he called the number in his father's billfold, looking for the owner of the ranch. He found out the man had passed away, the ranch had been sold, and the new owners were not looking for any help, especially if they were under twenty years old.

So, for the next two days the boys looked around town, trying to find ways to get a free meal, so they could save the money they had for lodging since it was turning cold. However, garbage cans behind a truck stop ended up being their best bet for food. The third day, Cooper walked into a grain elevator to see if there was any work to be had for two industrious boys. Instead, he found a bulletin board with adds from ranches looking for all kinds of help. After questioning the clerk behind the counter, he quickly pointed out a man named Ed Wilkinson, who owned a large ranch nearby.

The kindly looking man sat down on the tailgate of his truck and spoke to the boys. When he decided to hire them, he asked for their names. Right away, Paul introduced himself as Paul Darnell. When the man turned to Cooper, he responded, "Coop, Cooper Dodge, sir."

Smiling, the man shook his head before standing up, "I guess I'm not too sure those are your real names. Tell me, are either of you in trouble with the law?"

Both Cooper and Paul stated that they were not in trouble with the law, but just down on their luck with no families to turn to.

Nodding his head, the rancher replied. "Well, I guess I'm willing to take a chance. Jump on the back of the truck, and I'll bring you out to the ranch. We'll find you a place in the bunkhouse, give you a good hot meal, then put you to work in the morning. There's always a lot of work to do on a ranch as big as the Double D, so I guarantee you boys will learn a whole lot real fast."

As the Ford pickup pulled onto the road, Paul looked over at Cooper and laughed. "Cooper Dodge. That name still makes me laugh a little bit, but what the hell, I don't even have a clue what my real name ever was."

Cooper had to laugh, "If the deputy in the jail hadn't given me a magazine to read, my last name may have been Smith or Jones."

Paul nodded his head, "It suits you, my friend. It has a nice ring to it. From this point forward, you will always be known as my friend, Cooper Dodge."

Arriving at the ranch, Mr. Wilkinson turned the boys over to his top wrangler, John Winthrop.

After setting up the customary file for new employees, he walked them over to the large bunkhouse, assigning them bunks fourteen and fifteen.

After sitting down on bunk fourteen, he smiled and said, "You boys are lucky to have this job. I have been with the Wilkinson family for nearly ten years. These people treat you right and pay a fair wage. Both Ed and I expect you to earn that wage, and the food you are fed. I will not tolerate anyone abusing the Wilkinson hospitality or kindness. You screw up, I'll fire you on the spot, no questions asked. Right now, we have just seventeen men working on the ranch. All good cowboys and all willing to teach newcomers. So, the boss says you don't have much for clothing, but that's not a problem. We sometimes have workers that take off with just the clothes on their backs, and leave the rest in their lockers, or get new and don't have a use for the old ones. We wash them up, mend them if needed, and store them in the back room by bunk twenty-four. Go ahead and help yourself to whatever works for you. Make sure you grab a hat, you'll need one. Once you get paid, we expect you to go into town and buy yourself some boots. Until then just wear what you have on. We'll serve supper around five-thirty in the chow hall next door. Breakfast is always at five o'clock sharp, and then it's straight to work after that. I'll be the one handing out the work assignments each day. If you have any questions, make sure you ask."

After searching through the clothing rack, Cooper and Paul each found some nice clothing that fit them well, and they each grabbed a black cowboy hat. Although they were nervous about what they had just signed up for, many of their fears were put to rest during supper. The other crew members were polite and funny, and willing to share stories about how things were done on the ranch.

Over the next several weeks, Cooper and Paul were assigned to paint the Wilkinson home and the main garage, help stack hay bales into a warehouse, and in the evening, feed the cows after they had been milked.

Often, late in the evenings they sat around a large fire and listened to some of the hired hands play guitars, fiddles, and mandolins, as they sang old western ballads.

After about six weeks on the job, the boys were taught how to ride a horse, rope a steer, and shoot a pistol, in case they ran into snakes out on the prairie. Cooper took to horses like it was second nature, but Paul was thrown several times before he learned to let the horse know who was in charge. They were tremendously excited when they were each allowed to pick out a horse from the small herd that would be their ride as long as they worked on the ranch. Paul chose a black horse that had three white stockings, while Cooper picked out a buckskin that appeared to have a lot of spirit. They had several weeks to get accustomed to their new rides before everyone packed up for the long trek up to the mountain ranges, where about three hundred steers had spent the summer months. Now it was time to bring them down to the corrals before the snow set in.

Learning how to round up the strong-minded steers and the young new stock that had been added two months ago was a real experience. It took long hours in the saddle before all the animals were collected and ready to be driven back down to the ranch.

One evening after helping to clean up the chuck wagon, Cooper walked over to the horse corral to brush down his horse and feed it some carrots. He had only been there a couple of minutes when Paul came walking up. After sitting down on a large boulder, he looked over at his good friend.

"Coop, do you ever think about going back to New York to find your sister, or doing something else besides ranch work?"

Smiling, Cooper leaned against his horse. "Yeah, I think about my sister quite a bit, but I'm sure she is doing well. She was getting ready to start nursing school when Pa and I left. So, I'm sure she's doing alright."

"Coop, you know you could write to her. She might be interested in what happened to you and your Pa since you left," Paul responded as he looked up at the stars.

After tying off his horse, Coop sat down next to Paul. "Yeah, I have thought about that, but every time I start, I end up ripping up the letter. I just don't know how to tell her what Pa did and how it all ended. Hell, I can't even tell her where our Pa is buried because no one told me. I guess maybe someday I'll figure it out. As far as work goes, I always enjoyed watching the ships come into the navy yard when I was growing up. I wondered where they had been and what the sailors had seen. Who knows, maybe I'll join the navy in a few years."

Paul sat quiet for a moment before responding. "Yeah, I think sailing around the world could be interesting. I'll need to think about that too."

Returning from the cattle drive, all the men spent a good deal of time in town. Cooper and Paul were no different as they enjoyed the night life, and most bar tenders never asked their age since they were ranch workers. During those visits to town Paul instantly fell in love with a girl named Sadie Merchant. She was a gorgeous blonde with a smile that lit up her entire face. What was more interesting to Coop, was that she fell in love with Paul just as quickly.

Throughout the long winter, any time Paul was able to break away from the ranch, he was gone like a rocket and could be found in the company of Sadie.

As spring of 1938 rolled around, it was hard for Coop to realize they had already been working on the ranch for nearly eighteen months. He knew he had done more and matured farther than most boys that were seventeen years old, and he loved being a ranch hand.

After the cattle were brought back to the ranch in the fall, John Winthrop the ranch foreman, took Larry Baxter up into the high country to look at a spot to build a new summer bunk house and stable. They had been gone for two days when a massive snow storm blew down onto the ranch from the high mountains. The crew on the ranch worked day and night, attempting to round up all the milk cows and get them into the milking barns before they died in the blizzard. They knew the beef cattle were stronger and could manage in the nearby feed lot.

As the storm began to die out on the third day, Larry's horse walked into the yard, the saddle covered in blood. Ed Wilkinson was positive both Larry and John had succumbed to the storm, but was nervous about sending a search party into the mountains.

However, the following morning, Coop asked if he and Paul could head up to the high country to see what they could find. Although Mr. Wilkinson was positive nothing more could be done for his men, he listened seriously to Coop's plea. Ed knew Coop had all but adopted John as his father, and would probably go no matter what he decided. After a long talk about safety, and where they should search, Ed gave his blessing for the mission. During the night Coop and Paul loaded everything they felt was necessary, including rifles, pistols, and a good first aid kit in case they were attacked by wolves.

The following morning the two young men rode out, heading northeast into the mountains. With the wind still howling out of the valleys, the men tied on their hats and wore heavy scarves across their lower faces as they rode higher up into the Anaconda Mountains. There were many stories dating back to the 1860's of men that had been lost in these rugged mountains during a blizzard, never to be seen again. Paul and Cooper prayed they would not suffer the same fate.

As night began settling over the mountains, Coop and Paul set a course for an area they knew quite well, that had several caves they could take shelter in. By 4:30pm, the men were in the largest of the three caves, where they could get their horses out of the wind. Using small saws they had brought along, they cut branches off nearby trees to start a fire.

Throughout the long night, the sound of wolves howling in the dark was enough to make any man's blood run cold. The following morning as they loaded up their horses, they found wolf tracks a mere ten feet away from the entrance to the cave.

The wind had finally subsided and the sky was crystal clear, with the brilliant sun making it almost impossible to see. By 10:00am the men had made their way up one of the locations Ed had thought about building the summer crew quarters. They rode the horses around the flat area to see if the horses would stumble on a body that had been covered by the snow, but they found nothing. Looking over a map of the ridge line, the boys rode a bit father toward the northwest, where another small plateau was located. There was less snow cover on this area as the wind had blown much of it over the top of the ridge. Coop had ridden about half way across the plateau when his horse came to a full stop and began backing away.

Handing the reins to Paul, Coop walked forward slowly, until he saw what appeared to be the outline of the head and shoulders of a man, leaning against a large rock out cropping. Walking over and brushing the snow off the man, it became evident it was the body of Larry Baxter. There was a large gash on the back of his head, and his clothing had been torn and shredded by wolves. Paul looked down at Larry for a moment. "I'm guessing wolves attacked him while he was on his horse, then pulled him off and he slammed his head into the rocks"

Digging into the snow, Coop found Larry's pistol on the ground aside of him. The six-shooter had three empty chambers. Looking over at Paul, he nodded his head. "You probably have the scenario right." Walking back to his horse, Paul stumbled over something covered by the snow. Brushing it off, he found the carcass of a dead wolf.

"If there's one, there's probably more," Coop said, as he turned and looked farther down the ridge line. "Let's move farther north, there may be some other caves along the rocky outcroppings we don't know about."

They had gone about a hundred yards when Paul spotted what appeared to be a dead horse laying in the snow near a cave. Both men dismounted as they walked toward the horse a few yards in front of them. Paul was about to kneel down to see what he could find under the snow, when they heard a familiar voice. Turning back toward the north, they saw John Winthrop leaning against a large boulder near the entrance to a cave, with his left leg in a splint.

John held out his hand to the men as he smiled. "You guys are a sight for sore eyes. I was hoping someone would come looking for us, but coming up this high in the mountains in these conditions is risky as hell."

Paul explained about Larry's horse returning to the ranch, and the decision to start the search.

John shook his head. "That storm came up so fast we were totally caught off guard. My horse stumbled on some rocks under the snow and threw me off. That's when I broke my damn leg. I could see bones sticking out of her front leg as well, so I knew we had to put the old girl down. We could hear wolves in the distance, so we decided to take cover in the cave, but we knew they would come after Larry's horse first thing and there wasn't room inside. Larry decided he would head down the mountain to get help. It was a risky proposition, but we didn't have many choices. He was only gone about fifteen minutes when I heard three shots. I figured a pack of wolves had jumped him and he tried to fight his way out of it, but I was also sure he had lost. I'm surprised as hell his horse made it down back to the ranch."

Coop looked over the splint and said, "John, you can ride with me. It will be slow going, but I'm sure we can make it down before it gets too dark."

With Paul's help, they loaded John up behind Coop and began their slow descent down to the ranch. The temperature was dropping rapidly as Paul and Coop navigated their horses through the rocky terrain. The entire time, the call of hungry wolves echoed off the mountainside, making the men more nervous by the minute, as night was not far away. They were just about to cross a frozen stream when John placed his hand on Coops shoulder.

"To your left on that large boulder, look at the size of that son-of-a-bitch." Without saying another word, John took careful aim with the prized rifle he had removed from his dead horse. Squeezing the trigger ever so carefully, the rifle fired. Instantly, the large wolf yelped and rolled off the boulder.

With his Winchester already out of the scabbard, Paul took aim at another wolf that had been slowly pacing in front of the boulders. When it stopped to sniff the carcass of the wolf John had shot, Paul pulled the trigger. The animal barked and yelped as it collapsed in the snow, thrashing around as its rear legs refused to move. Quickly Paul chambered another round and fired at the wounded animal. The wolf leapt into the air about a foot before falling to the ground. After the sound of the gunshot diminished, everything was quiet in the shallow canyon. There was no doubt the rest of the pack had scattered, after seeing their leaders cut down.

It was about 9:00pm when the two horses slowly walked into the yard. Several of the ranch hands came running to help get John and his very cold rescuers into the house. Mrs. Wilkinson put on a pot of coffee and made a hot meal for the men.

About midnight, Coop and Paul made their way into the bunkhouse where their warm beds were waiting. As Coop laid his head on his pillow, he could not believe what he and Paul had accomplished against all the odds stacked against them. He felt bad about Larry, but knew there was nothing they could have done to change the outcome and was thankful they had persevered and were able to rescue John. They would return in Spring to bring Larry's remains down the mountain for burial, but for now he would be on eternal vigil on the mountain, overlooking the ranch he loved so much.

As spring turned into summer, Paul announced he and Sadie were going to get married. Cooper was ecstatic that his good friend had found peace in his soul, and was now going to settle down with a great woman. But it also gave Cooper time to think about his future. He loved the ranch, but the thought of joining the navy seemed to gnaw at him a little more with each passing day. Now with Paul married and starting a new life, Cooper decided it was time for him to move on.

He finally wrote a long letter to Dierdra, explaining all that had happened since he and his father left New York. He apologized for taking so long to write, and hoped she would understand. The last thing he wrote was that he had visited the Naval Recruiter in Missoula, lied about his age, and enlisted in the navy.

Paul was heartbroken to hear his best friend was going to leave the ranch, but realized the navy had been in his blood since he was a child. Sadie and Mrs. Wilkinson put together a grand goodbye party for Coop that lasted well into the early morning hours.

The next day Paul drove Cooper to the train station in Missoula. As the men walked along the boarding platform, Paul laughed. "You'll have much better accommodations this time then that Chevrolet we rode in riding west."

Cooper had to laugh as he shook his head. "I have often wondered where that car ended up. It was a comfortable ride though, and the interior was sharp. I wouldn't have minded owning that car."

As they arrived at Coopers rail car, the young men shook hands. Cooper smiled. "Never thought I was going to have a travelling partner like you, Paul. We covered a lot of miles and did a lot of things on the ranch. I will never forget you, old friend."

Paul gave Cooper a huge hug as he forced back his tears. "You rescued me from the hell of that orphanage and I will never forget that. No matter how you look at it, you gave me a new life that was more than I could ever have dreamed of. Take care, Cooper!"

Paul stood on the platform for several minutes, watching the train disappear down the tracks toward the west. Part of him wanted to be on the train with his friend, but going home to Sadie was a gift he never expected, and he wouldn't trade it for anything. Somehow he knew that he and Coop would be together again one day, he just wasn't sure how it would happen.

Cooper watched the mountains slide by as the train steadily moved west toward the Pacific Ocean and his new job with the navy. He already was missing Paul, but knew his friend was going to have a great life and so would he. He knew that joining the navy was the best thing he could do for himself. Already looking ahead, Cooper decided that on one of his first leaves, he would travel back to Montana to see Paul and Sadie. They were family and he would never forget them.

CHAPTER FIVE – TOKYO, JAPAN

May 11, 1939 2100 hours. Prince Kanin Kotohito's Office, Tokyo Japan

After hearing about General Masanobu's* attack against Russian forces on the border of Manchuria, Prince Kotohito* paced the floor behind his large wooden desk as he mumbled to himself regarding the future of Japan's military problems. After several minutes he waved the piece of paper he was holding up over his head and yelled, "Who gave the order for General Masanobu to do such a foolish thing? We had no plans to attack Russia in any way. They are the last enemy we want at this time. Does anyone in this room realize what General Masanobu has done?"

Standing up, General Hideki Tojo,* the Vice War Minister spoke. "I believe the general had the right idea, but he should have waited until we had enough troops and material on the ground to make the attack successful. Sir, we still have time to help him out if we move quickly!"

Admiral Osani Nagano,* Chief of the Navy General Staff, stood up and bowed. "Sir, I disagree with General Tojo. The navy has its hands full fighting the Chinese along the coast and up into the rivers. We do not have the time or equipment to begin moving complete armies from Japan to China. We need to tell General Masanobu to pull back his forces into Manchuria immediately, and hope Russia will not attack his rear guard."

"To retreat and run from Russia would be a major slap in the face for Japan" Hoime Sugiyama,* Japan's War Minister stated angrily. "Although this was not the plan the war ministry had in mind, it is now on the table, and we need to see it through. I suggest we move men and equipment immediately to bolster the sixth army. I have already prepared a list."

Before the Prince could reply, Prime Minister Fuimaro Konoye* stood up. "Japan is in a bad situation now. We must pull back the sixth army and apologize to Russia immediately, or the sixth army will cease to exist. The war council has bitten off more than it can chew by invading China in the first place. We must pull back, now!"

General Tojo stomped his foot on the floor as he glared at the Prime Minister. "Apologize to Russia? Then we must apologize to the world for what we are doing to create a new empire for the emperor, and the people of Japan. No, we cannot bend to that way of thinking! We must do as Sugiyama says, prepare reinforcement's for immediate transfer to China, and have the navy get every vessel possible to transport them before it's too late."

The Prime Minister realized it was better to back down to the fiery Tojo and accept his decision, than to make him a bitter enemy. As the military was increasing its hold on the government, having too many enemies in the military was not good for one's health.

"That is enough discussion," Prince Kotohito called out, before sitting down behind his desk. "Japan will never apologize to Russia or any other nation. I agree, we must send in reinforcements to bolster General Masanobu." Reaching out his hand, he said. "Give me your list General Sugiyama, it shall be so."

May 31, 1939 midnight Tokyo Japan.

With all military couriers reporting back that they had finished their deliveries to every Japanese military base, the long awaited JN-25 code was launched. The code contained 33,000 words, phrases and letters, and was to be strictly used for military purposes. Only one code book per base was handed out, to ensure the code did not accidentally fall into the wrong hands.

July 26, 1939 1000 hours. The White House, Washington D.C.

By now It became clear to FDR* and the State Department that no amount of negotiation with Japan was going to halt their drive into Mongolia, or have them consider leaving China all together. The president understood very well that any steps the United States took against Japan forced them deeper into a corner, and could precipitate further military action against the United States. At 1000 hours, Bill Friedman,* head of the cryptology department and his decoding staff, once more met with President Roosevelt in his second-floor office. The president had a cigarette in his classic holder as he held onto a cup of coffee Harry Hopkins had just poured.

Pointing to the chairs near his desk, the president said, "Have a seat and a cup of coffee gentlemen, we may be here for a while." Rolling his wheelchair over to a large map of China, he pointed toward a red line running across Mongolia. "I figured by now Stalin would have thrown the Japanese back into Manchuria, but they keep moving forward. What kind of information can you give me today?"

Bill Friedman stood up by the map, and pushed pins into the areas where Japan's forces had last been according to intercepts they had brought with them. "Mr. President, we decoded these intercepts at 0730 this morning, so they are up to date. We also know that today, the Japanese navy is transporting about another thousand men, with all their equipment from the sixty-fourth infantry division. We are guessing they will also end up in Mongolia, as commanders there have been asking for more help."

Before President Roosevelt looked over the latest crop of decoded messages, he looked at Friedman. "Has your team had any luck decoding the new Japanese code?"

Bill Friedman looked intently at the president as he responded. "No sir. It is a tough code, and there are many variables to it. I have my people working at it around the clock, but so far, we haven't been able to get even a foot hold on it."

Nodding his head, the president said, "Alright, let's continue. I don't suppose there are any intercepts here showing a desire for Japan to withdraw any types of forces from China."

Shaking his head, Friedman replied. "No, Mr. President. Everything we see supports the fact that Japan has no interest of getting out of China or withdrawing from Mongolia, and they are calling up more men for conscription. I'm sorry to say, sir, things are looking rather bleak."

Just as Friedman finished speaking, Secretary of State Cordell Hull entered the office, handing the president a manila envelope. "I think that should cover everything you have in mind, Mr. President."

After reading the paperwork, he handed it to Harry Hopkins. "Harry, what do you think?"

After quietly looking over the paperwork and rubbing his chin several times, he took a deep breath. "Yes sir. I agree with Mr. Hull."

After taking back the papers from Harry Hopkins, President Roosevelt said, "I am going to terminate the 1911 treaty of commerce we have with Japan. I have no choice but to give them a six-month notice, so the effective date will be January 25, 1940. I think that for now, this is the only way to get the attention of Tokyo and their war ministries."

One hour later, the proclamation Cordell Hull had proposed was on the way to Tokyo. Now it would be awaiting game to see how the Japanese would respond.

July 27, 1939, 0900 hours. Prince Kanin Kotohito's palace, Tokyo.

Prince Kotohito entered his office a few minutes after the war council had been seated. Walking toward his desk, he carried the order signed by President Roosevelt. Turning to face the members, he shook his head. "The United States has broken off the Treaty of Commerce we have had with them since 1911, effective January 25 next year. That means we will no longer be able to purchase their scrap iron, or any other types of ore from their mines. It also means we have lost our favorite nation trading agreement, and the possibility of using their court system to deal with trade agreements with other nations. For all intent, it is a knife in the back of Japan. According to the supply minister, as of this morning we have about six million tons of scrap iron on hand. Last year nearly seventy-five percent of our scrap iron and ninety-four percent of our copper came from the United States. These are numbers that are not easily replaced with the ship building program the navy has initiated."

General Tojo stood up and walked over to a map of the Pacific hanging on the wall, "We must begin buying more scrap from Australia, and iron ore from the Philippines. But overall, we must think about Malaysia. That is where our wealth of resources can be met. We must think about Malaysia!"

Admiral Nagano stood facing General Tojo. "We are already purchasing ore from Malaysian mines, but their government has placed a limit on how much we can buy. If you add that limit to what is being extracted in China, Korea, Manchuria, and our new mines on Sakhalin Island, we still do not have enough to build the equipment we need."

Tojo slammed his hand against the map. "Who said anything about buying. It is our destiny to control the Pacific Basin, and Malaysia is part of it. We must begin to be bold, we must invade Malaysia and seize the mines and the oil production."

General Sugiyama immediately stood up. "General Tojo, we are already bogged down in China, and our army has decided now to invade Mongolia and pick a fight with the Russians. Every day we expend resources that could be used for our future plans. We cannot invade Malaysia today, or in the next few years, if we do at all. We just do not have the strength to have a two front war right now. I agree we need to find new sources for scrap iron and iron ore, but attacking Malaysia now would bring the Dutch, British and I fear the United States down on us like a hammer."

Tojo nearly frothed at the mouth after the tongue-lashing he took from General Sugiyama. Shaking his finger at the map, he continued. "Bold, Japan needs to be bold, think bold and carry out those ideals, or we shall never control the Pacific!"

After everyone was seated, a new comer to the council, Admiral Isoroko Yamamoto stood up. Walking to the map he picked up the pointer. Sweeping it across the Pacific Basin he said. "The majority of the land mass in the Pacific Basin is in the western Pacific. There are only small islands in the eastern Pacific, controlled by several different nations. Of all the islands, only Hawaii has enough land mass to build bases that can be used to control the eastern approaches. I doubt there are over 350,000 people in all the eastern islands, including Hawaii. Most of them will flee when the might of Japan comes down upon them. Only Hawaii will become a problem for our military, and it can be dealt with. Once Hawaii is secured, our need for iron ore and scrap metal will fall, as our Imperial Fleet will rule the Pacific."

The room was quiet as the Admiral took his seat. Prince Kotohito stood up from his desk and looked at the map once again. "We shall contact Chile, Peru and Columbia to see if they can help with our need for scrap iron and additional ore." Looking over at Admiral Yamamoto, he added, "I fear there will be a time when we will need the fleet to guarantee Japan's place in the world, so we must be prepared and have all the resources on hand to accomplish the job!"

As the meeting broke up, most members of the council approached Yamamoto and shook hands. There was little doubt his words had made an impact and inspired the members of the council to think well beyond the bloody endless war in China.

August 3, 1939, 1100 hours, Admiral Richardson's office, Pearl Harbor, Hawaii*

Overall commander of the Pacific Fleet, Admiral James Richardson stood in his office peering through the large windows that looked out over Pearl Harbor. Staring at the ships moving back and forth through the channel, he turned back toward Commander Joseph Rochefort.*

"You know, Joe, one ship sunk in that channel would bottle up Pearl Harbor for months. Every damn day I wonder if those brass hats in Washington have any concept of what we're dealing with out here in the Pacific. After listening to what you had to say, I keep wondering what the top boys in Washington know about Japan that they're not telling us. If they expect us to defend this rock twenty-five hundred miles from the mainland, they're going to need to share what they know. I'm telling you, Joe, we're going to have to deal with the Japanese down the road, and Hawaii is going to be right in the middle of the entire affair." After walking back over to his desk and picking up his coffee mug, he shook his head. "I'm losing way too much sleep over the harbor and the fleet, and I need some answers, Joe. What do you recommend?"

Sitting down in the dark brown leather chair in front of the Admiral's desk, Rochefort replied. "I would recommend we get someone out here from the cryptologist office to let us know what they're dealing with and see if we can't be a recipient of the information they are decoding. Sir, you could contact the president and ask him to send us some people out here, or I could contact the office directly and talk to my boss. What do you think?"

Smiling, Admiral Richardson replied, "Joe, you never minded ruffling feathers, and so far, it has worked well for you. But I think you may be right, so I'll send a very carefully worded cable to the president, asking for a sit down with Bill Friedman and his people. We'll see how it comes out."

On August fifth, as Bill Friedman was reading overnight intercepts, his phone rang. He sat up straight and put down his coffee mug when he heard President Roosevelt on the line. "Bill, Jim Richardson out in Hawaii has some concerns regarding intercepts, and how they are handled. Apparently, Commander Rochefort thinks we are holding back on some essential information. I want you and Walt Tagway to fly out to Hawaii on the clipper and put his mind at ease. Get out there, do what you need to do, and get back here as soon as you can."

After a grueling three-day trip with little sleep, Bill Friedman and Walt Tagway walked into Admiral Richardson's office, where Commander Rochefort, two of his assistant cryptologists, and Major General Charles Herron,* commander of the Hawaiian Army, sat in a circle going over some new intercepts they had picked up overnight.

Admiral Richardson walked up to the two men and shook hands, "Welcome to Pearl Harbor, gentlemen. We are grateful you men made the long trip out here to talk with us."

Walt walked over to the large windows on the south wall of the office and shook his head. "That is quite the view you have there. I've never seen anything like it."

Admiral Richardson smiled as he pointed to a couple of chairs in the circle. It is beautiful and impressive, and we want to keep it that way. That's exactly why you and Mr. Friedman were asked to fly all the way out here. Both Commander Rochefort and I feel we are not getting the full information as to what's going on in the far east. How are we supposed to prepare ourselves, if we don't have the complete story as to what's going on with Japan and China?"

Bill Friedman shook his head, "Admiral, everything we decode goes up the chain of command as soon as we are finished with it. Copies go to the president, the war department, chief of naval intelligence and so on. We don't have the clearance to automatically send you decoded intercepts, as we don't know how they're going to be classified."

"And therein lies the problem, Bill. Some of these jackasses back in Washington don't know a battleship from a sampan. How the hell can these people make the proper decision when classifying these documents, when they don't know what they're reading?" As Admiral Richardson yelled, his face turned progressively darker shades of red.

Walt was not sure what to say to that, so he looked over at Commander Rochefort. "Do you have any intercepts from last night that you are curious about?"

"Yes, as a matter of fact I do." Commander Rochefort stated, as he pulled two intercepts from his stack, handing them over to Walt."

After looking over the intercepts, he turned to Bill Friedman. "Sir, two Dutch destroyers patrolling off the coast of Malaya spotted three Japanese ships, two destroyers and one light cruiser sailing south about 1630 hours local time yesterday. The message says the ships continued on a southerly course, until they disappeared over the horizon."

Admiral Richardson looked at Bill Friedman. "Now, we were able to pick up the messages ourselves and decode them. If you had received that message and we had not, would we have been contacted as to the movement of these ships? Simple question, Bill."

Shaking his head, Bill Friedman replied, "Admiral, I cannot be sure this information would have been sent directly to you. Again, we do not classify documents, and we do not disseminate them beyond Washington."

"That's about what I expected. Damn it, Bill, you need to go back to Washington and let those lead bottomed paper pushers realize that this is not a paper fleet they can shuffle around on their desks just for the fun of it! You guys need to help us out one way or the other, or by God, one of these days were going to be caught flat-footed at a damn serious time!"

Commander Rochefort handed Walt several more intercepts that had been received over night, and asked for his opinion on them. After carefully reading each one, he passed them over to his boss. "Looks to me like the Japanese are in real trouble in Mongolia. They haven't backed down from a fight, or lost a major ground battle since they started their offensive in 1937. It appears Tokyo doesn't want to send any more troops. This situation will need to be followed closely."

"Damn right it will need to be watched closely, but how the hell do we do it if we don't pick up the right broadcasts. Sometimes weather fronts move in and cut off our signal. That's why we need to be getting information from Washington. For God's sake, Bill, we're all on the same side here," Admiral Richardson stated boldly as he walked over to the windows to look out over the fleet. Continuing, he added, "Bill, I'm afraid one of these days we're going to wake up and be at war with Japan and they'll surprise us and wipe out the Pacific Fleet. Then what the hell do we do?"

Walt stood up, walking over to the large windows. "Sir, most of the military leaders in Washington do not believe the Japanese have the capabilities to make such an attack. They would need to navigate across thousands of miles of open ocean while being undetected. Their pilots are inferior to ours, and their ships might not hold up to such a long journey. Washington just doesn't believe they could ever attack us at Pearl Harbor. The Philippines, yes, but Pearl, no."

"Mr. Tagway, it's all noise, just noise with no real understanding of Japan," Admiral Richardson replied, slamming his hand down for emphasis. "As you said, they believe certain things, but what would they say if they were pinned down to making a decision right now, this very minute? At that point I believe we would be in for some real problems."

Over the next two days, Walt and Bill spent hours in the cryptology office with Commander Rochefort and his team, examining intercepts they gathered overnight. Bill Friedman became increasingly concerned, as he was positive many of the intercepts were only partial messages. He knew that in Washington, his code team was working off complete intercepts gathered from all the listening stations in the Pacific. It became increasingly clear that there needed to be a change in how information gleaned from intercepts in Washington was disseminated to the Pacific commands. But how he could change the minds of the military leaders in Washington that had become nothing more than federal bureaucrats? It was a serious problem indeed.

Arriving back in Washington, Bill asked for an immediate meeting with the president.

Joining the president in the East Sitting Room, Bill slid forward on his chair and began. "Mr. President, our meetings with Admiral Richardson and Commander Rochefort were extremely helpful in many ways. The problem sir, is that station Hypo does not always get full messages that they can de-code, in order to understand the entire story. We need to change the way we disseminate our information in order to get it into the hands of our overseas commanders much faster. They are on the ground, sir, they may need to make real time decisions and adjustments that our military leaders here in Washington just aren't in the position to understand."

Nodding his head, the president responded. "I understand all of that, Bill. But there are also times when our men here in Washington have a greater amount of information gathered from other sources that puts together a bigger picture. We need to have everything in place before we move, so we don't put our forces in danger. I will see what I can do to get more information passed on faster than we are doing now, but I simply can't guarantee exactly how much that will be. Get ahold of Admiral Richardson, and assure him he is not a forgotten man."

CHAPTER SIX –
SAN DIEGO, CALIFORNIA

Cooper was more than excited when he arrived at the sprawling naval base in San Diego, California. He could not wait to begin basic training and then move on to gunnery school, the advanced training he chose when he enlisted.

For a young man in his physical condition, basic training was a piece of cake. He aced his physical abilities test, and outran every recruit in the mile course. The eight weeks went by quickly, and in no time he was on his way to gunnery school.

There was a lot to be learned in gunnery school as they trained on everything from fifty caliber browning machine guns, twenty and forty-millimeter anti-aircraft weapons, all the way up to the new sixteen-inch guns that had been placed on the newest battleships in the fleet. Cooper hoped to be assigned to a battle ship as their compliment of weapons included everything they had learned about in training.

Going out to sea on a World War One destroyer, the men were given the chance to fire live ammunition during simulated anti-aircraft attacks. Cooper did well with the individually manned machine guns and the twenty-millimeter cannons. He was somewhat upset when he was on the forty-millimeter Bofors gun, as the reloading crew was screwing around instead of getting the ammunition loaded fast enough for the drill. But he still learned the concept of the weapon and knew he could make it work if he were assigned to one of the gun tubs.

The trainees also worked with the powerful three-and five-inch guns that could be used for anti-aircraft battles and shore bombardments, or against enemy vessels.

The most miserable part of the training was learning how to break down the weapons and clean them. It was a dirty job overseen by chief petty officers that wanted the weapons to shine like a mirror when they were reassembled.

After all the training was completed, each man anxiously waited to see if they were going to get assigned to a ship or to a shore-based unit.

Cooper tried to keep his hands from shaking as he carefully opened the envelope containing his orders. He wanted a battle ship, but in the end, a ship was a ship was a ship, so he smiled when he read the words Light Cruiser, USS *Honolulu* CL-48.

The ship was a Brooklyn-class light cruiser that was launched in 1937 and commissioned in 1938, and best of all, was currently berthed in San Diego.

Cooper was assigned as the gunner on a Bofors 40mm anti-aircraft battery, commonly referred to as a pom pom gun, because of the sound it made when fired. Each battery had two barrels and there were two batteries in each tub. There were four tubs on the *Honolulu*.

Each tub was manned by an officer or fire director, and each battery had five enlisted men. When the gun was actively firing on approaching aircraft, the tubs appeared to be a wild, frenetic circus of activity as each man did his job. Each tub could fire 150 rounds per minute.

The crew assigned to Cooper's tub were a gallant bunch of young men that all had joined the navy during the depression in order to have a job. They laughed and played tricks on each other to pass the time when things were quiet. But during drills or firing practice, they were dead serious and proved to be the best qualified tub on the *Honolulu*.

Going out to sea for the first time, Cooper was like a kid in a candy store. He marveled at the size of the waves, the rocking of the ship, not being able to see land in any direction, and the howling of the wind as the salt spray stung his face. At night he was totally mesmerized by the number of stars he could see across the wide Pacific Ocean.

Every day the gun crews would wipe down their weapon to make sure salt spray would not clog moving parts or get into the electrical control boxes.

Since the tubs were close to the side of the ship, Cooper found it to be a bit daring to be moving around the tub with waves breaking off the side of the ship just a few yards away. The rest of the crew laughed at him, although they privately admitted they had gone through the same experience when they were assigned to their first tub.

The third day out at sea, a plane from an aircraft carrier in the fleet flew by, pulling a large target panel behind it. The aiming crew was doing a great job of turning the battery so Cooper could keep the panel in his sights. When the Lieutenant ordered him to open fire, Coop pressed the trigger. He was amazed and excited as the cannons slid back and forth, firing their projectiles into the bright blue sky. Angry puffs of black smoke dotted the sky each time one of his rounds exploded. Keeping the target panel fixed in the center of his sighting screen, the rounds were bursting in a perfect pattern that would damage or bring down any aircraft attempting to attack the ship.

When he had finished firing for the day, Cooper could barely stand still as adrenaline coursed through his body like a freight train out of control. He hugged each man in the tub and yelled like a maniac as he shook his fists in the air. For the first time in his life, he felt like he was part of something much bigger than life itself. He knew each man on the crew was family and would fight together as a team.

That night Cooper wrote a long letter to Paul explaining what his day had been like and how great it made him feel. Working on the ranch with the other hands had been fun, and given him a sense of belonging he had been missing, but what he was doing now was hard work, exciting and very rewarding, and he knew the navy was his destiny.

After several weeks at sea running all kinds of war games, the *Honolulu* and several other ships sailed into the port of Lima, Peru for shore leave. As Cooper did not have duty, he went ashore with his friends to taste the local food, drink some of the native alcohol, and try to get a kiss from a pretty Peruvian girl. As Cooper walked up the gangway to the *Honolulu* he had accomplished all three goals and felt like shore leave had been a true success.

Back out to sea sailing south from Peru, Cooper saw the largest whales he could have ever imagined. One of them swam right alongside the ship as he was cleaning the tub. Then his eyes nearly popped out of his head as two more whales surfaced and all three were swimming side by side. Cooper had to smile when he realized he was getting the education of a life time while getting paid at the same time. He wished over and over that Paul were there to take this all in.

Turning farther to the west the swells became bigger and the *Honolulu* rolled and heaved as waves broke over the bow, sending sheets of water back over the ship. The fleet crashed through monstrous waves as rain poured down for several days. After escaping the storm, the aircraft carrier USS *Enterprise* launched a float plane that made several circles around the fleet before heading toward the *Honolulu* so their aft crane crew could practice picking up a float plane from the ocean and bring it up onto their deck. Cooper watched with fascination as the pilot dropped slowly out of the sky, setting his plane down just feet behind the cruiser. Quickly, the co-pilot hooked up the cables from the crane and sat back down in the cockpit. In just a few minutes the seaplane was sitting on the aft deck of the cruiser. After having lunch on the *Honolulu*, the crew returned to the plane. Within minutes, the crane crew had picked up the plane, swung it out over the stern of the ship and set it in the water. Quickly the co-pilot unhooked the cables and once again slid down into the cockpit. The pilot pushed the throttle forward, sending fuel to the large radial engine and the plane skipped across the surface of the ocean until it gained enough speed to take to the sky.

The pilot swung his plane to the north as he continued gaining altitude until the engine coughed. The pilot worked frantically attempting to figure out why his engine was missing so badly, but he was losing speed and altitude quickly. In desperation he made a quick turn in hopes of setting his disabled aircraft down in the water near the *Honolulu* so they could be plucked from the ocean.

As the pilot was finishing his turn, the engine roared to life for a mere second before shutting down completely. Now the aircraft was aiming directly toward the side of the ship near Coopers gun tub. The lieutenant ordered everyone to run as the plane closed in rapidly. At the last second, the pilot was able to redirect his aircraft slightly, so the right side of the plane slammed into the hull of the ship. The collision ripped off the right wing of the plane causing the crippled aircraft to somersault upside down into the crest of a monster wave.

Without giving the situation a moment of thought, Cooper and a sailor named Carl Smith jumped from the deck of the *Honolulu* into the cold water. Taking a mouthful of air, both men dove under the plane where the pilot was struggling with the canopy. Cooper grabbed the front of the canopy and pulled with all his strength. Seconds later the canopy tore free, allowing Cooper to help the pilot get out of his harness. Pulling the pilot free of the plane, Cooper helped him to the surface where several orange lifebuoys had been thrown into the water. As the men pulled the pilot up, Seaman Smith came to the surface for air. As he hung on to Cooper, he said, "Help me!"

In an instant, Cooper and Smith dove once more as the plane was beginning to sink faster. They pulled as hard as they could to get the co-pilots canopy open, but the collision had jammed it. Seeing the co-pilot slumped over his controls, Cooper grabbed hold of Smith pointing toward the surface. Breaking the surface of the ocean, both men were struggling to catch their breath. They held onto each other and worked to tread water as they watched one of the ship's rescue boats coming toward them.

With the rescue boat back up on deck, Cooper and Smith were taken to the infirmary where they were treated for hypothermia. Early that evening the skipper of the ship came down to see them. He thanked them for their bravery, and told them he was going to authorize a naval decoration for their outstanding performance.

Cooper looked at the commander and said, "Thank you, sir, but we lost the co-pilot."

The commander just shook his head. "Son, sometimes you just have to make a decision about who you can save and get it done. That means very simply that others may die. Regrettably, that's the situation you found yourself in today. You saved a good man and did your best to rescue his partner, but it just wasn't to be. It's even possible he was already dead from the impact with the ship."

Smith looked at the ships captain. "What do you tell the family of the co-pilot?" Shaking his head, the commander replied. "That is the toughest job of command, Smith. It's never an easy thing to do, especially when there was no chance to recover his body and send it home. Sometimes you learn that being in command of a ship is one God awful place to be."

After shaking hands with the men once more, the commander went back to his stateroom to begin his letter to the parents of the co-pilot.

That night, the letter Cooper wrote to Paul was anything but upbeat. He explained how he had watched the plane disappear into the depths of the ocean carrying the body of the co-pilot to his final resting place, hundreds of feet below the surface of the ocean. It was something Cooper would relive in his dreams for a very long time to come.

Returning to San Diego, the crew worked cleaning the ship for two days before being given shore leave for the next two weeks. Without giving it a thought, Cooper boarded a train that would get him back to Missoula to see his best friend.

Paul picked up Cooper from the station and drove him home. Sadie made them a great meal and looked forward to hearing all of Cooper's stories from the sea. The two men talked late into the night after Sadie went off to bed. After pouring them both another cup of coffee, Paul said. "So, do you think I would do well in the navy? Nothing is the same out at the ranch since you left. I keep telling Sadie I need a change, and she said maybe the navy would be good for me too."

Cooper laughed, "Everyone is different, but I love the navy and am very glad I made the change. We've been hearing the entire fleet may be moved to Hawaii in the next year, can you believe that?

Paul shook his head, "Hawaii, damn you lucky fool. Sadie would love to live there. Maybe we should give the navy a second look after all."

Returning to San Diego, Cooper was promoted to gunners mate first class, and awarded the Navy Commendation Medal for his bravery in rescuing the pilot.

The *Honolulu* went back out to sea, passing through the Panama Canal then heading up the east coast of the United States before arriving in Norfolk, Virginia. Having ten days shore leave, Cooper took a train to New York City to visit Dierdra. He was stunned to find her very unwelcoming and uncaring. After about an hour of listening to Dierdra berating him, Cooper picked up the phone to call for a cab so he could return to the train station.

Dierdra jumped up from the chair and yelled, "Sure, just run away again and take care of yourself. Sail around the world and care about no one but Carmine Santucci, or whatever name you want to go by now. When the heat gets turned on go ahead and run like father did, I don't care!"

Putting down the phone, Cooper looked at his very attractive sister. "Yes, I should have written to you earlier, and yes, I guess I should have found out where they were going to bury Pa, but I was scared they were going to put me in jail. So yeah, I ran, I ran as fast as I could like any scared fifteen year old kid would do. I'm sorry for everything I did that was wrong, and I mean that."

After a moment of thought, Dierdra said, "Fine, you can spend the night here if you wish."

Cooper shook his head. "Thanks for the offer, but I think it's best if I head back to the ship. The last thing I want to do is argue with you, it's not good for either of us. Marry your boyfriend, have a family and find peace in your life. That will make both me and Pa very happy."

Picking up the phone, Cooper called for a cab and walked out to the curb to wait for it.

Two days before the *Honolulu* was to sail, Cooper was having coffee with some of his friends in the galley when a Petty Officer walked in. "Damn it, Dodge. I've been looking all over for you. There is a woman by the name of Dierdra Santucci out at the main gate that wants to see you. She says she's your sister. What do you want me to do about her?"

Without saying a word, Cooper hustled off the ship, caught a ride to the front gate, and walked up to the fence, as his hands shook. Dierdra smiled, "Those are some pretty big ships, which one is yours?"

Cooper smiled. "You can't see it from here, but it's just like the USS *Nashville* berthed to your left. There are nine Brooklyn-class light cruisers.

Dierdra smiled for a moment, then looked down at the ground. "I saw a coffee shop about a block away, would you like to get some coffee?"

Immediately, Cooper took out his pass, showed it to the gate officer and walked off the base.

Sitting in a booth, Dierdra reached out her hand, placing it over his. "I never expected to have a brother named Cooper Dodge, but I think he's a pretty neat guy."

As tears rolled down his face, he squeezed Dierdra's hand. "I love you, sis, and I never meant to hurt you. You are all I have left in this world. I was totally terrified when Pa died. I was so far from home and had no way to contact you. I thought I would never see you again and it broke my heart."

Wiping her eyes, Dierdra replied. "I told my fiancé about our discussion and he was not too happy with me. After thinking about everything the two of us said, I realized I was the one being mean and uncaring. I hope we can start over and be brother and sister again."

Looking up at the ceiling for a moment, Cooper said. "So, is this Steven guy good to you?"

Nodding her head, Dierdra responded. "He's the best, and I really love him. I'll be sure and send you an invitation when we set a date. If you are close by, maybe you can come to the wedding, or if not, I can send you a piece of wedding cake."

Cooper laughed, feeling very happy that he and Dierdra had patched things up and were a family again. They talked for nearly two hours before Dierdra headed back to Little Italy.

Two days later, the *Honolulu* and three other ships departed Norfolk, sailing on a southern course toward the Caribbean. Then it would return through the canal and sail on to San Diego where the Pacific fleet was preparing to sail for Hawaii.

CHAPTER SEVEN – FEARS OF WAR DEEPEN

It was clear that the world was about to explode in 1939, and it was obvious Japan would be at the center of it. They had made up their minds to follow through with their plans to create an empire in the Pacific, and they were positive there would be no one that would step up and stop them, except maybe the United States, and even that could be doubtful.

On February 10, 1939, Japanese forces invaded Hainan Island of the coast of Indochina. The island was rich in many different types of raw materials, including many rubber plantations Japan would need for war production. The deep-water bay at Samah Bay would allow the navy to control all movement in the South China Sea, and stop China from importing war materials.

On March 18, 1939, Japanese forces invaded the Spratly Islands, seven hundred miles from Formosa. Although most of the Spratly Islands are uninhabitable for lack of fresh water, the Japanese built a large submarine and float plane base on Long Island. During the invasion, the Japanese also took control of the Parcel Islands. The islands had been the property of China for years. However, since China was at war with Japan and had no way to defend the islands, Japan claimed that the islands now belonged to them.

As the American fleet finished up war maneuvers in the Caribbean on April 15, 1939, Roosevelt sent the Atlantic Fleet to Hawaii. He hoped the presence of the American fleet would deter Japan from striking out against Hong Kong, or the Dutch East Indies.

About midday in Washington on August 23, 1939, Walt Tagway stood by a news ticker in the cryptology office in Washington D.C. After watching the long message print out, he tore the intercept from the ticker and sat down at his desk to decode it for his superiors. His eyes nearly bulged out of his head as he rechecked the message to make sure he had decoded it properly. Running over to Bill Friedman's office, Walt said, "This is dead serious, sir. Intercept 1379H from Moscow to Berlin. This morning German Foreign Minister Joachim Ribbentrop* and Russia's Minister of Foreign Affairs Vyacheslav Molotov,* signed a ten-year non-aggression pact in Moscow. We never saw this coming, sir. It has to be a prelude to something big."

Bill Friedman looked over the intercept as he pondered it carefully. "Russia appears to be slowly kicking Japan out of Mongolia. They certainly can't be afraid that Germany would attack Russia in the west to help the Japanese! There must be something deeper to this message than we know. Better get it to the president at once!"

In Tokyo, Prime Minister Konoye exploded when he read the intercept that was handed to him by Yosuke Matsuoka,* his Minister of Foreign affairs. "Germany has stabbed us in the back! How dare they sign a ten-year nonaggression pact with Russia. We have signed an Anti-Comintern Pact with Germany declaring we would help them stop the spread of communism around the world. What are Hitler and Ribbentrop up to? Send a message immediately asking Germany for an explanation as to why this has taken place. I feel there is more to this than meets the eye."

Since the beginning of July, the cryptology office in Washington had been carefully monitoring German troop movements along the Polish border, realizing something was in the wind, and it was not good. On the morning of August 28, 1929, Walt handed an intercept to Bill Friedman as he was standing quietly, examining a map of Europe. "Intercept 2101F Warsaw Poland to London, England and Paris, France. It states they have now called up all reserves, and sent all mobile forces toward the German border, to counteract the German build-up of troops."

Bill Friedman studied the intercept for a moment before shaking his head. "Are there any more intercepts from Berlin to Moscow, or Moscow to Berlin?"

Shaking his head, Walt replied. "Plenty of intercepts from Berlin to London, Paris and Rome, but all involve diplomatic material, nothing to do with military actions. Moscow has been extremely quiet."

Bill stared at the map for several minutes before replying, "Walt, I want you to stay here tonight to keep an eye on things. I'll send this message to Roosevelt, and maybe he can contact Berlin and settle things down, but I doubt it."

Through the night, Walt checked every message coming into the cryptology office from everywhere in the world, looking for any signs of trouble. It was becoming increasingly clear that Japan was beginning to feel the full weight of the Russian forces on their front lines, but they had not yet buckled.

At 0300 hours, August 29 in Washington D.C, a message from Moscow to Marshal Semyon Timoshenko* was decoded. It stated that the forces formerly discussed had now begun to move as planned, but gave no directions of movement. Without waiting for orders, Walt immediately sent a copy of the intercept to the White House.

Over the next two days, the only intercepts that were being decoded from Berlin and Moscow were normal diplomatic messages. That just added to the tension that was already building in Washington. The State Department sent messages nearly hourly to London and Warsaw, asking for updates, but was receiving back little or nothing that could give the president the information he wanted.

At 2245 hours on August 31, 1939, Susan Preston burst into Walt's office. Looking up from the intercepts he was working on, he was stunned by the look on Susan's face.

Her face was white, and her hands shook as she handed Walt an intercept from Warsaw, Poland. It said, "September 1, 1939, 0600 hours local time, German infantry and armor have crossed the Polish frontier in force. German aircraft are attacking Polish positions and cities in the path of the ground offensive. Situation in doubt!"

Within seconds, every intercept machine in the building was running, as messages were being picked up from every European capital. Susan looked at Walt, "It has begun, so what do we do now? France and England have a defense agreement with Poland, what will they do?"

Understanding that Poland was not going to be the only country German forces would attack in the near future, he took a deep breath. "We work, Susan. Call Bill and get him in here. I'll take these over to the White House myself."

Arriving at the White House, Walt was taken straight to the president's office on the second floor. He was working on one of his stamp collections as Walt walked into the room. "Looking up from his desk, the smile disappeared from his face. "What is it, Walt?"

Stepping forward, he handed the president several of the intercepts his staff had hurriedly decoded. Shaking his head, the president asked. "Have you contacted anyone else yet?"

Walt shook his head, "No sir. We called Bill to come in, and then I came straight over here."

Looking over at Harry Hopkins, President Roosevelt said, "Go ahead, Harry. Call everyone we have on the list and have them meet here at 0600. Get Prime Minister Chamberlin* on the phone as soon as possible as well. Call my son and tell him to be here by 0430 so I can be ready for the meeting, I think this is going to be a very long and excruciating day."

Returning to the cryptology office, Walt, Bill and Susan slowly sifted through unending piles of intercepts that were continuing to arrive. The ones that appeared to be important were decoded immediately, while others that did not appear to be as urgent, were placed in baskets on a shelf in Bill's office. It became increasingly clear that Polish forces were not fairing that well under the pressure of the German Blitzkrieg. What was far scarier, was that it appeared neither England or France were doing anything to come to Poland's aid as was agreed upon in March of 1939. If they did not act soon, Poland would disappear from the face of the map, and the Polish government would become hostages of the Third Reich.

Throughout the day, Japanese code breakers that were being trained by the Polish military in Warsaw, sent urgent messages to Tokyo regarding the German onslaught. Tokyo instructed them to remain in place, and that their safety was being assured by Germany.

But having their decoders trapped in Poland was not Japan's only difficulty in September. After a grueling three-day air battle, where nearly three hundred Russian and Japanese aircraft fought death defying combat in the skies over Mongolia, an armistice was reached in the war on September 16, 1939. Both sides agreed to pull back behind the original Manchuria and Mongolian borders. Japan claimed they had 8,717 killed or missing, with 10,997 wounded. Russian casualties were reported at 8, 931 killed or missing, and 15,952 wounded, but the fighting had finally ended.

With the Japanese sixth army all but wiped out during the short war, Japanese leaders were completely humiliated. Once the pull back of troops was complete, General Tguji Masanobu was recalled to Tokyo where he was seriously reprimanded. Many staff officers felt the General's reprimanded should possibly include a public execution. However, Tojo and many other militant staff officers believed in keeping the general around. After much discussion, it was agreed that General Masanobu had a solid knowledge of combat and leadership skills that were still needed. He would occupy many high level jobs in the Japanese military in Tokyo during the upcoming war.

With Japan's war with Russia over in the east, early on the morning of September 17, 1939, Russian troops rushed across the Polish border. Quickly, Russian Foreign Affairs Minister Vyacheslav Molotov announced to the world that the nation of Poland and the Polish Government no longer existed, as was agreed upon and written in the fine print of the Hitler-Stalin non-aggression pact of August 23, 1939. After twenty days of fighting, Poland is partitioned between Russia and Germany. Russia will occupy three-fifths of the country and control 13.5 million residents.

After finishing a call from England's Prime Minister Chamberlin, President Roosevelt set down the phone receiver and looked up at Cordell Hull. "Cordell, I believe the world has gone insane. Both the British and the French had offered Poland help if they should be attacked by Germany. Now it is apparent that neither country is prepared to follow through. To be honest, I don't believe either country is strong enough militarily to do any good. After all, Germany has had time to build and train an army that is probably the strongest on the continent. Add Russia to the mix, and no one is safe in Europe tonight." Moving his wheelchair over to the large map of Europe, the president continued. "I'm afraid the lights in Europe have gone out. And there is little doubt that the remaining lights there are in the Pacific will also soon go dark. The world is entering a dark time, and it would seem other than America, there is no one else out there left to help. Somehow, someway, we must become the arsenal of defense for the free world. Otherwise, we will fall into an abyss such as the world has never witnessed before."

On November 4, 1939, President Roosevelt rounds up enough support in congress to pass America's fourth Neutrality Act. It allowed belligerent nations to buy the weapons of war on a cash and carry basis on their own ships. This final act effectively did away with all the previous neutrality acts that had been passed in the 1930s. In his plea to congress, President Roosevelt said, "America's neutrality laws, as they stood in 1939, might actually give passive aid to an aggressor, while denying help to victimized nations." The revised neutrality act passed the House on November 2, 1939, with a vote of 243 to 181.

Although the news of Germany's attack on Belgium and France in May of 1940 shocked the entire world, in Japan it was met with a sense of wonder and awe. While reading decoded intercepts from Europe, Prince Konoye began studying maps of Indonesia. Suddenly, he realized what he had thought about for so long but always rejected, was now becoming a possibility. The slicing Blitzkrieg attacks of Germany, throughout France, Belgium, Luxembourg, the Netherlands and Denmark greatly encouraged him, as he realized that none of the allies that had promised to respond were raising one finger.

He realized what General Tojo had said was accurate. Seizing Malaysia was the answer to all of Japan's lack of natural resources. Now that Holland, Belgium, and France were under the thumb of the Nazi's, there was little their far east military could do to stop Japan's new found might.

CHAPTER EIGHT –
1940 THE WAR EXPANDS

In March of 1940, President Roosevelt was becoming very concerned over the actions of Japan in the Pacific. He realized at the present time the only real force to deal with Japan was America's Pacific Fleet, and it was stationed in San Diego, California. We had bases in Hawaii and the Philippines, but neither of them had any form of military power that could deal a damaging blow to Japan's growing military might if a war began. What worried the president most, was that Japan had a lethal history of attacking without issuing a declaration of war. They had done it in 1894 against China, in 1904 against Russia, in 1931 against Manchuria and now against China again in 1937, which was sending dangerous ripples around the entire world. The last thing the president wanted was for the United States to suffer the same consequences as the earlier enemies of Imperial Japan.

Calling in his advisors, Roosevelt laid out the problem as he saw it. He explained to everyone that moving the fleet to Pearl Harbor as a deterrent to Japan might be a good idea. Admiral Stark, the Chief of Naval Operations, and Frank Knox, Secretary of the Navy, vehemently argued against the plan. Their main argument was the lack of fuel in Hawaii, the lack of repair shops and equipment, not to mention the incredibly long supply line to the west coast. Secretary Stimson was unsure as to how the fleet could be protected from enemy attack that far away from the United States as there were times when intercepts in Washington differed from those received in Hawaii. Changes needed to be made.

In order for the United States to keep a closer eye on Japanese operations, major listening and cryptology stations were set up around the Pacific. Station Hypo in Hawaii, Station Frumel in Melbourne, Australia, and Station Cast on the island of Corregidor in the Philippine Islands. There were two more general listening stations set up, one on the Island of Guam and the other on Bainbridge Island in Puget Sound, Washington.

Commander Joseph Rochefort was put in charge of station Hypo in Hawaii, which was located in the basement of the old administration building at Pearl Harbor. It was so damp and dark, many of the employees referred to it as the dungeon. Rochefort believed in the work that came out of the dungeon and met regularly with Admiral James Richardson, commander of Pearl Harbor at the time. Rochefort was a bit of an eccentric, who often wore a burgundy smoking jacket and bedroom slippers while he was at work. Nevertheless, he was an extremely talented code breaker, but often found himself at odds with Washington over the way uncoded materials were handled and disseminated. However, no one in Washington or Pearl Harbor ever doubted the excellent work that was coming out of Rochefort's tightly operated station Hypo.

With all the recommended changes in place, everyone in the inner circle at the White House agreed with Roosevelt, that having the massive fleet that close to the heart of Japan would make the Japanese war ministers take a long look before they forced any major issues. They also agreed that with listening stations around the Pacific Rim, and Commander Rochefort in Hawaii, there was no doubt that the United States would always have ample advanced warning of any moves the Japanese combined fleet attempted. Although the discussion went on for several days, the decision was finally made to have the fleet make the move gradually, and over a period of time, so as not to make Japan feel we were coming after them, or to disturb the Hawaiian population.

The first contingent of ships consisted of one aircraft carrier, two heavy cruiser divisions, and two destroyer squadrons, along with all the supporting vessels and staff a small fleet would require to operate. A large building program went into operation, constructing an oil tank farm, new docks, maintenance buildings, warehouses, dormitories and every type of building a new modern naval base would need to operate, keeping in mind that the balance of the fleet would be moving in on a date and time not yet decided.

The commander of the fleet, Admiral James Richardson, was still very much opposed to the idea and protested loudly, but was instructed by the president to get on board with the plan.

It did not take long for the battleships and the rest of the fleet to make their final move to Hawaii. The American public and press were told the fleet was only going to be there for a few weeks of much needed training, which was later changed to a couple of months.

Uncomfortable with having a fleet that was short of fuel and ammunition, Richardson wrote a letter to Admiral Stark, stating the fleet could not be sufficiently prepared for war in Hawaii.

After getting no reply, Richardson wrote a more scathing letter to his boss, Admiral Stark. To this letter Admiral Stark replied as follows.

"Why are you in the Hawaii area?

Answer: You are there because of the deterrent effect which it is thought your presence may have on the Japs going into the East Indies."

To how long the fleet would be in Hawaii, Stark just said to leave it alone that it was a delicate matter, and that if the president wanted the fleet in Hawaii, there it would stay."

In January 1941, Admiral Richardson would write one more letter complaining about having the fleet in Hawaii, but this time it was to President Roosevelt. Immediately, the president relieved Richardson of his command and sent Admiral Husband Kimmel* to replace him.

Along with problems regarding the Pacific fleet and the naval chain of command, things also looked glum in Washington as Hitler's forces continued swallowing up Europe at an alarming rate. The only true light on the horizon was that Winston Churchill* had been appointed as British Prime Minister on May 10, so now there was somebody at Ten Downing Street that had the guts and the fortitude to fight the Nazis.

President Roosevelt sat in the Oval Office with Harry Hopkins on May 11, going over the days agenda when Henry Stimson arrived on schedule at 11:00am. After exchanging the usual pleasantries, Stimson stood in front of the president's desk. "Mr. President, most everyone in the war department is coming to realize that aircraft are going to be the big weapon in the coming war. Hitler has used the Luftwaffe to keep his Panzers moving, and destroy whatever the enemy has on the ground in front of them. Sir, right now we have roughly 3,900 aircraft of all types. The Air-Corp has 1200 bombers and most of them are old and obsolete. We have only twenty-three of the new B-17's, and we are still depending on a bunch of open cockpit fighter aircraft. Sir, before Germany launched its attack against France, they had 1000 new Messerschmidt ME 109's sitting on their airfields. They could wipe out our planes in a matter of days. Mr. President, with Churchill coming to power, he may very well ask us for planes we do not have."

President Roosevelt removed his glasses and rubbed his eyes before looking up at his secretary of war. "Henry, we have discussed our war needs over and over and have attempted to shift money where we can to pay for what everyone is demanding. The problem is, there is no other money available to shift. I have Speaker Bankhead* and Senate Majority Leader Barkley* coming for a meeting at 2:00pm. When they arrive, I'm going to hand them a request for an extraordinary credit of one billion, one hundred eighty-two thousand dollars. In that request, I am asking for 50,000 aircraft of all types. The remainder of the request will go to build ships, procure rifles and ammunition, build necessary buildings, and squeeze out whatever else we can get. Since the democrats control both houses, I see no reason why the proposal should not pass right on through."

Henry Stimson nodded his head as he felt a wave of relief wash over him. "Mr. President, that is a great relief, but there is no doubt in my mind that I will need to come back to this office to ask for more funding down the road. The threat is too great, and we're going to have a brand-new military we need to build from the ground up."

President Roosevelt nodded as he placed his glasses on his head. "Don't worry, Henry, every mother and father in this country are willing to pay whatever it takes to keep their sons and daughters out of a war no one in America wants."

At 2:00pm, both the speaker of the house and the senate majority leader arrived in the oval office. After looking over the wish list the president handed them, Speaker Bankhead said, "Mr. President, there is not one person in the congress that does not understand the predicament America has found itself in. However, I'm sure there will be many questions from our constituents as to this large proposal. I suggest you address a joint session of congress on the sixteenth of the month that can be broadcast nationwide to allow Americans to understand the need for this money."

The speech on May 16, 1941 was well accepted by congress and most of the American people. However, the American First Committee slammed the president and congress for the outrageous spending, as they still felt war could and should be avoided.

On August 1, 1940, Japan's new Foreign Minister Yosuke Matsuoka* made a proclamation that Japan was announcing the creation of the Greater East Asia Co-prosperity Sphere, that would include French Indo China and the Dutch East Indies. His speech was followed up by a story in the Yomiuri,* Tokyo's top newspaper, that said, "Japan must remove all elements in East Asia which will interfere with its plans. Britain, the United States, France, and the Netherlands must be forced out of the far east. Asia is for the Asians!"

As Walt read the intercept that included Matsuoka's declaration, he walked over to Bill Friedman's office. Handing over the intercept, he said, "Bill, the Japanese have finally declared that GEAPS, the Greater east Asia Co-prosperity sphere actually exists. What do you make of that?"

Bill Friedman looked out the window for a moment before replying. "Like it or not, the Japanese now have drawn out some big plans for their military to follow through with. Now that France, England and the Dutch are all tied up with Hitler, Tokyo is going to seize every one of their holdings in the far east to import the raw materials they don't have. Who the hell is going to stop them? Who stepped in when they seized Hainan Island? Not a damn soul. Put together an overview of what we are seeing and get it to the White House and the War Department as soon as possible. Damn it, Walt, we're going to end up in a war with Japan one way or the other, and we may not be ready."

CHAPTER NINE -
THE USS *HONOLULU* MEETS HONOLULU

April 10, 1940 The Pacific Fleet is now combined in Pearl Harbor

About two months before the *Honolulu* was scheduled to sail for Hawaii, Cooper received a letter from Paul. It was short and to the point.

"Cooper, I joined the navy a week ago, as there is no doubt a war is on the way. We found a place in San Diego for Sadie to move into. I start basic training in a week and have much to get done before we leave here. Will write you as soon as I can. Paul."

Cooper was excited about having Paul enlist in the navy. He hoped that down the line they could be assigned to the same ship. But for now, there was a tremendous amount of work that needed to be done. With every ship from the fleet heading to Pearl Harbor, they were being loaded with every extra piece of equipment possible. No unused areas inside the ship, nor any unused deck space were going to be left empty. Trucks and cranes worked all night delivering ammunition, engine parts, clothing, or any other type of equipment the fleet would need while setting up operations. By dawn, the loading process was just about finished. With the fuel tanks topped off, the crew was given one last shore leave to acquire items that may not be available in Hawaii for the time being.

Cooper tried to find Sadie's phone number, but with so many navy families moving in and out of San Diego at the moment, many new numbers were getting lost in the shuffle. Although calling cross country was expensive, Cooper wanted to hear Dierdra's voice one more time before leaving the mainland. It was evident Dierdra was concerned for Cooper's safety, as there was no doubt in her mind that a war with Japan was right around the corner. Cooper did all he could to console his frightened sister, but was positive her fears were going to come to fruition.

As the *Honolulu* departed San Diego, most of the crew was upbeat and excited about going to Hawaii. They had all read magazine stories of hula girls, tropical walks on the beach with a lady friend, and the warm trade winds that made the island a true paradise.

Just four days out at sea, one of the engines began to cause problems. The skipper cut speed down to fifteen knots while the mechanics attempted to solve the problem. Regrettably, they informed the skipper that the engine would need a rebuild when they reached Hawaii, as they did not have the equipment to complete the job. So, the six-day journey tuned into a nine-day trip, but the weather was fine, winds were calm, and the crew enjoyed some extra time working on their sun tans, where ever they could find room on the ship.

The decks of the Honolulu were filled with sailors waiting to get a glimpse of this new paradise as the ship entered Pearl Harbor. They were impressed to see all eight battleships tied up along Ford Island with several support ships. The locks behind Ford Island were filled with destroyers, cruisers, one aircraft carrier and many more support ships. Every sailor agreed it was a powerful armada and Japan would have to be crazy to attempt to fight it.

After the *Honolulu* was unloaded, the ship was pulled into one of the repair docks for an engine rebuild. The skipper announced that since the repairs could take a month or more, any man that wanted to be reassigned to another ship need just apply for a transfer.

Cooper was unsure of what he wanted to do, so he stayed with the ship for the first two weeks, painting and doing other light maintenance work. One evening as Cooper relaxed on the bow of the ship, he was paged over the PA system to report to the gangway. As he approached the officer of the deck, he saluted and said "Seaman Dodge reporting as ordered, sir."

The officer simply nodded his head as he pointed toward the dock. "Seaman apprentice Darnell is here to see you."

After saluting the flag, Cooper ran down the gangway, grabbing hold of Paul and giving him a bear hug. "Where the hell did you come from, Paul. Damn, it is sure good to see you."

Paul laughed as he slapped Cooper on the back. "When I finished gunnery school, I was given orders to the *Tennessee* so she would have a full crew complement. Damn, she is a big ship, and I still don't know my way around her very well. You should come over and take a tour."

Cooper smiled, "Yeah, I think I'd like to see a battleship up close, I wanted to be on one when I was assigned to the *Honolulu*. So, what kind of gunnery do you do?"

Paul smiled, "I'm a loader on a 40mm pom pom gun tub. We were able to practice on the way out here, she really puts out some fire."

Cooper nodded his head, "Hell yeah, I know. I'm a gunner on a 40mm myself."

The next day Cooper was given permission to tour the *Tennessee*. He could not believe how much bigger the ship was compared to the *Honolulu*. After eating midday chow, the men ran into Lieutenant Crowder, the officer in charge of Paul's gun tub. After introductions, Paul asked if there was still an opening on any 40mm gun tubs.

Lieutenant Crowder nodded his head. "Seaman Jones was just promoted to a position on the carrier *Lexington*. So that means there is a gunners spot open in your tub, Darnell." Looking at Cooper he said, "The job is yours if you want it. Don't worry about the paper work, I'll handle everything. Since the *Honolulu* is down for repairs, you can move your sea bag over here first thing in the morning. Glad to have you aboard, Dodge."

Three days later most of the fleet sailed out of Pearl Harbor for a training mission south of the Hawaiian Islands. The seas were rough, but the *Tennessee* handled them well. Cooper loved sitting in his gun tub watching the massive fourteen-inch guns lobbing shells well beyond the horizon. The roar of the massive guns shook the gun tub with every blast, but you could not have a better ringside seat to watch the fireworks.

Returning to Pearl, Paul had two letters from Sadie waiting for him. Reading the second letter he gave out a yell as he grabbed Cooper and swung him around. "Can you believe it, I'm going to be a daddy, me Paul Darnell, I'm going to be a daddy. And better yet, Sadie and two friends are coming out here to Hawaii to share a house. It may not be the best set up, but having Sadie here is going to be fantastic!"

Cooper was excited for Paul, but was envious of Paul's success in life. In most cases Cooper had done his best to drive off any women that were interested in him, but now that he was maturing, he wanted to have a relationship with a woman he could count on to always be there for him. With the number of single men now coming to Hawaii with the fleet, Cooper figured his chances of meeting that special woman here was now next to impossible.

One evening when Paul was off with Sadie, Cooper went for a stroll down on Waikiki. Finding an open bench near a beach bar, Cooper purchased a bottle of beer and sat down to relax. While reading a story about the navy in a newspaper that had been left on the bench, he was paying little attention to anything around him. Eventually, a woman's voice broke his concentration.

Looking up, he observed a young woman of Polynesian descent standing several feet away. Closing the paper, Cooper smiled, "I'm so sorry, Miss. I was so engrossed in the article, I didn't understand what you said. Please forgive me."

Laughing, the woman pointed toward the bench. "I asked if I could join you."

Standing up, Cooper motioned toward the bench, "Yes please, that would be nice."

Sitting down. the woman took a swallow of beer from the bottle she was holding. "So, where are you from, sailor?"

"Kind of all over, but originally, New York City. Have you ever been to the forty-eight states?" Cooper inquired as he examined the woman's face.

Laughing she responded. "Actually, my mother was Hawaiian and my father is a naval officer, so I have lived in many places. San Diego, Charleston and Key West, just to mention a few. Actually, this is my first time in Hawaii. My mother paid for me to come and live with my grandparents so I could learn some of the Polynesian ways. I go to college where I'm studying to be a nurse, plus I work part time at a woman's fashion store. it keeps me busy and gives me some extra cash. So, what is your name, sailor? My name is Lily, Lily McDermitt, a true American name that my grandparents don't really care for. They call me Konane, which means bright moonlight"

"Well, the name fits you very well, you are a very radiant woman." Cooper replied. "My name is Cooper Dodge now. I changed it after I left New York. Originally it was Carmine Santucci."

"Hmm, I think I like Cooper Dodge much better. It's a strong name that people will remember. It fits you Cooper Dodge. May I call you Coop?" Lily asked, as she felt a very real liking for this Italian sailor from New York. "Do you have a girlfriend, Cooper Dodge?"

"No, I've never been that lucky, but I need to ask and hope I'm not out of line. Do you have a boyfriend?" As he waited for her reply, he was really hoping she would say no.

"I think we are both in luck, because, no, I do not have a boyfriend. I approached you tonight because you looked interesting and were just minding your own business, despite all the pretty girls on the beach, something most naval boys do not do." Lily responded, feeling very excited that Cooper was not attached to anyone.

Cooper and Lily continued seeing each other when ever their schedules allowed them free time, and they always made the most of it. Paul and Sadie loved Lily and enjoyed spending time with her also.

As rumors of war in the Pacific continued to become a daily conversation in and around Pearl Harbor, the fleet spent the majority of its time out at sea preparing for any eventuality. Every sailor on those powerful vessels hoped the rumors were wrong and they would not be called upon to fight, but they also wanted to be ready just in case.

However, now orders had come down from the Commander in Chief, Pacific Command, also known as Cincpac, that armed guards were to be posted around the clock on every ship. The torpedo nets across the entrance of the harbor were to be closed and secured after ship traffic had passed by. Ready boxes near each gun were to be stocked with ammunition, but they were still to remain locked.

April 15, 1940 Prime Minister Konoye's office in the War Ministry

After another heated round of discussions regarding how Japan was to deal with the United States, Prime Minister Konoye shook his head. "Each time we meet we get nowhere, although the United States continues to tighten its strangle hold on Japan."

With Prince Kotohito present for the discussions, it quickly became obvious that he was not happy with what he was hearing. Turning to Vice Admiral Yamamoto, he said, "Admiral, it appears you have stuck to the plan you presented us nearly a year ago. Do you think your plan can work and bring the United States to its knees?"

Both General Tojo and Admiral Fukudome stood up, arguing that it was clear Yamamoto's plan was reckless, dangerous and put far too many of Japan's war resources on the line for one attack. Raising his hand into the air, the Prime Minister responded. "We shall see what the Admiral has to say."

Walking up to the large map, Yamamoto pointed to Hawaii. This is where we need to strike the fatal blow. My staff have reworked my original plan several times to make sure it is fool proof. We shall attack at dawn on a Sunday of our choice. The fleet will contain six carriers. They will travel to Hawaii via a northern route, avoiding all merchant vessels. Their main targets will be battleships and carriers. They will fly off the carriers in three separate attacks. Once all the planes are recovered, the fleet will leave and sail back to Japan, while making strikes on the Philippines and Wake Island as they pass by. We can make changes as we move forward, but this is the plan we now wish to put in place."

The room was quiet as the Admiral took his seat. Prince Kotohito stood up from his red leather chair and looked at the map once again. "We are still working on contracts with several Pacific Rim nations for iron ore and scrap metal, but I am sure they will be in place shortly. Then we can build a fleet that can rule the Pacific."

Admiral Fukudome stood up next, arguing that six carriers were too many, and that one of the large carriers should stay back in home waters to protect Japan. Admiral Yamamoto once again stood up and bowed slightly. "If we do not take six carriers, our mission will fail. We must be able to put nearly three hundred planes in the air to overcome defense issues on Oahu. It is six carriers or the mission will not be possible."

Prime Minister Konoye nodded his head. "I feel the Admiral's plan is sound, but no doubt dangerous. Nevertheless, he is the only one that has put together an aggressive plan against the United States and outlined how it shall be carried out. I will notify the emperor that we have a plan."

As the war ministers began to leave the office, it was evident there was no clear agreement on Yamamoto's plan. However, everyone took time to wish Yamamoto the best of luck with the Emperor.

Several days later, Yamamoto was summoned to meet with Emperor Hirohito. He realized his entire plan rested on the presentation he was going to give today. Although confident of the organization of the attack, it still came down to the emperor's decision.

Arriving at the Fukiage Palace, Yamamoto sought out the emperors closest aides, inquiring as to what the emperor expected from him, but no one was able to give him the answers he sought as these were surely uncharted waters.

Yamamoto was seated in the ornate waiting room for just a short time, before being called into see his Imperial Majesty, Emperor Hirohito. Entering the ornate office, Yamamoto bowed and recited a blessing most visitors used when meeting their emperor.

The young emperor stood up from his desk. "You may be seated, Admiral Yamamoto. I have heard a lot about you and have many questions regarding your plan."

Walking up to a plastic covered map of the Pacific, he pointed toward Hawaii. "Everyone in the war council says Pearl Harbor is the place we must attack to take America out of the war. It is roughly 4,000 miles across the roughest part of the Pacific Ocean, and the possibility of storms only increases the risks we may face. Do you believe we can sail that distance and still do enough damage to the American fleet to take them out of the war?"

Admiral Yamamoto stood up and traced the route across the map with a grease pen that the fleet would follow. Taking a deep breath, the Admiral looked at his emperor. "Your majesty, Japan has the ships and the men to make such a trip. However, I do not think everything has been worked out properly yet. They talk of four or five carriers, but I believe there should be six. The battleship Admirals talk of five battleships to accompany the fleet, I think there should be just two. The plan right now is to have eight oilers, I believe there should be nine to be on the safe side. The mix of aircraft is still a question we will need to resolve, depending on what ships are in the harbor when we depart Japan. It is mostly agreed that we will attack at dawn on a weekend, preferably a Sunday morning. We should launch our aircraft when we are two hundred miles northwest of Hawaii. That would give our planes the optimum time to fulfill their assigned missions. We should launch our aircraft in two separate waves to ensure maximum damage. Originally, I believed we should have three separate waves, but now I believe two larger waves will be less costly for the fleet. However, as the carriers will burn no aviation fuel all the way to Hawaii, they will have enough fuel for the planes if the task force commander decides a third attack is called for. Once the second flight is sent off, the fleet will begin its withdrawal to the west. The first attack group will know in advance where to rendezvous with the returning fleet."

The emperor stood quiet for a moment as he took in everything Yamamoto had told him. Pointing to the waters around the launch area, the emperor went on. "What is the possibility of the fleet being discovered by American submarines?"

Yamamoto nodded his head. "That is always a risk. However, the United States Navy has been doing most of their submarine and anti-submarine training to the south and southwest of Hawaii. It is my belief that they will never expect an attack from the dangerous seas to the north. Plus, while we are launching our attacks, we can spread out the light cruisers and destroyers to create a curtain around our fleet to watch for enemy submarines. We can also put up some patrol aircraft to search, once the attack flights have struck their targets. I do not believe submarines will be a problem."

The emperor appeared to be satisfied with everything Yamamoto had explained to him. Walking over to the large glass windows, the emperor stood quiet for a moment before asking. "If this attack is successful, and we put the American fleet out of action, what kind of prognosis can you give me for our future war efforts?"

Yamamoto knew that question was going to be asked, but he also understood the emperor may not like his response, but he was ready to answer. "Your majesty, an attack on Pearl Harbor will no doubt anger the American people, and they will demand their government act swiftly to bring the war to our shores. I have been to America, and I am well aware of their industrial might. The best I can promise you is that after the attack on Pearl Harbor, I'll be able to run wild in the Pacific for six months, but after that, I can guarantee you nothing. I gave this same answer to Prince Kotohito about two weeks ago."

Turning back toward his desk, the emperor no longer had the confident look on his face he had earlier. Turning to Yamamoto, he asked. "After those six months, what will be the fate of Japan?"

Yamamoto looked his emperor face to face. "By that time, we will be dealing with the British and the Australians, as well as the United States. There will be many naval battles, some of which we shall win. But there may be a question as to how much of the newly conquered territory we gained during the first six months can be defended properly. If we are strung out across thousands of miles of ocean, things may become bleak sooner than we would like."

Nodding his head, the emperor asked, "If we should need to consider talks to end the war, how do you think the United States would respond?"

Shaking his head Admiral Yamamoto replied. "I have no good answer for you on that question. However I feel their terms would be the toughest possible, and it would mean the end of Japan's Greater East Asia Co-prosperity Sphere. They would seek strict retribution for the attack on Pearl Harbor, and all the losses they will have sustained up to that point."

Sitting down behind his desk, the emperor nodded his head. "You have put much careful thought into this plan, and have looked at everything with an open mind. I feel we must move forward with the attack so we are able to create a Pacific for the Asian people as we have discussed many times. Begin moving forward Admiral, and if there are any issues I feel need more serious discussion, my palace shall be in touch with you."

September 10, 1940, 0900 hours, Tokyo, Japan

With the surrender of France to Germany on June 25, there instantly became a void as to who controlled France's overseas colonies. Nobody was more interested than Japan, as there were raw materials to be gathered and ports to be seized, and here was a possibility to shut down the Kunming Haiphong Railroad the Chinese military was using to bring in war supplies and oil.

Prime Minister Konoye paced his office quietly, as Admiral Yamamoto, General Tojo, and General Sugiyama sat quietly in their seats. After taking one more look at the map of southeast Asia, the Prime Minister turned toward his small audience. "We began talks with French General Henri Petain,* the leader of the Vichy Government in southern France, regarding the possibility of allowing Japan to move into French Indochina. As the talks continued, Petain had decided he would approve Japan's request. However, it now appears that agreement has fallen apart.

General Charles De Gaulle* has claimed to be leader of the French Government in exile, and refuses to negotiate with us, or accept any agreement Petain might make. We had hoped to peacefully negotiate a surrender of French Indochina, but that is now out of the question. It appears we have no other choice but to take Indochina by force. We have a strike force of 6,000 men on Hainan Island, and enough trained men ready to go so we can send a larger force by sea to back them up. When can we be ready to commence the attack?"

General Sugiyama stood up immediately. "Sir, we could be ready to invade by September 25 if the navy can supply us transports and two carriers to provide us with air support."

As quickly as he sat down, Admiral Yamamoto stood up. "Sir, the navy can supply the general with whatever he needs to make the invasion possible as he has suggested, but we need to keep one thing in mind. The naval command will be sending you a memo on September 22, informing you we now have less than a two-year supply of bunker oil remaining. Being cut off from

United States oil has taken a large amount of fuel out of our inventory. We must find a way to get more oil, and do it quickly."

Nodding his head, the Prime Minister smiled. We have already sent several envoys to Java asking them to increase the amount of oil they are selling to us. I hope to hear more about the negotiations in the next few days. Gentlemen, it appears we are all in agreement. We shall set the date for invasion of Indochina for September 25.

Having a clear consensus from his top officers, on September 25, 1940, Japan invaded North Vietnam with 6,000 troops that had been stationed on Hainan Island. The invading force quickly pushed inland, turning north toward Haiphong. A force of 25,000 men under the command of General Takuma Nishimura,* was already on its way from Japan with strong air cover from aircraft carriers. They landed on the same well secured beaches and began driving inland toward the capital city of Hanoi. In short order, Japanese forces took control of the Kunming Haiphong Railroad from the port of Haiphong and Hanoi to the Chinese border. That effectively closed the back door on China's ability to bring military supplies from outside sources. All French military forces and political leaders in Hanoi were safely evacuated.

Batavia, Java, September 9, 1940

As a confident looking Japanese foreign affairs delegation entered the capital building in Batavia, they knew what they wanted, and did not intend to leave until their demands were met. On the other side of the table sat a group of oil executives and government officials from Java.

The British oil minister began the discussion. "We have read your proposal and understand your need for more crude oil. However, you must realize we supply many nations in this part of the world with oil, which makes up one hundred percent of what we produce. We have been sending you 4.5 million barrels of oil a year, and we just cannot send any more.

The Japanese minister smiled slightly as he leaned forward. "You must understand that Japan's industry and military are using more oil than ever before. If we are to keep growing, we need to have you send us 22 million barrels of oil starting this coming year."

The oil minister looked stunned upon hearing the number. He shook his head and said, "Do you realize that is nearly forty percent of our entire annual output? That number is not possible."

After debating back and forth for a good part of the day, the Japanese minister looked menacingly at the delegation across the table. "We need oil for our ships, and our navy is growing incredibly fast. You must come up with a number we can deal with, or there is always the possibility of war, where we will just seize what we want. You must make up your mind on this matter quickly."

The following day when the two delegations met again, the oil minister promised they could sell Japan 14.5 million barrels of oil a year, roughly the amount the United States had cut in the embargo. Temporarily pleased with the deal, the Japanese delegation left for Tokyo, knowing the day was coming when they would have the forces to seize all the oil and natural resources of Java, and place them under the Greater East Asia Co-prosperity Sphere. It was clear to the British oil executives that time was not on their side.

September 19-25, 1940, Washington D.C.

Throughout the day on September 19, 1940, Walt and his team studied intercepts from the far east very carefully. It was mid-afternoon when Walt walked into Bill Friedman's office. "Sir, it appears a large Japanese convoy of ships, including troop transports, supply ships, and aircraft carriers, is sailing south from Japan. We know talks have broken down between Japan and the French government, so all indications suggest that Japan is going to land troops somewhere in French Indochina. Our best bet is they will land in the north. Everyone on the floor agrees that Japan is about to make a big move."

Bill Friedman read several of the intercepts, as well as the statement his team had put together. After nodding his head, he replied, "I'll get a packet put together for the White House immediately."

On September 25, 1940, the cryptology office in Washington was buzzing as every cryptologist was busy reading intercepts from every major news source in Europe, as well as the many foreign embassies still operating on the continent.

Bill Friedman stood center office taking decoded intercepts from everyone in the room as they finished them. Walking over to Walt's desk he leaned against the wall. "Something is happening Walt. We have Italian Foreign Minister Galeazzo Ciano* and Japanese Special Envoy Kuruso Saburo* in Berlin, and Ribbentrop is telling the foreign press there will be a major announcement on Friday, but he has not given any clues as to what it could be. What do you think is happening?"

Walt set down his coffee mug and shook his head. "I'm not sure, but whatever it is, it's not good. I don't see Germany sending forces to Japan to help them when they invade Indochina or the Dutch East Indies. No, there is something else going on, and right now we got nothing."

On Friday, September 27, all eyes were on Berlin as every reporter crowded around the Reichstag to see what was going to be announced. Around noon, German Foreign Minister Joachim Von Ribbentrop appeared on the steps of the Reichstag holding a document. Approaching the microphone, he stated that Germany, Italy, and Japan had just finished signing a historical defense pact. It stated that if one of the nations was attacked by a foreign power, it was an attack on all three nations. It became known as the Tripartite Act.

President Roosevelt sat at his desk in the Oval Office when he was buzzed by his secretary that Prime Minister Winston Churchill was on the phone. The president knew exactly what the call was about, as the message had been carried by the BBC and its affiliates, as well as NBC and CBS radio in the United States.

Picking up the phone the president said, "My dear Winston, what can I do for you today?"

"Mr. President, it appears all our eggs have been thrown into one basket now. We'll need to create some sort of an alliance if we are to defeat this serious threat!" Prime Minister Churchill spoke emphatically, hoping to back Roosevelt into a tight corner.

President Roosevelt smiled slightly at the Prime Minister's comment as he gathered his thoughts. "Mr. Prime Minister, I fully understand the situation you are in. However, I cannot unilaterally join you in the war on the continent without approval from congress. As you realize, our programs allowing you to purchase war equipment for penny's on the dollar is close to breaking the rules of neutrality. It has only been twenty-two years since the war ended in 1918, and most Americans are not ready to send our boys over to Europe to fight another war. We will continue to supply you as congress allows, but to commit troops and ships to fight is out of the question."

The conversation continued for some time, with Churchill realizing the only way America would ever come into the war, was if it were attacked.

October 29, 1940, Department of War Auditorium, Washington D.C.

On September 16, 1940, congress passed the selective service act which stated every man in the United States between the ages of 21 and 45 needed to register for the military draft. On October 29, the lottery numbers that had been placed in blue celluloid capsules were dumped into a ten-gallon fish bowl. A blindfolded Secretary of War stirred the bowl with a wooden spoon. He then drew out a capsule, handing it to President Roosevelt. He opened it and read number 158 out loud. A woman in the audience shrieked when she heard the number, as she knew her son Robert Bell* had been assigned that number. That evening 6,175 men were the first called up for military service that would see duty during World War Two.

Ironically, President Roosevelt was involved in a presidential campaign at the time. In a campaign speech the following night, he promised not to send American boys into a foreign war.

CHAPTER TEN – THE THREAT GROWS

The roar of warming engines reverberated throughout the sprawling naval base near Hiroshima, as twenty Aichi dive bombers, known as Vals to the allied forces, awaited orders to take off.

Keisuke sat quietly in the cockpit of plane 1165, watching his instruments as the propeller attached to the huge radial engine spun in front of him. Today was the first day his entire crew would take to the skies as a team, and Keisuke wanted to make sure everything was perfect. Looking out through the heavy glass canopy, he could see the first planes beginning to taxi toward the runway.

Masashi Kaneko, his second seat man, spoke into the intercom. "Keisuke, we know you are one of the top-rated pilots in this new wing. Show us today how good you really are."

Smiling, Keisuke replied. "Starting today my friend, I will only be as good as you are as my spotter. Put me on target each time we attack and the crew of bomber 1165 will be known by everyone at headquarters."

Nodding his head, Masashi replied. "You will have clear targets I can assure you."

As the aircraft rolled forward, Haruto Ishii, the third seat spotter and gunner looked up at the cloud bank that was building off to the north. He understood there were times when they would have to fly through ominous weather to reach their targets several hundred miles away, but the dark clouds still sent a shiver down his spine.

"Keisuke, are we headed north today? It looks like the weather could be rough."

Keisuke smiled, aware of Haruto's nervousness regarding bad weather. "No, we are heading south to attack an old freighter. Do not fret my brother, I will not let anything happen to you."

By now plane 1165 stood next in line to take off. As the warrant officer at the end of the runway waved his green flag, Keisuke released the brake, shoving his throttles forward. Quickly, the aircraft rose into the morning sky, climbing to a predetermined altitude of 12,000 feet. After crossing over Kochi Island, the squadron turned south toward the Ryukyu Islands.

Although the squadron was now flying through broken cumulus clouds, Keisuke was still able to make out the many small islands that made up the several hundred-mile chain of islands.

Finally, Lieutenant Kimura came on the radio, giving out the coordinates to where the target ship was anchored. Zooming in with his spotting scope, Masashi found the vessel anchored about ten feet off the coast of a small rocky island. As the first planes in the squadron made their attacks. Keisuke was upset by the number of misses taking place. Just before he began his dive, Masashi gave him a quick course change that took the 1165 slightly over the island. Dropping the nose over to begin the dive, Keisuke could feel a slight tug on the plane from the wind as it blew between the more mountainous islands. Holding the aircraft steady in the dive, the crew watched the long steel deck coming up at them at an incredible speed. As usual, Keisuke pulled the red lever at 3,000 feet and slid the plane off to the west about 300 feet above the water.

Both Masashi and Haruto were screaming for joy, as they watched the sand bag slam into the deck of the target ship, right in the middle of the large red circle. Today there were no small wing bombs to drop, so the squadron climbed back to 4,000 feet and practiced aerial dog fighting. Although a dive bomber was not built to fight other aircraft, it had two 7.7-millimeter front facing machine guns, and one rear facing machine gun operated by the third man in the cockpit. It was well known that the rear facing machine gunner was always a favorite target of an enemy fighter. Taking him out made the heavier dive bomber a much easier target to dispose of.

Returning to Hiroshima, Lieutenant Kimura called all his pilots together, less than happy about their overall performance. He paced the classroom for several moments before looking at his pilots. "Three! Just three hits on the target. Yes, there were two strikes on the side of the vessel, but a real war ship would have heavy armor plating that would have reduced the impacts of those bombs. This ship was not moving, and if it had been, it might have lived to fight another day. Every pilot in this squadron was handpicked for a special mission that will be coming up shortly. If you cannot perform and strike your targets within the next month, you will be relieved and transferred out. So, starting tomorrow you must do your best every day."

As every pilot in the squadron saw himself as special, and the last thing anyone wanted was to suffer the embarrassment of being relieved. The following day the planes attacked two target ships in the islands off Nagasaki. The lecture had done wonders, as all but two planes struck their assigned targets. By the end of the month, only one pilot and his crew were transferred out of the squadron. It was a happy time for the crews, as they were honing their skills every day.

Taking a four-day leave, Keisuke traveled to Tokyo to pick up his wife Etsuko, and bring her to their new home on the naval base. She was very excited about being a naval aviators wife, and starting a new life with her husband. One day they went on an adventure to Kanawa Island. After exiting the ferry, they walked for a while before sitting down on a large bench near the water. After sipping some wine they had brought along to share, Etsuko looked directly at her husband. "How do you feel when you are in your plane, knowing you are preparing to kill other people?"

Keisuke was taken back by her brutally honest question. After gathering his thoughts, he replied. "Japan will only use it's sea power for good, to defend our empire, and fight only if attacked. Then I will be able to do my job without question."

Etsuko was not sure how far to push the conversation, as Keisuke had never been touched by the realities of war the way she had. A year ago, her brother had been killed in China and was hailed as a hero that was defending the empire. She knew nothing about how he had perished, but felt the continual expansion of the war in China was not defending the safety of the empire. She was angry with the ever-increasing power the militarists used as a strangle hold in Tokyo to build a war machine like nothing Japan had ever seen over thousands of years.

After taking a long breath, she asked. "What if you are asked to bomb villages or cities in China? What will you do? There could be old people and children, even babies in those towns. What would you do? Is it your job to kill those people?"

Keisuke was getting a bit upset with his new wife, as it was not the place of a woman to get involved in such matters questioning the actions of the Imperial Government.

"That is difficult to answer." Keisuke said, as he looked into his wife's questioning eyes. "I do not believe our government would ever ask pilots like me to bomb innocent people. They would make sure everyone had departed the cities before we attacked, so we would strictly be bombing enemy forces."

Hearing the tension in her husbands voice, Etsuko realized she had pushed the subject as far as she dared without causing problems between them. Hoping to smooth out the uncomfortable tension that had crept into their little holiday, Etsuko stood up and stretched out her hand. "Let's walk and figure out names for our child, the baby will be here before we know it."

Smiling, Keisuke grabbed her hand and began following her along the path that ran near the water. They took turns swapping names and making jokes until they reached an attractive open-air restaurant. After sharing a special meal Etsuko had chosen from the menu, the couple walked through several shops and outdoor booths until it was time to catch the ferry back to Hiroshima.

Arriving back at their humble home, Etsuko went to bed, as it had been a long day for her. However Keisuke sat on the small stoop on the front of the house, quietly contemplating everything his wife had asked him. There was no doubt in his mind that he and his wife had a difference of opinion on how the government in Tokyo was handling the war in China. She no longer trusted the war ministry, and for good reasons, but no matter how Keisuke looked at the situation, it was his job to support the government and do what it asked of him, as he was one of their highly trained pilots.

About a month later, Masashi walked out to the flight line to attach a newer, clearer lens to his spotting scope. As the sun was beginning to set and no one else was on the flight line, Keisuke checked to see if he could help his spotter. Once the work was completed, Masashi said. "Commander, now I should be able to see a gnat on the back of a bald China-man's head before we drop our bomb."

Keisuke laughed as he leaned up against the side of the plane. "My friend, would you ever wish to drop a bomb on that bald China-man's head?"

After a moment of thought, Masashi replied. "If it meant winning the war and saving lives of the Imperial Army, yes, I would. It would be my duty to do so, don't you agree?"

Kicking at a small stone that was laying on the tarmac, Keisuke said. "But when we drop that bomb, how do we know that killing that bald man, or any other will end the war and keep our families in Japan safe?"

Masashi wrinkled up his forehead as he stared as his plane commander. "What has gotten into you, lieutenant? You have always impressed me as a pilot that would do his duty without question, and would be proud to be part of the Greater East Asia Co-prosperity Sphere."

Keisuke smiled as he nodded his head. "Relax, your commander has not lost his nerve, or his desire to be the best dive bomber pilot in the Japanese navy." Realizing he had to be careful not to implicate his wife as an anti-government dissenter, he continued. "The skills we have learned can do nothing but ensure our empire will last a thousand years. I want to be part of that in every way, I just want to make sure the crew of the 1165 stays faithful to our mission to the emperor."

Nodding his head, Masashi replied. "You have nothing to worry about, my friend. Our emperor will never ask us to do anything that would tarnish our empire or cast doubt and suspicions on our intentions."

Several days later, Lieutenant Kimura assembled the air crews in a hangar. After uncovering a chart, he turned toward his men. "Today you will enter the next phase of your training. You will learn how to takeoff, and drop 500-pound bombs. These bombs will be used to attack enemy aircraft carriers, cruisers, destroyers, and auxiliary vessels. But the explosive power of these bombs is wasted on a battleship unless you can obtain a lucky hit. The weight of these weapons will affect the takeoff and dive skills you have already learned. As you will need to adjust your take off skills, you will be moved over to another runway that is set up to teach you how to take off and land from a carrier. The bright orange lines on the runway equal the length of one of our glorious carriers. There are three cables stretched across the runway that are hooked to hydraulic pistons. As you land, you will now use your tail hook to grab one of the wires.

Approaching plane 1165, Keisuke observed the huge practice bomb attached to the underbelly of his aircraft. As he knelt beside it, Haruto knelt beside him. "The emperor is giving us great responsibilities now. We must learn to use this tool efficiently, so we can be ready to attack the enemy carriers that will be thrust against us in the coming war with the United States."

Keisuke scowled as he looked at his rear gunner. "Why would the United States seek to attack Japan? There is no reason for a war with a nation the size of America."

As the men crawled out from under the plane, Haruto responded. "The leaders of the United States will never allow the emperor to continue building the Greater East Asia Co-prosperity Alliance. You will see, they will bring war to the Japanese people, and we will need to send them back with their tails between their legs, begging for forgiveness. It shall be so, Keisuke, it shall be so."

Once Masashi arrived, the men climbed aboard their bomber and prepared for takeoff. Several planes in front of 1165 were still on the ground as they passed the orange stripe, infuriating Lieutenant Kimura. Not wanting to make the same mistake, Keisuke brought his engine up to a stiffer RPM than he ever had before as he released the brakes. The 1165 shot down the shortened runway like a scared jack rabbit, bringing the tail of the plane up from the deck quicker than it ever had before. Continuing to pour fuel to the engine, the 1165 became airborne well before the orange stripe. Both Haruto and Masashi cheered as Keisuke followed the squadron up to 12,000 feet. It did not take long for Keisuke to realize how differently the aircraft operated with the extra 500 pounds hanging from the bomb rack, but he was able to adjust, and easily control his plane. Today, the bombs they carried were going to be dropped on a small uninhabited island in the Ryukyu Islands. Lieutenant Kimura led his squadron around the island once, so the pilots could take a good look at the target before dropping their bomb. Once again, the sky was filled with low hanging cumulus clouds, but nothing that Keisuke had not overcome in past practice sessions. As the planes started back on a southerly course, Lieutenant Kimura gave the signal to attack. One by one the pilots nosed over their aircraft and began a steep dive, hoping to land their bombs inside the flagged area in the center of the small island. Like all the bombers, the 1165 nosed over much quicker with the extra weight, but Masashi called out clear and precise adjustments, helping Keisuke to bring the 1165 right where it needed to be. With small mountain peaks surrounding the bombing range, it was essential the pilots drop their bombs from nothing lower than 3200 feet.

As soon as Keisuke pulled his red lever, he pulled back on the stick, pouring fuel to the engine as he began turning toward the south. All three men were pushed back in their seats by the force of the turn as Keisuke watched the last peak disappear underneath the 1165, with just 125 feet to spare. As the 1165 continued climbing to join the squadron, Keisuke made one more turn which laid his plane over on its side. In horror, the men were able to see bomber 1148 slam into the mountain peak they had just missed. Flames shot skyward for several hundred feet as the fuel tanks exploded. Debris from the explosion scattered in every direction as what remained of the aircraft and its crew slid down the side of the mountain.

It was a quiet flight back to base, with every man contemplating what had just happened to one of their important aircrews. Keisuke shook his head to get himself refocused for the landing as he stared down at the orange stripe that represented the fantail of the ship. Seconds later, the tail hook of 1165 grabbed the number two wire, bringing the bomber to a stop. After maneuvering his plane over to the parking area, Keisuke looked down at his shaking hands. He had never experienced fear in the sky before, but now he had watched a plane destroyed with its entire crew, and he had learned what it was going to be like landing on a carrier, and being responsible for the lives of his crew.

After practicing carrier landings for several days on the concrete runway, Lieutenant Kimura felt his pilots were ready for the real thing. On a Friday morning the squadron took off heading out over the Sea of Japan where the carrier *Soryu* was on maneuvers with the fleet. Lieutenant Kimura landed perfectly, making it all look very easy. Several pilots in front of Keisuke were waved off by the landing crew, forcing them to go around and try a second time.

Listening to the landing crew on the radio, Keisuke began pulling back on the throttle as he watched the rolling, heaving deck of the carrier. He felt like calling off the landing and going around for a second try, but he also understood nothing was going to change with the attitude of the deck. It would be something he would have to conquer each time he landed his aircraft. It was evident that the landing crew was happy with the way 1165 was lined up, as they encouraged Keisuke to continue his approach. Moments later, the 1165 cleared the ramp and dropped down onto the deck as Keisuke cut the power to his engine. Immediately the tail hook grabbed the wire bringing the aircraft to a nice managed stop. Deck handlers quickly signaled where they wanted the 1165 moved so the deck could be ready for the next approaching aircraft.

With everyone on board, the crews were treated to a typical carrier meal before getting a tour of the vessel. By 1700 hours, Lieutenant Kimura rolled down the pitching deck, leading his squadron back to Hiroshima for a debriefing before allowing everyone to have a weekend off.

Etsuko was happy to have her husband home for two long days. Knowing training would soon be over, she knew Keisuke would then be assigned to a carrier, and would be gone for long periods of time. She knew being assigned to a carrier was exactly what her husband wanted, and had lived for, but she still had a nagging feeling the day would come when he would have to make tough decisions regarding what he was ordered to do and what he believed in.

On Monday morning, everyone in the squadron held their breath, waiting to see what carrier they would be calling home. As in any military unit rumors traveled at a blistering speed, with no substantiation to back them up. Finally, Lieutenant Kimura called everyone together in the shade on the north side of the main hangar. The first order of business was to introduce the crew of aircraft 1112. They had completed training in Yokohama and would fill in for the lost crew of aircraft 1148.

The lieutenant then stood smiling for several seconds without saying a word as he watched his crews begin to get restless and call him funny names. Finally, he held up his hand and bowed toward his men. The crews were ecstatic as they yelled their approval and slapped each other on the back as the lieutenant said one word, "Akagi!" The newest and largest carrier in the combined fleet.

After the men stopped cheering, Lieutenant Kimura nodded his head. "You have all earned this privilege. No other squadron in the training program has scored higher points than you. Now go out to the fleet and make the emperor proud of you."

CHAPTER ELEVEN – THE AKAGI

Although Keisuke missed his wife tremendously, and knew he was not going to be home for the birth of his first child, he was enjoying life on a carrier. He had become accustomed to the pitching deck as he set down his aircraft, and enjoyed the drills and practice raids the squadrons went through. It was always interesting when the level bombers, torpedo bombers, fighter aircraft and his dive bombers worked together on a training mission. It was interesting to watch each of the different type of aircraft complete their missions while the other crews were heavily involved in support roles.

Now many daily lectures included segments regarding American politics, their navy and Pearl Harbor. The crews began studying photos and charts of Pearl Harbor, and other military installations around the island of Oahu.

Whenever the *Akagi* was within flying distance of Tokyo, Commander Minoru Genda,* third chief of staff of Japan's air self-defense force, would fly out to the carrier and meet with its top officers. Few people on the ship realized he was one of the secret general staff of the navy working on preparations for the attack on Pearl Harbor.

One evening as Genda walked around the hangar deck of the *Akagi*, he noticed Keisuke speaking with his mechanic regarding an adjustment to the rudder. It was clear the mechanic was not agreeing with the adjustment Keisuke was asking for.

As Genda approached, both men jumped to attention and saluted. After returning their salutes, he looked at the mechanic. "Have you ever flown a dive bomber?"

Looking down at the deck for a moment the mechanic replied, "No Commander, I am not a pilot, but you must understand that—"

Before he could finish Genda raised his hand. "I have heard your pilot's request and explanation for the adjustment. It is he who flies this beautiful piece of equipment and understands how it reacts to small and large bomb loads. It is he who needs to worry how his aircraft will respond when going into a deep dive. I suggest you make the adjustment, and if it does not work, the two of you can work out a compromise. Does that make asense to you?"

The mechanic nodded his head. "It shall be done, Commander." Turning to Keisuke he continued, "I will adjust your rudder as requested. Forgive me for not listening to you."

Keisuke nodded his head and gave his mechanic a slap on the shoulder. "Together we shall have the best dive bomber in the fleet. You need not apologize." After both men bowed, Genda smiled before continuing his walk.

Quickly, Keisuke called out, "Commander, may I have some of your time?"

Smiling at the young pilot, Genda replied, "Actually, I need some coffee. Let's go to the officers wardroom and we can talk there."

Sitting down with steaming cups of coffee, Genda asked, "So, what is bothering you, Keisuke, are you having problems back home?"

"No Commander, everything is fine with my family. But I am concerned about some things. I keep hearing rumors regarding Japan's future in the world." Keisuke began. "I keep hearing reports that we shall soon be going to war with the United States and Britain, but I do not believe they would ever attack us, so how would that be possible?"

Genda's face turned hard and cold as he stared at Keisuke. "Japan's future relies on controlling every aspect of the Pacific. If we are going to make the Greater East Asian Co-prosperity Sphere rich and successful for all Asian people, we will need to push out all the other nations that are robbing the Pacific of its treasures. Only we should be allowed to mine them and use them as we see fit. So, it will be the mission of our Imperial forces to push all non-Asians out of the Pacific."

Keisuke thought about what he had just been told. "Does that mean we will be attacking foreign nations to destroy them?"

Genda gave a slight smile, "Yes, Keisuke, we will all be involved in making the Pacific a true home for all Asians. We will give outsiders an opportunity to leave, and our great leaders in Tokyo believe it shall all work out. Do not fear Keisuke, you will do well."

In April of 1941, Japanese forces in China were involved in attacking the headquarters of the nineteenth Chinese Army but were bogged down. It appeared the only way the stalemate could be broken, was through the use of air power. Dive bombers from the *Akagi* and *Soryu* were assigned to attack Chinese positions all along the defensive line. The 1165 was fitted with three one-hundred-pound high explosive bombs. Fighter aircraft from both carriers escorted their bombers to the prescribed targets. Each bomber was to make two passes over the targets, hitting separate targets on each pass.

As Lieutenant Kimura gave the order to attack, each pilot dropped down from 13,000 feet. With the rudder readjusted, the 1165 was much easier to handle during the dive, as the plane plunged toward earth. Clearing the clouds at 9,000 feet, Keisuke could see the lead planes dropping their bombs on a village about two miles behind the battle lines. Taking aim at a large building on the west side of the town, at 3,000 feet, Keisuke pulled the red lever. As the 1165 screamed low across an open field, beginning to gain altitude, the crew could see the building erupt in a massive ball of flame. Keisuke did not have time to think about what he had just done, as he was attempting to avoid anti-aircraft fire as he climbed to 12,000 feet before attacking once more dropping his wing bombs.

On the second attack, Lieutenant Kimura assigned the crew of the 1165 to strike a small bridge just to the west of the village. Once again making a perfect dive, Keisuke released his bombs and turned north, but nearly froze when he looked down to see the bridge and road flooded with civilians attempting to escape the fighting.

Masashi yelled, "Keisuke, what is the matter, pull up, pull up!"

Hearing his co-pilot's pleas, Keisuke pulled back on his stick, sending power to the engine so they could climb away from the angry Chinese forces that were firing at them, and fly back toward their carrier.

That evening, Keisuke laid quietly on his bunk, wondering how many civilians he had killed. How many were women and children, how many were old people escaping with just the few essential belongings they could still carry. No one on that road was a combatant, no one on that road had been given notice they were going to be attacked. As tears ran down Keisuke's face, he was sure this was not going to be the last time he was going to be ordered to attack innocent civilians and it made him sick. The glamour and thrill of being a pilot for the emperor no longer excited him. Now he knew all the stories he had heard about atrocities by Japanese bomber pilots were true.

After tossing and turning for an hour or more, Keisuke went for a walk around the ship. Soon he was walking into the hangar bay where the mechanics were working at a fevered pitch repairing damaged aircraft.

Approaching 1165, he watched his mechanic rivet a new piece of sheet metal to the underside of the plane. Walking over to the mechanic, he said. "So, there was some battle damage that needed to be repaired?"

The mechanic bowed and replied. "Yes, you were struck several times by ground fire. I removed eight bullets and a piece of shrapnel from an antiaircraft gun. The shrapnel missed your rudder cable by half an inch. You were lucky it stopped where it did or you would have gone down. You must pull up faster after dropping your bombs. Japan cannot lose a good pilot like you, Keisuke."

Giving his mechanic a slap on the back, he replied, "And Japan has need of good mechanics like you who keep the planes flying. I shall be more careful in the future."

After getting a breath of fresh air near one of the elevators, Keisuke went back to his quarters. The talk with his mechanic had only served to make him feel worse. He not only killed innocent people today, he had almost killed his crew when he froze for a few moments. Settling into his bunk, he hoped he could do better during his next mission.

Over the next few days, Keisuke bombed and strafed several Chinese military positions that were threatening to overrun Japanese positions. These were the types of missions that made him feel like a true Japanese patriot, since saving Japanese soldiers was most important.

A week later his squadron was chosen to attack a hill where Chinese soldiers had dug in and were holding up a Japanese offensive. Lieutenant Kimura brought the squadron in at 16,000 feet, hoping to avoid some of the heavy antiaircraft fire. As they approached the hill, Lieutenant Kimura said, "Planes 1165, 1166 and 1158, attack the antiaircraft guns on the north side of the village. The rest of you follow me down the hill."

Keisuke followed the other two planes as they headed for the village. Heavy smoke from all the antiaircraft guns was blowing into the village, creating a problem for Masashi to get an accurate sighting. As 1165 dropped past 9,000 feet Keisuke called out, "Any last adjustments?"

But Masashi did not answer as he was struggling to get a good sighting so they would bomb the target accurately.

Getting frustrated as the plane approached 8,000 feet, Keisuke yelled into the intercom. "Tell me quick, any adjustments?"

After getting what Masashi thought was a good sighting, he called back, "Keep her on this glide path, we are lined up perfectly."

At 2,500 feet, Keisuke released his bombs and began to pull up. As he circled around to the west to strafe several Chinese military trucks, he looked back over the village. He was horrified to see the school nearly a half block away from the antiaircraft guns burning, as children and teachers ran. Keying his microphone button, he yelled. "Masashi, what did we just do?"

"It was the smoke, I couldn't see clearly. I thought the steeple on the school was the steeple on the building where the guns were located," Masashi called back in a calm voice.

"You were wrong, we bombed a school and killed children," Keisuke yelled, as tears ran down his face.

Warrant Officer Haruto said. "That is the price the Chinese must pay for putting their guns so close to a school. We have done nothing wrong, take us back to the ship, Keisuke."

That night Keisuke prayed to the Japanese Gods to give him strength, because he knew the worst was to come when the war with the United States arrived.

While in training for some future attack no one had information about, once again Keisuke needed to learn a new way to handle his aircraft. His plane was designated to carry the new 1800-pound anti-ship bomb. It was the largest bomb in the Japanese arsenal, and only a few of them had been made. Normally, his plane could carry bombs up to 830 pounds, so now he had to figure out how to handle the extra thousand pounds.

Many of the unoccupied islands in the Japanese chain were small, containing small inlets that forced pilots to work exceptionally hard to hit their targets lined up alone the shore line. The pilots practiced attacking these areas with weighted sand bags to assure the pilots could hit their targets, despite gusty winds and possible anti-aircraft fire. However, only a select few officers and pilots knew they were practicing for an attack against the United States fleet at Pearl Harbor.

To assure security for the training was maintained, all letters and photos being sent home by ship crews were closely censored to assure no one back home had an inkling as to what the fleet was practicing for.

CHAPTER TWELVE - THE PLAN IS SET

With final approval from the emperor, Admiral Yamamoto and the Prime Minister called a formal meeting to outline the plans for an attack on Pearl Harbor. Admiral Yamamoto was outranked by many officers in Japan's military structure, and had created many enemies among the army hard liners that followed now Prime Minister General Tojo's every step. However, confidently and without worry, he stood in front all of them today as supreme commander of the mission. He knew there would need to be small changes to his plan, especially in regards to what ships were in Pearl Harbor on the day of attack, but otherwise, everything else he was going to tell these officers was chiseled in granite, and there would be no changes.

However, the Prime Minister took the floor. "I had a meeting with the emperor yesterday afternoon. When we were finished discussing the situation, he read me a poem he wrote that we must consider. The emperor wrote, 'If all people are brethren, then why are the winds and the waves so restless.'"

Immediately, Yamamoto jumped up from his chair, stating that if the emperor does not want war and there is a chance for peace, we must listen to his words. Quickly, everyone in the room began speaking out that it was too late to change what was happening and they must continue with their plans. Once the Prime Minister restored order, he looked at Yamamoto. "The emperor never said we should not move forward. He just feels it is important we take all precautions to avoid it if possible. The others are right. You must go forward as you had planned."

After clearing his throat and looking around the room at everyone, Yamamoto began. "The American fleet at Pearl Harbor will be attacked by the combined fleet. The probable date will be Sunday, December 7, this year. We shall attack at dawn, when most American forces are attending worship services or sleeping. We shall use 353 aircraft launched from our six newest and largest carriers. The *Akagi* will be the flag ship of the task force. Our attack aircraft will include 40 torpedo bombers, each armed with our new long lance torpedo, modified so they do not plunge to the bottom of the harbor. There will be 103 level bombers, 131 dive-bombers and 79 fighter aircraft.

The fleet will consist of the six carriers, two heavy cruisers, thirty-five submarines, two light cruisers, nine oilers, two battleships and eleven destroyers.

The ships of the fleet will begin assembling in Hitokappo Bay in the Kurile Islands on November 19th. The fleet shall sail at 0700 hours on the morning of November 27th. The army will sweep the coastal areas of Iturup Island, removing all residents and fisherman, to ensure secrecy. All unessential radio equipment will be removed from ships and planes during the voyage, so there is no possibility of anyone breaking radio silence by accident. All communication between ships shall be done by flag and signal light. While the fleet is at sea, we will have several transmitting stations around Japan sending out and receiving false radio broadcasts, to make anyone listening think the combined fleet is in our home waters. It will be essential for the commanders of each ship to put a strenuous training schedule in place, to keep the pilots and their repair crews in top condition, as this will be a long voyage. I will be with the fleet in Hitokappo Bay aboard the *Yamato*, to help work out any last-minute details, But I will not sail with the fleet. We will pick an overall commander of the fleet no later than June.

As the emperor still believes there is a chance that peace may be attained through negotiations, we have set the date of December 2 as an end to all serious negotiations. If negotiations have resulted in an agreement, the fleet will be immediately notified to turn back. Any officer failing to turn back when ordered will be seriously reprimanded."

Before Yamamoto could continue, several staff officers jumped up from their chairs, arguing that turning back would be a sign of weakness on Japan's part, and terribly bad for the morale of the pilots and crews after such hard training, and all that time at sea.

Prince Konoye was about to speak, but was cut off by Yamamoto's booming voice. "Sit down, sit down all of you. If the emperor tells us to call off the attack, we shall do as we are ordered! We will never defy the order of our divine emperor. Any officer in this room that feels he cannot follow this directive should leave the room at once and resign!"

Yamamoto stood defiantly at the front of the room, waiting to see who might get up and leave. Seeing everyone settle back into their chairs, Yamamoto finished his orders. "If negotiations fail, a message shall be sent out from headquarters on December second to all ships of the Japanese fleet. It will read, 'Climb Mount Nitaka.' That will be the directive from headquarters to proceed as planned. After all aircraft are recovered, the fleet will leave Hawaiian waters at flank speed toward the west. The fleet will conduct air attacks against Wake Island and the Philippines on the return trip.

We will be conducting large scale maneuvers in June at a time and place not yet chosen. At that time, we shall pick an overall commander to lead the attack."

When the meeting broke up, there were still some battleship officers that believed the attack could never be carried out by air power alone. They believed the only way to gain the inevitable upper hand at the outset of the war was to use the massive fire power of their battleships. They would remain quiet until June, and then attempt to influence the war games that only through the addition of battleships, could this planned attack succeed.

Yamamoto understood very well that there was still a lot of disagreement to the proposed plan, but he hoped to bring everyone on board through personal visits over the next months.

The plan to broadcast false radio messages began in earnest the following week.

June 1, 1941, Battleship Yamato, Inland Sea of Japan

For several days, high ranking officers from every branch of the Japanese military had been arriving aboard the *Yamato,* Yamamoto's flag ship. With every one once more assembled, Yamamoto went over the plan to attack Pearl Harbor, down to the exact minute. When he was finished, he asked if there were any discussion. As expected, the Admiral's that still insisted wars would always be fought by battleships once again gave their arguments as to why the plan was dangerous and should be reconsidered. Admiral Nagumo, who had been appointed as overall commander of the attack force argued vehemently why the plan would work, asserting that anyone still arguing against it was unpatriotic and should resign. That comment upset many of the officers and brought about loud angry rebukes and wild accusations.

Quickly, a visibly angry Yamamoto jumped up stomping his foot. Breathing heavily, he looked over the assembled officers and told them all to sit down. Placing his hands on his hips, the Admiral looked sternly toward the officers that had protested the loudest. "We are not here today to accept or reject this plan. As you are all aware, this plan has been approved by our emperor. It will be incumbent on every officer in the war ministry to do his job so that the mission will succeed. As I have told you before, if anyone cannot accept the plan he should leave now and resign." As most officers involved in the screaming match hung their heads, Yamamoto half smiled. "Every man that voiced his opinion today is a patriot. You all want to see Japan be successful, that is why you voiced an opinion. But now we must put that aside and move forward together as one."

With order reestablished, Yamamoto motioned at two sailors standing nearby. Dutifully they pulled a large tarp from a massive platform that contained an accurate sand table of the Hawaiian Islands, all the military bases, and the routes the planes would use to attack. In an instant, every officer circled around the table and began to smile and nod their heads as Yamamoto's staff officers used long pointers to explain each step of the attack and answer questions. The man that appeared to be mesmerized the most by the sand table was Captain Mitsuo Fuchida.* He had worked with the attack planners to assemble the proper attack squadrons and figure out how many aircraft were needed. Now he knew all his hard work had paid dividends.

Standing next to Fuchida was one of the chief planners of the attack, Captain Minoru Genda. He had asked that Fuchida be given the honor of leading the first planes into the attack, and stay above Pearl as long as he could, to record an accurate picture of what damage had been done to the American fleet. The two men shook hands and smiled as they looked over the sand table. Fuchida looked over at Genda and said, "This will bring glory to the Japanese Empire, you have done well."

Modernization of equipment for Pearl Harbor attack

Through out the 1930s and into 1940, aerial torpedoes usually plunged to a depth of 70 feet before leveling off at a preset depth of 30 to 50 feet. The problem was the average depth of Pearl Harbor is only 47 feet. So, designers had to figure out a way to keep the torpedoes from dropping into the mud at the bottom of the harbor and still hit their targets. New mounting brackets were built for each torpedo bomber so the torpedoes hitting the water from an airplane did not sink to such drastic depths. Additionally each torpedo was fitted with wooden fins that changed how far the weapon would sink before leveling off. (There is an actual unexploded Japanese torpedo in the Pearl Harbor Museum with the wooden fins still intact.)

Many of the dive bombers were fitted with an 1800 pound reconverted naval shell as a bomb. As Japan was beginning to construct battleships with 18" rifles, they no longer needed the smaller 14–16-inch shells they had in stock. Most of the shells were converted to bombs to ensure the weapons would penetrate the heavy armored decks of American battle ships. It is unknown how many of them were dropped at Pearl Harbor, but there is evidence from bomb fragments that were found after the attack that some did strike American ships.

CHAPTER THIRTEEN – THINGS ARE HEATING UP

January 10-24, 1941, Washington D.C.

Regardless of how President Roosevelt felt about Germany, he knew it was impossible for the United States to get involved in a shooting war with them at this time. However, if the shipping convoys were not able to bring the supplies of war to England, there was a definite possibility all resistance on the continent would collapse, and even England could be subdued by the German military. The Geneva convention was very clear as to how far a country could go helping a warring nation, before it to was considered a belligerent nation, allowing a declaration of war to exist.

For several months, as Winston Churchill pleaded with President Roosevelt to get involved in the war against Germany, it was also evident the American people wanted nothing to do with another European conflict.

During this time, Roosevelt asked Attorney General Francis Biddle* and secretary of State Cordell Hull to study the Geneva convention carefully to see exactly how far America could go to help England before they were involved in a shooting war.

After Francis Biddle laid out what could be done and still wave the flag of neutrality, FDR called in senate and house leaders to discuss a plan he had named, Lend – Lease The program would allow the United States to give war supplies to countries whose defense was vital to the security of the United States, with an agreement that the equipment would be paid for after the war was over.

Roosevelt felt that arming Britain and other nations at war in Europe would free the United States to prepare for a war that was undoubtedly coming in the Pacific with Japan. Many congressional leaders felt it was not enough, while others felt it was dragging the United States down a rabbit hole they could not back out of. After the meetings went late into the night, Senate Majority leader Albon Barclay* and Speaker of the House Sam Rayborn* promised the president they would conduct the proper hearings, then get it to a vote as soon as possible. The bill was given the designation HR-1776.

As expected, there were plenty of fiery arguments among democrats and republicans, as well as women's groups who demanded the bill be killed instead of American boys. However, the bill was finally passed in March, and the president signed it the very same day.

Strangely, as HR-1776 was being argued, on January 24, Secretary of the Navy Frank Knox sent Secretary of War Stimson a letter, warning of a surprise attack on Pearl Harbor. As clear and concise as the letter was in some respects, when it came to solid facts about an actual attack, it was rather vague, and contained no date or possible time line.

Confused War Warnings

On March 1, 1941, Admiral Kimmel called General. Frederick L. Martin* and Admiral. Patrick N.L. Bellinger* to his office to discuss security of Pearl Harbor. After the meeting was finished, Bellinger and Martin departed to figure out the best way to handle security for the Hawaiian Islands.

The *Martin-Bellinger Report* was returned in April, and proved to be surprisingly accurate. They told Kimmel the attack would most likely come at dawn on a weekend, most likely a Sunday. The attack would come from the north, and the enemy would most likely use six aircraft carriers. They would use a mixture of high-level bombers, dive bombers and torpedo planes. The report suggested a 360-degree search of the ocean around the islands, using B17's which could fly out to 600 miles. The problem was that they would need 180 planes to make the plan operational, but that was more than all the B17's in the United States, and Hawaii only had 12. They also wanted to do short range searches out to 300 miles using PBY aircraft. Again, the problem was that they needed 170-200 PBY's to make the plan work, and there were only 81 in Hawaii.

As intelligence on Japanese naval capabilities was beginning to take shape, during a briefing in November it was said that the United States air patrols are very good to the south and southwest of Oahu. But generally, were inadequate to the north of the islands.

Admiral Kimmel took the report to heart, but understood what the report was asking for was just not going to work. He agreed to place more planes in the air to patrol the ocean frontier, but could not guarantee they could fly out as far as 300 miles.

By November of 1941, there was plenty of evidence that Japan was getting ready to do something big, but no one could possibly have guessed just what, as there were so many targets of opportunity they could strike at. Most officials were still of the mind that Japan could never sail halfway across the Pacific and strike at Pearl Harbor by air. In 1941, many military leaders still had the very definite opinion that Japanese men made inferior pilots, and their eye sight was so poor they could never navigate the long distances that would be required to attack Pearl Harbor. Nevertheless, there were other top navy and army officers in Washington that believed Japan was quite capable of carrying out such an attack and made their concerns known. After a very raucous meeting with General Marshall* and Admiral. Stark* it was decided that a warning should be sent to all overseas commanders in the Pacific. Marshall wrote one for the Army, and Stark wrote one for the Navy. They both dealt with the same information, but Admiral Stark's message was much more to the point. It read as follows.

> *27 November*
> *From: CNO*
> *To: All Overseas Commanders.*
> *This dispatch is to be considered a war warning. Negotiations with Japan looking toward stabilization of conditions in the Pacific has ceased and an aggressive move by Japan is expected within the next few days. The number and equipment of Japanese troops and organization of naval task forces indicates*

an amphibious expedition against either the Philippines, Thai of Kra Peninsula or possibly Borneo. Execute an appropriate defense deployment preparatory to carrying out the tasks assigned in WPL-46. Inform district and army authorities. A similar warning is being sent by the war department.

The warning sent by the war department was much different. General Marshall wrote the following.

Japanese future action unpredictable, but hostile action possible at any moment. If hostilities cannot, repeat cannot, be avoided the United States desires that Japan commit the first overt act. This policy should not, repeat not, be construed as restricting you to a course of action that might jeopardize your defense. Prior to hostile action you are directed to undertake such reconnaissance and other measures as you deem necessary, but those measure should be carried out so as not, repeat not, to alarm civilian population or disclose intent, and report measures taken. Should hostilities occur you will carry out the tasks assigned in Rainbow five so far as they pertain to Japan.

When the dispatch arrived at Pearl Harbor, Admiral Kimmel immediately called in all his top officers, including Admiral William (Bull) Halsey.* He read the memo to everyone twice, and asked for suggestions as to how to respond. There were suggestions to send the fleet back to San Diego, or to rotate half the fleet out to sea on a weekly basis, or to add more air reconnaissance covering a 360-degree search of the ocean around the islands at a distance of 250 miles. The last idea was shot down by Kimmel immediately, as he stated they did not have enough planes, fuel or pilots, and there would be no time to do the maintenance required to keep the planes flying at that rate of usage. Several officers even stated the general's warning sounded like double talk. However, Kimmel stated emphatically that the chief of staff was not into double talk.

Everyone in the meeting felt good that Admiral Stark had not specifically mentioned the Hawaiian Islands verbally in the report, so they all felt they were safe from any such attack, and most agreed that the Philippines or Wake Island would be Japan's possible target. As no clear consensus was agreed upon, Admiral Kimmel ordered all naval staff in the Hawaiian Islands to go on full alert status.

Kimmel stated years later that the term War Warning used in the dispatch never had a standing in official navy designations, so he was unsure of what to make of it.

General Short felt that the army memo he read was concerned about sabotage on the island from Japanese people already living there, and felt there was nothing in the warning regarding an attack from the outside on the Hawaiian Islands. He had all aircraft not being readied for flight be placed in groups in the center of the airfield where they could be guarded by soldiers. He had concertina wire and guards placed on all beaches where an invasion could take place, and assigned well-armed guards on armories and ammunition storage areas. General Short sent a very well laid out message to the War Department, explaining all the plans he had put into effect to counter possible sabotage on the islands. No one in the War Department contacted him to explain that was not what the war warning was about.

Later, on November 27, Kimmel had a meeting with General Short, General Frederick L. Martin, Commanding General of the Hawaiian Air Forces; Colonel James A. Mollison,* General Martin's Chief of Staff; Admiral Claude C. Bloch,* Commandant of the Fourteenth Naval District; and Admiral Charles H. McMorris,* Kimmel's Chief of War Plans. The intent of the meeting was to decide what should be done to reinforce Midway and Wake Islands. The best plan they came up with was to send pursuit planes by carrier to the islands from Pearl's already under equipped Air Force Squadrons. Just before the meeting broke up, the following exchange took place, as documented in the Pearl Harbor Investigation.

> *Kimmel turned to Admiral McMorris asking,*
> *"McMorris, what is your idea of the chances of a surprise raid on Oahu?"*
> *McMorris replied, "I should say none, Admiral."*

Admiral Kimmel kept finding himself in a precarious position, as his own operations people were giving him reports that appeared to conflict with the reports and warnings he was receiving from Washington. He called meeting after meeting with his top advisors in Hawaii, trying to piece things together. During nearly every meeting he would say, "Why can't Washington give us the complete story and let us figure things out for ourselves!"

At Pearl Harbor on December 2, 1941, just five days before the attack, Rear Admiral Edwin T. Layton,* the Pacific Fleet Intelligence Officer, briefed Admiral Kimmel. Layton presented Kimmel with a summary showing the approximate position of Japanese fleet units in the Pacific, based on radio traffic intercepts they had been listening to, not realizing they were fake messages being sent out by Tokyo.

During the report, using Layton's observations, Kimmel noted that a large Japanese force accompanied by troopships was moving along the coast of Thailand, but there was no trace of either of the Imperial Navy's top five carrier divisions anywhere in the Pacific. It was evident to Kimmel that Layton's report contained no accurate information on movement of Japan's carrier divisions or their possible positions. Upset at what he was seeing and hearing from his Intelligence Officer, the following conversation between them took place. (Factual account taken from Admiral Layton's testimony in the Pearl Harbor Investigation.)

> *Adm. Kimmel:* "What? You don't know where the carriers are?"
> *Adm. Layton:* "No sir."
> *Adm. Kimmel:* "You haven't any idea where they are?"
> *Adm. Layton:* "No sir, that's why I have Homeland Waters with a question mark. I don't know."
> *Adm. Kimmel:* "You mean to say that you are the Intelligence Officer of the Pacific Fleet and you don't know where the carriers are at?"
> *Adm. Layton:* "No sir, I don't."
> *Adm. Kimmel:* "For all you know, they could be coming around Diamond Head right now, and you wouldn't know it?"
> *Adm. Layton:* "Yes sir, but I hope they'd have been sighted by now."
> *Adm Kimmel half smiled, replying, "Yes I understand."*

Kimmel was continually told by his cryptology office that there had been no radio traffic from Japan's main carrier forces in several weeks, and all naval units at sea had changed their call signs twice over the last month. However, Kimmel understood Japan would not suddenly pull their major carrier forces back into home waters with no communications during a period when they had so many different operations taking place.

CHAPTER FOURTEEN – ALERTS AND CONFUSION

Operations on board the USS *Tennessee* were about as confused as Admiral Kimmel's office. The ship went on alert so often the men were beginning to take the alerts for granted, and officers were not much better. Eight hours on and eight hours off began to wear out the men as no one could give them any good reason for all the alerts.

As was customary in the United States Navy at the time, each battleship was required to have a dance band. Actually, that was not much of a problem, since many of the young boys that enlisted had played in high school or college bands. Many sailors hearing about bands on the battleships brought their instruments with them when they boarded. However most of the large instruments were provided by the navy. So, as the *Tennessee* was at sea this week, Captain Reordan had to work out a schedule to cut band members free from their responsibilities so they could practice with their band. Saturday night, December 6, 1941, was the battle of the bands at Block Arena, a very big deal for all navy members on Oahu. The big prize for winning was allowing the crew of that particular ship to sleep in Sunday morning, and not have to stand reveille. As rivalries always begin with contests, the *Tennessee's* band was determined this time around to defeat the band from the *Arizona*, considered to be one of the best bands in the U.S. Navy.

Cooper was getting frustrated as he and Lily were planning to be married, but he was not able to tell her when he would be coming home on shore leave. Day after day he sat in the gun tub next to Paul, as Lieutenant Crowder scanned the skies over Ford Island for anything that looked suspicious.

Looked suspicious? Cooper thought to himself. If the Japanese were attacking and his lieutenant was just thinking about them now, the war would be over before it ever got started.

The alerts also meant search aircraft from Ford Island were taking off at regular intervals to patrol the approaches to the island, while nearly every submarine was out patrolling the waters around Oahu. Cooper wondered with all the security in place, how could they miss a Japanese fleet big enough to attack Pearl Harbor.

As Lieutenant Crowder put down his binoculars for a minute, Cooper said, "Sir, our weapon is loaded, but the ready box is locked and the ammunition elevator isn't operating. How are we supposed to fight off an aerial attack set up this way?"

Lieutenant Crowder glared over at Cooper. "I follow orders like everyone else in this man's navy. Have our weapons ready for action, but keep the ammunition locked down so there are no accidents. That's what I was ordered to do, and that's what I'm doing. If you don't like it, I can send you up to the old man and you can discuss it with him!"

Paul stepped forward, "Sir, Cooper is not asking anything the other gunners haven't already been asking. It seems like we're going around in circles doing these alerts, but everything we need to do our jobs is locked away and not at our disposal. It makes no sense, sir."

Lieutenant Crowder shook his head, "Look, the *Tennessee* is heading out to sea in the rotation. Maybe by the time we come back in, everything will be rectified and we can go back to normal. Just bear with all of this, we need to be ready if we're attacked."

The next morning at 0600 hours, the *Tennessee, Maryland* and *Nevada* sailed out of Pearl Harbor with their escort ships. The fleet took a wide turn to the southwest as large thunderheads began to build. Captain Charles Reordan sat is his tall chair peering out into the South Pacific. He knew it was entirely possible that a Japanese Fleet was lurking out there farther to the west, but the Pacific was a massive ocean and two fleets could pass each other just a hundred miles apart and never see one another. Although he had been a battleship officer nearly his entire career, he had come to realize the importance of air coverage, and he wished there was a carrier in the fleet with them tonight. For now, all he could do was look west into the dark gray ocean and hope he was not in the gun sites of a Japanese battleship.

As evening settled over the Pacific, the rain had stopped, but the heavy cloud cover made the night as black as a coal mine. From the 40mm antiaircraft gun tub, Cooper could hear the rushing of the water off the side of the battleship as it charged forward into the blackness, but seeing the actual water barely eight feet below him was next to impossible.

As the ships remained at full battle alert, crews worked rotating shifts of eight hours on and eight hours off. So tonight, Cooper and Paul had the late watch in the gun tub. Cooper had actually been able to sleep fairly well after his last watch, so he was wide awake, unlike Paul. The way Paul looked, he was certain his best friend hadn't slept much, if at all in the last few days. Now he would have to struggle throughout the black night to stay awake.

Looking over at the other gun in the tub, Cooper noticed Gunners Mate Farcy was sound asleep in the gunners seat. Grabbing hold of a broom handle, Cooper gave his friend a solid poke. Farcy jumped up while looking around him. Turning to face Cooper, he said, "Damn, did I fall asleep again, I just can't stay awake tonight."

Cooper nodded his head, "Yeah, Paul is doing a lot of pacing behind the tub trying to stay awake, too. Farcy, you don't dare let an officer find you sleeping while we're on alert. You'll wind up with a court martial, clear as day."

Standing up and turning into the wind, Farcy said, "Cooper, do you think we're going to be at war in the near future?"

Cooper took in a deep breath. "I hope not. Lily and I are getting married on Friday after we get back in port. I asked for leave on the sixth and seventh but was turned down, so we' ll have to postpone our honeymoon for now. But I get shore leave Saturday night so we can spend some time together until I have to return to the ship. No, I hope someday I will be sitting on the front porch with my grandkids, telling them how everyone was so sure we were going to war and never did."

Shaking his head, Farcy said, "But what if the Japs do attack us? Then what the hell happens? I mean, what happens to us?"

"You know, Farcy. I don't even want to think about that. But if war comes, we'll just do what we have been training for and we should be fine. At least, that's what I hope happens."

About 0200 hours, Captain Reordan approached the gun tub as he patrolled his ship. He was happy to see everyone awake and bantering with one another. When Paul saw him approach, he yelled out, "Attention!"

"No, no, as you were, men. How are things going down here tonight?" the captain inquired.

"Well sir, except for the fact that we can't see a damn thing out there, I guess things are alright. I'd sure hate to sail into a battle this way though," Cooper responded with a slight smile.

"Can't say I can argue about that. Our meteorologist back at Pearl says the clouds should break up in the morning, and that will be a big relief for all of us. Earlier, I heard the *Nevada* was almost hit by a destroyer that got off course. That's the last damn thing we need right now," the captain said, before walking farther down the deck.

As dawn broke over the South Pacific, Cooper was greeted with a big surprise. Just a short distance away was the USS *Honolulu*. The repair work had been completed and the mechanics had taken her out for a shakedown cruise. There was no doubt that everything was performing properly as the ship passed the *Tennessee*, doing a full thirty knots as the bow sliced through the ten-foot waves. The skipper of the *Honolulu* spent the day circling back and forth inside the convoy, allowing the mechanics to give the ship a passing grade so it could rejoin the Pacific fleet. Although Cooper missed some of the crew members on the cruiser, he had now found a home on a battle wagon and was completely satisfied with his surroundings.

After a week at sea, everyone on the *Tennessee* was ready to return to port as they were looking at a weekend of liberty passes in Honolulu. Of course, Cooper was more excited than his ship mates, as he and Lily were set to be married in the Pearl Harbor Chapel Friday evening.

Bringing the ships into the harbor was a bit tedious, as Admiral Kimmel had ordered all of his battleships to turn around and face the harbor entrance before they were tied down. He felt that if the base was attacked and the ships had steam in their boilers, they would be able to exit the harbor quickly and escape destruction or damage. As usual, the *Tennessee* was berthed against the anchor platform near Ford Island with the *West Virginia* tied solidly up against its starboard side. Directly behind the *Tennessee* was the *Arizona* with the repair ship *Vestal* tied up on the *Arizona's* starboard side.

In front of the *Tennessee* was the *Maryland* with the *Oklahoma* tied up on her starboard side. The *California* was berthed all alone just in front of the *Maryland* and the *Oklahoma*.

Late in the afternoon of Thursday, December 4, 1941, the battleship USS *Nevada* stately sailed up the channel from the Pacific Ocean into Pearl Harbor. She was the last of the eight battleships stationed at Pearl to return after a long week of training, so she was backed into place behind the *Arizona* and tied up all alone. The *Pennsylvania* was still in dry dock going through a complete overhaul. The old battleship *Utah* had been berthed on the south side of Ford Island by herself for several weeks. All her heavy guns and most of her superstructure had been removed to make it a bombing target for training pilots.

Although all ship crews had trained to install anti-torpedo nets on the exposed sides of their ships when tying up for an extended period of time, the decision had been made that nets were not necessary while berthed in Pearl Harbor, because everyone in command still felt Pearl was too shallow for a torpedo attack, as it was just forty-seven feet at its deepest. Also, with the new gates over the harbor entrance, it was impossible for an enemy submarine to enter without being seen, and too narrow for an enemy submarine to maneuver around the harbor to make an attack. Regardless of arguments to the contrary, on December 4, most United States naval experts considered an aerial attack on Pearl Harbor well out of the question.

Captain Francis W. Scanland,* skipper of the *Nevada,* took his vessel out to sea more than other battleship commanders. He was certain and vocal that the United States was going to be involved in a war with the Japanese more sooner than later, and he wanted to know that his crew would be up to the task when called upon. They spent hours south of the Hawaiian Islands on antiaircraft drills, gunnery practice, submarine detection, and setting up combat drills against enemy battleships, exactly what the *Nevada* was built for. Most sailors at Pearl Harbor understood that Captain Scanland had no time for men that were goldbricks, or men that could not only perform the job they were assigned to, and at least two other major tasks aboard his vessel. While out at sea, the men crossed trained every day to assure they would be ready to handle whatever position they could be called upon to fill in battle.

As soon as the crew of the Tennessee was released from duty, Cooper and Paul caught the first ferry over to the mainland. Cooper and Lily spent the better part of Friday going over last-minute problems, ensuring everything was going to be perfect for their wedding.

With the chapel filled with friends, Cooper and Lily walked down the aisle, with Paul and Sadie as their best man and maid of honor. After going out to a traditional Hawaiian wedding dinner, the happy couple joined the rambunctious crowds on Waikiki in their wedding wear. After countless toasts and dancing the night away in several hotel ballrooms, the couple retired to an expensive hotel in the middle of Waikiki Beach.

It was nearly noon when Cooper and Lily were ready to greet the world as Mr. and Mrs. Cooper Dodge. Sadie and Paul joined them for an elegant champagne buffet, compliments of the hotel, and that was a good thing because the wedding had cost Cooper more than a whole months pay.

Regrettably, the day went by too fast for Cooper, but finally, he was standing on the front stoop of Lily's grandparent's house, kissing his new bride goodbye. He could not tell her when he would get his next shore leave, or if the fleet was heading back out to sea on Monday. However, Lily didn't care about specifics, all she knew was the next time the *Tennessee* had shore leave, her husband would be home with her and they could begin working out their future.

Arriving back on the *Tennessee*, Paul was assigned mid-watch, midnight to 0800 hours, and Cooper was assigned morning watch 0800 hours to 1600 hours. Cooper kind of shook his head because he knew first thing in the morning all the drunks would return to the ship, and it could get a bit disorderly.

CHAPTER FIFTEEN –
FINAL MESSAGE

On the evening of December 5, 1941, Commander Alwin Kramer* and Colonel Rufus Bratton* are working in the cryptology office in Washington D.C. Late in the evening, one of the decoding clerks walks into the office, handing a newly decoded Japanese message to Commander Kramer. She says, "Tomorrow morning the Japanese are going to begin sending a message to the embassy here in Washington in fourteen parts."

Commander Kramer reads the entire message before handing it to Colonel. Bratton. After some thought, Commander Kramer turns to the clerk and says, "Make sure we have staff on board tomorrow morning to begin decoding and typing the messages as soon as they begin arriving."

Both Kramer and Bratton are intrigued and speculate as to what could be in the message, but neither man has an answer. They both decide to be in the office by 0700 Saturday morning, so they can see the contents of the messages as soon as they begin to come in.

The Japanese have no idea the United States has broken their main diplomatic code, and have devised a decoding machine to read it, code named Purple. By this point the United States was decoding and reading the diplomatic codes faster than the Japanese embassy in Washington.

Saturday morning, December 6, 1941, the messages began to arrive around 0730 hours. It began by explaining to the embassy that the fourteenth part would be withheld until Sunday morning, and should be presented to the President no later than 1300 hours, Washington time.

As quickly as a piece of the message was decoded and typed, Kramer and

Bratton read them before placing them in a file. After piecing everything together, Commander Kramer tells Colonel Bratton the Japanese are going to attack the United States on Sunday morning. Bratton asks if he can prove his scenario, and Kramer replies, no, but he was going to share everything from the first thirteen parts to everyone on the message list. By 2100 hours on Saturday night, Commander Kramer begins making the rounds of Washington, contacting everyone on the approved list. He is not allowed to speak to the President, so Harry Hopkins delivers the message to the president to read. When he returns with the briefcase, Hopkins tells Kramer the president wants to see the fourteenth part as soon as it comes in. That is pretty much the same answer he gets from everyone else on the list. However, as Hopkins returns to the library, FDR shakes his head, saying simply, "This means war."

On Sunday morning, December 7, after the fourteenth part arrives, Colonel Bratton types it out and begins searching for Chief of Staff General Marshall. After Marshall reads the fourteenth part of the Japanese intercept, he quickly scribbles a note on a piece of paper, handing it to Colonel Bratton, instructing him to get the message to all overseas commanders.

The memo stated, "The Japanese are presenting at 1pm eastern standard time today, what amounts to an ultimatum. Also, they are under orders to destroy their code machines immediately. Just what significance the hour set may have we do not know, but be on alert accordingly."

After Bratton has the message coded, he takes the paper to the message center. He is informed that atmospheric conditions around the Pacific that morning were very bad, and very few messages were going through. Bratton insisted they try again, but the only places that replied they had received the message were the Panama Canal and the Philippines.

The officer in the information center tells Bratton they could send it as a telegram instead, and Bratton reluctantly agrees. The only problem was, the telegram was not marked urgent, so it was sent as a non-urgent telegram. It arrived in Kimmel's Office in Pearl Harbor several hours after the attack had ended.

Secretary of State's office, December 7, 1941

On November 26, 1941, the Secretary of State handed to the Japanese representatives a document which stated the principles governing the policies of the Government of the United States toward the situation on the far east, and setting out suggestions for a comprehensive peaceful settlement covering the entire Pacific area.

The Japanese ambassador asked for an appointment for the Japanese representatives to see Cordell Hull to discuss the November 26 letter at 1300 hours on December 7. Due to the time it took for the Japanese to decode the fourteenth part of the message, the appointment was changed to 1345 hours, Washington time. The Japanese representatives finally arrived at the office of the Secretary of State at 1405 hours. They were received by the Secretary of State at 1420 hours.

By that time Cordell Hull had been informed of the attack on Pearl Harbor, and had confirmed it through the White House. Neither of the Japanese representatives were aware the attack had already taken place.

Entering Hull's office, Ambassador Nomura realized something was wrong. After handing to Hull what was understood to be a reply to the document handed to him by the Secretary of State on November 26, he and Special Envoy Kurusu sat down.

Secretary Hull carefully read the document handed to him by Nomura and immediately turned to face him. With complete outrage in his voice, Hull responds. His exact words are as follows."I must say that in all my conversations with you over the last nine months I have never uttered one word of untruth. This is borne out absolutely by the record. In all my 50 years of public service I have never seen a document that was more crowded with infamous and distortions on a scale so huge, that I never imagined until today that any government on this planet was capable of uttering them."

As Ambassador Numura began to speak, Cordell Hull lowered his head while waving his hand saying, "Go, just go."

As the Japanese ambassadors left the office, it was the first time they found out Pearl Harbor had already been attacked. They returned to the Japanese

Embassy under Army armed guard so that no angry Americans might attempt to attack them. Numura strongly claimed until his death he knew nothing about the attack or why the preset time of 1300 hours was so important.

CHAPTER SIXTEEN – WHERE TO ASSIGN PLANES

On December 3, 1941, another memo from the Chief of Naval Operations arrived in Hawaii. It read, "Highly possible information has been received that categorical and urgent instructions were sent yesterday to Japanese consular posts at Hong Kong, Singapore, Batavia, Manila, Washington and London to destroy most of their code ciphers at once, and burn confidential and serious documents."

Both Kimmel and Short understood this memo to be a basic piggyback to the November 27 memo, that it contained nothing new, and once again did not mention Pearl Harbor specifically.

Although there were many disagreements regarding the war warnings at Pearl Harbor, one issue that most top leaders agreed upon, was how to reinforce Midway and Wake Islands. Admiral Kimmel felt that any attack on the islands would start with some type of aerial attack by Japanese carrier forces. So, he felt the need was to send more fighter planes to the islands.

Throughout the end of November, meetings were being held on a regular basis to discuss the situation and take all suggestions under consideration. The one part of the plan that was most hotly discussed, was the need to send off two carriers to deliver the planes, thus leaving Pearl without any mobile fighter planes.

During these discussions, Admiral Kimmel continually referred to the Martin-Bellinger report that had been compiled by General Frederick Martin and Rear Admiral Patrick N.L. Bellinger. The report argued the need for air reconnaissance to search the ocean frontiers west of Hawaii for any signs of threatening Japanese naval activity. Kimmel continually applied the report to Midway, which sat 1299 miles west of Pearl, and Wake, which was 2289 miles farther to the west of Pearl. These islands were truly in the frontier and were much more vulnerable than Pearl was.

However, neither Kimmel or General Short were willing to give up any of the planes assigned to their commands, as they would not be able to continue the search grids they had been flying since the war warnings came out. It appeared the only solution left was to send out Marine fighters. The Marines argued vehemently that they were severely short of planes to do the patrolling they were required to complete, and giving up twenty-four planes was just not something they could do.

However, being under strict control of the navy, all the arguments the Marines could muster pretty much fell on deaf ears.

When it was time to fly the planes out to the carriers, they would be flown to their respective carriers by naval pilots that were well trained in landing with the use of a tail hook.

So it was decided that Admiral Halsey would take twelve marine fighter planes to Midway Island on the USS *Enterprise*, and Admiral Newton would deliver twelve fighters to Wake on the USS *Lexington*.

However, the three war warnings that had been sent directly to Pearl and other outlying stations across the Pacific, allowed serious concerns as to what Washington knew, and what the Japanese were actually going to do. All those questions weighed heavily on the minds of Admiral Kimmel, Admiral Halsey and many more of the fleet commanders.

Knowing that relations with Japan were deteriorating by the day, Halsey was concerned about being caught at sea when and if a real shooting war began. The round trip to Midway would take twelve days, and he was sure Japan would have every submarine possible in the waters around Hawaii prior to the beginning of hostilities, making his task force a sitting duck.

With Halsey's task force set to sail on November 28, 1941, he and Kimmel had one last conference on November 26. Halsey was looking for guidance and direction from his former classmate at the naval academy regarding what he should do if war broke out while he was at sea, or if he ran into

Japanese ships along the way. It was easy to see that Halsey was looking for clearly defined orders he could fall back on if he became involved in a shooting conflict.

Kimmel understood exactly what his top battle admiral had in mind, but he also realized he had no orders or directives from Washington as to how to handle the type of situation Halsey was rightfully concerned about, and rightfully so. Kimmel ducked the question for the moment as he looked out the windows at the fleet. Turning back toward his desk Kimmel looked up at his old friend and said, "Bill, get out there and deliver those planes, then probe and get back here as soon as you can. Do you want me to assign a couple battleships to join your task force?"

"Hell no!" Halsey replied, "If we're going to probe, let's probe and do it quickly, those old battle wagons will just slow us down."

Realizing Halsey was right, Kimmel looked intently at his trusted Admiral. "Bill, then get out there and see what you can find. With the *Lexington* heading to Wake and the *Saratoga* still in Puget Sound for repair, the *Enterprise* is the only effective combat mobile task force in the central Pacific. Get out there, then get back here as soon as you can and let us know what you've seen."

Walking over to the table by the door to Kimmel's office to pick up his hat, Halsey was still feeling unsure regarding his orders. So, once more he asked, "Kim, what the hell do I do if I run into the Japanese fleet while we're out there?"

After a moment of thought, Kimmel looked eye to eye with Halsey, "Bill, just use your common sense."

Halsey nodded his head, replying, "By God, at least there's one commander in this man's navy that has not lost his nerve." As Halsey turned to walk out of Kimmel's office, he boldly stated, "If I see as much as a Japanese Sampan, I'll blow it out of the water!"

Early on the morning of November 28, 1941, Halsey's task force departed Pearl Harbor on an easterly course, in order to throw off anyone that might be observing ship movement. Several hours later, the fleet turned to the west, sailing close to Oahu so it could take on the marine fighters. After placing them securely down in the hangar deck, Halsey began steaming at full speed for Midway Island.

In order to keep the mission somewhat of a secret, none of the men aboard the ships had been told what their next mission was going to be, so they all figured they would be just out overnight, so most had packed little more than a toothbrush and one change of underclothing.

They were not told about their mission until late on the first day, well after the marine fighters had been stowed.

As the *Lexington* and its screening fleet had just arrived back in Pearl, there were many issues that needed attention before the task force was ready to sail again. As was customary, a returning admiral would always visit the fleet admiral to brief him on every issue regarding his last voyage. So, Admiral John H. Newton followed protocol and made an appointment to visit with Admiral Kimmel the day after arrival.

Upon entering Kimmel's office, it was clear to see the admiral was under a tremendous amount of stress. After listening to everything that had happened on the *Lexington's* last assignment, Kimmel was very satisfied. Standing up, he walked over to a large map, explaining where Halsey had sailed, and explained that the Lexington would be delivering twelve aircraft to Wake Island once all preparations were made. Kimmel explained about the precarious situation the United States found itself in with the Japanese government, and told Admiral Newton to take all necessary precautions while out at sea.

With fueling, replenishment and repairs completed, Task Force 12 sailed clear of Pearl Harbor on the morning of December 1. Under orders from Kimmel, Admiral Newton followed the same sailing plan as Halsey. After picking up his twelve aircraft, Admiral Newton poured power to his engines so he could get out to sea and complete his mission.

The *Enterprise* arrived off the coast of Midway Island as scheduled, sent off the aircraft and retrieved their pilots in near record time, as Halsey fully realized something big was about to happen.

Leaving Midway Island for the first two days, Halsey used a zigzag pattern so he could search more of the ocean between Midway and Pearl Harbor, but all he was coming up with was open ocean.

On the morning of the fourth day, Halsey sat in the admiral's chair on the bridge having a cup of coffee when one of his radio men approached. "Sir, I just received this message from Pearl over the radio, but it makes no sense."

Looking very concerned, Halsey looked at the Petty Officer, "What does it say?"

Holding up the message the Petty Officer read, "Sir, it says, Air Raid Pearl Harbor, this is no drill!"

Halsey could feel the blood drain from his face. Getting out of the chair he looked at his Petty Officer. Get me confirmation of that report ASAP." Turning to his flight officer, he said, "We just might be at war, Commander. Send up additional patrols to search for submarine activity. Have a dozen planes fueled and ready to fly to Pearl once we find out what's going on." Turning to the ship's captain, he ordered all engines to flank speed, and head to Pearl on a straight course.

About thirty minutes later the Petty Officer returned to the bridge looking very glum. Walking up to Halsey, he said, "It has been confirmed, Admiral. The Japanese struck right about 0800 hours. They have attacked every airfield, and are pounding the harbor relentlessly."

Halsey shook his head as he looked out over the ocean. "The *Lexington* should be just about ready to turn around at Wake, but that still leaves them three days away. At flank speed, we can be back in place to support Kimmel by late tomorrow morning, but that may be too late."

After trying several times, Halsey was finally able to get through to Kimmel. After getting an idea of the amount of damage that had been sustained, he asked if there was a need for aircraft to defend the base. Kimmel agreed that he could use whatever the *Enterprise* could send him.

Knowing his planes would be at the short end of their fuel supply, Halsey had twelve planes that were armed and ready to be launched. They arrived at Pearl just as the attack was taking place and suffered terrible losses.

Later on December 7, with approval from Admiral Kimmel, Halsey sends six fighters to Pearl to help defend the base should the Japanese return the following morning.

Approaching the harbor, the pilots could still see fires burning aboard many of the ships, but everything else had been blacked out all over the island. Following the plan that had been put in place, the pilots turned on their lights, slowed their speed, and dropped down to just above the water. Several of the planes had just reached the main section of the harbor, when every gun along the shore line, and every gun still operable on the ships opened fire. Some of the planes exploded in midair, while others crashed into the harbor. A few pilots attempted to climb as quickly as they could, but that just allowed gunners to have a clear view of the bottoms of their planes as they were ripped apart.

Officers ran up and down the line, demanding their men cease firing as they were friendly aircraft, but most of the men disregarded the directive, being sure it was a Japanese sneak attack.

It wasn't until morning that the men saw the floating wreckage and bodies in the water, and realized what they had done. Back on the *Enterprise* when Halsey learned what had happened, he was furious, and made it quite clear he would launch no more planes to enter the islands airspace.

When the *Enterprise* arrived, Halsey sent off planes to patrol toward the north where it was now known the Japanese fleet had been. However, after an all-day search, no sign of the fleet remained.

The Enterprise sailed into Pearl Harbor that night in order to refuel and replenish their supplies, as the Japanese had failed to destroy the huge fuel depot and supply warehouses. Not wanting to be caught in the harbor if the Japanese returned, every bit of work that was needed had to be finished before daylight so they could escape under cover of darkness.

During his brief visit, Halsey told Kimmel, "Before we're through with them, the Japanese language will be spoken only in hell!"

With the *Lexington* finished with their mission, Admiral Newton turned his task force back toward Hawaii. Just after 0800 hours the following morning, the officer of the watch delivered a message to the admiral that made him go stiff. Opening the message, he read the same words Admiral. Halsey read. "Air raid Pearl Harbor, this is no drill!" Turning to his lieutenant, he inquired, "Lieutenant, has this been confirmed?"

Nodding his head, the officer replied, "That is why it was slightly delayed, sir. We wanted to confirm this before we delivered it to you. It is accurate, sir."

Sitting down in his elevated chair on the bridge, he looked at his radio control officer. "Patch me through to the task force." Once that patch was created, Admiral Newton keyed the mic and spoke. "Now hear this, now hear this, this is Admiral Newton. We have just received word and confirmed, that Pearl Harbor has been attacked by the Japanese. There is no way for us to know what kind of damage has been created by the attack, but it's important for you to know we are now at war, and all war time regulations are now in place. Not knowing where the enemy fleet is located, we are now at General Quarters. All hands man your battle stations."

Immediately, the klaxon began to sound on all ships in Task Force 12. Sailors ran to their battle stations, loaded their weapons and prepared for war, wherever it may come from.

After the war was over and the investigations on the attack were under way, Admiral Newton reported that although Kimmel had explained about the possibility of war with the Japanese before sailing to Midway, he himself had never seen or been allowed to read the war warnings that had been sent from Washington.

As Halsey and Newton went out on their missions, Kimmel was accurate about the carrier situation. The *Saratoga* was in Puget Sound for repairs, the *Yorktown* had just arrived in Norfolk, Virginia after an Atlantic Patrol and was in need of resupply. The *Ranger* was also returning to Norfolk for necessary repair work and the *Wasp* was the only carrier left in the Atlantic and Caribbean. The newest carrier, the *Hornet*, was still undergoing sea trials before being assigned to the fleet.

Wheeler Field, November 29, 1941

Although General Short had done just about everything possible to prevent sabotage on parked aircraft on Oahu, he still had a nagging fear that sabotage might not be the only risk to the Hawaiian Air Force. On November 29, Short held a meeting with General Gorden Austin, commander of Pursuit Squadron 47, stationed at Wheeler Field.

After looking over the planes sitting on the tarmac, Short said, "General, is there any way we can get some of these aircraft dispersed, just in case there is an aerial attack?"

After giving the question some thought, General Austin replied. "Well sir, we could send several over to auxiliary fields we have on Maui and Lanai. We could also send a few up to the base at Haleiwa, but there are no quarters up there for pilots and crews."

Short nodded his head. "That sounds like a plan to me. Get it done, General!"

Immediately, General Austin looked over plane crews and decided which planes were going to be moved. He finally called Lieutenant George Welch* and Lieutenant Kenneth Taylor* into his office.

"Gentlemen, take your P-40 Tomahawks up to Haleiwa and stand by."

The two men looked at one another for a moment before Welch said, "Sir, what are we supposed to do up there?"

As General Austin continued shuffling some papers, he replied, "Stand by and listen for the phone to ring. That's all, gentlemen."

Note from the author: The conversation above between General Austin and Welch and Taylor is factual, based on the investigation reports.

As the lieutenants left the office, Welch shook his head. "It's those damn card games. Somebody loses their shirt and they complain to the old man, and now we pay the price for it."

Taylor nodded his head, replying, "Yup, that's it."

The maintenance people assigned to Haleiwa pitched tents and made due with what they had. However, Welch and Taylor refused to live that way. As Taylor had just taken delivery of a new Buick, the men decided they could run back and forth to the field quickly if needed.

Besides, there was a huge party taking place at Wheeler's Officer's Club on Saturday night December 6, and Welch and Taylor were in no mood to miss the event of the fall season. As the party began to break up, a decision was made to have a poker game in the back room of the Officers Club. It looked like sweet pickings to Welch and Taylor, so they opted to join in the game.

As dawn of December 7 was just beginning to break over the island, a very tired and hung over Welch and Taylor walked toward their barracks. They may have violated orders, but they had filled their pockets with a good supply of cash that had been lacking in games over the last month and they knew no one involved in the game was going to cry to the General. Dog tired, the men took off all but their tuxedo pants collapsing onto their bunks.

CHAPTER SEVENTEEN – *TORA TORA TORA*

Hitokappu Bay in Japan's Kuril Islands November 1941

By mid-November, the Japanese navy had made the seas and bays around Iturup Island in the Kuril Islands off limits to all fishermen. Marines had occupied the island to assure no one was living there or attempted to land.

Hitokappu Bay had been selected as the rendezvous sight for the combined fleet that was going to attack Pearl Harbor. The convoy consisted of 27 ships, including the seven destroyers: *Akigumo, Kagero, Shiranuii, Tanikaze, Urakaze, Kasumi* and *Arage.* Two battleships, the *Hijei* and *Kirishima,* two heavy cruisers, the *Tone* and *Chikuma,* one light cruiser, the *Abukuma,* plus the six carriers, *Akagi, Kaga, Shokaku, Zuikaku, Hiryu* and *Soryu.* The balance of the 27 ships were oilers and repair vessels.

Admiral Yamamoto sailed to the bay on the battleship *Yamato* to help sort out any last minute details, and to have a meeting and dinner with the skippers of all the ships the night before they sailed. He also had extra oilers sent to the bay to top off the fuel tanks on all the ships. The situation was still a gamble as planners knew full well the fleet could run into severe weather on the way to Pearl, with waves large enough to capsize a ship not properly weighted.

On the evening of November 26, in a room highly decorated for the occasion, each officer was dressed in his most splendid uniform. After one of the most elegant meals the officers had in a long time, the business meeting began. Yamamoto's top meteorologist gave out weather reports for the first two days of the voyage, while telling the skippers they will attempt to update the fleet with the best information they have along the way. Intelligence officers informed the skippers of what ships were in Pearl Harbor right then, and what they were expecting on the seventh, again with updates to follow.

When they were all finished, Yamamoto takes the podium. Looking dead serious, he explains that the United States and the Emperor are still working on negotiations to prevent a war. Immediately there are murmurs among the officers. Yamamoto holds up his hand and says that all negotiations are to be completed no later than December 2, Pearl Harbor time. He says if negotiations are completed and agreed upon, the fleet will be notified to turn around. However, if negotiations fail, the fleet will be sent the message, "Climb Mount Nitaka," which means hostilities are to begin on December 7, 1941 Hawaiian Time. He ends with a stern warning that any officer failing to follow orders and turn around if ordered to do so will be executed upon return to Japan.

Around 0400 hours, Japanese time, on November 27, 1941, with Hitokappu Bay shrouded in medium fog, the fleet turns east, sailing for Pearl Harbor. Yamamoto leaves the bay, sailing to visit many of Japan's naval bases so the other commands think nothing out of the ordinary is happening.

Radio monitoring stations all around Japan have their antennas pointed east, in the hopes of catching any American radio broadcast sending information regarding the whereabouts of the combined fleet. Meanwhile, code stations in Japan continue sending out false reports of the combined fleet being situated in the inland sea, throwing off American intelligence gatherers.

The die has now been cast, or as some historians have said, "The bombs were in the air, they just hadn't landed yet."

Saturday December 6, 1941, The White House, Washington D.C.

After a long week of trying to break through the grid lock with the Japanese government to prevent an all-out war, President Roosevelt retired to his study on the second floor of the White House.

Firmly convinced the war every one dreaded was now at hand, he gathered up his speech writers and Secretary of State Cordell Hull. FDR was convinced the only way now to avoid the war was to send a personal letter to the Japanese Emperor, asking for his assistance in averting a conflict. The letter was several pages long, going over many of the points the United States had been arguing with the Japanese government over the last six months. Following is the closing statement from that letter.

> *"I address myself to Your Majesty at this moment in the fervent hope that Your Majesty may, as I am doing, give thought in this definite emergency to ways of dispelling the dark clouds. I am confident that both of us, for the sake of the peoples not only of our great countries but for the sake of humanity in neighboring territories, have a sacred duty to restore traditional amity and prevent further death and destruction in the world."*

After Cordell Hull left to send the message, the president went to the dining room to join Eleanor for dinner. After sitting down, he looked at his wife saying, "The son of man has just sent his final message to the son of God."

The message was not only sent to the emperor, but a copy was also sent to United States Ambassador Joseph Grew in Tokyo. This late in the day on December 6, the Japanese government had locked down all communications coming from the United States. Grew did not receive the message for several hours after it arrived. When he did receive it, he immediately called the palace, requesting an immediate conference with the emperor. He was told it would not be possible until the next day.

As the sun began to rise above the horizon of the eastern Pacific, it was clear for everyone on the island of Oahu to believe, Sunday December 7, 1941 was going to be another glorious day in paradise. Employees at the large hotels on Waikiki were busy on the beach raking the sand, making sure each grain was in its proper place before the tourists awoke to enjoy a quiet Hawaiian style breakfast buffet. Store and bar owners lucky enough to have their businesses located in Waikiki's famous shopping districts, were busy cleaning sidewalks and curbs, while rolling out their awnings, to make every inch of Ala Wai Boulevard, Kalakaua, Kuhio, or Ewa Avenues, looked attractive to entice customers to spend their hard-earned vacation money. Soft Hawaiian music added to the Polynesian charm, as it emanated from strategically located loud speakers along the busy thoroughfares. By 0800 hours, it was impossible to find any evidence of the typical raucous Saturday night naval crowd that filled the streets and bars. Every business entrepreneur in Waikiki loved the weekends when the fleet was in port, as the hungry, thirsty sailors filled their coffers well beyond what the average tourists could ever accomplish.

Yes, there were the occasional Saturday night fights between drunken sailors, soldiers, marines, and air corps personnel, but the military police and shore patrol were always quick to break up the battles. Any damage claims by business owners were always paid back from fines levied against the perpetrators by their senior officers, or by military court martial. Bar owners along the famous Waikiki Beach always had to take these issues into consideration as a price of doing business on an island that supported thousands of young military personnel. Most of the young men were away from home for the first time in their lives, and always had steam to blow off after spending long duration's at sea.

Of course, on Sunday mornings all was forgotten as a vast majority of the young men on the island attended church services, and were on their best behavior as their finances had suddenly run dry.

Sunday was a day for the families of military members to enjoy picnics on the beach, allowing children to play in the ocean while their parents soaked up the warming rays of the sun, as they relaxed on the beach with their favorite adult beverages. Wives and girlfriends spent hours searching stores for those special gifts only available in Hawaii, that they could send home to family members back in the states. Although there had been rumors of war with the Japanese for several months, nothing on the island this glorious Sunday morning gave people any reason to be concerned.

However, out in the Pacific Ocean just a few miles from the entrance to the Pearl Harbor channel where the USS *Ward* slowly patrolled, everyone appeared to be on edge.

At the Pearl Harbor intelligence office this Sunday morning, there was a huge cause for concern that only a select few military officials on the island knew about. A dozen new B-17's from the mainland needed to be guided in as they would be running low on fuel. Honolulu radio station KGMB had stayed on all night at the request of the army, so the navigators had a signal to home in on as they were at the westerly portion of their trip. The last thing General Short wanted was to have one of the new planes fall into the ocean, destroying the plane and killing the crew because they ran out of fuel.

Cooper and Paul jumped from their racks at 0630 hours. They showered and put on their best naval whites as ordered by every ship commander in the harbor until at least 1200 hours.

Once they finished getting dressed, the men ducked into the mess to grab a cup of coffee before reveille at 0800 hours. After that, they would stand deck watch until 1300 hours.

Paul shook his head, "Damn, its sticky in here this morning."

Cooper laughed, "Well, you could go back to Minnesota where its probably zero degrees with two feet of snow on the ground. I remember what it was like in New York this time of year. I hated walking to school and having to shovel snow for some of the old people so my folks would have a few extra dollars. Some days it was so cold I would shove old newspapers in my pant legs to give me a little extra warmth."

Paul had to laugh as he sipped on his coffee. "Yeah, I guess I can put up with a little humidity inside this metal box. For sure, I don't miss the snow and cold of Minnesota or Montana. I think we got a pretty good gig going on right now. Finishing their coffee, the men raced up several flights of stairs as they made their way to the flag pole on the aft deck of the ship.

Most of the band was already assembled, as Lieutenant Crowder, commander of the deck watch, gave the two late arrivals the evil eye. "Guys, if you had not shown up for reveille today, I would have sent both of you to Brazil to catch crocodiles with your bare hands. I guess three minutes to spare is not too bad."

As the men took their positions below the flag pole with the rope, something caught Paul's attention to the northwest. Motioning to the lieutenant, Paul called out, "Aren't those planes coming in pretty low for a Sunday morning, sir?"

As Paul finished speaking, they all stood in awe as they watched a torpedo drop from one of the lead planes. Throwing his hat across the deck,

Lieutenant Crowder pulled his .45 pistol from its holster, and yelled. "Damn it, those are Japs!" He fired off a full magazine of bullets toward the planes as the men ran back toward the superstructure of the ship. Jumping into the aft communications office, Lieutenant Crowder grabbed hold of the microphone for the ships intercom. "Battle stations, battle stations, general quarters, we are under attack, man your battle stations!"

0342 hours, December 7, 1941 Defensive Sea area, East of Pearl Harbor

While patrolling the defensive sea area east of Pearl Harbor at 0342 hours on December 7, 1941, Ensign R.C. McCloy,* skipper of the USS *Condor*, a wooden mine sweeper, observed a small wake on the surface of the ocean, not very far off the ships starboard side. After examining it for a minute, he radioed the Destroyer USS *Ward* that was also patrolling a short distance away, "Sighted suspected submerged submarine on westerly course, speed nine knots, time, 0348 hours."

Lieutenant Commander William Outerbridge,* skipper of the *Ward* immediately sails to the position. He conducts a search of the area until 0443 hours, and finds nothing. Having been up all night, Outerbridge decides to turn in and get some rest. He turns command of the bridge over to his executive officer, Lieutenant Goebbner.*

About 0645 hours, the skipper of the navy tug USS *Antares* notifies the *Ward* that what appears to be a small Japanese submarine may be trailing the tug as it prepares to enter the harbor. Scanning the ocean behind the *Antares,* Lt. Goebbner sights what he believes could be the periscope of a Japanese submarine aft of the tug, and forward of the target rack it was towing.

Lieutenant Goebbner immediately sends a runner to wake the skipper. When Outerbridge arrives on the bridge, he checks out the area between the *Antares* and the target rack, and quickly identifies it as a Japanese submarine. He immediately calls the crew to General Quarters, and instructs Lt. Goebbner to inform the *Antares* and Commander Fourteenth Naval District that they are attacking a Japanese submarine. He orders the front four-inch gun to commence firing. The first round falls short, but the second round strikes the conning tower of the sub as the crew begins to submerge. As the *Ward* passes over the area where the sub began its dive, Commander Outerbridge orders the crew to roll depth charges. After two depth charge attacks, a large patch of oil appears on the surface surrounded by debris.

While continuing to patrol the area looking for more submarines, Commander Outerbridge sends another notice to the commander of the Fourteenth Naval District at 0651 hours local time.

"We have depth charged submarine operating in defensive sea area."

Getting no reply, at 0653 hours, Commander Outerbridge sends another message to Commander Fourteenth Naval District. "Attacked, fired upon, depth charged and sunk submarine operating in defensive sea area."

This time the message is received and given to Lieutenant Harold Kaminsky.* He immediately calls Captain John Earl,* Admiral Kimmel's Chief of Staff. Earl asks if there is any confirmation to the attack by any other warships in the vicinity of the *Ward*. Kaminsky replies, "No." Irritated by the call, Captain Earl replies that there have been so many false sightings over the past month and none of them have had any credence, so he wanted confirmation.

Lieutenant Kaminsky argues this report is the real thing, closer than any other report, and it was right off the harbor entrance, and there is oil and debris on the surface.

Captain Earl adds that Outerbridge is a green skipper and may be a bit jumpy, and that he would pass the message on to Captain Bloch,* Commander of the Fourteenth Naval District.

Angered by what Lieutenant Kaminsky feels was an inappropriate response by Captain Earl, the lieutenant argues that he feels all commands on Oahu needed to be notified right away.

Captain Earl angrily responds, "Confirmation Kaminsky, I want confirmation!"

Ending the phone call, Captain Earl in fact does call Admiral Claude Bloch. The Admiral agrees the skipper of the *Ward* is a green ship commander, and sides with Captain Earl that they need confirmation. After hanging up, Captain Earl notifies the destroyer USS *Monaghan* to leave Pearl Harbor, and give assistance to the skipper of the *Ward*. No one else is notified of the *Ward's* encounter until after the Japanese attack begins.

When Admiral Kimmel is notified of the USS *Ward's* report after the attack has begun, he explodes saying, "A Japanese submarine in that close to our defensive area is a big deal, a very big deal." Although it is way to late, he demands to know why he was not notified of the Japanese submarine sighting immediately after the report first arrived.

Opana Point Radar Station, North Coast of Hawaii

In 1939, the United States military began experimenting with Electronic Aircraft Warning Services, otherwise known as RADAR. The entire project was under the direction of Colonel Wilfred Tetley.* By 1941, the most trusted system they had tested was the SCR-270 that could detect aircraft out as far as 150 miles. The radar station was a huge, heavy piece of machinery that took four large trucks to transport all the equipment necessary to assemble the system to where it would be set up.

Knowing that a war with Japan was all but inevitable, five of the first units were shipped to Hawaii. The units were set up at Kawaiola, Wainae, Kaawa, Kokohead and Schofield Barracks. At this point in time, there were no real well-trained crews ready to operate the equipment, so two-man crews were rotated on each unit around the clock in order for them to gather on the job training.

After much discussion, it was decided the unit at Schofield Barracks would be more reliable if it were transferred to Opana Point on the north coast of Hawaii. The point is 532 ft. above sea level, and is the highest point on the island. Operating the radar from there would give the screen a full sweep of the Pacific Ocean, north of Oahu.

The move was made on Thanksgiving Day, which ironically was the same day the Japanese combined fleet pulled anchor, and sailed from Hitokappu Bay in the Kuril Islands for the attack on Pearl Harbor.

There were no other buildings or resources on Opana Point, so the crews were driven up to the point whenever the radar unit was supposed to be in operation

Opana point radar station 0702 hours, December 7, 1941, north shore of

Oahu

The nightly training program was set to end at 0700 hours as usual on Sunday morning, December 7. However, for some reason this morning, the truck did not show up on time to pick up privates Joseph Lockhard* and George Eliot.*

Since there was nothing else to do, George Eliot decided to leave the system on to get a little more training. Lockhart rebuked him, saying, "Come on, George, our problem was over at 0700, turn that damn thing off."

At 0702 hours, George called for Lockhart to take a look at what was on the screen. They both agreed it was bigger than anything they had ever seen before. Going to the plotting board behind them, they plotted the course and speed of the aircraft.

Feeling something was not right, Eliot called the Operations Center at Fort Schafter to explain what they were seeing. As the regular switch board operator was not on duty, Private Joseph McDonald* was manning the position. When Eliot explained what they were seeing on the screen, McDonald explained that the night problem had ended at 0700 hours and everyone was gone. Eliot insisted that this information needed to be handed over to someone in charge as the flight was coming from the north, three points to the east, and bigger than anything they had seen before.

Looking around the Operations Center, McDonald noticed Lieutenant Kermit Tyler* sitting by one of the phones reading a newspaper. After McDonald relayed the message to Lieutenant Tyler, he responded that it was nothing to get excited about. McDonald told Eliot what Lieutenant Tyler's answer was, and hung up.

As the blip on the screen began to grow, Lockhard called back to the Operations Center, demanding to talk to someone. Hearing the nervousness in Lockhard's voice, McDonald walked over to the Lieutenant, asking if he should call the plotters back in to work, and was told no, that the radar was simply picking up a flight of B-17s coming in from the states. McDonald returned to the switch board giving Lockhard the message, but that did not satisfy him. He demanded to talk to the Lieutenant himself. When McDonald transfers the call, Lieutenant Tyler gives Lockhard the same message, that it's a flight of B17s coming in from the states and not to worry about it.

After the call is disconnected, McDonald feels like he should call an officer of higher rank at Fort Schafter, but changed his mind, knowing he could be court martialed for going over his commanding officer. McDonald said later, "After all, who would listen to a private!"

At 0745 hours, McDonald's job was completed on the switch board. For some reason he could not explain, he felt the blip was Japanese planes coming to attack, but had no way to substantiate his feelings. Fifteen minutes later, he knew his gut feeling had been correct.

Back at Opana Point, Eliot and Lockhard tracked the blip until it filled the entire screen. They lost the blip due to ground clutter at 0740 hours. About that time, Eliot turned off the station as the truck arrived to pick them up for breakfast and a warm cot. They had barely arrived at their base at Kawailoa for breakfast when they heard the attack had begun. They had the truck driver take them back to Opana Point, where they spent the rest of the morning tracking and plotting aircraft.

CHAPTER EIGHTEEN - THE MORNING OF GLORY

On this glorious Sunday morning just two hundred miles north of Oahu, Keisuke had made several laps around the hanger deck, taken a quick shower and put on his new flying suit. Under the suit he wore a white T-shirt that had the names of many of his ancestors embroidered with red thread. His mother had worked on it for months to make sure her son was protected when he flew into combat. Legend said that the names would ward off enemy weapons and bring Keisuke back home to them safe and sound.

Keisuke visited the Shinto shrine on board the *Akagi* asking his ancestors for firmness and braveness under fire. However, like most pilots, Keisuke did not believe he would be coming back from such a major attack. Walking past the mail drop box, Keisuke removed an envelope from inside his coveralls, kissed it, then dropped it in the box for Etsuko and their unborn child.

Following the rest of the pilots to the ready rooms, the men donned heavy flight suits, winter head wear, insulated foot wear, and heavily insulated gloves. At 14,000 feet, the temperatures would be cold this time of year so the air crews needed to be prepared.

Leaving the ready rooms, the men climbed the last set of stairs to the flight deck. The maintenance and weapons crews cheered loudly as the air crews arrived on deck. Although there was some light fog drifting back and forth with the light southerly breeze, the pilots felt the warmth of the men that had worked for so long to prepare their aircraft.

Dive bomber 1165 sat in the fourth row of planes as the crew chief checked and rechecked everything on the plane just one more time. Keisuke had never seen his plane look so clean and shiny before, and he felt it would be an honor to fly this plane into the opening battle against the United States. Maybe his bomb hitting the right target today could make all the difference between a long or short war. He stood on the deck, bowing his head and praying one more time to his ancestors so he could make a difference and be able to be proud of his accomplishment.

After settling down into the cockpit, the crew chief buckled Keisuke into his seat. He then handed him a white head band with a large red sun on the front of it. It was signed by his entire maintenance crew so they could ride along with him into battle. Smiling at his crew chief he said. "I shall wear this for good luck and you will also be remembered in history after today."

A buzzer sounded on the deck as a flag was raised, which meant prepare for battle. Only the men kneeling below the planes waiting to remove the wheel chocks now remained on the deck.

Instantly, a roar rose from all the carriers in the task force as aircraft engines sprang to life. Keisuke was proud of the way his engine fired up and settled down to an even rumble in just a few minutes. Although many of the pilots kept their canopies open, just in case they had to abort the take off and ditch in the ocean, Keisuke pulled his closed so he could concentrate on the moment and remember everything about this glorious day. A moment later the buzzer sounded once more as the actual combat flag flown by Admiral Togo Heihachiro* in 1904, when the Japanese Navy defeated the Russian Navy at Tsushima was raised. Every pilot saluted the flag as the chocks were pulled from their wheels.

A lump arose in Keisuke's throat as he watched Commander Fuchida's plane roll down the heaving deck into history at exactly 0610 hours. Then the deck spotters waved at individual planes to follow their leader to Pearl Harbor. One by one the rows of planes in front of 1165 screamed down the carrier lifting off into the morning sky, and now it was Keisuke's turn. Throwing the throttle forward and releasing the brake, the 1165 rolled down the pitching carrier with the rear wheel rising up from the deck just as he passed the bridge. A second before reaching the end of the deck Keisuke pulled back on the stick and they were airborne. Ensign Masashi quickly pointed out where Keisuke was supposed to fall into place with all the other planes of the attack force. After gaining a little altitude and moving a short distance to his starboard side, the 1165 slid perfectly into position with the other dive bombers.

Soon the heavy clouds began to disappear, allowing the aircrews to see a magnificent sunrise that reminded many of the men of their glorious flag. Keisuke and his crew saluted the flag as another good luck charm that would assure them victory today.

Playing with their radios, it did not take long for the co-pilots to pick up Honolulu's KGMB radio station that had broadcast all night to guide in the B-17's from the states. They quickly adjusted their tracking devices to home in on their target signal. The men smiled as they listened to the soothing island music that came in crystal clear on their headsets.

About 0720 hours, the island of Oahu appeared on their port side. Some low hanging light clouds were still slowly gliding toward the northwest, but were not going to cause a problem. Every pilot had their eyes wide open as they searched the horizon for any sign of American fighters coming up to challenge them, but everything appeared to be curiously quiet.

Commander Fuchida in the lead plane was beginning to feel overwhelmed that they might just have successfully achieved complete surprise. He reached down taking hold of his radio hand set and waited just a few more minutes before broadcasting TO, TO, TO, which is a Japanese idiom calling men to fight. At 0749 hours, he made his historical message, "TORA, TORA, TORA," notifying everyone complete surprise had been attained.

Back on the *Akagi*, Admiral Nagumo and his staff took a minute for a small celebration, but turning to his top aides he says. "A message was to be sent to the American's no later than 1300 hours Washington time. We can only hope all has gone well."

Sitting in the large conference room on the battleship *Yamato* in the inland sea off the coast of Hiroshima, Yamamoto smiled slightly but was also concerned that the message had arrived at the White House on time. Now it was a waiting game to see what kind of damage would be done on the American fleet. He knew that Commander Fuchida was flying circles around the

Harbor and would report everything as he saw it happen. Before the reports began coming in, Yamamoto went outside on the main deck to get some fresh air.

At 0755 hours, Japanese planes begin to dive in different directions to accomplish the tasks assigned to them. No one needed to take evasive action as there was no antiaircraft fire or fighters to contend with.

With the first torpedo bombers dropping their weapons, men on the ground began to run to take cover or get to their battle stations in order to repulse the attack.

On Ford Island, Commander Logan Ramsey* was about to head over to the mess hall to get some breakfast, when the sound of explosions over Battleship Row made him turn back. Seeing the Japanese planes diving on the harbor, he ran up to the information desk inside the administration building, picking up a pencil he wrote his historical message and told the operator, "Send this message out to all commands and repeat it twice, "AIR RAID PEARL HARBOR, THIS IS NO DRILL!"

By now torpedo planes are dropping from the sky like angry dragon flies unloading their lethal redesigned long lance torpedoes at Battleship Row. The *Oklahoma's* port side was shredded after being struck by nine torpedoes. Twelve minutes after being struck by the first torpedo, she rolled over trapping hundreds of men inside. The *West Virginia* was hit by six torpedoes and two high caliber bombs. She sank into the mud quickly trapping many men inside. The *California* took two torpedoes and two large caliber bombs. However, she sank slowly allowing men to escape the doomed vessel. The *Nevada* was struck by one torpedo and six multipurpose bombs. She was the only battleship to get underway but was beached on Barber's Point as she had been so badly damaged. As the *Tennessee* and *Maryland* were both tied up between the quay and another battleship, neither one of them could be torpedoed, however, both ships were struck by two 500-pound bombs.

With the *Pennsylvania* being in dry dock with the destroyers *Cassin* and *Downs* it also could not be torpedoed but was struck by a 500-pound bomb. Most of the damage to the *Pennsylvania* occurred after the *Cassin* was struck by several 500-pound bombs blowing it apart.

The old retired battleship USS *Utah* now being used as a target platform, was struck by two torpedoes and countless bombs. By 0807, hours, she had rolled over entombing fifty-eight men.

The *Arizona* was struck by one of the 1800-pound reconstituted armor piercing naval shells at 0808 hours. The weapon penetrated down several decks where it detonated near the black powder bag storage area.

Griffin Westberry, a powder handler on the *Arizona* had awakened at 0705 hours. Although the crew was allowed to sleep in on December 7 for winning the battle of the bands competition the night before, Griffin just could not sleep. Quietly, he showered and put on his dress white uniform that was the custom among the fleet. Entering the main passage leaving his berthing station, he could smell coffee and bacon wafting down the mid-ship ladder from the crews mess. With just a few men taking part in the breakfast, Griffin was through the serving line in a matter of minutes. The coffee was fresh, hot and tasted nearly like any fine restaurant would serve. After cleaning his plate, he walked back to the serving line to get another warm cinnamon roll and butter. He stopped part way back to his table and looked around the mess. Nothing appeared to be unusual and most of the men were involved in quiet conversations. Yet something did not feel right as he sat back down. Normally, he would have taken his time and savored a warm cinnamon roll and hot coffee, but the nagging feeling that something was not right continued to gnaw at him. Suddenly, all he could think of was getting up to the main deck for a breath of fresh air. After gulping down the rest of his coffee, Griffin hurried over to turn in his dirty dishes and head for the exit door. He had just turned and grabbed the railing to the stairway that led up to the main deck when an explosion threw him backward down to the floor. The ship shuddered for a moment before a second explosion struck farther aft. Pulling himself up from the floor, he ran back down the companion way to the mess hall to take a look out of one of the port holes. He was stunned as he saw Japanese planes dropping down from every angle toward Battleship Row. He spun around and yelled, "The Japanese are attacking us, there are planes all around the harbor!"

He had no sooner said it when the call come over the ships loud speaker,

"Air raid, man your battle stations!" Running back out of the mess area, Griffin ran to the next stairway leading down into the ship to get to his battle station in the powder handling room. He had just turned the corner on the third deck when a powerful explosion sent him careening down the passageway toward the stern of the ship. The explosion was like nothing he had ever experienced in his life. He could feel the ship raise up for a moment then fall back into the water with a terrible jolt. Suddenly the passageway was filled with thick black acrid smoke that attempted to squeeze the life out of his lungs.

Pulling himself back up from the floor, Griffin was disorientated, unsure of which way was forward and witch way was aft. The one thing he was sure of, was the heat in the passageway was rising by the minute. Without warning a wall of flame thrust itself down the passageway, searing everything in its path. Without much thought, Griffin turned to his right thinking that had to be the aft of the ship. Feeling his way down the dark smoke-filled passageway was taking more time than he would have liked as the wall of flame appeared to be gaining on him.

Suddenly his toes ran into a knee knocker, meaning he was moving from one compartment to the next one. He knew full well there had to be a water tight door on the other side of the bulkhead he could close to stop the advancing flames. After stepping over the knee knocker he reached around to his left side, grabbing hold of the huge steel door. With a mighty push he slammed the door shut against the frame, then grabbed the sealing handles pulling them down into place. Immediately, the smoke cleared as it was using a stairway just a few feet away as a chimney.

Without wasting a moment, Griffin ran toward the stairway and began climbing back up to the second deck. He had just cleared the hatch when the door he had sealed blew open with the force of a bomb tearing the door from its hinges. The flames swirled around in the small opening before gathering strength from the fresh oxygen supply and rising up the stair way toward the hatch Griffin had just cleared. Quickly, Griffin kicked down the hatch cover and spun the wheel, dogging the hatch down in place.

He was not fully acquainted with the area of the ship he was now in, but it was filling with smoke rapidly as several more explosions rocked the battleship. He knew going forward was suicide, but he was not sure if there were any other hatches in the passageway that led up to the main deck. If he went all the way to the back of the ship without finding a hatch, odds are he would certainly die of smoke inhalation before he could find his way back forward. Closing his burning eyes, Griffin leaned back against the bulkhead for a moment trying to decide what to do as fear began to take over his mind. Griffin shook his head several times trying to restore his logical thinking, but more and more it was becoming tougher to do. Opening his eyes, he turned again toward the right and said to himself, "It's now or never."

Once again, he turned toward his right, held his hands out in front of him, and began moving down the dark smokey corridor. Moments later he could hear a groaning sound as if air was being forced out through a smaller opening. Moving another five feet, Griffin stood beside a steel door covered with iron mesh. The water tight door behind it was open, allowing the smoke and debris to make its way into the engine room several decks below him. Pulling the mesh door open, Griffin found a battle lantern hanging on the wall for emergency purposes. Grabbing the lantern, Griffin scanned the bright stream of light around the walkway above the engine room, looking for some type of escape hatch. In the distance about twenty feet down the walkway he could see a shaft of light coming from a hatch overhead. Immediately, he began walking toward the hatch when the light disappeared. Now he could feel the super-hot steam escaping from broken steam lines and it was getting hard to breathe.

Placing the strap from the lantern around his neck, Griffin began climbing the small ladder that led up to the hatch. When he reached the top, he could see the light moving to his left on the second deck. He was not alone, and it appeared those men knew where they were going. In a split second Griffin was up and moving along the passage way as steam from the engine room was turning the ship into an oven. Suddenly, another explosion below Griffin rocked the ship buckling the floor plates he was standing on. Seconds later he was laying on the floor as smoke and flames began creeping through a damaged bulkhead about ten feet in front of him.

Low crawling forward to keep below the building flames, Griffin at least found the air closer to the floor less contaminated and cooler, soothing his burning lungs. After passing below the wicked flames, Griffin came upon a body on the floor. Several large pieces of metal from the last explosion had ripped into the sailors neck and there was nothing that could be done for the man. Laying on the floor, Griffin could see the smoke above him moving rapidly down the passage way toward some type of chimney. Was it something he could fit through, or was it just a ventilation duct. The only way to know was to get back on his feet and continue moving. Second by second the passageway was getting lighter and the smoke was rolling out of the ship at an incredible speed.

Seeing the bright light from the deck hatch overhead, Griffin began to run but his left foot caught another knee knocker, sending him sprawling across the floor. Just as he was about to get up, he heard a voice say.

"Same thing that happened to me. So close yet so far away. My left leg is broken and the bones are sticking out of the calf. I'm done for it, mate! Can you help me, I don't want to die in here like my buddy did when that bulkhead exploded."

Seeing a broken battle lantern on the floor, Griffin knew the sailor and his dead friend had been the men he was following. Reaching down, Griffin picked up the sailor and led him over to the ladder. "Use your right leg to climb, I'll push you up and be your left leg. You can do this!"

The first two rungs were awkward for the injured man, but quickly he caught on and made slow but positive progress up to the main deck. Reaching the teak deck, the injured man spun around, grabbing Griffin by the shirt collar and pulling him out into the fresh air.

The men laid on the deck for several minutes trying to catch their breath. Moments later Griffin realized the flames that were consuming the mighty battleship were beginning to surround them. Without saying a word, Griffin stood up, threw the injured man over his shoulder and began walking toward the side of the main deck. Just as Griffin stopped to think about how to get off the ship, another explosion threw both men overboard into the water. Although the water felt good to Griffin, the salt water burned the injured man's leg and he screamed as he desperately clutched Griffins arm so he wouldn't sink.

Several men on Ford Island that had escaped the raging fires of the Arizona jumped into the water to help pull their injured shipmate to safety. It felt like a dream come true as Griffin laid on the cool damp grass on Ford Island. He coughed over and over as his lungs worked desperately to get rid of the acrid smoke and toxins he had been inhaling.

Moments later two men returned with a stretcher from the hospital. Griffin help load the man on the stretcher and carry him to an ambulance that was just coming their way. As Griffin prepared to push the stretcher into the ambulance, the sailor grabbed his wrist. "Name, what's your name sailor?"

Smiling, Griffin replied, "Griffin Westberry from Los Angeles, California. How about you?"

"Ricky Giuliano, formerly from New York. Now my Pops helps operate the El Rancho Hotel and Casino in a place called Las Vegas, Nevada. When this war is over come and see me and you got yourself a job. We could use a good guy like you."

As the ambulance drove off, Griffin had to laugh regarding what Ricky had just told him. Whoever heard of a place called Las Vegas in the middle of the Nevadan desert, and who would be stupid enough to build a resort and casino there? Griffin sat down under a banyan tree with twenty more sailors, watching their ship, their home, sinking into the mud of Pearl Harbor, as flames and continual explosions tore the ship to shreds. No one spoke and no one attempted to walk away. They all sat there quietly contemplating what had happened to their shipmates that were unable to escape the raging inferno.

On the *Tennessee*, Cooper and Paul were running full speed along the main deck heading toward their gun tub, but had to throw themselves to the deck several times as Japanese pilots attempted to strafe them. Reaching the tub, they found Farcy and one of the loaders lying on the deck with numerous machine gun bullets in their bodies, but that was not the worst news. As the Japanese pilots had machine gunned the crew, they had worked over the gun tub with 20mm ammunition, so it was a total wreck. Leaning against the side of the mangled wreck, Cooper struggled to catch his breath.

Slapping Paul on the back, he yelled, "Let's try and get to the tub up near the funnel on the port side. We can fire east and west without hitting the *West Virginia!*"

Immediately, both men began climbing ladders heading for the top of the ship. Not knowing where his men were going after seeing his gun tub destroyed, Lieutenant Crowder followed them.

Reaching the tub, several crew members were laying on the deck nearby watching the attack. Looking at the men, Cooper yelled, "What the hell are you doing, why aren't you fighting back?"

One of the loaders yelled, "We don't have a gunners mate, we don't know how to use the weapon and the ready box is locked."

Overhearing what had just been said, Lieutenant Crowder shot off the lock on the ready box as Cooper jumped into the gunners seat. Just as Paul slammed the first rounds into the weapon, a low flying plane released a bomb near the front of the ship. The *Tennessee* shuddered as smoke arose from the foredeck. Paul spun around screaming, as a piece of shrapnel ripped open his upper left forearm. Grabbing a piece of a rag from the cleaning equipment, Lieutenant Crowder bandaged the arm the best he could, allowing Paul to stay in action.

With the air line up at full pressure, Cooper pointed toward several planes coming from the northeast. As the crew began to rotate the gun tub toward the diving aircraft, Cooper yelled at Paul, "Jump in the other gunners seat, we need all four barrels firing!"

Without saying a word to Lieutenant Crowder, Paul jumped into the gunners seat and opened the air valve. Nodding his head, Paul yelled, "Let's go!" Immediately, all four barrels on the tub began throwing high explosive shells at the diving planes. The lead plane broke off its dive, climbing to the south as the second plane dropped low over the harbor with a streak of black smoke trailing behind it.

With the *West Virginia* beginning to settle lower and lower into the mud, the *Tennessee* began to list as the ships were still tied to one another. Quickly, crew members from the *Tennessee* began using fire axes to chop the heavy mooring lines that held the two ships together. Thankfully the sharp axes ended the tug of war, forcing the lines to snap allowing the massive battleship to right itself,

Breathing a sigh of relief, the men could now shoot in every direction without hitting the West Virginia. In seconds, the men that were working on the tub looked like they had been working together for years. The gun swirled, the azimuth on the barrels rose and dropped with precision as Cooper and Paul continued hammering away at any plane that flew into their view.

Suddenly, there was massive explosion directly behind the *Tennessee*. A wall of white-hot flame soared hundreds of feet into the air and out across the channel as if the devil himself was making a grand entrance from hell itself. Instead, the entire port side of the *Arizona* appeared to have vanished as the behemoth began settling into the muddy bottom of the harbor. Initially, the ship listed hard to port before righting itself, then settling straight up on the muddy bottom. She was encircled by millions of gallons of burning oil with flames that rose hundreds of feet into the clear blue sky. Millions of pounds of black powder, plus thousands of barrels of propulsion oil had all exploded at one time, blowing out the bottom and part of the port side of the vessel. Men that had survived the destruction of the *Arizona* came walking out of passage ways with the skin burned off their arms and faces, many of them had their clothes burned off and were not even aware of the condition they were in. Many died quickly, dropping to the deck where they stood.

Incredibly, some survivors of the blast that were not badly wounded jumped into the harbor and swam to nearby Ford Island. Some survivors that were badly wounded and horribly burned refused to get into the water, knowing the salt water would only make their wounds hurt much worse. Quickly, a parade of small boats began to arrive at the Arizona's fan tail, taking survivors across the channel to the mainland where they could be taken to the base hospital.

The roar of the exploding *Arizona* was deafening, like nothing any one had heard before. It shook the *Tennessee* as if some massive giant was shaking the ship like a toy, buckling some interior bulkheads, bursting light bulbs, jamming gears on many of the ammunition elevators and causing water pipes to leak. Cooper looked over his shoulder in disbelief as he watched the *Arizona* all but disappear in a matter of minutes, but even that was not the worst of it. In a matter of seconds, the shock wave from the explosion rolled across the harbor like a sledge hammer. People were knocked off their feet, and debris picked up by the shock wave flew through the air like missiles, killing people on ships as far away as the Maryland. Even Japanese pilots caught in the shock wave several thousand feet above the harbor reported their aircraft bounced out of control for a moment as they passed on through it.

What appeared to be an eternity for the survivors of the *Arizona* and everyone that watched the scenario take place, actually played out over just fourteen minutes. The ship came to a rest in the bottom of Pearl Harbor, taking 1,177 of her crew with her. Just 335 men survived the inferno.

With the gun tub pointed back to the northeast, Lieutenant Crowder pointed at a plane making a dive on Battleship Row. Raising the altitude of the guns, both Cooper and Paul hammered away at the diving aircraft, keeping the plane perfectly in their range finders. They could see shells bursting all around the plane, yet it continued dropping down out of the sky.

Inside the diving Japanese aircraft, Keisuke had the foredeck of the Tennessee lined up perfectly to be the recipient of his massive bomb. He smiled as he watched the ship getting larger and larger as the 1165 continued dropping down from 15,000 feet.

Suddenly, a round from one of the 40mm cannons exploded just a few feet away from the starboard fuselage. Ensign Masashi screamed out in pain as a large piece of steel from the exploding shell, along with pieces of the aircraft's skin tore into his abdomen and throat. The next exploding round shattered the rear canopy, sending hundreds of pieces of shattered Plexiglas throughout Haruto's section of the cockpit. Thousands of shards of flying glass turned into deadly missiles that penetrated his face and neck, but more importantly his eyes. Unable to see as blood flowed down his mangled face, Haruto slid his hand down into a leg pocket of his flight suit, withdrawing a small pistol. As the plane rocked back and forth from the loss of aerodynamic stability, he placed the weapon tightly against his head and pulled the trigger.

Unable to hear the gunshot because of the powerful wind, Keisuke continued calling him on the radio, hoping he could take over the spotting job since Masashi was already dead. A moment later, a 40mm round exploded in front of the propeller, shattering the blades. As many parts of the blades flew back into the engine, the powerful Mitsubishi engine ceased to run. Keisuke sat motionless for a moment as he looked at the foot long section of prop that was sticking out of his chest. He knew now he would never live in glory for what he was hoping to accomplish at Pearl Harbor, and his family back home would never know what happened to him.

In deep pain Keisuke reached over, pulling back the red lever that released the massive bomb underneath the 1165. He felt the plane twist a little as the huge bomb fell away, heading down toward Battleship Row. Although Masashi had not been able to aim the bomb, Keisuke hoped it might hit the California or maybe even the Maryland.

As the 1165 rolled over on its port side to begin it's death spiral, the massive 1800-pound bomb slammed into the surface of the harbor roughly three hundred feet from the *Maryland's* bow, creating a large water spout. A moment later an explosion rocked Ford Island about two hundred yards from Battleship Row. The 1165 burrowed into the grass near the side of the runway without damaging any military equipment. A thick cloud of black smoke rose over the island as flames consumed what was left of the plane while cremating the three men that now would not even become a footnote in history.

The first attack flight contained 51 dive bombers, 43 fighters, 40 torpedo planes for a total of 183 aircraft. The second flight consisted of 54 high level bombers, 80 dive bombers and 36 fighters for a total of 170 aircraft. In total, the Japanese launched 353 aircraft against American bases on Oahu.

December 7, 1941, 0825 hours, Haleiwa Field Hawaii North Coast
Saturday evening December 6 was the annual officers ball at Wheeler Field. It was the social event of the year, and any officer not on duty was all but required to attend. Lieutenant Ken Taylor and Lieutenant George Welch had been in a funk all week after being assigned to Haleiwa Field as they would not be able to attend the gala. Finally, the men decided that since Wheeler and

Haleiwa were only about ten minutes apart, they would tell the maintenance chief where they were going to be in case something bad happened.

Wearing their finest new tuxedos, the two officers fit in perfectly with the crowd while dancing and drinking the night away. They had every intention of returning to Haleiwa after the Gala broke up, but were enticed to attend a late-night poker game in the back room.

As dawn was just breaking over Oahu, the men decided to sleep in their quarters at Wheeler instead of driving back to Haleiwa. They had barely laid down when they were awakened by explosions and low flying aircraft at 0751hours, when Wheeler Field came under attack. As the men threw on uniform shirts, Taylor called Haleiwa to tell them to get their planes fired up and ready to fly. Welch quickly ran to get Taylor's new Buick and bring it around to the barracks door. In just under ten minutes, the men were running from the car toward their planes, still wearing their tuxedo pants. The only thing they were unhappy about was that the planes held only a half tank of fuel, but the guns were fully loaded.

Quickly, the men roared down the runway, screaming skyward toward the Japanese attackers. Welch scored their first victories as he dropped down out of the clouds hammering away on a dive bomber that had not dropped its bomb yet. The plane exploded, dropping down into the harbor. Rolling over to his left he caught a torpedo bomber unaware of his presence and blew the canopy off the plane. With the crew dead, the plane fell off to the earth.

Meanwhile, Taylor jumped a Zero from behind, destroying its engine. The fighter rolled over to its port side and dropped from the sky. The plane that smashed into one of the hangers at Hickam field is thought to have been that plane.

Now that the Zero pilots were aware there were American fighters in the sky, they went after the P-40 pilots with a vengeance. Both Taylor and Welch did a good job of avoiding the enemy fighters, but they were beginning to run out of fuel. Making a wide turn to the north, the pilots quickly made their way to Wheeler Field, where crews waited to refuel and rearm the planes.

With the aircraft ready to go, the second wave of Japanese aircraft were just beginning to arrive. Seeing the enemy planes arriving, the flight line supervisor gave Taylor and Welch a direct order not to take off. After a heated argument between Taylor and the flight line supervisor, both aircraft once again roared back into the skies. Within minutes, Welch shot down several high-level bombers and Taylor destroyed another Zero. Soon several other American planes joined into the battle, making life for the second attack group much more dangerous.

During a dog fight over Hickam Field, several bullets penetrated Taylor's canopy, tearing up his right arm and sending shrapnel down into his right leg. He dropped down making his way back to Wheeler Field. He was credited with two confirmed kills, but it is surely possible he shot down other planes that were not verified. He was awarded the Purple Heart and the Distinguished Flying Cross. He was nominated for the Congressional Medal of Honor, but the flight supervisor would not drop his charge of taking off without permission, so the Medal of Honor could not be awarded.

Welch continued chasing the enemy and damaging as many planes as possible until he ran out of ammunition. He was credited with four kills, but like Taylor, it's conceivable he damaged other planes that crashed into the ocean before returning to the carriers. Welch was awarded the Distinguished Flying Cross, however, he was not nominated for the Congressional Medal of Honor.

Japanese Miniature Submarine

After the situation with the USS *Ward*, Captain Earl decided to send another ship out to the security area to help patrol. The only destroyer to have enough steam up to get moving immediately was the USS *Monaghan*. At 0826 the *Monaghan* began heading for the harbor entrance.

At 0833 hours, the Seaplane Tender USS *Curtis* reported seeing the conning tower and periscope of a Japanese miniature submarine in the harbor near Berthing Station X-22. Immediately, the *Curtis* and USS Tangier another sea plane tender, took the vessel under fire.

Making a quick mid-course direction change, the *Monaghan* turned to attack the sub. Seeing the vessel just a short way under the surface of the harbor, deck gun number two fired one round which misses the sub but strikes the derrick barge moored at Beaconing Point. Commander Buford* told the crew to stand by for ramming at 0835 hours. Just before the *Monaghan* rammed the sub at 0837 hours, the skipper of the sub fired a torpedo which ran aground near the derrick barge without exploding. After seeing the sub go down, Buford ordered full reverse and depth charged the vessel to make sure it was finished.

Buford then left Pearl Harbor to patrol with the Ward. The *Monaghan* received slight damage to its stern from the depth charge attack due to the shallowness of the harbor. The remains of the sub and its crew were dredged up later in December and buried in the sea wall of the harbor. It was dug up during a construction project years later and buried away from the harbor.

CHAPTER NINETEEN – THE WIVES

Lily awoke from a very sound sleep at 0715 hours on Sunday morning. After sitting on the edge of the bed for a few minutes, she decided to get dressed and go to an earlier church service. She showered and dressed quickly, so she could make the service that was scheduled to begin at 0830 hours.

Like always, she would take her next-door neighbor Dorothy Madison with her, and pick up Sadie along the way. Being a bit early, it gave Lily a chance to have a cup of coffee and look over the morning newspaper somewhat before leaving the house she and Cooper had rented.

She looked at the photo of the USS *Tennessee* hanging on the wall near the refrigerator. There was Cooper and the rest of the crew sitting on the foredeck with the massive main gun turret directly behind them. She had circled Cooper and Paul's smiling faces. They looked like a couple of kids with a new bicycle on Christmas Day. She always thought the *Tennessee* was a most terrifying weapon. But today it was just one of seven more battleships berthed in Pearl Harbor.

Just as Lily finished her coffee, Dorothy Madison walked into the kitchen. Sitting down by the table she said, "So, is Cooper coming home today? Stan has deck duty today, but it should be pretty quiet on the Arizona, since the news this morning said their band won the 'Battle of the Bands' competition last night, so they got to sleep in. He should be in a pretty good mood when he comes home tonight."

Lily laughed as she shook her head. "Well, that won't make Coop very happy at all. He had several bets on the competition and was hoping to sleep in late this morning. Plus, I'm guessing he'll have to eat a little crow over the next few days. But no, Cooper will not be home until Tuesday, and that's if Kimmel does not send them back out to sea again."

Looking over at the clock above the kitchen sink, Lily said, "Well, I suppose we should get going or Sadie will wonder where we are."

As Lily unlocked the car, she heard a strange noise that caught her attention. Looking over at Dorothy, she said, "Does that sound like planes coming in rather low?"

Nodding her head, Dorothy responded, "Yeah, it sure does, and it sounds like a bunch of them."

Walking out to the street to get a better view toward the northwest, Lily stood there in bewilderment. The planes she was watching looked nothing like the planes she saw flying over the island every day. Then in horror she saw the lead plane drop a bomb on Ford Island. As the plane rose up into the sky, she yelled out to Dorothy.

"Oh my God, those are Japanese planes. They're attacking Pearl Harbor!"

Dorothy shook her head in disbelief, saying, "Honey that's just not possible. Where would those planes have come from? And look how many there are."

Lily stood frozen on the street as she watched torpedo planes and high-altitude bombers attacking Battleship Row like a swarm of hornets. By now, explosions rocked the harbor, sending shock waves up the hill toward the area where many dependents rented homes. Lily covered her ears as she dropped to her knees screaming in horror, "My God, make it stop, make it stop. Dear God, this can't be happening, please Lord, make it stop!"

Just as Dorothy pulled Lily up from the street, a very low flying Japanese plane screamed overhead. Moments later, a small bomb struck a house down the block from Lily and Cooper's house, completely destroying it. The explosion blew out windows and doors in many nearby homes, sending deadly shards of glass and sharp splinters of wood flying throughout the neighborhood. Minutes later, bloody people stumbled out of several homes, screaming in pain as large pieces of glass protruded from their faces, arms and chests.

Dorothy attempted to pull Lily off the street toward a large bush for cover, screaming, "They're going to kill us all, we're all going to die!"

Lily struggled to get away from Dorothy, as she wanted to run down to the Radford Drive gate leading into the naval base. She had barely pulled free when another plane came screaming overhead, even lower than the first one, and firing its machine guns. Several people screamed out in pain as machine gun bullets tore into their bodies. A moment later a car came down the hill with the front left tire blown out, then slammed into a tree a short distance away. As smoke poured from under the hood, Sadie scrambled from the burning vehicle stumbling down the road toward the base.

"Sadie, Sadie!" Lily called out, as she ran toward her friend who had blood on the side of her face. "Honey, are you alright?"

Sadie looked dazed as she struggled to maintain her balance. "Lily, that pilot tried to kill me! He machine gunned the car, blowing out the front tire and smashing three windows in the car, including the one next to me. What are we going to do? I want to see Paul and he's out there with Cooper. We have to get to them!"

Lily took Sadie over to the curb, sitting her down. Brushing back her long hair, Lily could see several small cuts on her forehead. Reaching down into her purse she removed a clean white handkerchief and held it against the wounds to stop the bleeding. She then took out several band aids, applying them to Sadie's forehead. "Forcing a smile, Lily brushed Sadie's hair with her hand saying, "See, it's good to have a nurse for a friend, we come prepared."

After giving Lily a hug, Sadie said, "We need to get down there, we need to help our men somehow. We can't just leave them out there alone!"

The three women had gone just a short distance when a massive explosion rocked the harbor. They stopped and stared in horror as a massive wall of fire climbed up into the sky, throwing debris in every direction. A moment later they were struck by the tremendous shock wave which literally drove them back several feet, causing Sadie to lose her balance and fall.

Dorothy screamed in horror as she watched what was left of the Arizona disappear behind the thick black smoke and raging inferno. Dropping to her knees, she screamed, "Oh my God, Stan! Oh my God!"

Lily and Sadie held on to Dorothy as she wept and continued screaming, as it was evident there was nothing right now that was going to console her broken heart. Several minutes later, Dorothy's niece arrived on the hill. After staring in disbelief at the Arizona for a moment, she knelt down by Dorothy. Then looking at Lily, she said. "Let me take her back to my place where she can lay down, that would be best for her."

After Dorothy was taken away, Lily stood up saying, "Enough!"

Quickly, she took off down the hill until she reached several police cars that were keeping everyone back from the naval yard gates.

Sadie looked at the officer and yelled, "Our husbands are out there. You need to let us through this very minute!"

The officer looked at Sadie. "Look Ma'am, there are hundreds of husbands out there and there is not a damn thing you or I can do to help them right now. The best thing you can do is go home and pray for them, but you can't go onto the base. Just look what's going on out there!"

Sadie looked out toward Battleship Row and watched the massive fires as Japanese planes continued hammering away at the ships and Ford Island. She watched the puffs of antiaircraft fire exploding above the harbor as the Japanese pilots twisted and turned trying to avoid it. It was a ghastly sight her mind just could not comprehend.

Suddenly, there was a small explosion nearly overhead from where they were standing. They watched as the Japanese torpedo bomber burned, minus half a starboard wing, leaving a trail of greasy black smoke in the sky before smashing into a house about two blocks away from Lily's home. The house burst into a massive ball of flame as the high grade aviation fuel from the bomber exploded.

Sadie placed her hands over her face and began to cry as she leaned against the patrol car. Lily placed her arms around her best friend, holding her tight as she watched an ambulance come down the hill with its red lights flashing. Lifting Sadie's head with her hand Lily said, "I've got an idea, come with me."

Stepping in front of the ambulance, Lily raised her hand for it to stop. The driver leaned out of the ambulance and yelled. "Are you crazy, lady? I got to get down on to the base, they're in need of ambulances down there, now get the hell out of the way!"

Lily stepped up to the driver's door and yelled back, "Do you think they just might be in need of trained nurses that can help with the wounded down there?"

Nodding his head, the driver replied, "Yeah maybe, are you two nurses?"

Lily pulled out her ID card from the hospital and said, "Does this answer your question? Now, do you think we've wasted enough time here already?"

"Yeah, yeah. Climb in the back, I'll get you to the hospital," the driver replied as he prepared to continue on his way.

The marines guarding the gate to the base never said a word and just pointed toward the hospital and stood off to the side. Arriving at the hospital, Lily and Sadie jumped from the back of the truck as two corpsmen came running out toward the ambulance. The one with Petty Officer insignia's looked at the women. "Are you gals nurses?"

They both nodded their heads. Before they could say another word, the Petty Officer continued, "Get inside get gowned up, we've got badly wounded patients already, and there will be hundreds more on the way! See Doctor Winstead or Chief Nurse Freiling, they will point you in the right direction."

After entering the building, Sadie pulled Lily off to the side. "Lily, I don't know a scissors from a stethoscope. What the hell am I supposed to do?"

Turning toward her friend, Lily replied, "Be brave and help where you can. Help bandage men the best you know how and no one will know the difference. You can do this, Sadie."

After gowning up, the women ran into Doctor Winstead. Looking at Lily, he said, "You come with me, we're going to surgery." Looking at Sadie, he said, "See Nurse Freiling in the burn ward, she's already overwhelmed."

There were two other naval doctors working in the surgical ward when Lily and the doctor walked up to their first patient. The note around his neck indicated he had two shots of morphine. The doctor looked at the man's right leg and matter of factly, said, "Well Lily, let's do our first amputation of the day, I'm sure there will be many more to come."

Walking into the burn ward, Sadie was nearly overcome with the amount of blood on the floor and the bloody sheets that were covering the men. Nurse Freiling said, "Lady, I don't believe for a minute you are a nurse, but today you're going to learn more about life and death than you ever thought possible. Now come with me."

Using Sadie's help, Nurse Freiling and several other corpsmen worked feverishly, trying to deal with the awful burns that were already starting to stack up. As Sadie approached one of the patients, he reached out grabbing her arm. "Please, get the picture out of my shirt pocket."

Unbuttoning the pocket, she handed the sailor the photo of a beautiful blonde sitting on a boat in a swim suit. Smiling, the man said. "Tell her I love her, and let her know I still want to marry her."

Sadie smiled, "Hang tight, sailor. We'll fix you up and you can tell her yourself."

"No, I'm dying and you all know it, please..." With that the sailors head rolled to the side.

Seeing Sadie cry, Nurse Freiling said, "Get used to it, sweetheart, you better get prepared because the worst is yet to come. Have you seen what's going on out there? Suck it up, lady because you are in the den of the tiger now!"

Just as Dr. Winstead was about to make a second incision on the patient he was working on, the entire building shook. Windows exploded and light fixtures shook, breaking bulbs as items sitting on tables and shelves crashed to the floor. An ambulance parked by the emergency room door tipped over on its side, killing one of the corpsmen as the side of the vehicle was crushed by the shock wave caused by the blast.

Everything in the surgical room came to a stop as someone yelled out, "What the hell was that!"

A army military police officer that was dropping off several injured soldiers, said, "It's the *Shaw* in dry dock. Good lord, I have never seen an explosion like that before." As he finished speaking, several pieces of the ship came crashing down on top of the hospital, and blew out windows wounding several men already in line for treatment.

When the building quit shaking, Dr. Winstead said, "Well, the war no one wanted is now upon us. God help us because our fleet is no more." Taking a deep breath, he continued on with the surgery.

When they heard that a second attack group was flying over the harbor, everyone felt sick, afraid, and discouraged. Ambulance drivers arriving at the hospital were telling stories of Japanese landings on the north side of Oahu, and that American forces were retreating as they were quickly being overwhelmed.

As fast as possible, many patients were being loaded into ambulances to be transferred to Tripler Army Hospital at Fort Schafter. The hospital was not much larger than the one at Hospital Point, but today, it allowed the naval hospital to gain some badly needed bed space. The major problem was that Tripler was already taking in all the wounded from Hickam Field, Schofield Barracks and the severely wounded from Fort Schafter, so it was quickly being overwhelmed. The decision was made to transfer non-critical patients to the civilian Ewa Plantation hospital, and the Aiea Plantation Hospital, where space was still available.

Out in the Harbor, whale boats from the hospital ship USS *Solace* moved up and down Battleship Row, plucking wounded sailors out of the water and delivering them to the ship. One of the whale boats caught fire in the burning oil near the *Arizona* and was lost along with the three men on board.

Surprisingly, the *Solace* was not touched during the attacks, and was able to supply much needed emergency medical treatment to sailors that were in critical condition.

At CINCPAC Headquarters, officers raced about the building using phones while attempting to get a handle on what all was happening on the island for Admiral Kimmel. While Kimmel was at his desk sorting through papers, a telegraph runner came into the room holding a telegram envelope, stating the message came from the Chief of Staff in Washington. Kimmel opens it and finds the message Colonel Bratton had sent for General Marshall. After reading the message, he said, "Gentlemen, I have a telegram from the Chief of Staff." After clearing his throat, he read it out loud.

"The Japanese are presenting at 1pm eastern standard time today, what amounts to an ultimatum. Also, they are under orders to destroy their code

machines immediately. Just what significance the hour set may have we do not know, but be on alert accordingly. Signed, Chief of Staff. George C. Marshall."

Every officer in the room stood quietly in place, shocked at what they had just heard from the Pacific Fleet Commander. By this time the second wave of Japanese aircraft had nearly completed their attack. Kimmel stood up from his desk and walked to the large window overlooking the harbor. As he watches his fleet being decimated, a bullet comes through the window, striking a button on his uniform. One of his aides picks it up off the floor and says, "Sir, its bent!"

Kimmel never looks at the bullet, he simply says, "It would have been more merciful had it killed me."

Back at the hospital, Reverend Henry McCloud, one of the chaplains assigned to Pearl Harbor, arrives at the hospital as he watches the attack continuing to unfold across the harbor. He walked among the wounded, consoling them while saying prayers over the dead. Seeing the grief on the faces of the doctors and nurses, he walked among them, encouraging each of them to be brave and continue on with their work and not despair. Wherever possible, he lent a hand to help the staff, hoping his assistance might save the life of a young man. By 1100 hours, the hospital was completely overwhelmed and was running out of morphine, bandages, bed sheets and many other essential items.

The walls along the corridor outside the surgical department were lined with bodies covered in blankets, tarps or ponchos, but they soon ran out of room. Doctor Winstead ordered additional bodies be stacked in the basement until other arrangement could be made.

Outside the back door of the hospital, four 55-gallon drums were filled with arms and legs, and the surgical teams were still not finished amputating. During the first three hours after the attack began, the hospital treated 960 casualties and admitted 452. (Note: The number of casualties treated and the story regarding the 55-gallon drums were obtained from the factual record.)

A corpsmen working in the surgical ward said later that at one point the large amputation saw had cut through so many bones it was hot to the touch.

By now, Sadie was handling many burn patients on her own without needing to talk to nurse Freiling. As the morning turned into afternoon, Nurse Freiling put her arm around Sadie, "How you holding up, kid? Do you need anything?"

Sadie shook her head, "No, not unless you can assure me that my Paul is safe and sound. Other than that, there is nothing anyone can do for me. The problem is, with each new case I deal with, the more my doubts grow that Paul will survive."

Nurse Freiling smiled at Sadie. "Honey, maybe you should go home instead of dealing with all of this."

Sadie shook her head. "I have no one to go home to. Lily is my best friend and she's doing what she knows best. So, without her I would be lost. Besides, these men need me, and right now I need each one of them more than you will ever understand."

Without saying another word, Sadie finished the glass of water she was drinking, then went on to the next patient that had just been carried into the ward.

About 1400 hours, Lieutenant Norman, a tall Army officer from Fort Worth, Texas entered the hospital. Seeing Doctor Winstead looking at toe tags of the wounded, he walked over to the tired surgeon.

"Doctor, you need to pack up your patients and prepare to move out of here as soon as possible. That's an order from base command!"

Doctor Winstead looked at the lieutenant, asking, "Exactly which officer with his head up his ass made that ridiculous decision? Get the hell out of my hospital unless you are here to help!"

Stunned by the reply, Lieutenant Norman replied. "Sir, we have word the Japanese are landing a large force of infantry just to the north of Diamond Point. There's nothing out there that can stop them, so I have been sent here to set up a defense perimeter to slow them down. That means the hospital will be directly in the line of fire. You must evacuate now!"

Realizing the lieutenant was just the delivery man, not the person making the decision, Doctor Winstead shook his head. "Son, take a look around you. Do you see any way we can evacuate this place, and there are more men on the way. Tell me, Lieutenant, where can we go where we would have the equipment to save lives? I realize you have a job to do, but your request is just not possible.

The lieutenant was just about to speak when Reverend McCloud stepped forward.

"Lieutenant, we have boys here that are fighting for their lives, and more on the way as the doctor said. Every person here on Oahu will need to make tough decisions today as to how they will survive, and what they can do to help those in need. If the Japanese are indeed coming, we will have to deal with them when they get here. But for now, you must do what you need to do, and let us continue what we are doing. And we all must pray that this day has an outcome we can all live with. Go now, and may God be with you and your men."

Placing his steel helmet back on his head, Lieutenant Norman nodded slightly while turning to leave the hospital.

Outside, military trucks continued to roll up by the hospital with 200 soldiers, machine guns, mortar tubes, sand bags and cases of ammunition. The scared men went right to work constructing a defensive perimeter as Lieutenant Norman continued barking out orders and giving directions. From time to time, he would look over at the hospital and shake his head as more ambulances arrived with horribly wounded soldiers and sailors.

About 1600 hours, a sergeant arrived at the hospital with a jeep and a truck. Walking inside, he asked if there were any non-military people working there. Reverend McCloud said they had two women volunteers that had been there nearly all day and had been doing an outstanding job.

The sergeant said that all non-military personnel were to evacuate the base by no later than 1700 hours, with no exceptions. He stated they would be given a ride to where ever they wanted to go, but they had to leave, orders from Commander of the Fourteenth Naval District. Neither Lily or Sadie wanted to leave, but Reverend McCloud explained that no one knew what was going to happen when the sun went down, so it was best that they leave.

After climbing into the jeep, the driver asked where they wanted to go. Lily explained where they lived, so the driver was quickly on his way. Approaching the Radford Drive Gate, two nervous soldiers pointed their rifles at the driver, demanding to know what the password was. After giving the password, the men were still not sure if they should let him pass by. After several more minutes of arguing, Lily was finally able to convince the men to let them leave without shots being fired or having anyone arrested.

Stopping in front of Lily's house, the women climbed out of the jeep and began walking toward the house. Jumping from the jeep, the driver called them back. "Ladies, this is really important. When you get inside, stay inside. Don't go walking around in the dark tonight or you will risk getting shot. There are also rumors that Japanese operatives are on the island poisoning the water supply, so you might want to get as much water as you can before it's too late. And keep your curtains closed so no one can see any lights after dark."

Before either of the women could say a word, the driver jumped back into the jeep, let the clutch fly, and spun the vehicle around, heading back toward the base.

The women were barely in the house when there was a knock on the back door. Pulling back the curtain, Lily saw a nervous Dorothy standing outside with a load of blankets and pillows.

Lily barely had the door open, when Dorothy charged forward nearly knocking Sadie to the floor. "I am so glad to see you two are alright. My niece left several hours ago and I was scared to be by myself, can I stay with you?"

Giving Dorothy a hug Lily said, "Of course you can, the more the safer, tonight." Quickly, Lily began filling the bathtub with water, as Dorothy and Sadie filled every large container Lily had in the house. Listening to the radio, everything on Oahu sounded rather bleak. The announcer talked about the Japanese landing near Diamond Head, and another landing on the north shore near Haleiwa. He said paratroopers had landed near Wheeler Field and had taken it under control. None of the women could explain the next news item, but the announcer reported that the local civil defense coordinator stated there were rumors of dogs barking in code, sending messages to Japanese Operatives. (Note: True radio report.)

The women decided to sleep on the floor together, so they would be at the lowest point in the house. They tipped the bed on its side and barricaded the bedroom window, then slid the heavy dresser against the door for protection. When they were comfortably settled on the floor, Sadie looked at Dorothy. "So, how are you doing now."

Dorothy forced a small smile as she replied. "Several times today I walked down toward the Radford Street Gate and watched the ship burn. Each time, I knew in my heart that Stan was dead because it would have been impossible to escape such a nightmare. Next year Stan would have had thirty-five years in the navy and we were going to find a nice quiet place to settle down. I loved moving around with Stan as much as he loved the navy, so we had a good life together. Our daughter and her family live near Denver, Colorado, so as soon as I can, I'm going to pack up what I want to keep and sail back to the states and live with them for a while. It will give me time to figure out what I want to do. Of course, being without Stan will be the hardest part to get over."

Rolling over on the makeshift bed, Sadie closed her eyes as tears flowed down her face. She placed her hands over her abdomen, where their little child was beginning to grow, knowing in the next few days she may have to rearrange her entire life, the same as Dorothy. It killed her to think of Paul being burned to death on the *Tennessee,* but after working with the sailors today, she knew in her heart it would be best if Paul was dead and not burned so horribly as many of the survivors. It felt horrible to think that way, but she was trying to be a realist.

Lily held onto Dorothy for some time trying to give her comfort, but her heart would not allow her to think of Cooper being dead. She was carrying his child and she insisted Cooper would be there to raise their child, it just had to be that way.

During the long dark night, shots rang out all around the neighborhood as people ran back and forth chasing imaginary Japanese infiltrators. Several times throughout the night, Lily heard bullets strike the back of the house.

The soldier that brought them home had been right, the streets were simply not safe for anyone tonight.

Down by the hospital, Lieutenant Norman walked back and forth along his skirmish line, attempting to keep his men calm. He knew it would not take much to set them off as he could feel the tension in the air. Kneeling down by one of the machine gun operators, he asked the private how he was doing.

The scared soldier looked up at him. "When are they coming, sir? I thought I heard Japanese voices a little while ago, but now it's quiet. Shouldn't they be around Diamond Head already?"

"We don't know what's all going on. Just stay calm and we'll take it one step at a time. Who knows, maybe they didn't land on the island, maybe it's all a mistake," the nervous lieutenant replied.

"Look behind us at the fires, sir. Do you think that's a mistake, do you think that was an accident? No sir, they're here, and I can feel them out there getting closer," the soldier replied, as he placed his finger closer to the trigger of his machine gun.

Moving on, the lieutenant prayed that dawn would come soon so no one would get killed by accident tonight. Everyone was scared, not thinking accurately, and wanting revenge for the attack. It was a bad combination that could explode any moment, and it did.

About 0100 hours, every weapon on the right side of the line opened up, but Lieutenant Norman could not see any return fire coming from the east. Running down the line, he yelled, "Cease fire, cease fire, hold your fire!"

One of his riflemen jumped up from the ground, yelling, "We got them sir, we saw them running this way and we watched them go down. We got the bastard's, sir, we got them sure as hell. They were just about fifty yards out when we opened fire. Yeah, we got the bastards for sure!"

Just as the man quit talking, a sickening sound rolled across the open field. In the distance you could hear a man yelling, "I'm hit. Medic! Damn, I'm hit!"

After ordering his men to put their weapons down, the Lieutenant took six men along with him to search the field. They had gone about forty yards when they came across five bodies lying on the ground. It was evident that three of them were dead, but two were badly injured. After sending several men to the hospital for stretchers, Lieutenant Norman knelt down beside one of the men.

"What were you doing out here? Where the hell did you come from?"

"We were standing guard on the channel when we saw a Japanese ship coming toward us. We didn't know what to do, so we just ran, sir. You got to tell someone the Japs are in the main harbor channel. They're coming to finish what they started."

When his men arrived with the stretchers, the lieutenant had the wounded men removed. Looking at the rest of the men, he said, "No one else gets killed out here tonight, and these bodies will have to wait until morning." After getting everyone re-situated behind the skirmish line, he went over to his radio set to call in the incident. Regrettably, he was told that had been the third such shooting incident of the night, claiming a Japanese ship was coming up the channel.

Around 0430 hours, an American jeep drove down the small dirt road near the tank farm to the north of the hospital. It did not have any lights on, so everyone nervously allowed it to pass without shooting at it. After reaching the high fence separating the tank farm from Hospital Point, the driver turned on his lights and made a turn to go back the way it had come. Once again, men on the right side of the line opened fire. Just as quickly, the lights went out on the jeep as it disappeared from the road.

Lieutenant Norman scanned the area with his binoculars, but was unable to make out any sign of the jeep. Sitting down in the ditch on the east side of the dirt road, the two military police officers sat quietly in their vehicle, not sure what to do next. After giving it some serious thought, the driver restarted the jeep, slammed his foot down on the throttle and drove back onto the main road. In a matter of minutes, the jeep disappeared around the north side of the tank farm and out of sight from the trigger-happy infantry.

Returning to Hickam Field, they reported everything at the tank farm was fine, but the nine bullet holes in the jeep and a hissing radiator proved otherwise.

At 0630 hours on Hospital Point, Lieutenant Norman received orders to load up all his equipment and return to Fort Shafter. After retrieving the bodies from the field, the lieutenant could see the horror on the faces of his men that had done the shooting. He knew there was nothing that could be said to take away the guilt that was haunting them, yet he understood the fear they were feeling as they laid in that dark field, not knowing if the Japanese were going to attack at any moment. This war was just starting and it was impossible to know who was going to survive and what these green army recruits were going to experience before the fighting would come to an end. But one thing Lieutenant Norman knew to be true, they would never get over the haunting feeling that they killed their own men out of fright.

Out on Battleship Row, fires still raged on several of the ships as tug boats worked close by trying to knock down the flames. All across the harbor, the sound of pneumatic hammers and drills could be heard as they ripped away at the armored plates on the underbelly of the Oklahoma. It was a slow tedious job and everyone knew that time was running out for survivors. Doing a horrible job, several small barges sailed among the damaged ships continuing to pull bodies and other human remains from the oily water.

CHAPTER TWENTY –
SECOND ATTACK

Cooper and Paul sat back in their gun tub, watching the Japanese planes disappearing off to the northwest. Lieutenant Crowder and the gun loaders dropped down to the deck, attempting to catch their breath for a moment. A few seconds later, Paul sat up straight pointing toward the north. "Here come the son-of-a-bitches again!"

Immediately, Cooper and Paul began firing at the attackers, as did more gunners all around the harbor. Along with the additional antiaircraft guns, there were now several American fighters attacking the Japanese planes before they could break formation. It was evident that this group of Japanese pilots were not as willing to fly through the heavy flak and attack with the sheer determination as the first flight. It was nice to see several Japanese planes falling out of the sky or turning back toward the north, trailing columns of greasy black smoke.

Paul could tell something was drastically wrong inside the *Tennessee* as his gun misfired on several occasions. Suddenly Paul's gun quit firing altogether. He looked at Cooper, yelling, "What the hell do I do now?"

Cooper was sure his weapon was going to suffer the same fate quickly, but yelled back. "Check your air valve. Turn it off and then back on again to see what happens!"

After Paul turned his air back on again, it was evident the weapon was now out of commission. Seconds later, Coopers gun suffered the same dilemma. He also tried the air valve but the gun failed to react.

Over the horrendous noise in the harbor, Lieutenant Crowder leaned over the wall of the tub yelling, "What the fuck guys, why are you stopping?"

Cooper threw his arms up into the air as he yelled back, "Air sir, we got no damn air pressure on either gun!"

Slamming his fist into the wall of the tub, Lieutenant Crowder yelled back, "What are we supposed to do, throw these damn shells at the fucking Japs?"

While the men were discussing the problems, one of the ammunition handlers came running out the door leading to the upper section of the super structure. "Lieutenant, the main air distribution line coming up from the engine room has been cut by shrapnel. They turned it off in the main steam trunk down by turret two. Were done, sir!"

Completing his announcement, all the ammunition handlers scrambled for cover back inside the ship.

As Paul jumped from the gun tub, he turned toward the angry lieutenant. "Sir, what the—"

He never finished his question, as another explosion on the *Arizona* sent a wall of hot steel and debris flying in the direction of the *Tennessee*. Cooper ducked down into the gun tub, screaming as the super-heated air from the explosion burned his back. It seemed like forever as the roar once again blotted out every other sound in the harbor.

When the wall of debris had passed them by, Cooper slowly raised himself up from the gun tub and looked around. The hoses that pumped air to the guns were torn loose and dangling from the weapons. The outside barrel on Cooper's gun was bent, and a large piece of shrapnel still nearly red hot was jammed into the ammunition loading box. He was surprised the ammunition in the box had not exploded. If it had, it would have certainly torn him to shreds.

Wiping soot and dirt from his face, Cooper called out for Paul, but heard no response. Slowly standing up, Cooper looked across the deck to where Paul had been standing. He gasped in horror as he looked at the remains of his best friend now sprawled in a large pool of blood. Paul's face was all but burned off from the super-heated air that had rushed over him. His left arm was gone at the elbow and his right shoulder was shattered with bones protruding from the skin. A large piece of shrapnel from the Arizona had embedded itself in his abdomen, nearly disemboweling him on the spot.

Turning toward Lieutenant Crowder, Cooper could not believe what he was seeing. His body had been torn completely in half by the storm of steel that had flown across the deck. The upper half of his torso was laying on the deck with his arms torn off, while the lower half was actually leaning up against the railing a few feet from where he had been standing. His shoes still had a good shine on them, and what was left of his dress white slacks still had a fairly good crease.

Cooper attempted to shield his face with his hand from the extreme heat coming off the Arizona, but quickly decided he might burn to death if he stayed where he was. As he passed by Paul's body toward the superstructure door, Cooper stopped for a moment.

"I'll let Sadie know you died a hero. She deserves to know you fought back until the very end. Good bye, old friend."

After ducking inside the ship, Cooper pulled the door closed to keep out the intense heat. It was obvious everyone had evacuated the area, not knowing what was going to happen next with the *Arizona,* or if the *West Virginia* just might suffer the same fate. After dropping down several levels in the ship, Cooper ran into Chief Petty Officer Keppers. Before Cooper could say a word, Keppers grabbed him by the arm. "Cooper, where is Darnell and Lieutenant Crowder, have you seen them?"

Cooper nodded his head. "They're bodies are up on deck five. That last blast from the *Arizona* tore them to shreds."

After looking at Cooper's burns, the chief said, "Cooper, a lot of men have abandoned ship. I need some men that can fight fire down below. Do you think you can still work?"

Without giving it any thought, Cooper nodded his head. "What do you want me to do, Chief?"

After grabbing two other men that were attempting to leave the ship, the Chief led them down to an area directly above the engine room. "That last explosion on the *Arizona* started fires in the crane equipment room. We've got to get in there and knock it down before it can get to the starboard fuel bunker. Let's go, we can't wait."

After placing an oxygen mask over his head and tightening the web belt to hold the tank in place, Cooper wanted to yell out in pain as the oxygen tank and belts ran directly across his torn and blistered skin, but he just clenched his jaw and took several deep breaths.

As Chief Keppers opened the door to the equipment room, a surge of extremely hot air rolled out over the top of the men and down the passageway. Cooper turned on the nozzle and began pulling the heavy charged line into the room. He went after a work bench first that contained a pile of burning rags, coveralls, cans of grease and other lubricants. He swirled the nozzle around and around until he had begun to beat back the intense flames. He then noticed that the biggest part of the fire was the burning paint that had been applied to the walls over and over in Navy tradition. Starting in the corner by the work bench, the men worked west, knocking down the flames on the wall. However, the heat from the fires on the *Arizona* quickly turned the water into a cloud of hot steam that burned the men's arms and faces that were unprotected. In about forty-five minutes the fire was knocked down, but no one could be sure the old paint would not reignite, as it had in several other compartments.

Slamming the door closed, the chief said, "Follow me, boys, we have a real emergency farther forward."

The men ran down the passage way to another ladder that led toward the ammunition bunkers in the middle of the ship. Smoke was coming out of a large air handling vent overhead. Several sailors with axes were attempting to break through the metal sheeting. The bigger they tore the hole, the more smoke rolled down into the passageway.

Chief Keppers looked at Cooper, "We think the smoke is coming from a fire in or near the aft steering room. If that fire follows this duct work into these ammo bunkers, we'll go up like the *Arizona*. Once they make the hole a bit bigger, you'll have to get up in there and work your way aft, looking for fire. It's a straight run, but there are many trunk lines that break off the main run. Find out where the fire is and attack it. If you can't, back the hell out and let us know what you see."

Cooper was not in the frame of mind to be cooked alive inside the ventilation shaft, but somebody had to do it. After using the ladder to get up to the shaft, one of the men handed him a large flash light. When he was ready to move, the fire hose was fed into the metal shaft aside of him. With the tank on his already burned back, Cooper had a hard time crawling forward, and every inch closer toward the stern of the ship, the smoke became thicker and much hotter. The flashlight no longer gave him much help, so he tucked it into the strap around his waist, knowing it may come in handy farther down the vent.

A few minutes later the air became very hot, giving Cooper the idea that he was very near the fire, but unfortunately, he was at a tee in the duct work. Were the flames still ahead or were they to his left or right? For the first time in his life, he was scared beyond anything he had ever been before, and he felt like panicking, but he knew there were hundreds of men counting on him to keep the ship from being blown apart.

Several more minutes passed before he was able to see flames peeking out through the black smoke. He was not sure where the fire was coming from as he pulled the nozzle up to his chest and turned it on. Dirt and soot splashed up into his face as the steady stream of water bounced off the bottom and sides of the massive vent. With the smoke dissipating somewhat, Cooper could see the flames were coming up from a vent screen that led to a compartment one deck below. The massive vent he was laying in was acting like a huge chimney. The closer he came to the screen, the hotter the bottom of the vent shaft became. It was impossible for Cooper to aim his nozzle at any one particular burning spot, but he continued moving it back and forth over the screen, hoping to keep the flames down. Several minutes later, the door to the compartment burst open as several men wearing firefighting suits entered with two large hoses.

Turning off his nozzle, Cooper began working his way back to the opening where he had entered the ventilation shaft. It was tough going as he had to kick the hose back with his feet so he could keep working his way back in the total darkness. Finally reaching the hole, Cooper dropped down to the floor where he laid spread eagle on the deck, completely exhausted. After a moment he looked up at the Chief.

"The fire is in a compartment one deck down. Firefighters are in the room right now. The fire was probably caused by heat from the Arizona, we should be good."

Chief Keppers smiled as he knelt down beside Cooper, to wipe some of the gunk off his face. Looking up at the chief, Cooper said, "I don't care what's going on outside, I need fresh air!"

Nodding his head toward a couple sailors standing nearby, they scooped Cooper up from the floor, carrying him toward a door facing Ford Island. Cooper could still hear planes roaring around overhead and explosions destroying America's magnificent fleet. As he gasped for air, tears ran down his face as he thought about all the brave men like Paul and Lieutenant Crowder that had died today. All he wanted to do right now was find another gun he could use to shoot back at the bastards. They had to be stopped before more men were killed.

Looking up over Ford Island, he saw a Japanese bomber being chased by an American P-40 with its machine guns blazing. Suddenly a column of black smoke began to billow from under the engine bonnet of the Japanese aircraft. The pilot pulled up and toward the north, but the P-40 hung right with him. As the bomber reached the entrance to Pearl Harbor, the engine coughed several times before quitting completely. The aircraft nosed over, slamming into the Pacific Ocean where it exploded. Victory to the American pilot he thought. At least not all the Japanese are going to get home to a hero's welcome.

Walking forward toward the bow, Cooper noticed a .40-millimeter tub with just one gunner. Running over to the tub, he grabbed one of the loaders by the arm. "Does this gun still work?"

"Yeah, it does. The gunners mate was killed by some shrapnel," the sailor answered as he looked at Coopers filthy ripped and mangled uniform.

Without saying a word, Cooper jumped into the gun tub, not caring that the seat and controls were covered in blood. Grabbing the controls, he looked at the loaders standing nearby. "Fill this thing up and lets go after the son-of-a-bitches!"

With the first rounds dropped into the loading box, Cooper began hammering away at several planes that were making a pass over the dry dock area, when the *Shaw* exploded. The explosion was so violent that it shook the *Tennessee* clear across the harbor, while it threw pieces of the ship hundreds of feet into the air. The loaders stood aside of the gun tube, frozen in place as they watched the smoke and flames rise higher and higher into the sky. Cooper could not believe what he was seeing or feeling, when the shock wave of the blast rolled across the harbor. For a second, Cooper thought it was going to rattle his eyes right out of his head. After taking a quick breath, he raised the azimuth of the guns so they could follow the flight path of the two planes. The pilot of the first plane rolled over on his starboard side to make a run over Hickam Field, while the second pilot climbed toward the south.

Seconds later, the plane that turned toward the south shuddered as a column of black smoke appeared underneath it. The pilot continued pouring fuel to his engine as he disappeared over Ford Island. Cooper could not be sure the plane was going to crash, but at least the pilot was going to have a tough flight back to his carrier.

Swinging the tub back toward the northwest, the men fired at two other planes that were flying over CINCPAC as they flew back toward the fleet. The pilots were probably reaching the limits of the .40 millimeter guns, but at least the shell explosions gave them something to think about for a few minutes.

And then, everything began to calm down. The last antiaircraft guns went silent, no more planes dove down out of the blue sky, no more machine gun ammunition was ricocheting off the steel ships, and the bombs had ceased to explode. All that was left were the roaring fires on the ships that had been so violently attacked. For the first time, Cooper saw the small whale boats idling up and down Battleship Row, plucking survivors and bodies from the water before the burning oil overtook them.

Feeling exhausted, Cooper peered across the harbor. Looking at the other gunner, he said, "The bastards are coming back, they didn't bomb the oil tank farms yet. They'll be coming, sure as shit!" Looking at the loaders, he yelled,

"More ammo, get more ammo up here now! Dammit, we need to be ready when they come back!"

Although the man operating the other gun stepped clear of the tub to have a cigarette, Cooper sat in place with his hands on his knees, ready to fire at a moment's notice. But they didn't come back. It seemed that the attack of a lifetime was over and no one really knew what to do. An hour later Cooper stood up and shook his head as he looked at the Chief. "This makes no sense, what the hell were they thinking about? They never came back to finish the job, what the hell?"

"Yeah, they have done some damage, but we can still operate out of here, and we've got all the oil we need to fuel the carriers when they return. We ain't out of this war by a long shot!" Chief Keppers replied, as he gave Cooper a gentle pat on the back.

"Dodge, you deserve a shower and a change into clean dungarees. Most of the showers are still operating, and there is hot water with the boilers up to power. Grab a sandwich and a cup of coffee, then report to me on the fore-deck at 1200 hours."

Cooper dragged himself to his quarters, stripping off the filthy, ripped dress white uniform he was wearing. Luckily, the showers in his compartments head were still working, and the hot water felt like a gift from God. Walking into one of the mess areas, he spotted trays stacked high with cold sandwiches. He grabbed two and a cup of coffee, then found a place to sit where he could be alone. He noticed no matter where men were sitting, not a word was being said. They ate and left, while others filed in following the same procedure. Many of the men wore battle dressings over injuries, or had blood covering their uniforms from helping the wounded, while others had large burns on their arms and faces, but no one compared wounds. No one knew what to say, it was just a glance and a nod of the head that let you know there was still life inside that shaken body. Some men knew where they were going when they left, others hadn't a clue what to do next, so they just went to the south side of the ship facing Ford Island and sat on the deck, waiting for someone to select them for a job.

Joining Chief Keppers on the foredeck, Cooper asked. "What's our mission, Chief?"

"Not a nice one, Dodge. We go looking for bodies or wounded men that have not been able to get to sick bay. We'll start with your gun tube," the chief stated, as he led his men up a ladder to the higher decks.

Cooper still couldn't believe what he was seeing as he looked down at Paul's mutilated body. What was he going to tell Sadie? He knew beyond a doubt that she wasn't going to handle it well, and that Lily would need to be there to console her. He thought about the baby Sadie was carrying, and how the child would never know its fantastic father, except through stories from family members. That was no way for a child to grow up, but what happened today had made countless widows and orphans, and it all just made Cooper sick.

Carefully, the men rolled Paul's lifeless body onto a tarp alongside Lieutenant Crowder. They then walked around the area, picking up body parts adding them to the tarps. After tying them closed, they were taken down to the foredeck, where medics were working to identify the bodies. Cooper made it easy for them in this case, as he knew exactly who each man was.

It was nearly early evening when the last dead man was delivered to the foredeck. When the medics had completed their job, the officer of the deck ordered the deck cleared as they all were expecting another attack around dusk.

Cooper leaned back against the forward main turret, looking over at the bottom of the *Oklahoma* as it stuck out of the water. Crews were already using different pieces of equipment in an attempt to find out which was the best method of cutting through the heavy armor plate. It was clear to Cooper that it was going to be a long and tedious job.

As darkness closed in around Pearl Harbor, everyone was on edge. Every gun that could fire was manned and ready, and guns that had needed minor repair were back on line. The gun tub assigned to Cooper and Paul near the stern was still uninhabitable because of the fires on the *Arizona*, so after cleaning up all the blood and debris from inside the tub Cooper had been in when the attack ended, he sat silently watching the sky for any signs of returning Japanese planes.

Around 2200 hours local time, a lieutenant walked up to the tub. "Alright, listen up and hear me good! Sometime in the next hour there will be planes flying up the main channel with their lights on. They are replacement fighters from the *Enterprise.* Do not shoot at them, I repeat, do not shoot at them!" After making sure everyone understood, the lieutenant took off for the next gun battery.

What the lieutenant had just told them bothered Cooper very much. He could hear gun shots echoing across the harbor from the mainland. He knew nervous men were firing at anything that moved, or were seeing hordes of Japanese soldiers in the dark. He was terrified of what might happen when some of those trigger hungry men heard aircraft engines over the channel. He prayed that everyone had gotten the word, and that the pilots would be able to safely land on Ford Island.

Although fires still lit up a good part of the harbor, Cooper figured with a blackout order being strictly enforced on Oahu and the other Hawaiian Islands, the next probable shining light bulb was half way across the Pacific in Los Angeles. There was a slight wind out of the west, so the nearly toxic odor of thick black bunker oil drifted along Battleship Row making everyone nauseous. But worst of all were the taps coming from trapped men inside the West Virginia. Some sounded like Morse Code, while others were solid strikes against pipes or bulkheads. Cooper shivered when he thought about being trapped inside the ship in total darkness, behind water tight doors they could no longer open, as the oxygen was slowly being used up. How long could they survive? How many men were in each compartment? What was it going to be like when you were the last man alive, too weak to beat on the wall anymore, as you struggled for each ounce of oxygen, knowing death was imminent. Would it be now, or the next breath? Would you make it until morning? But when was morning in such utter blackness. Cooper looked over the side of the ship toward the West Virginia for a moment. He shook his head as he thought of those men. They were under water, the companion way outside their compartments were filled with water, and they were sitting in an island with no way to escape. Rescue parties could not even attempt to start until the holes in the hull were sealed by qualified underwater welders, and then the ship would need to be refloated by pumping out all the water that covered so many lower decks. It was a gruesome thought but one every sailor would think about after today.

At 2100 hours local time, a flight of six F4F-4 Wildcats arrived near Oahu. In the total blackness the pilots were somewhat confused as to where the entrance to the harbor was. Lieutenant Hebel* led the planes over Oahu once, looking for Ford Island. The sound of the planes overhead made everyone near Pearl Harbor nervous. Hebel radioed the tower on Ford Island they had finally spotted the island and were going to make one more circuit over the main island before coming in from the north. The tower operator explicitly told them not to do that. He repeated that the plan was for them to approach Ford Island with lights on, flying low directly up the channel. Hebel either did not get the message, or was still planning to land from the north. As he began making a second circuit over the island, gunners became anxious and everyone opened up. Hebel's plane was quickly shot up very badly. He pulled up turning to the north to avoid the flak, hoping to land at Wheeler Field, only to be met by heavy small arms fire. The plane suffered severe damage and was brought down. Hebel was killed in the crash.

Hebel's wing man, Lieutenant Menges,* was shot down crashing into the Palms Hotel in Pearl City. While he was killed in the crash, no occupants of the hotel were injured. Lieutenant Hermann's* plane was so seriously damaged he could hardly keep it in the air, but managed a controlled crash into the water on the west side of Ford Island, but was able to walk away from it. Lieutenant Flynn* pulled up and away from the entrance to the harbor, crash landing in a sugar cane field where he was chased down by soldiers with guns. Only his constant swearing at them kept him from getting killed, as the sergeant in charge realized anyone that could swear like that was undoubtedly an American. Lieutenant Allen* attempted to jump from his damaged aircraft over the harbor. As his chute did not open all the way, he was injured badly when he slammed into the water inside Pearl Harbor. Although seriously injured, he swam through burning oil to get to the Mine Sweeper USS Vireo. He died the following morning.

Lieutenant Daniels* closed in on Ford Island following instructions, but was taking serious fire. Trying to avoid some of the fire, he nearly struck the beached USS *Nevada*. Seeing what was happening, the tower operator told him to come in low and fast. With only partial flaps working, he landed hard and slid off the runway, but survived. He was the only pilot of the six to reach Ford Island intact, but the plane was too badly damaged to repair. As Daniels was crawling out of his plane, a soldier carrying an M-1 rifle thought he was a Japanese and prepared to fire on him. However, as Lieutenant Hermann was still walking back to the tower after his watery crash, he walked up to the soldier and took the rifle away from him, slamming it down on top of his steel helmet, thus saving Lieutenant Daniels. All six planes were destroyed, three pilots were killed, and two of the surviving three pilots required medical attention.

The gunners on the *Tennessee* never fired, but Cooper sat in horror as he watched his fellow Americans being shot up and killed by other Americans through a drastic mistake. He put his head down over his firing controls and wept, having had enough.

Chief Keppers attempted to send Cooper down to his quarters to lay down for a while as he was in no condition to continue, but Cooper refused. He stayed in the gun tub until just before midnight when he was relieved from duty.

As Cooper walked down across the deck toward his quarters, all he could hear was the tapping and pounding coming from inside the West Virginia, a sound that would haunt him for the rest of his life.

CHAPTER TWENTY-ONE – FIGHTING BACK

At 0618 hours on the morning of December 7, twelve U.S. Douglas SBD Dauntless dive bombers in nine groups of two were launched from the carrier Enterprise en-route back to Pearl Harbor. The planes were part of Scouting and Bombing Squadron Six. Their mission was to scout ahead of the carrier for the possibility of any lurking Japanese war ships, especially submarines, then land at Hickam field. The planes were set to scout a 90 degree sector search from 045 degrees to 135 degrees for 150 miles. After completing the mission, they were to practice navigation runs by homing in on radio station KGMB's signal.

Everything had gone off like clock work for the crews and they had not sighted any Japanese or civilian ships during their search. They began to approach the southwest coast of Oahu between 0815 and 0830hours heading toward Ewa Field.

Before they could understand what was happening, they flew directly into the attack on Pearl Harbor that was well underway.

Pilots of Japanese Zero's from the carrier Soryu were searching for their next targets when they spotted the much heavier and poorly armed SBD's coming in from the ocean. A forbidding radio transmission from one of the SBD's set the mood for the rest of the air group. Ensign Manuel Gonzales* shouted into his microphone, "Do not attack me, this is Six Baker three, I am an American plane." Gonzales and his radioman and gunner, Leonard J. Kozelek* were never seen again after several Zeros pounced on them.

The SBD dauntless was never made to truly engage in aerial combat, but it did have weapons to defend itself. The aircraft was designed with two .50 caliber machine guns in its nose cowling and a 30 caliber machine gun operated by the radioman /gunner in the rear seat of the cockpit.

Ensign John H.L. Vogt* charged his weapons and without hesitation flew his SBD into a group of Japanese aircraft that were in the process of forming up for their return flight to the carriers. Marines and sailors at Ewa watched in astonishment as Vogt began attacking an enemy Zero in a sudden twisting turning pattern from 4,000 feet down to 25 feet above the ground.

The pilots were locked in a desperate fight for survival as they screamed back and forth across the sky above Ewa. Marine Lt. Colonel Claude Larkin,* commander of the base at Ewa reported that he watched the two planes strike one another during a tight maneuver. With the SBD to damaged to continue on, Vogt and his radioman Sidney Pierce* were able to bail out of the crippled aircraft, but unfortunately they were to low. The men perished when their parachutes failed to open completely.

Investigators searching through Japanese records of the attack after the war ended stated there were reports of several near misses, but no reports of a collision with an SBD. Japanese reports indicate only three Zeros in their first wave were lost, but none of them were reported lost near Ewa. According to after action reports it's possible Vogt's aircraft was shot down by Shinichi Suzuki,* a pilot from the carrier Soryu.

While the fighting was taking place over Ewa, a second flight of SBD's was nearing Barbers Point on a different course. Lieutenant Clarence E. Dickinson* and his wingman Ensign John R. McCarthey,* were flying a steady course when McCarthey observed several Zeros. He dropped down under Dickinson so his gunner could get a more straight on shot at the attacking aircraft, however that move placed his SBD directly in the line of enemy fire he could not escape from. With in seconds McCarthy's wounded aircraft began to smoke and became hard to keep under control. The plane spun out of control heading toward the ground. McCarthey figured the only way to survive the situation was to bail out, which he did. However his radioman Mitchell Cohn* was not able to bail out and went down with the plane. Cohn was killed instantly in the grinding impact. McCarthey survived bailing out but broke his leg on impact when he landed.

With his wingman gone, Dickinson was jumped by four enemy aircraft all at once. He attempted to dive away from the encounter, getting off several short bursts from his weapons at a Zero that crossed over in front of him. His back seat gunner William C. Miller* fired a stream of bullets at one of the attacking Zeros doing severe damage to the plane. The other two Japanese fighters went after the SBD with a vengeance, firing several long bursts of machine gun fire into the rear fuselage. Sometime during the wicked exchange of fire, Miller was critically wounded and put out of action.

Suddenly, Dickinson's left fuel tank caught fire and several of the control cables were damaged beyond usage. In a last-ditch attempt to escape the never-ending fire from the Japanese planes, Dickinson struggled to make a hard right turn away from his pursuers. Unfortunately, the SBD did not respond the way Dickenson had planned and went into a tail spin. Realizing Miller was gone and he was out of options, at 1,000 feet, Dickenson climbed out on the wing throwing himself clear of his burning, spiraling SBD.

With his chute operating properly, Dickinson was down on the ground in short order. The chute did not have a tremendous amount of time to slow his decent, but luckily Dickinson landed on a dirt embankment just a short distance east of Ewa. After gathering his thoughts and brushing off dirt from his uniform, he gathered up his parachute and began walking out of the pineapple field he landed in toward a nearby road. Mr. and Mrs. Otto Hein,* near by residents of Ewa were driving near the airfield. They were unaware that a major dog fight was going on above them. Seeing Dickinson walking along the road, they stopped their blue sedan to talk to him. After hearing what was happening, the couple told Dickinson to climb aboard and they drove him back to Pearl Harbor, parachute and all.

Regrettably, two more of the battling SBD's were sent to the ground in flames by planes of the first attack wave. Surviving pilots reported that as they flew over Barbers Point, they witnessed several Japanese pilots going after Ensign Walter M. Willis* and his gunner Fred J. Ducolon.* No one could report the plane being shot down, but neither man was ever seen again.

The last SBD pilot to become a casualty was Ensign Edward T. Deacon.* His aircraft became victim to friendly ground fire by army gunners at Fort Weaver, close to the entrance of Pearl Harbor. With his plane badly damaged but still flyable, Deacon was able to ditch the plane in shallow water several hundred yards from shore. He and his radioman swam back toward the beach where they were rescued.

Across Oahu at Haleiwa two obsolete P-36 pursuit planes still powered by radial engines roared off into the morning sky. They were manned by Lieutenant Harry W. Brown* and Lieutenant Robert J. Rogers,* both members of the Forty-seventh Pursuit Squadron. They flew toward Kaena Point, which is the farthest west coast line of Oahu. It was at that point that Rogers spotted a mixed group of Japanese aircraft. Immediately, two Japanese pilots charged out of formation in an attempt to take out Rogers and his fighter. Lieutenant Brown readied himself then dove directly into the middle of the Japanese squadron, knocking down one of the Japanese fighters with ease.

Meanwhile, Rogers got himself into position, firing a steady burst of machine gun fire into another Japanese plane. Immediately, the plane began to smoke and dove in a controlled dive away from Rogers. Neither Rogers or Brown could report that the damaged planes crashed.

Lieutenant Brown then charged into position with Lieutenant Malcolm A. Moore* who was also flying a P-36. The two men engaged two enemy Zeros in an amazing dog fight that covered a vast distance of sky. Again, neither Brown or Malcolm could testify that the damaged planes crashed. However, after the war, Japanese records indicated neither plane had returned to any of the attacking aircraft carriers.

At Kaneohe, a flight of nine Zeros, led by Lieutenant Fusata Iida* destroyed all the P-40 fighters on the ground. As Iida was flying very low and beginning to pull up and away from the base preparing to attack Bellows Field, a group of marines using rifles and BAR's took his plane under fire.

Several BAR rounds penetrated Iida's fuel tank, doing tremendous damage to the fuel system of his aircraft. Realizing he would never be able to return to his carrier, Iida decided to dive his doomed aircraft into Kaneohe's armory.

Coming down at a tremendous velocity, a wing of his plane made a glancing blow off the street, causing the plane to strike an earthen embankment.

Later that day as the aircraft wreckage was being removed, Iida's body was recovered from the plane and shoved into a garbage can, because the men had nothing else close by to place it in. Iida's body and those of sixteen other Americans were left outside the sickbay entrance. There is no record of how Iida's body was disposed of.

The overhead doors to the fire station at Pearl Harbor had been smashed by 20mm cannon fire, but no one inside had been wounded, nor were the trucks damaged. Commander Loren Creighton was in charge of the station that morning, but he was unsure about sending out trucks with all the shooting going on.

When the call came in regarding fires in the dry docks with the USS *Cassin, Downes,* and the *Shaw,* the decision was made for him. He had Senior Chief Alvarez assemble his crew and take the nearly new 1940 Chevrolet firetruck over to the dry docks. Screaming down Harbor Road, the red lights and sirens make for a perfect target for a diving Japanese bomber that still had its general purpose 100-pound bombs at the ready. The men standing on the back of the truck could see the pilot lining up the truck for a hit, but were unable to jump clear of the speeding truck without getting killed. Both men pulled themselves in as close as they could to the hose bed as they watched the first bomb fall from the undercarriage of the bomber.

The driver of the truck, Fireman First Class Alfred Dinkins, saw the bomb drop from the plane. Swinging the steering wheel to the left, the tires bounced up over the curb sending the speeding truck flying toward two Quonset huts with a narrow alley between them. As the bomb crashed into the road, the truck missed the alley, smashing into the corrugated steel side of the second building. Shrapnel from the bomb tore off the large red light in the center of the cab roof and broke off the right side spot light, however all the fire fighters escaped injury.

As the pilot turned back toward the harbor planning his second attack, Dinkins threw the truck into reverse, backing up about fifty feet before barreling down the narrow alley. As the pilot returned to attack the truck again,

Dinkins was three blocks north and turning east onto a narrow dirt road that was partially camouflaged by low hanging palm trees. The second bomb fell directly on an empty Quonset hut, penetrating the roof and exploding inside directly behind the fire truck.

Quickly, Dinkins drove the truck back onto Harbor Road, running up through the gears as quickly as he could. This time the plane strafed the Chevrolet, blowing out the right front tire and puncturing the water tank. As Dinkins fought to control the heavy truck, the Japanese pilot decided enough was enough and flew back to the harbor. After fighting the truck to a controlled stop, Dinkins shook his head and swore before putting the truck back in gear. It was an ugly ride with the right tire gone, but fifteen minutes later Dinkins rolled the truck up to a fire hydrant about a block from the dry docks. Without saying a word, the men went right to work pulling hoses and attaching nozzles as Dinkins and Chief Alvarez checked over the pump to see if it was still serviceable. Feeling confident it would work properly, the men opened the hydrant and began sending water to the hoses.

Immediately, the men began spraying water into the dry dock on the foredeck of the *Shaw*. Unknown to them there was a serious fire burning deep inside the ship. Suddenly, all the ammunition in a forward bunker ignited. The explosion was overwhelming, sending fire and debris hundreds of feet into the air and over a wide area. The brave firefighters were thrown back like rag dolls, their bodies ripped apart. The front of the Chevrolet was blown off as the truck was pushed back twenty feet before it rolled over, puncturing the fuel tank. The fires from the *Shaw* and the ruptured fuel tank turned the truck into a twisted pile of metal. There were no survivors from the valiant crew.

The USS *Hoga** was a combination tug boat and firefighting vessel assigned to Pearl Harbor. Sunday, December 7, 1941 started out like most every other Sunday for the crew. Although there were no ships moving in or out of the harbor needing assistance, the crew had the main boiler fired in case a call came in for an emergency move. Tied up to the 1010 dock that morning the crew had a front row seat to the attack as it unfolded. As soon as the attack began, Tug Master Robert Brown* took the *Hoga* out into the harbor to assist in any way they could. They first picked up two sailors from the *Arizona* and took them back to the pier. They then went over to the burning *Arizona* where the crew of the USS *Vestal* was fighting desperately to break the mooring lines free from the burning battleship. After tying several lines from the *Hoga* to the *Vestal*, the skipper ordered full reverse breaking the lines free. With the *Vestal* in mid-channel and operating under her own power, the skipper of the *Hoga* set her free.

The *Hoga* was then dispatched to the USS *Oglala* in the east loch. She had been damaged by a bomb that fell between her and the USS *Helena*. Moments later a torpedo meant for the *Helena* exploded under the *Oglala's* hull. The explosion from the torpedo tore a hole in the bottom of the hull, flooding the aft section of the ship while lifting all the deck plates right up to mid-ship. There was concern the ship might roll over and sink in the east loch causing problems for ship movement.

The crew of the *Hoga* tied on to the *Oglala* and dragged the severely damaged ship to the 1010 dock where she was secured to prevent her from sinking.

Meanwhile the *Vestal* was taking on more water than the crew could deal with. The skipper was sure she was going to sink, so once more he called upon the *Hoga*. By the time the *Hoga* could be tied on to the *Vestal*, it was clear the ship was going to go down, but they did not want it to roll over. So, the *Hoga* pushed the *Vestal* to the Aiea Shoals in the southwest portion of the harbor. The *Vestal* came to rest in 35 feet of water without rolling over.

By this time the *Nevada* had made its gallant run for the sea but had been damaged by a pounding from Japanese bombers and fighters and had been beached on Hospital Point. After releasing the *Vestal*, the *Hoga's* crew went to work attempting to knock down fires on the *Arizona* and pull men from the oily water. However, it was quickly realized the *Nevada* could not stay where it was, as the outgoing current was attempting to push the rear of the ship on to the rocky shoreline where the stern could still cause problems for traffic navigating the narrow harbor channel.

Once more the *Hoga* was called into action. Arriving at the *Nevada* it was essential that fires on the stern of the ship be knocked out before moving the vessel could be completed. The *Hoga* was tied to the battleship with its engines in reverse to keep the stern from swinging any more to the east. Naval Tug *YT-130* was also dispatched to the *Nevada* to lend a helping hand. Once the fires were extinguished and a good portion of the water pumped from the *Nevada* to make her buoyant, the two tugs pulled tremendously hard to pull the battleship off the muddy shore line and back into the harbor. The decision was made to beach the ship on Waipi'o Point in the west channel directly across from Ford Island. By 1045 hours local time, the *Nevada* settled into the mud.

With the *Hoga* tied to the *Nevada*, fire crews, fought blazes on the forecastle and pilot house with four lines for over an hour before breaking loose from the beached battleship.

The *Hoga* then returned to Battleship Row, fighting fires on the *Maryland,* the *Tennessee,* and finally back to the *Arizona.* The *Hoga* fought fires on the *Arizona* from 1600 hours on Sunday until 1300 hours on Tuesday. After 72 continuous hours of fighting fire, the *Hoga* patrolled the harbor assisting in body removal and searching for possible Japanese mini-subs believed to be hiding in the harbor.

Although the *Hoga* was strafed several times there was no major damage done to the vessel. Worst of all, the crew was not able to shoot back or defend itself as the ship did not contain any offensive or antiaircraft weapons.

Sailors assigned to Pearl Harbor stood near the 1010 dock watching in horror as the attack unfolded with no way to help out. Many sailors commandeered officers whale boats that were tied up to the pier. They sailed back and forth between the ships, rescuing sailors in the water and retrieving the dead. The men were daring as hell, sailing right into the middle of the burning oil with the wooden boats in order to save lives. One whale boat near the Arizona caught fire as it was removing living survivors from the rear of the ship. Knowing the boat would not make it back to the mainland with the number of men it had on board, the operator chose to beach it on Ford Island. The men had not run far from the burning boat before the fuel tank exploded. Several brave boat operators were killed by strafing or bombs that fell near Battleship Row.

Doris Miller,* an African American mess attendant on the USS *West Vir-*

ginia was helping in the laundry when the first torpedoes struck. Leaving the laundry, Miller helped evacuate wounded men from the ship, placing them on the foredeck. After seeing a man on a machine gun go down, Miller ran to the gun and began firing at the diving Japanese planes without one minute of training on the weapon. No one knows if he shot down a plane for sure, but one Zero that came in very close to Miller's gun left streaming fuel as it climbed away from the harbor. He was awarded the Navy Cross for his actions.

At midnight on December 7, Reverend McCloud sat quietly in a chair near the x-ray department. The rush of wounded had nearly come to an end, as at least for now as darkness had stopped most of the rescue operation. Several nurses offered him cups of coffee, but he always refused with a smile. His heart was broken by what he had witnessed throughout the long day, and he wondered how many more men out in the harbor were dying or in need of medical care.

One of the female x-ray technicians stopped alongside Reverend McCloud's chair and knelt down beside him. Taking hold of his hand, the young lieutenant said. "Reverend, you need to go in the staff locker room and take off that uniform, get a hot shower and let me give you a hospital surgical outfit to wear for the time being. There is nothing more you can do for now. Leave the men to us, we will take care of them."

For the first time, Reverend McCloud looked down at himself, horrified to see how much blood covered his perfectly tailored uniform and spit shined shoes. Looking up at the officer, he said, "My God in heaven!" After a moment of thought, he replied, "No, I'll go back to my quarters to shower and change, thank you for the offer."

The lieutenant looked dead serious at Reverend McCloud. "No, you can't do that. You won't get a block away from the hospital without some nervous marine making you our next casualty. It is unsafe out there for man or beast. After you get cleaned up and dressed, I'll set you up with a cot and a blanket in the storage room for the night."

After hearing several random gun shots, Reverend McCloud nodded his head. "Thank you, I do not wish to put some brave young man into a bad position." After removing his uniform, he placed it in a bag, telling the lieutenant, "Burn it, throw it away, I never wish to see that uniform ever again!"

Around 0700 hours December 8, Reverend McCloud rolled out of his cot and prepared for a day he knew full well would be filled with death and tragedy. After making a quick round of the hospital, he drove back to his quarters where he showered, shaved and put on a Navy work uniform. After a quick breakfast, he drove down to the pier hoping to get a ride across the harbor to Ford Island. As he stood on the pier, he stared at the destruction that met him head on. It looked bad from Hospital Point, but seeing the burning *Arizona* and the other damaged battleships close-up made him feel sick. All he could think of were the lives that had been lost in a matter of minutes without a hint of warning. He wondered how any reasonable nation on God's earth could be capable of such a barbaric attack.

Ten minutes later, a whale boat pulled up to the pier unloading sailors that looked like they had been through hell. Some of them wore blood-stained uniforms, while others wore uniforms covered in soot and grime. None of them smiled or showed any resemblance to the once jovial young sailors that had manned the pride of the American fleet. A lieutenant commander getting off the boat did not even return the salutes of the men waiting to get on board. Instead, he patted each man on the back saying, "Go help your brothers, there is much you can still do."

The smell of the thick black oil that covered a large portion of the harbor made most of the men on the boat nauseous, causing a few of them to hang over the side of the boat and vomit. Reaching Ford Island, Reverend McCloud saw a truck driver preparing to drive off, so he ran over and climbed into the passenger seat of the truck. Looking at the driver, he smiled and said, "Hospital please, driver!"

The young man looked back and nodded his head. "Prepare yourself, Padre, what you are about to see will make you wish you hadn't come over here. It's the worst thing I have ever seen in my life. Some of those men would have been better off dead. It's a damn shame, Padre."

Walking into the hospital, Reverend McCloud observed a nurse in her forties wearing the rank of major sitting behind a desk writing in a file. She looked up at Reverend McCloud with red swollen eyes and closed the file. "I just wrote time of death in this young sailor's file. I have done that way too many times over the last twenty-four hours. I'm tired, my spirit is broken, and I just don't want to see anymore. Tell me why, Reverend, tell me why. I need an explanation if I am to go on."

Kneeling down in front of the crying nurse, Reverend McCloud took her in his arms, holding her as she wept. Speaking softly in her ear, he replied. "I wish I had an answer, but I do not. I asked myself that all day yesterday in the base hospital, but I never came up with a reason, and I'm sure I never will. I believe only God knows why he allowed this to happen. I'm afraid all we can do is help heal these brave boys, and comfort those we cannot help."

Leaning back in the chair, the nurse half smiled. "Thank you for coming, Reverend. There is much work to be done here."

Moving on into the hospital, the scene was much like the main hospital on Oahu. The only difference was there were no longer long lines of men needing emergency care. Only a few men trickled in that had just been rescued from sunken ships, or had been trapped behind water tight doors.

Walking toward the back of the hospital, Reverend McCloud heard a nurse arguing with a patient. He walked over to see what assistance he could render to end the discussion. He was taken back to see the sailor had lost his right arm at the shoulder, his left leg at the knee and the right side of his face had been burned away, including his nose and eye.

The nurse looked at Reverend McCloud. "Sorry Reverend, but he continues to take off his oxygen mask, pulls out his IV needle, and refuses to take the antibiotics the doctor prescribed, which is important to reduce the chance of infection."

Placing his hand on the nurses shoulder, Reverend McCloud said, "Let me talk to the boy. Go take a break and get a cup of coffee, you look exhausted."

After the nurse left, Reverend McCloud sat down next to the terribly wounded sailor. The man looked at Reverend McCloud with his one eye, saying, "She don't get it, Reverend, but I know you will. I have burns over nearly all of my body and I know I'm going to die. There is nothing they can do to save me, and I don't know why I'm still here. But I am going soon, God told me last night he has a place prepared for me. Do you believe me?"

Nodding his head, Reverend McCloud replied, "Yes, I do. What's your name, son, and where are you from?"

"Peter, Peter Albrecht from Springfield, Missouri. My pop runs a large concrete factory there. I was supposed to take over the plant when I came home, but that dream my folks always had is over now. Tell me, Reverend. What is heaven like, give me some idea of what I'm to look forward to. I need something to hang on to, something I can wrap my brain around, something that makes sense, because none of this makes sense anymore. What did I do to deserve this?

The man wheezed as each breath became tougher. Reverend McCloud shook his head. "Peter, none of us know why God allowed this to happen, and we never will. But I can assure you that today you will be with God in paradise, and your suffering will be over. You will be whole again, and there will be angels there to wait on you if you need anything."

Peter struggled to breathe as he smiled. "That sounds good, Reverend, real good. Pray with me now because it's time for me to..."

As Peter closed his eye, his head rolled to the right. Reaching in his pocket for his small bottle of holy water, he anointed Peter's body and pulled the sheet over his head. Looking up toward the ceiling, Reverend McCloud said, "God, give me strength."

About a half hour later he came upon another young man that had been horribly burned when the *Arizona* exploded. As he stopped by the bed, the man rolled his head slightly, saying, "Whose there? My eyes are gone but I can sense when someone is nearby."

Pulling up a chair, Reverend McCloud sat down next to the bed. After introducing himself, he asked, "Son, is there anything I can do for you?"

"Yeah, write my folks a letter. Tell them their son Billy was not a coward. I did what I could do to save my buddies, but it just wasn't enough. Tell them I love them and will miss them," the young man replied, as he coughed several times. "The doctors say I inhaled super-heated air and my lungs are just about gone. I know that I'm dying, and I'm happy about that. I don't want to be a burden to anyone. The doctor could not believe I made it through the night. I'm guessing with so many men arriving at the Pearly Gates yesterday, they didn't have time to call me home. I never was much for church going and that really made mom angry. I just hope God doesn't hold that against me. Do you think he will?"

Smiling as he fought to hold back his tears, Reverend McCloud replied. "No Billy, you have nothing to worry about. Go to him in peace and know he is waiting for you, and he will end your suffering. You are free to go, Billy."

"Thanks, Padre." Billy said, nodding his head. "Hey, do you think they play baseball in heaven? I was a pretty good short stop in college before I enlisted. I was hoping to try out for the big leagues when my hitch was over."

Laughing slightly, Reverend McCloud replied, "I have it on good information they have several leagues up there, so you'll play short stop again."

"Okay Padre, you made my day. Go now and talk to some of the other boys, but stop back before you leave." Billy said, with a smile on his face.

Reverend McCloud talked to several more men before he decided it was time to leave so he could see what assistance he could give out on Battleship Row. As he walked by Billy's bed, he observed a nurse stripping off the sheets.

"Where is Billy? I promised him I would stop by before I left." The reverend asked.

Another nurse looked at Reverend McCloud, saying. "I came to take his vitals and he brushed my hand aside and said something like, "Tell the Reverend I have a game to warm up for tonight." Do you know what he was talking about?"

As tears ran down his face, Reverend McCloud replied. "Yeah, yeah I do."

Leaving the hospital, Reverend McCloud sat down on a bench near the hospital, attempting to sort out everything he had just been through. He never imagined he was going to experience anything like this when his bishop asked him to take on the job.

After taking several long breaths of air, he walked over toward Battleship Row where crews were still working down in the dark bowels of the ships seeking out survivors or carrying out the dead. Stopping by a chief petty officer, he asked what he could do to help.

Without really looking to see who was talking to him, the chief smugly said. "Put on a hard hat and a set of coveralls then report back to me." Finding the gear on the back of a truck, Reverend McCloud put them on and walked back to the chief.

Shaking his head, the chief said. "Alright, I'll get you on one of the crews waiting to go. These ships are very dangerous with buckled decks, hanging battle damage and the possibility of unexploded ordnance. It's a mine field in there, so you'll need to watch your footing."

"Got the risks down, chief, now where do you want me to go." Reverend McCloud stated boldly.

The chief shook his head at a man that appeared to be in too much of a damn hurry to risk everything to search a dangerous ship. A moment later, a lieutenant came walking over, "Is this the new man we were promised, because my crew is ready to go back into the *West Virginia*."

Before the chief could respond, Reverend McCloud replied. "Yes sir, all rested up and ready to get to work. The names McCloud, Henry McCloud."

After shaking hands, the two men walked up the makeshift bridge they had built leading onto the quay. The lieutenant said, "Alright McCloud, you know the drill. We put this belt around your waist, and a rope is strung through one of the 'D' rings." This gives you some latitude to move around, but do not go down ladders to lower compartments, and for God's sake don't remove that rope or you may never get out of that damn ship. Follow the orders of the petty officer and you will do alright."

Seconds later, the eight-man team began walking down the ladder into a pitch-black passage way. The men worked their way forward, searching with their flashlights while yelling out for survivors or pushing open jammed doors. The combination of temperature and humidity inside the ship was beyond anything Reverend McCloud had ever experienced, and the smell of oil was overwhelming. When they finished the deck, they dropped down one more level and began working their way aft, searching compartment after compartment. Standing by an open hatch leading down, Reverend McCloud said, "How do we search down there? I can hear banging coming from somewhere down there in a lower compartment."

The petty officer turned angrily saying, "McCloud, how the hell do you think we can go down there and get them out? We can't pump the water out because the harbor will just push more in until the holes in the hull are patched, and that ain't going to happen any time soon. Those guys must be behind water tight doors with water all around them. They're dead, they just don't realize it yet."

Reverend McCloud was about to unload on the petty officer until the man behind him said, "It sucks like hell, McCloud, but that's the plain truth. It kills me to know we are so close and yet so far away. I don't even want to know what's going through their minds."

Halfway back in the passage, one of the men heard a faint knock that appeared to be coming from a compartment on the right side of the passage way. After examining the door, the petty officer said. "The deck here is raised, so we must be nearly directly above where a torpedo struck the ship. Come on, put your shoulders into this door!" he yelled out as he pried against it using a five-foot-long pry bar. On the third try the door flew open. Inside the room were three bodies. Two of them had been hit by shrapnel that penetrated the deck floor when the torpedo exploded. The third man was severely wounded and had lost a lot of blood. Quickly, the team bandaged the worst of the sailor's wounds and placed him on a stretcher for a trip out of the ship. Picking up two large tarps, the men returned to the compartment to pick up the two bodies. It was then that Reverend McCloud observed the odor of quick decomposition, due to the excessive heat and humidity. Mixing the odor with that of the fuel oil, his head began to spin, forcing him down to one knee.

One of the men took hold of his arm, lifting him back to his feet. "It's kind of an acquired smell, but you will get used to it. I know it's there, but my mind just ignores it."

About a half hour later they found another dead sailor on the floor of the passage way. Apparently, he had been in the lower part of the ship and mortally wounded by the blast, but had made his way to this passage before succumbing to his injuries. He was badly burned with his uniform melted into the skin of his chest. It was a horrible sight that no one wanted to look at.

Fifteen minutes before the shift was over, they heard a man yelling quite a distance in front of them. When they reached a junction of the ship where ladders went up and down and several passageways intersected, they found a man hanging upside down from a ladder with his left leg broken in several places and his left shoulder dislocated. Carefully, the men picked him up, splinted his leg and tied off his broken shoulder. As the Reverend finished tying the shoulder, the man smiled. "I've been hanging there since probably 0830 yesterday. I was on my way to my battle station when the explosion forced me to lose my grip on the railing. I twisted around as the ship shuddered and that was that. I've been drifting out of consciousness for the last twelve hours. I'm not sure how long I could have lasted. Thank God you guys found me."

Smiling at the young man that probably had never even shaved yet, Reverend McCloud replied, "Yes, thank God indeed."

The sun was beginning to set over the eastern horizon of the Pacific when the search crew finished the last passage way that was on the day's schedule. Before they walked up the ladder to the deck above, Reverend McCloud walked over to another open water tight door leading down to the flooded part of the ship. Removing his small bottle of holy water, he poured some into the oil fouled water and said a prayer for all those that were dead below, and those that were surely going to die before they could be rescued. Several of the men watching the small prayer service instantly recognized Reverend McCloud from the Sunday services they attended. They all gathered around the open hatch joining in with the prayers. The crew was happy the reverend had joined in with the search, and felt it was because of him that they had found two men alive. They were saddened that three other men had perished, but were glad survivors had been removed from the baking temperatures of the ship.

Sitting on the main deck sucking in fresh air, Reverend McCloud refused to take credit for finding the men alive. He reminded them the men would have been found with or without him, but he was not sure some of the men wanted to believe that. At this point, Reverend McCloud did not care what they believed, as long as it gave them something to cling to as they performed this miserable task.

Before leaving the ship, the chief walked up to Reverend McCloud. "You lied to me, Padre, you told me you were one of the rescue workers. I can't believe you could do that."

Reverend McCloud laughed loudly as he placed his hand on the chief's shoulder. "I never lied to you, chief. I simply asked if I could help. You told me to get a hard hat and coveralls. I did that and you put me to work, for which I am eternally grateful. You just assumed I was a rescue worker."

The chief pointed his finger at Reverend McCloud, yelling, "This is a dangerous job, there is no way you should have been down inside that ship. You put everyone at risk."

Smiling, the reverend replied, "Everyone told me a punk kid like me couldn't make it through the seminary. People told me a punk kid like me would end up in jail someday and spend my life in prison. But then here I am an ordained minister working for the man that created heaven and earth. So, do you think God is going to let a jewel like me get injured, or hurt someone else? I should think not. Hope to see you in my place of work next Sunday, chief"

As Reverend McCloud walked away, the chief had to laugh. After nearly twenty years in this man's navy, he had finally met his match and it was not an enlisted man, nor was it an officer, it was a mild-mannered minister that suckered him. As he turned back toward the *West Virginia*, he said to himself, "Well, what the hell, sure wish I had twenty more like him."

Over the next week, Reverend McCloud spent the majority of his time performing funerals or attending burial services up in the Cemetery of the Pacific. What he hated most was the placing of multiple wooden coffins in a mass grave where a marker would simply say, unidentified, and then the name of the ship. But there was nothing the military could do now but bury the dead as best they could in order to prevent disease.

At the end of December, Reverend McCloud's bishop wrote to him asking if he was ready to be reassigned in Pennsylvania. It was an easy letter for him to respond to. He simply wrote, "This is where I am needed most, this is where I belong, thanks for the offer."

Military Airfields and Bases December 7, 1941
Wheeler Field

Wheeler Air Corp Base was the home for the forty-sixth pursuit squadron. December 7 began like any other Sunday morning. Some crews were allowed to sleep in, while others were assigned to guard duty or other essential jobs. As several men were walking over to the hangers to relieve soldiers that had been on guard duty all night, one of them pointed out a large flight of planes in the distance heading toward Pearl Harbor. At 0755 hours, they heard the first bomb explode on Ford Island, just seconds before they noticed Japanese Zeros circling the airfield at about 15,000 feet. By 0758, dive bombers that had come in at 12,000 feet were rapidly dropping down to 500 feet where they released their 250-pound all-purpose bombs cratering the runways. It is estimated that twenty-five Japanese bombers dropped thirty-five bombs and fired an unknown quantity of machine gun bullets and 20 milliliter cannon rounds at targets.

Since General Short had ordered all planes not being readied for flight to be lined up on the ground, wing tip to wing tip, to prevent sabotage, they were an easy target. They were viciously attacked by bombers and fighter planes, over and over. Other bombers went after the hangers, dropping their bombs while strafing anyone that was in sight.

As all the antiaircraft batteries at Wheeler were to be manned by members of the ninety-eighth Coastal Defense Artillery, the angry soldiers quickly realized there was no ammunition for their guns. Orders had come down a week earlier, requiring all ammunition for the weapons to be secured in the central ammunition storage bunkers off base.

With the Air Corp beginning to transition from the older P36 fighters to the new P40 fighters, the Japanese went after the P40's first. As the planes exploded and burned, the wind blew the smoke from the planes and the burning hangers over the parked P36 fighters, keeping the Japanese from seeing them. Most pilots began a race in futility to get to their aircraft to fight back, but regrettably, most of them were killed by machine gun fire as they ran across the open airfield. However, there were a few pilots that managed to get their aircraft running. Unfortunately, as they headed down the runway they were blown apart before they could gain altitude. Seven pilots were actually able to get airborne and were credited with knocking down four enemy aircraft.

The base housing area was not attacked, although some machine gun bullets that were probably meant for the hanger did strike several buildings. The large canvas tents that had been erected between hangers two and three to house new soldiers assigned to the base were strafed several times, killing many of the occupants.

Officers and enlisted men fought fires while dragging wounded men to safety, only to be killed by enemy strafing. Some air crews struggled valiantly to pull necessary equipment from burning hangers, while other crews attempted to pull planes that were down for service toward dispersing bunkers.

Men that were able to get rifles and pistols from locked cases went to roof tops or other areas of the base to shoot back at the planes when they came in low. The last plane to strike the base was at 0945 hours. All the Japanese planes armed with 20mm canons fired explosive incendiary rounds that were extremely effective at low altitudes. Once fuel tanks on planes were ruptured by machine gun fire, the incendiary rounds created massive fires. Wheeler had fifty men killed and seventy-five wounded. A total of 83 aircraft were destroyed.

Bellows Airfield

Bellows Airfield, home of the Forty-fourth Pursuit Squadron and the Eighty-sixth Observation Squadron was attacked at 0830 hours, with Japanese planes coming in low over the water. As Bellows was just 35 feet above sea level, the planes were able to stay low right up until the last minute. They immediately attacked the parked aircraft with machine gun and cannon fire. A single fighter broke off from the main attack to strafe the tent area which was empty at the time.

At 0900 hours, nine Japanese fighters attacked from the ocean, all equipped with belly tanks. They broke off in groups of three to attack predetermined areas of the field. Several bombs were dropped on the runways, but none landed dead center, allowing the runways to remain operable. Several hangers received heavy damage from small all-purpose bombs.

After the attack was over the clean-up began. Along with the empty shell casings left behind by the attackers were hundreds of metal clips that held the machine gun belts together. All the belt clips had been manufactured in the United States. Twelve planes were destroyed on the ground, while three were able to get airborne and shoot down one enemy aircraft. The twelve planes on the ground would have been worthless in the air, as all their machine guns had been removed on Saturday for cleaning after an extensive training session on Friday.

Bellows was no different than Wheeler, as there was no ammunition for antiaircraft weapons. The only return fire came from soldiers with rifles and BAR's. One BAR operator did hit a Zero as the low flying plane was seen flying off to the northwest, trailing a huge stream of fuel. The three American fighters that fought back were all eventually shot down by overwhelming Japanese opposition.

On Monday December 8, as soldiers began reinforcing the coastline defenses, several men noticed a Japanese sailor struggling in the surf. After taking him into custody, he was transferred to Pearl Harbor for interrogation. He operated one of the five two-man submarines that were supposed to penetrate the harbor's defenses in order to attack ships. He said after his gyro quit working on Saturday, he became lost and struck a rock pile underwater, becoming stuck. Sometime during the attack, a bomb exploded near his sub, breaking it loose from the rocks. Since the sub was badly damaged it began to sink. Both men were able to escape from the sub, but he lost sight of his assistant in the rough surf. Both the assistant sub operator and the damaged sub washed ashore over the next 24 hours. The sub contained two 18" torpedoes and one 300-pound bomb. The bomb was to be used if they felt they could not get out of the harbor. They were to sail up to an American ship and detonate the bomb next to its hull.

The submarine is on display at Pearl Harbor. During the attack, two Americans were killed and six were wounded.

Ewa Subsidiary Field, (pronounced Eva)

Ewa is slightly inland from the coast, southwest of Pearl Harbor. Many of the attacking aircraft flew over the base to attack the harbor. It was struck two minutes before Pearl Harbor, making it the first base to be struck during the attack. Japanese planners figured Ewa's fighters would cause them the most problem so the base was considered a primary target. Nine out of its twelve F4F Wildcat fighters were destroyed on the ground, along with 33 other aircraft including trainers, transports, and utility aircraft.

Witnesses said pilots came in low at about 20-25 feet off the ground, firing short bursts from their machine guns and cannons at each plane they came across. Again, incendiary rounds created massive damage. As with the other bases there was no antiaircraft ammunition, so just rifles and BAR'S were used to fight back. The runway was cratered badly, but planes could still take off and land, placing one wheel on the grass.

Since Barbers Point just west of the harbor was the rendezvous point for many of the Japanese planes returning to their fleet, Ewa was strafed over and over as departing pilots emptied out their remaining machine guns on the base before flying out over the ocean. Four men were killed in the attack.

Kaneohe Marine Base

Kaneohe is located on the east side of Oahu on Mokapu Point. The control tower was strafed at 0757 hours local time by nine fighters that also attacked four float planes moored out in the harbor. They then attacked the ramp where five float planes were being readied for flight.

At the time of the attack, the base was undergoing a complete restoration and expansion. However, on December 7, the base only had thirty-three PBY float planes. Twenty-four were completely destroyed on the ground, while six others were damaged so badly, they were unable to fly. Three other PBY's were out on patrol during the attack and were able to stay clear of the island until the all clear was sounded.

At 0930 hours, nine two seat bombers came in over Kahuka Point about 1500 feet in the air. They attacked Hangers 11 and 12. That is where the largest number of men were killed on the base. Some had run into the hangers for protection, while others were attempting to get machine gun ammunition out of the master lockers. Two bombs ripped through the steel roof of the hanger exploding on contact. Another bomb exploded between the hangars, tearing up more steel roofing while one more crashed through the ceiling of an adjoining hangar, but it was a dud.

At 1000 hours, a large group of Japanese planes roared down on the base firing machine guns and cannons. Several enemy aircraft were seen flying off to the northwest trailing fuel or black smoke from ground fire. That group of pilots also viciously attacked civilian cars filled with off duty marines and sailors attempting to return to the base. The second wave of Japanese planes went after the balance of the parked planes, hangars, repair shops and barracks, using bombs and cannon fire.

The Japanese pilots shot many men attempting to put out fires or attempting to save aircraft. The battle history says many men died in 'reckless resistance,' attempting to fire back at the attacking planes. When one man went down, another would run out from his cover to take over the position.

It was the only base on Hawaii to be left in complete and utter shambles.

Fort Shafter

It was evident after the attack that the Japanese never intended to land troops on Oahu. Otherwise, they most certainly would have gone after the 34,000 men that were stationed at Fort Shafter.

The fort had been assigned the job of information center for all the radar units on Oahu. Unfortunately, the base is more known for Lieutenant Kermit Tyler's response at 0750 hours, "Yeah, well, don't worry about it," when Private Lockhart called from Opana Point radar station concerned about a large blip of planes coming in from the ocean. Tyler was convinced it was the B-17's coming in from the United States mainland and never checked into it.

The base was also home to the U.S. Army's Pacific Command, and home to the Twenty-fourth, and Twenty-fifth Infantry Divisions. When the attack began, General Short and all his staff moved into the bomb-proof command center at Aliamann Crater about three miles west of the base. The command center stayed in the crater for an entire week before moving back to Shafter. When the attack began, Short ordered both infantry units to move out to preassigned positions along the coastline to prevent an invasion.

As antiaircraft ammunition for the guns on Fort Shafter was also locked up off site, the only weapons to respond to the attack were rifles and BAR's from the roof tops. Several Japanese planes did strafe and bomb the area of the base known as Palm Circle, without creating any major damage or killing anyone. Most of the casualties on the base were caused by shells from five-inch naval guns that were fired from ships at Pearl Harbor. One five-inch shell struck a barracks, killing a soldier that had been sent inside to bring out more weapons.

Other than pock marks from machine gun bullets, Fort Shafter remained intact.

Schofield Barracks

Attacking Japanese planes strafed the engineer and artillery command centers near the quadrangle, and they also went after officer's quarters and the hospital, creating some minor damage. The planes also strafed the nearby small town of Wahiawi, killing two civilians and wounding nine more. Two low flying Japanese planes hit by fire from the roof tops of Schofield Barracks crash landed near the town. As at the other bases, men smashed locks on ready boxes to get ammunition for their small weapons, as there was no ammunition present for the antiaircraft guns. Five men were killed fighting from the roof tops.

Ford Island

Ford Island was not only occupied by marine and naval personnel, it was also the home base for the United States Coast Guard. Early on Sunday morning, the 125-foot coast guard vessel *Tiger* helped the USS *Ward* as it tracked the Japanese submarine near the entrance to Pearl Harbor. When the attack began, the skipper of the *Tiger* positioned his vessel at the entrance to the harbor, blocking it so no unauthorized vessels could enter. No weapons on the *Tiger* fired at any attacking Japanese planes. At 0900 hours, the 327-foot cutter Tanay which was berthed at the Honolulu Harbor six miles from Pearl Harbor got into the war. Although the vessel never got underway, its five-inch guns and machine guns fired at Japanese planes as they circled out over the ocean. However there is no recorded evidence that they scored any hits. Ford Island was struck at the beginning of the attack, wiping out float planes on the east ramp and 33 planes on the ground.

The new medical dispensary building, constructed on the southwest corner of the island near the shore line, was severely damaged during the attack by a large near-miss bomb that was probably meant for the *California*. Although the building sustained major damage, the staff continued treating a nonstop line of wounded men from the island and Battleship Row.

Seaplane Hangar 6 and Standard Hangar 38 were both completely demolished. Every building on the island suffered damage from strafing or shrapnel from bombs striking runways and the parking ramp. Surprisingly, only one man was killed on Ford Island. Many more died on the island as sailors from Battleship Row made their way ashore to escape their burning ships.

Hickam Field

The Japanese planes struck Hickam with a vengeance at 0758 hours with Zeroes and Val dive bombers hitting simultaneously. As at the other air bases around Oahu, they used 20mm incendiary rounds to start fires in the groups of aircraft lined up wing tip to wing tip in the center of the field to prevent sabotage. Besides the P-40 and P-36 fighters lined up on the field, they found America's larger planes like B-17s, B-18s and the Army's A-20 bombers sitting together in a group. Within minutes, the flight line was a whirlwind of fire and smoke. Forty-two aircraft were destroyed on the ground. Several planes were able to get into the air, but there is no record of what the pilots may have shot down. As at other bases, men were killed attempting to set up machine guns around the base to fight back.

There was a strong effort to not only disable the planes, but the Japanese pilots were intent on killing American pilots and aircrews. Thirty-five men were killed by strafing in the mess hall while having breakfast. The Army's largest barracks of any airfield in the United States was built at Hickam. It was struck by an estimated 27 general purpose 100-pound bombs, killing and wounding many men still in bed. Three out of five hangars were completely destroyed, while many other buildings such as the fire hall, chapel, the Hawaiian Air Depot, guard house, and every barracks was damaged.

However, as at Pearl Harbor, the attacking aircraft failed to destroy the large repair shops or strike the large fuel tank farm behind the base, a critical error.

The first attack lasted about fifteen minutes and the second about 30 minutes, with the last plane leaving at 0945 hours. In the end, 121 men were killed, 274 were wounded, and 37 were listed as missing.

B-17 Bombers Coming from the Mainland

On the evening of December 6, 1941, orders were given by General Short to have the main air traffic tower at Hickam Field, and the operations center at Fort Shafter manned and ready for operations by 0430 hours. He explained there was a flight of new B-17 bombers arriving from the states sometime between 0430 and 0800 hours, and he wanted to make sure the pilots were guided in properly after flying all night across the open Pacific. The planes were to make a refueling stop at Hickam before flying on to become part of General MacArthur's air force in the Philippines.

The navigators of the B-17's were told to lock onto Honolulu's most powerful radio station, KGMB 590am. The station had agreed to stay on the air all night long, allowing the B-17's to have a signal to home in on.

Major Truman Landon* was the officer in charge of the air group. He was very pleased and relieved when his navigator found the frequency, and locked on to the signal. Even with the extra-large fuel tanks installed in the bomb bays, the massive bombers were beginning to run low on fuel.

At 0759 hours, Major Landon sees columns of smoke coming from Pearl Harbor as he watches planes flying in erratic formations over the harbor. He looks at his co-pilot and says, "What kind of air traffic control do you call this?" Instantly, his radio operator tells him Pearl Harbor is under attack from the Japanese. Moments later, several Japanese fighters fly out to meet the incoming bombers. Thinking they are friendly planes, the B-17 crews excitedly wave at the pilots, seconds before the first machine gun bullets are fired at their unarmed planes.

Quickly, Major Landon notifies the other eleven pilots that Pearl is under attack. He tells them they are on their own, and to get down on the ground as quickly as they can.

While taking evasive action, Major Landon says loudly, "A hell of a way to fly into a war, out of gas and no ammunition!"

Two of the pilots immediately turn away from the group and find a safe place to land at the subsidiary base near Haleiwa. A third pilot attempts to follow them, but suffers damage to his fuel system. He sets his plane down safely on a golf course near Kahuku. The balance of the bombers decided to risk landing at Hickam. Two are completely destroyed after hitting the ground, but the other seven make it to the ground intact, but with heavy damage. After the attack, the pilots state they were not sure who did the most damage to their planes, the Japanese or the American antiaircraft gunners, thinking they were Japanese bombers. Luckily, the crews of the destroyed bombers were able to escape from their planes before they blew up. Although several men were injured from flak or Japanese bullets, none of the injuries were serious.

CHAPTER TWENTY-TWO – AFTERMATH

The Japanese fleet was now sailing west toward home waters when the last planes were returning from Pearl Harbor. As the planes had to fly farther than when they took off, several planes streaming fuel or having serious battle damage were not able to return to their carriers. Pilots that ditched in the sea were on their own as Admiral Nagumo had strict orders not to stop to pick up downed pilots as American submarines might now be searching for the Japanese fleet.

When Fuchida landed on the *Akagi* he was stunned to see a third attack force was not being readied. Looking at Genda he asked what was going on, since there was still much to be attacked. Genda ran up to the bridge to speak with Nagumo. Several other officers on the bridge listening to Genda's demands that a third attack was needed, agreed with him.

Nagumo thought about the third wave for just a moment before rejecting the idea. He stated that today this war had just begun and it would be a long war. He added that he had been entrusted with bringing these ships across the Pacific Ocean to attack the American fleet, and he had accomplished that mission. So now he must return the fleet safely to Japan. Nagumo ended by saying they had accomplished all they came for and pushed their luck to the limit. As the war was just starting the fleet must be kept intact.

No doubt Nagumo also kept in mind reports from pilots of the second wave regarding the amount of flak over the harbor and the tenacity of the remaining American fighter pilots. He knew 74 planes returned with serious damage, and 24 were considered a total loss. Twenty-nine other aircraft had been shot down and 64 men were dead or missing. Regardless of their great victory over the Americans, Nagumo realized that 20 percent of the First Air Wing had been destroyed. It was a loss that bothered him very much, and he was not about to risk more of his fleet as they had no idea where the American carriers were located.

Back in Japan aboard the battleship Yamato, men were celebrating as reports of their great victory came in over the fleet's radio broadcasts. After one of the officers handed Yamamoto a glass of Saki, he pushed it away. Standing up, he said, "American radio broadcasts are saying the attack began before our declaration of war was given to the White House. I cannot imagine anything that would infuriate the American people more than that." It has been rumored that Yamamoto also said, "I fear all we have done is to awaken a sleeping giant and fill him with a terrible resolve." However this quote has never been verified or found in any factual document.

Lily was the first to arise from the makeshift bed the women had slept on the night before. Making her way into the kitchen, she started a pot of coffee before walking out onto the road. She slowly walked down the hill a short-way where she could get a good look at the harbor. She cried as she watched flames still roaring from the broken ships, as thick black smoke continued billowing out over the Pacific Ocean. She could see the *Tennessee* where Cooper and Paul were stationed sitting stately aside of the sunken *West Virginia*, as if it had not been touched by the attack. Small whale boats sailed back and forth across the harbor among the damaged ships, removing the wounded and dead. She prayed that Cooper and Paul were not among them.

A few minutes later Lily returned to the house to find Dorothy and Sadie pouring cups of steaming coffee.

As Dorothy handed a cup to Lily, she said. "I don't want to go down there and take a look. I know in my heart Stan is dead, and I may never see his face again. I need to think about moving on now no matter how terrible that sounds."

Sadie walked up to Lily. "How does the *Tennessee* look this morning?"

Lily tried to force a smile. "It looks good, it doesn't look like it was hit at all, but there is no way of knowing that for sure."

After some silence Lily walked over to the radio hoping to hear the latest news regarding the attack. The announcer gave a few details about damage in the Honolulu area, but also reported the news of Japanese invasions on Oahu all turned out to be untrue. He went on to report that officials at Pearl Harbor and Fort Schafter were not yet ready to release any information regarding losses or damage. He added that President Roosevelt had given a speech to congress asking for a declaration of war against the Japanese, and played the taped broadcast.

> *Mr. Vice President, Mr. Speaker, members of the Senate and the House of Representatives:*
>
> *Yesterday, December 7th, 1941 - a date which will live in infamy - the United States of America was suddenly and deliberately attacked by naval and air forces of the Empire of Japan.*
>
> *The United States was at peace with that nation, and, at the solicitation of Japan, was still in conversation with its government and its Emperor looking toward the maintenance of peace in the Pacific.*
>
> *Indeed, one hour after Japanese air squadrons had commenced bombing in the American island of Oahu, the Japanese Ambassador to the United States and his colleague delivered to our Secretary of State a formal reply to a recent American message. And, while this reply stated that it seemed useless to continue the existing diplomatic negotiations, it contained no threat or hint of war or of armed attack.*
>
> *It will be recorded that the distance of Hawaii from Japan makes it obvious that the attack was deliberately planned many days or even weeks ago. During the intervening time the Japanese Government has deliberately sought to deceive the United States by false statements and expressions of hope for continued peace.*
>
> *The attack yesterday on the Hawaiian Islands has caused severe damage to American naval and military forces. I regret to tell you that very many American lives have been lost. In addi-*

tion, American ships have been reported torpedoed on the high seas between San Francisco and Honolulu.

Yesterday the Japanese Government also launched an attack against Malaya.

Last night Japanese forces attacked Hong Kong.

Last night Japanese forces attacked Guam.

Last night Japanese forces attacked the Philippine Islands.

Last night the Japanese attacked Wake Island.

And this morning the Japanese attacked Midway Island.

Japan has therefore undertaken a surprise offensive extending throughout the Pacific area. The facts of yesterday and today speak for themselves. The people of the United States have already formed their opinions and well understand the implications to the very life and safety of our nation.

As Commander-in-Chief of the Army and Navy I have directed that all measures be taken for our defense, that always will our whole nation remember the character of the onslaught against us.

No matter how long it may take us to overcome this premeditated invasion, the American people, in their righteous might, will win through to absolute victory.

I believe that I interpret the will of the Congress and of the people when I assert that we will not only defend ourselves to the uttermost but will make it very certain that this form of treachery shall never again endanger us.

Hostilities exist. There is no blinking at the fact that our people, our territory and our interests are in grave danger.

With confidence in our armed forces, with the unbounding determination of our people, we will gain the inevitable triumph. So help us God.

I ask that the Congress declare that since the unprovoked and dastardly attack by Japan on Sunday, December 7th, 1941, *a state of war has existed between the United States and the Japanese Empire.*

After a moment of silence, the announcer stated congress had voted to affirm the declaration with a yes vote of 82 to 0 in the Senate, and 388 to 1 in the House. The lone dissenter was Jeanette Rankins, a Republican from Montana that had been a life-long pacifist. She also had voted no to the declaration of war during World War One.

After finishing their coffee, both Dorothy and Sadie left Lily's house heading home to an uncertain future. No-body could say for certain how long it would take the navy to put together a list of the dead, wounded and missing. Now it was a waiting game of the worst type.

Aboard the *Tennessee*, officers had put together a rotating list to keep the weapons manned in case the Japanese returned. Cooper had drawn an early watch so he was able to hit his rack about 0100 hours. He was somewhere between numb and defeated when he laid his head on the pillow. His mind ran back and forth over the events of the day, Paul's tortured body, what Lily and Sadie must be thinking right now, and what was going to happen to him now that all the battleships were out of commission. After tossing and turning for over an hour, Cooper finally drifted off to a fitful sleep.

After his morning watch, Cooper walked up to Chief Keppers, "Chief, when do you think I could get over to the mainland and let Lily know I'm alright. She must be going crazy not knowing what's happening."

Chief Keppers nodded his head. "You are not the first one to ask me that question, Dodge. Problem is there isn't an answer to that question as yet. But I can give you permission to go onto Ford Island where there is a bank of phones to call your wife. The line may be long but that's the best I can do for you."

Without saying another word, Cooper left the ship heading toward the Naval Air Station on Ford Island. Surprisingly, the line to use a phone was rather short when he arrived, and the men were being respectful and keeping their calls short as possible. Cooper's hands shook as he dialed the phone, as he was not sure how Lily was going to react.

On the second ring, Lily picked up the phone, "Hello, can I help you?"

Cooper nearly choked when he replied, "Lily, I love you so damn much!"

Lily screamed out, "Oh my God, Coop where are you? Come home this very minute. I miss you and love you more than you will ever know. Are you alright? Is Paul alright?"

Cooper took a moment to clear his head before answering. "I'm fine sweetheart, I have some burns on my back, but they'll be fine. I don't know when I will be allowed to come home, but I will be there as soon as I can. But sweetheart, Paul… Paul is dead."

Lily gasped, placing her hand over her mouth as tears ran down her face. "How? How did he die?"

"He was in the line of fire when there was a major explosion on the Arizona. He was literally blown apart and burned beyond recognition. It was the ghastliest sight I have ever seen. I don't think he felt a thing since it all happened so fast." Cooper explained, as Lily listened and cried. After taking a deep breath, Cooper continued. "I don't know how long it will take the navy to notify all the families, but maybe you could let Sadie know, so she can have some piece of mind. I hate to lay this on you, but it might be for the best."

Lily was quiet for a moment before replying. "Dorothy from next door can go with me to talk with Sadie. She has come to the conclusion that Stan didn't make it on the Arizona. Please come home as soon as you can. I love you, Cooper."

That afternoon, Lily and Dorothy drove over to Sadie's house. As Sadie opened the door to let them in, she looked at Lily's face. "No, please God, no. Don't tell me Paul is dead."

Dorothy grabbed Sadie before she could fall to the floor. Sadie wailed in grief as she placed her hands over her abdomen where Paul's baby was growing. "Oh God, why was it Paul? Why did this happen, I want Paul back safe and sound."

Sitting next to Sadie, Lily held her best friend tightly as they both cried together. Lily knew Sadie was not going to be consoled easily, as she and Paul loved each other very much. Nearly an hour later, Sadie looked at Lily, "I need to lay down, but please don't go."

It was mid-afternoon, when Sadie walked into the living room and sat down next to Lily. After taking a deep breath, she said, "After Paul is buried, I think I will go back to Montana to be with my parents. There is nothing here for me anymore but memories. I'll book passage as soon as I am allowed. But I want to remain friends with you, so you must promise to write to me."

Lily nodded her head. "I will write to you all the time, sweetheart. I want to know what's happening with that baby. I am going to miss you very much, Sadie, but I understand why you want to leave. I think I would do the same thing."

Dorothy nodded her head. "After I hear about Stan, I'm going to leave Hawaii also. I'm not sure where I'll go just yet. Most likely to Denver to visit my daughter for a while, but I can't stay here."

On December 9, the decision was made that anyone on the *Tennessee* that had family on the mainland could have a five day leave to visit them. However, they were all told that when their leaves were completed, they would have to see the Fleet Personnel Office for reassignment. There was no reason to keep all of them onboard, as no one could say for sure how long it would take to raise the *West Virginia* so the *Tennessee* could be freed.

After packing all his belongings, Cooper caught the second whale boat for the mainland. He jumped in a cab with several other men for the short ride to his home. Cooper had barely climbed out of the cab, when Lily came running from the house. She threw her arms around Coopers neck and wept uncontrollably as Cooper held her tight.

There was not a lot to do on Oahu, as martial law had been proclaimed by the governor. He had placed a ration on gasoline as there was no way of knowing when another supply ship might arrive. Every beach now had barbed wire along the water's edge as soldiers walked guard, and jeeps with machine guns patrolled the beautiful seashore twenty-four hours a day. Even many of the wonderful restaurants along the ocean were forced to close in order to keep private citizens out of the way in case of an attack. Diamond Head was closed to the public as the army had turned the entire area into a coastal watch base with many antiaircraft batteries scattered throughout the mountain.

Nevertheless, Lily and Cooper spent several joyful days walking through the many parks on Oahu, while finding great spots for picnics. As all shore leaves go, this one also came to an end. Lily drove Cooper down to the main gate where many other wives were dropping off their husbands in a tearful goodbye.

After kissing Cooper several times, Lily looked sternly at her husband. "You need to let me know as soon as possible what your new assignment is going to be, or I'll drive myself crazy imagining the worst."

Cooper smiled and kissed his beautiful wife one more time. "Yes, I promise I will let you know as soon as I can. Go home and spend some time with Sadie and Dorothy, because the cruise ship is going to be here next week, and after that they will be gone. Remember I will always love you, Lily, you are all I have."

After one more kiss, Cooper picked up his sea bag and walked onto the base. A truck took all the men to the Fleet Personnel Office where they waited in several long lines before reaching the officer with their orders.

As Cooper walked up to the lieutenant, he said, "Dodge, Cooper reporting for new orders."

The lieutenant smiled as he handed Cooper a file. "Dodge, you have been assigned to the carrier *Lexington* as a gunner. She will be arriving about the twenty-seventh, and only be in the harbor for a few days, I'm guessing. Until then you will be assigned to Facility A3. When you arrive there the Chief Petty Officer will give you the low down on what you will be doing until the Lexington arrives."

After Cooper was settled into the barracks with other men that were going to the Lexington, the chief called those men together. "Until the Lexington arrives, you will be helping where ever needed in cleaning up the mess from the attack. There's lots to do, and construction crews are already beginning to repair the damage. Any questions?"

Before Cooper could get his hand in the air, another man asked. "Why are we going to the Lexington? Doesn't the ship already have a full complement of men?"

The chief nodded his head. "It does. But a lot of the men from the Lexington are being sent back to the states as the backbone for a crew that will be manning a new carrier joining the fleet. We can't turn a ship over to a completely green crew and expect it to operate efficiently."

Cooper was more than satisfied with the answer, as it made good sense. For the next several days, the men worked long hours attempting to put the base back into an efficient operating order. Late on the night of December 13, the *Lexington* sailed into Pearl Harbor to refuel and resupply. The following morning all the new men were marched aboard and assigned to their quarters and their new jobs. As the *Lexington* had no 40mm antiaircraft guns, Cooper was assigned to a five-inch battery near the bow of the ship along the flight deck. He was told the *Lexington* was going to have a refit in April where many of the five-inch guns were going to be replaced by 20mm Oerlikon antiair-craft guns. He was promised one of the new weapons as he had experience with the forty-millimeter guns on the *Tennessee*.

Cooper sent a letter to Lily soon afterward, explaining his new assign-ment and sharing everything he had experienced since arriving on the aircraft carrier. He was impressed with its size and the number of airplanes down in the hangar deck.

December 20, Lily arose with a terrible knot in her stomach. She knew that in just four hours she would be taking Sadie and Dorothy to the Cruise Tour Terminal in Honolulu. Odds were, she may never see either of them again and the pain of the loss was nearly overwhelming.

The drive to the boarding terminal was way too quiet for Lily's liking, but she understood that each of them were lost in their own thoughts of grief, separation, and fear of the unknown.

When Lily parked her car there was a rather long line waiting to clear cus-toms and board the SS *Lurline*, that had serviced Hawaii since the mid-thir-ties. It was a gleaming white ship that carried 715 passengers to and from Los Angeles on a regular schedule that had only been disrupted once, and that was after the attack on Pearl Harbor.

The three women walked slowly to the boarding line. When they arrived, Lily gave both women the absolute best hug she could muster. As tears rolled down their faces, Sadie said, "I don't know what I would have done without you since we arrived. You have been the best."

Dorothy kissed Lily on the cheek, saying, "It's hard to believe such a beautiful place could have taken my Stanley away. I shall never return." With that, she walked into the boarding line.

Lily looked at Sadie and said, "Please write often, I want to hear all about the baby and what's happening in your life. Our friendship can't end like this."

Sadie smiled as she kissed Lily on the cheek. "And you must tell me about that baby you are going to have also. Maybe after the war is over, we can get together and let our babies get to know each other. You have my address so you know where to find me."

Lily was about to respond when a ship attendant asked Sadie to please get in line. After another hug, Sadie boarded the ship, throwing Lily a big kiss. Lily walked to her car and wept as she could feel her heart breaking.

CHAPTER TWENTY-THREE - LADY LEX

The aircraft carrier *Lexington*, nicknamed 'The Lady Lex,' was the fourth ship in the history of the United States Navy to bear that name. She was one of two Lexington class carriers to be built for the navy in the 1920s. The *Lexington,* displaying 49,000 tons with a length of 888 feet, was commissioned on December 14, 1927. She was a powerful ship capable of making a top speed of 30 knots, and held a crew of 2791, including the air crews. The Lex had a cruising range of 10,000 miles at a reduced speed of ten knots. Her hangar held 91 aircraft and had two large elevators used to bring the aircraft to the flight deck. While under construction, the *Lexington* was given such a massive power plant that during the winter of 1929-1930 she was tied up to a pier in Tacoma, Washington helping to power the city because of major blackout problems.

Her sister ship was the USS *Saratoga*. On December 7, 1941, the Saratoga was just approaching North Island in San Diego after completing a full over haul at Puget Sound Naval Base in Washington. She would not arrive at Pearl Harbor to join the Pacific Fleet until June 6, 1942.

Cooper found the crew of the *Lexington* to be a hard-working jovial bunch of men that really loved their ship. They went out of their way to make new men comfortable and were always willing to pitch in when or where help was needed. Cooper felt the *Lexington* was a happy ship.

Late on the night of the fifteenth, the *Lexington* quietly slipped away from the 1010 dock sailing back out into the Pacific Ocean on a desperate mission. Along with her escort ships, the *Lexington* was dispatched to attack Japanese bases in the Marshall Islands to help relieve pressure on Wake Island. For the first two days out at sea, Coopers five-inch gun and several other units practiced their firing tactics so they would be ready when they arrived on station. Cooper felt he was working with a good crew and was sure they could do the job well when they met the enemy.

The task force sailed at nearly flank speed the entire time, knowing the men on Wake were in a tough situation. Regrettably, before the task force was able to lend its firepower to the battle, Major James Devereux surrendered to the Japanese. Upon hearing of the surrender, the *Lexington's* task force was recalled.

On February 6, 1942, the carrier *Yorktown* sailed into Pearl Harbor to join the fleet. She did not have long to wait to be on the attack. On February 16, 1942, the combined *Lexington-Yorktown* task force sailed toward Rabaul on New Britain, for a scheduled February 21, 1942 attack. Rabaul was a massive Japanese fortress in the Pacific. It had a deep-water bay allowing major warships to come in for repairs and replenishment without going all the way back to Japan. Their construction crews had built nine major airstrips on the island, along with deep bunkers capable of holding tons of all types of ammunition. Fuel was stored in above ground tanks and underground bunkers that were nearly impossible to see from the air. Although the United Stated bombed and shelled Rabaul countless times, the base never fell to the allies. The commander of Rabaul formerly surrendered the base after the emperor's speech ending the war in 1945.

As the *Lexington* with task force 11 neared Rabaul on February 20, it was spotted by Japanese pilots on routine patrol. The task force was attacked by two waves of enemy aircraft, nine aircraft to a wave. However, the early morning forward combat air patrol from the *Lexington* had spotted the planes and easily vectored the carriers fighters right into the path of the oncoming Japanese planes.

Fighter planes roared into the sky from the deck of the *Lexington* to join the ships early morning combat patrols about fifty miles out from the task force, as gunnery crews went to general quarters preparing their weapons for combat.

From the weapons deck, Cooper could see the Japanese planes approaching as the American fighters dove down on them from about 10,000 feet. The sky was alive with swirling aircraft making unbelievable aerobatic maneuvers to avoid being shot at. Soon, the first Japanese plane dropped toward the ocean trailing a long column of black smoke. Moments later there was another Japanese plane going down, followed by several more.

By the time the battle was over, the air combat fighters had brought down 17 enemy aircraft without losing one of its own. It was proof enough that American pilots were as good as the vaunted Japanese pilots. However, Tokyo liked to proclaim their best pilots were the first and second air wings which were assigned to the six aircraft carriers of their combined fleet.

The men on the *Lexington* manning antiaircraft guns stayed on the alert as their fighters returned to the ship. It was easy to see some of the planes had received battle damage, but nothing that could not be repaired by the maintenance people down on the hangar deck.

The crew of the *Lexington* was excited to hear that Lieutenant E.H. (Butch) O'Hare* had become an ace in his first air battle. He would be awarded the Congressional Medal of Honor for shooting down five planes in one day.

With the battle over, the combined task force sailed toward the southeast in hopes of finding Japanese task forces preparing to land troops and equipment on New Guinea. The patrol was scheduled to last until March 6. The day after arriving off the east coast of New Guinea, Task Force 17 with the *Yorktown* once again joined them.

Headquarters at Pearl Harbor had been looking for a way to give Japan a taste of its own medicine by attacking a major base with a surprise aerial attack. After gathering a large amount of information on Japanese transport movements, it was decided the fleet would strike at New Guinea.

The combined fleets sailed south past New Guinea before turning east along the New Guinea southern coast line, placing the Owen Stanley mountains between the Japanese bases and the fleet. With perfect weather on March 10, waves of American fighters, level bombers, dive bombers and torpedo bombers rose into the early morning sky at 0749 hours. The *Lexington* launched thirty Dauntless SBD bombers from two different squadrons, along with thirteen Devastator torpedo bombers and eight Grumman Wildcat fighters as an escort. The flight rendezvoused with a similar number of planes from the *Yorktown* over the Owen Stanley Mountains. The carrier planes were joined by eight American B-17 bombers flown out of Garbutt Townsville Australia that were normally assigned to Port Moresby, and eight Royal Australian Air Force Hudson Bombers of squadron thirty-two also out of Port Moresby.

The planes struck Salamaua and Lae at 0922 hours. The SBD's from the *Lexington* attacked two Japanese transports and an armed merchant cruiser. Antiaircraft fire brought down one SBD but the Wildcats put the battery out of commission in a matter of minutes.

A second group of SBD's from the *Lexington* attacked a mine layer and another transport. Because fog began to cover windshields and their telescopic bombing sights, many of the SBD's missed their targets completely. Off Salamaua, one SBD had good success dropping its bomb right on top of a Japanese transport ship setting off a massive explosion. The ship began listing heavily to starboard before going down by the aft. Other torpedo bombers from the *Lexington* struck transports at Lae destroying one naval transport and one civilian merchant ship.

Several destroyers and light escort ships turned on their smoke generators to cover their escape to the north where the American planes could not chase them down due to lack of fuel. When the planes began to leave, three beached landing transports were on fire and a seaplane tender was listing dead in the water. The light cruiser *Yubari* was damaged enough so that the only way it could be repaired was to get it to a dry dock in Japan. Off the coast of Salamaua, two destroyers were dead in the water with light fires on board, while one transport was sunk, and a second listing badly. Fires roared on the island from buildings and equipment warehouses that took a severe beating. In the end, just one American SBD was lost.

Too late to do any good, a flight of Japanese fighters arrived over New Guinea's north coast from Rabaul. They searched for the American fleet but did not know they had come over the steep Owen Stanley mountains.

All the sailors like Cooper manning the antiaircraft batteries scanned the skies for any Japanese planes, but not one enemy aircraft appeared, as they had no idea where the American fleet had launched from.

Considering the mission a victory, temporary Commander in Chief of Pacific Naval Forces William S. Pye,* recalled the task forces to Pearl Harbor as equipment that was needed to refit the ships had arrived. The ships had barely tied up to the 1010 dock on March 26, 1942, before workers stormed aboard to remove all the old equipment. Crews worked twenty-four hours a day as Nimitz wanted the *Lexington* group back out to sea no later than April 15, 1942.

Regrettably, the attacks did not stop the Japanese from reinforcing Lae and Salamaua. By the end of 1942, the bases were strongly held by nearly 40,000 Japanese marines. They would be a major pain in the side of General Douglas MacArthur during the entire New Guinea operation.

Top military officials in Washington, along with Admiral Nimitz's staff at Pearl Harbor, all realized the Japanese still had to be dealt a major loss or their southerly expansion would soon land on Australian soil, cutting off all assistance from America.

During the refit Cooper was able to get a three-day shore leave, to see his wife. Lily was extremely happy to see her husband back from a battle, although he could tell her nothing about it. However, it was clear to her it had been a success based on Cooper's state of mind.

It was nice to have some of the restaurants along the ocean open again, allowing Cooper and Lily to have a nice romantic dinner while hearing the waves crashing on the beach. Although Cooper never said a word about it, he couldn't help think of the pilots and sailors they had killed that went to the bottom of this very ocean he and Lily were enjoying. Suddenly, he realized that this war was going to affect him in ways he had never anticipated.

During his leave, Cooper and Lily took time to visit the cemetery up in the crater where Paul and the other sailors and marines that had been killed on December 7 were buried. Although he knew how violent the attack had been, he was surprised to see so many temporary markers that said, 'Un-known.' It made him think for the first time about ships that go down at sea taking their crews with them. They would never have a grave for family and friends to visit, and they would always be listed as missing in action. It made him sick to think about it, but he already knew it was a fact of war, as he had seen Japanese ships near New Guinea going down with most of their crews onboard. He prayed that what ever happened to the *Lexington* at sea, he would always return to Pearl Harbor where he could have his own grave.

With his brief shore leave completed, Cooper returned to a ship that was quickly changing from the way he had known it when he first climbed aboard. Up on the main mast of the ship, several radar arrays were being installed, and many of the five-inch guns had been replaced with 1.1-inch antiaircraft guns and the powerful 20mm Oerlikon cannons. Cooper's new weapon was located down in the gun deck amidship on the port side. As the weapon was a single barreled unit, all Cooper had to worry about was that ammo loaders could keep up with the speed of his weapon, since it could fire 450 rounds per minute. Cooper could not wait to go out to sea to try his new 20mm cannon, so he would be prepared when they sailed into combat again.

On the evening of April 14, Lily was headed home from her new part time job at a nearby clinic. Instead of taking the short way home, she decided to drive down Pearl Harbor highway to get a look at the *Lexington*. As there was little traffic, she slowed so she could watch cranes delivering loads of boxes and other equipment up to the decks of the *Lexington* and the *Yorktown*. She could see men moving about the flight deck working on several projects. She wished Cooper could come home just one more time before they sailed, but he had told her that was not going to be the case. After watching for several minutes, Lily drove on home, saying a prayer for Cooper and the crew of the *Lexington*.

By 2100 hours, all the work had been completed aboard the *Lexington*. Cooper walked up to the now quiet flight deck and sat down in the gun pit on the starboard side of the ship just below the ships island. He was bone tired but his mind kept going over all the things he had heard and seen during the last two days.

While he was helping load extra pallets of ammunition for gunnery practice during the day, other sailors told him about all the extra rations that had also been brought on board. Stories abounded about the ships officers carrying clip boards, checking and rechecking every inch of the ship in preparation for something no one was aware of. If all that was not enough, officers from Nimitz's headquarters on the mainland had come aboard several times in the last few days, guarded by armed Shore Patrol Officers and carrying satchels that were cuffed to their wrists. Every sailor on board the *Lexington* could feel the pressure building and the scuttlebutt machine was now in full operation.

Like all the other men on board, Cooper understood the *Lexington* was going to be out to sea for an extended period of time, and combat with the Japanese was almost a sure thing. Looking up the hill toward the north of Pearl Harbor in the gathering dusk, Cooper was sure his sweet Lily was already in bed sound asleep. He wished he could be with her right now as he was a bit nervous regarding what was going to happen with the huge carrier task force in the coming days. One more night with Lily before they sailed would have been a true pleasure.

No matter how he felt about everything, Cooper was confident the crew of the *Lexington* had handled themselves well during their last foray against the Japanese, but then again, it was only the pilots that tasted the sting of combat, as no enemy aircraft had come close to the fleet. True, he had fired back at the enemy from the deck of the *Tennessee,* but that was in port where his ship was protected from torpedo attacks by the other battleships around him, and the water was shallow without large waves or sharks to worry about if you ended up in the ocean. Now they were about to sail into war where no one could predict the outcome of a battle or who would live and who would die. Cooper had already experienced death on the *Tennessee,* and it was not something he was looking forward to again.

He knew carriers were well built fighting ships, but he also understood they did not have the wide thick belt of armor plating around the hull like a battleship that could withstand the blows of three or four torpedoes without sinking. With a carrier, one well-placed torpedo along with a couple of 500-hundred-pound bomb hits could do enough damage to send it to the bottom. Secondly, the wide flat deck of a carrier was a great target from 10,000 feet, where with a battleship the top deck was full of turrets and other equipment, making it possible for a bomb to bounce off and explode in the water, or do very little damage to the hardened gun turrets. Every ship was a trade off, but now with aircraft becoming the prominent weapon of war, carriers had become a seriously coveted target for any pilot. Granted, Cooper had never seen a carrier self-destruct, but when he thought of all the ammunition and fuel detonating at one time as it did on the Arizona, it frightened him greatly.

Taking a deep breath, Cooper finally stood up, throwing a kiss toward Lily. Deep in thought of what was yet to come, Cooper strolled down to his berthing compartment for some well-earned sleep, unaware of what the morning may bring.

On the morning of April 15, Lily decided to drive to work along the Pearl Harbor highway to get another look at the *Lexington* where her husband was working. Coming down the hill, she gasped. Sometime during her long restless night in bed, the Lexington and Yorktown's fleet had sortied from the harbor, which now looked almost empty as the fleet of 48 ships and their compliment of 139 planes had sailed off on a mission known only to a small group of officers. Stopping at one of the gates to the base, a shore patrol officer walked up to Lily as she exited her car.

"Ma'am this is a restricted area, you will have to leave immediately."

Lily nodded her head, saying, "I know, but I noticed the *Lexington* and *Yorktown* sailed last night. My husband is on the *Lexington*, do you know where they were going?"

The shore patrol officer shook his head. "Ma'am, I haven't a clue. Only the men over there in the crystal palace have any idea of what the fleet is up to. I just hope they're going out there to kick ass on the Japs and teach them a lesson."

Smiling slightly, Lily nodded her head in agreement, returning to her car without saying another word. She continued her drive to work almost in a daze, wondering where Cooper was right now and where was he going. In her heart, she knew this time the *Lexington* was going to be right in the middle of this damn war, and there was nothing she or anyone else could do to change a thing.

During the layover for remodeling, Captain Frederick C. Sherman* became the new skipper of the *Lexington*. He was known to be a hard-nosed officer that always demanded the most from his men, but always treated his crews with the utmost respect.

Right on target, the *Lexington's* task force sailed from Pearl Harbor on April 15, 1942, around 0200 hours, joining up again with the *Yorktown* to create Task Force 17. The antiaircraft gunners on the remodeled *Lexington* were given drills for the next several days until Captain Sherman was convinced the men could operate their new weapons and radar proficiently.

Scott Dowdle, a swift and nimble farm boy from just outside Irving Texas, was assigned as Coopers chief loader. Being a confident smart ass with the gift of gab and a large smile, he easily fit in with the rest of the crew. When the Lexington went out into the Pacific for Sea Trials before rejoining the fleet, Cooper was amazed at how fast Scott could reload the 75 round ammunition drums on his weapon to keep him firing. Dowdle always made sure there were enough ammunition drums in the ready box so he would not have to rely on drums coming up from the ships magazine right away.

Cooper and Scott became good friends quickly, as the need to work together efficiently during combat cemented their relationship. Coming from a large cattle ranch in Texas, Scott was totally interested in Cooper's stories about starting out in New York City, and ending up on a ranch as a cattle driver in Montana. He loved Cooper's total honesty and the fact that he and Cooper had something in common.

Late on April 18, 1942, the sailors of Task Force 17 were elated to hear that Lieutenant Colonel James Doolittle had launched a raid of B-25 bombers against the Japanese homeland and it was considered a success. No one could understand how B-25 bombers could get to Japan when you consider the distance from Pearl Harbor to Tokyo. All any one knew was that President Roosevelt told the press the planes were based at America's newest base in Shangri-la.

The seas had been very rough the first few days out into the deep Pacific, and Cooper's stomach was not taking it well. Nevertheless, being on a war footing, all the antiaircraft guns were manned 24 hours a day. Although still feeling a bit nauseous, Cooper never missed his assigned duties. However, there were times he found it a bit unnerving sitting behind his weapon on the gun deck. Over and over, large waves smashed by the massive bow of the ship sent large plumes of water breaking off the ships side. The angry white water just a few decks below was driven back by the wind, throwing copious amounts of salt spray over him and his weapon in the process.

However, Cooper and Scott were thankful they were on the huge *Lexington* as they watched their destroyer escorts bob up and down, earning them the nick name, 'Tin Can.' Cooper was sure his stomach would never allow him to operate on a ship that bounced and crashed on every wave or ripple in the Pacific Ocean.

Originally, the fleet was to have several more days allowing new pilots and deck crews to work together before going into action, but at 2345 hours on April 30, 1942, Task Force 17 had now sailed into the southwest Pacific as the fleet commanders prepared for war.

As Admiral Nimitz was getting disturbing messages regarding heavy Japanese ship movements in the Coral Sea, he and his advisors realized the American Navy was going to have to make its presence known and shove the Japanese Navy back to the north. So, to answer the challenge, on May 1, 1942, the combined *Yorktown - Lexington* task forces sailed west back toward the Coral Sea to search for enemy forces possibly covering projected troop movements along the coast.

Waking up to a brilliant blue sky and warmer temperatures, Cooper took a few laps around the flight deck in between launches of aircraft. It had been just sixteen days since they had left Pearl, and just eight days since they had turned west. It appeared every man in the task force was holding their combined breath playing a waiting game of enormous proportions. They all had the same questions… when, where and how would it happen.

About mid-morning, everyone understood that things were about to change. Admiral Nimitz had ordered the task force to turn south and catch the Japanese task force that was spotted sailing toward Australia. The task force consisted of 26 ships, including two large fleet carriers the *Shoho* and the *Shokaku* with 128 combat planes.

CHAPTER TWENTY-FOUR – BATTLE OF THE CORAL SEA

The battle of the Coral Sea was a confusing situation for both the American and Japanese commanders. Reconnaissance pilots for both nations sent out erroneous reports of ship sightings that made matters worse for the decision makers. Every admiral was well aware this battle was going to be the first sea battle in history, where two opposing fleets never saw one another, and all the fighting was done with aircraft. No fleet commander wanted to go down on the wrong side of history. For the first time in sea warfare, not one large caliber gun was used against ships on either side. It proved the old saying, 'Fear the Lord and Dreadnought was now over. (Dreadnought was a slang term for a battleship.)

The attitude of the crew turned from slightly jovial to dead seriousness in a matter of hours. Pilots began spending an incredible amount of time in their ready rooms, listening to officers lay out the plan of attack and what they could expect from the Japanese pilots they would be going up against. Odds are they would be running into carriers from Japan's Combined Fleet, containing pilots many foreign news reporters claimed to be the best in the world.

On May 5, Admiral Frank Jack Fletcher* removed the *Yorktown* and its escort ships from the combined fleet. He kept the designation name of Task Force 17, while giving Task Force 11 once again to the *Lexington*. Fletcher was to sweep the area north of Guadalcanal for any signs of Japanese naval operations. Seeing no activity, Fletcher turned the convoy south where it was to meet Task Force 44 at a predetermined point 370 miles south of Guadalcanal. Along with the *Neosho*, Task Force 44 consisted of several destroyers and an Australian cruiser attack group under the command of Australian Admiral Crace. On the way there, four Wildcat fighters from the *Yorktown* observed a Japanese flying boat skirting the edges of the task force. They rushed in and shot it down before the pilot was able to send a message out regarding the presence of the convoy. However, as the plane never returned to its base in the Shortland Islands,* the Japanese were sure it had run into an American task force and had been shot down. This incident put Admiral Takagi* on the alert, who had been positive an American fighting force was nearby.

As Task Force 17 was now entering what was considered Japan's new backyard, both carriers began sending off additional advance search aircraft to seek out Japan's surface fleet or any submarines that might take advantage of the large American task force.

Picket ships comprised of destroyers and destroyer escorts sailed on the peripheral edges of the convoy, as well as weaving back and forth throughout the moving mass of ships watching for any telltale wakes created by Japanese periscopes. Additionally, anti-submarine crews on the ships stood at the ready on the fan tail awaiting orders to roll depth charges.

Sitting on the gun deck behind his 20 mm cannon in the dead of night, Cooper looked up at the blanket of stars that covered the night sky. Like nearly every other man aboard the *Lexington,* Cooper's favorite constellation was the southern cross. He knew war was inevitable in the next few days, but tonight looking up at the shimmering cross it gave his soul a sense of peace.

Sitting next to Cooper on the floor of the gun deck was Scott, smoking his trade mark pipe, staring straight ahead at the black shadows of the war ships that closed in a bit tighter to the carriers at night. Scott was happy the seas were running at a moderate rate with swells of just four to six feet. That seriously reduced the possibility of a collision in the darkness. Both men quickly turned their attention to a destroyer escort that had come up along-side the *Lexington* at a rather rapid pace with thick smoke billowing from her funnel. They watched s signalman use the large signal light near the bridge of the ship to send a message to the bridge of the *Lexington.* Of course, the usual bright light was covered over with a red lens so it could not be seen from a far distance. When the message had been sent, the skipper of the escort ship poured fuel to his engines, disappearing off into the night.

After blowing out a mouth full of smoke, Scott looked over at Cooper, "What do you think that was about?"

Cooper shook his head. "I could make out the flashes of light, but I don't know Morse Code. Maybe he was telling the skipper to have a good night, and asked what was for breakfast tomorrow."

Scott laughed as he withdrew the pipe from his mouth. After watching the destroyer escort disappear into the blackness, he responded, "Yeah, maybe."

After a moment of thought, Cooper said, "No, I'm thinking they told the bridge that all is safe ahead, and to keep up flank speed."

Finishing his load of tobacco, Scott cleaned out his pipe and leaned back against the short wall behind the gun deck. Looking once more up at the stars he said. "Yeah, who really knows. Hey Coop, when do you think we're going to run into the Japs? To be honest, my gut tells me we're sailing right in to a hornets nest." After a moment of silence, Scott continued. "Coop, I want you to know I got your back. You fire that thing accurately, and I'll keep dumping full drums on as fast as I can. Nothing will keep me from my job!"

Smiling, Cooper replied. "And you best know I got your back, too. I'll never leave you hanging, my friend."

As dawn broke across the western Pacific, the morning crew walked down onto the gun deck to relieve the weary sailors. The gunner relieving Cooper said. "Great breakfast this morning. Only half the scrambled powdered eggs are burned, and all the toast is. The bacon is rubbery and the oatmeal is going to the Seabee's for concrete when we're through with it. But hey, the coffee is hot so what more does a man need!"

Scott laughed as he pulled the man's helmet down over his eyes. "Come on, Dwight. You loved it, be honest. This isn't the Ritz Carlton, you know."

All the men laughed as Cooper and Scott walked across the flight deck toward the massive island that stood several decks above. To Cooper it didn't matter what was for breakfast after being out on the gun deck all night getting hit by the ocean spray. A little chow, a hot shower to remove all the layers of salt, followed by some sack time would make him a new man ready for his next watch.

With the skies cleared of enemy aircraft, Admiral Fletcher ordered the *Neosho* alongside to replenish his fuel supply. While the refueling operation was in progress, Fletcher received a message from Pearl that a Japanese task force with carriers was moving south in the Coral Sea to aid in the landing of Japanese marines on the south coast of New Guinea near Port Moresby. After refueling all the ships in the task force on May 6, Fletcher intended to sail north toward the Louisiade Islands* where he would prepare for action on May 7.

As Fletcher moved north, Admiral Takagi's carrier force sailed down the east side of the Solomon Islands past San Cristobal Island* and entered the Coral Sea. He had also refueled on May 6 near Rennell Island* in preparation for a battle with the American carriers he was positive would take place on the seventh.

Late on May 6, the *Lexington* and its escorts rendezvoused with Fletcher's task force once again. Fletcher was sure the Japanese task force was still farther north near Bougainville,* so he allowed ships from Task Force 11 to refuel. To his regret, none of the air recon patrols were able to make a sighting because they were not in range of the Japanese aircraft.

Little did Fletcher know that his task force was sighted around 1000 hours by a Japanese flying boat that made good use of cloud cover to get an exceptional view of the American ships. Takagi received the message at 1050 hours. However, Takagi understood that Fletcher's task force was at the extreme fuel limits of his aircraft, and several more of his ships were already requesting to be refueled. Takagi was upset with the situation, but knew there was no way he could engage the American carriers at this time. Additionally, his intelligence people were saying Fletcher's Task Force was heading south, increasing the distance his planes would have to fly. His decision was very sound, because while Takagi was mulling over his plans to attack, Task Force 17 was proceeding into an area with thick low hanging clouds that would make spotting the fleet impossible. Instead, Takagi sent Admiral Hara* with two carriers and two destroyers to go after Fletcher's task force at flank speed, so they could attack the following morning,

On May 6, as Japanese ships began to gather for the invasion of Port Moresby, B-17 bombers out of Australia attacked the approaching ships several times throughout the day, including a Japanese task force under command of Admiral Goto.* Regrettably, none of the bombs dropped hit any targets.

After the last B-17 attack, General MacArthur contacted Fletcher giving him the exact location of the Japanese invasion force which included the newest Japanese carrier, the *Shoho*. The invasion fleet was just 489 miles northwest of Task Force 17. Fletcher was now convinced that Japan's main carriers were accompanying the invasion force, and he wanted blood.

As all the ships in task force 17 had been refueled at 1800 hours, Fletcher sent the *Neosho* and the destroyer *Sims** to sail further south to a prearranged meeting site. At that point Task Force 17 sailed northwest toward Rossel Island* in the Louisiade island group. With today's technology it seems improbable that at 2000 hours, both fleets were just 70 nautical miles apart and neither commander was aware of it.

Also, at 2000 hours, Hara decided he would reverse his course to meet his commander Admiral Takagi, who was now headed in his direction. Early on the morning of May 7, the *Kamikawa Maru** a sea plane tender, set up a quick base on the unoccupied Deboyne Islands* to help support the invasion as they approached Port Moresby*.

Early morning May 7, 1942, *Lexington's* morning air search planes radioed they had discovered a Japanese carrier task force. Immediately, Captain Sherman and his planners on board the *Lexington* began trailing the Japanese task force so they could set up an attack.

Throughout the very early morning hours, armors and plane handling crews brought up the planes for the first attack against the Japanese task force. Each aircraft was checked and double checked to make sure every plane would leave the deck without a problem. A slight haze greeted the pilots of the *Yorktown* and *Lexington* as they walked across the flight deck to their waiting aircraft. The time was 0540 hours as the pilots slid into their cockpits. After the plane handlers buckled in their respective pilots, they knelt down on the flight deck, preparing to pull away the wheel chocks so the planes could move on down the flight deck. The pilots sat anxiously in their cockpits waiting for the order to fire up their engines. It appeared like hours passed before the order came at 0549. One after another the engines spun over creating a cloud of smoke that rolled back off the end of the flight deck. The rear portion of the flight deck was severely crowded with fully armed aircraft, so pilots had the longest deck possible for take-off. Now that jammed parking area was dangerously alive with deadly spinning propellers. With the engines warmed up, most of the pilots pulled their canopies closed as they knew the air would be somewhat cold as they screamed down the flight deck and climbed to 12,000 feet.

Satisfied that the engines were properly warmed up, at exactly 0552 hours, Captain Sherman gave the order to launch. One by one the planes screamed down the flight deck, taking to the predawn sky until soon the flight deck was relatively empty and quiet.

At 0625 hours on May 7, 1942, Fletcher sent Admiral Crace's cruisers, now designated as Task Force 17.3, to set up a blocking formation in the Jomad Passage*. Setting up the blocking task force was a risky gamble as Crace would not have any air support. Plus loosing Crace's ships diminished the number of antiaircraft weapons that would be on hand when the battle started. Fletcher's decision was a calculated one because he did not want the invasion force coming through the back door while his carriers were busy attacking the Japanese fleet.

Now, feeling confident the Japanese carriers were north of his position, at 0619 hours, Fletcher ordered the *Yorktown* to launch 10 Douglas SBD Dauntless Dive Bombers to begin scouting out the area. In true form, Hara still believed Fletcher was south of him. He sent a message to Admiral Takagi, asking for aircraft to search the seas in that area. After much consideration and discussing the situation with his staff, Takagi sent 12 Nakajima torpedo bombers around 0600 hours. At nearly the same time, Goto had his cruisers launch four Kawanishi Float planes to search southeast of the Louisiades.

From the quickly established float plane base in the Deboyne Islands, two float planes joined the search along with four more from Tulagi, and three bombers from Rabaul. Both fleet commanders were now ready for a type of aerial war that had never been fought before. Never in the history of warfare had two fleets engaged one another across hundreds of miles of open ocean. Japanese pilots sat in their aircraft on the flight deck ready for takeoff at a moment's notice once enemy ships were discovered.

Knowing the fleet was going to be in combat soon, at 0735 hours Admiral Fletcher ordered the fleet to begin sailing in a zigzag routine to make torpedo attacks much more difficult.

After a long wait, at 0742 hours, a scout plane from Shokaku radioed he had seen the American Fleet 163 miles from Takagi's fleet. The pilot reported seeing one carrier, one cruiser and three destroyers. The pilot from a second scout plane radioed confirmation of the sighting. Fortunately for Fletcher, what the Japanese had discovered was Task Force 44, and had somehow identified the *Neosho* as a carrier.

After getting permission to attack, Admiral Hara set in motion what would be a long day of aerial attacks. Seventy-eight planes screamed down the flight deck of the *Shokaku* and *Zuikaku* about 0800 hours.

Twenty minutes after the attacking force had left the Japanese carriers, another float plane radioed he had discovered Fletcher's task force. Not quite sure if the report was accurate, a float plane from the Japanese cruiser *Kinugasa** verified the report.

Now the Japanese leadership were baffled by the contradicting messages. After much discussion they decided to continue with the first attack as planned. However, to be on the safe side, they turned their two main carriers toward the northwest to get in better range of the American fleet if the reports were accurate. They had to consider that an American task force might divide into two attacking forces they may have to contend with.

The *Yorktown* had sent off search planes at first light. About 0815 hours, Lieutenant John Nielson,* pilot of an SBD, sent in a report that he had sighted Goto's task force. However, he made a mistake in coding the message, stating there were two carriers and four heavy cruisers 225miles to the northwest. At 0930 hours, every ship in the task force went to general quarters. At 0957 hours, the fleet changed speed to 15 knots.

At 0915 hours, the Japanese attack force launched from Goto's fleet finds Task Force 44, but searched in vain for the reported carriers. Admiral Takagi finally realizes the American fleet is now somewhere between him and the invasion force. At 1154 hours, he orders all torpedo bombers and fighters leave the area of Task Force 44 and return to their ships with their ordinance intact, while dive bombers are allowed to attack the *Neosho* and *Sims*.

Four dive bombers drop down on the *Sims* from 10,000 feet. The dive bombers were totally accurate, hitting the *Sims* with three large anti-ship bombs usually reserved for battleships and carriers. Within minutes, the *Sims* broke in half and drifted to the bottom of the Coral Sea. Only fourteen of her 192-man crew were able to survive the massive punishment.

The *Neosho,* attempting to use evasive action, was struck by seven bombs. With her top deck in total shambles and fires raging below decks, the *Neosho* quickly took on a noticeable list as she went dead in the water. As the *Neosho* began to sink, the skipper radioed Admiral Fletcher of their situation. However, a large portion of the message was garbled. Fletcher was not able to glean any information as to who or what had attacked the ship. The last thing that was broadcast from the *Neosho* was its position, but with the turmoil on the bridge, the wrong coordinates were given to Admiral Fletcher.

From all the information that had been gathered, Fletcher decides the Japanese fleet has indeed been located and ordered every readied aircraft to be launched. As of 1015 hours, eighteen Grumman F4F Wildcats, 53 SBD Dauntlessness dive bombers and 22 Douglas TBD torpedo bombers were in the air.

Regrettably, at 1019 hours local time, Lieutenant Nielson returns to the carrier to realize he had made a grievous coding error. Although Goto's force included the carrier *Shoho,* he thought he had observed two heavy cruisers and four destroyers and for sure it was the main task force. By now it was too late to make any adjustments to the attacking force.

At about 1012 hours, a report from a search aircraft reported a carrier, ten transports and 16 miscellaneous warships 35 miles south of Nielsen's original report. As several patrolling B-17s agreed with Nielsen's report on the ship sighting, Fletcher was somewhat confused but was still convinced Nielsen's sighting was the main fleet, although the main fleet was still quite a ways to the east.

At 1040 hours, the American planes that had been launched against the *Shoho* report finding her near Misima Island,* so they immediately prepare for an attack. Four Zeros and four Mitsubishi fighter aircraft were flying coverage for the task force. All the rest of the *Shoho's* aircraft are down on the hangar deck being armed for an eventual strike against the American fleet. Quickly Goto's cruisers move in to provide a diamond shaped coverage of the lone carrier.

The *Lexington's* air group was the first to attack. The attack was led by Commander William B. Ault.* The *Shoho* was pummeled by two 1,000-pound bombs and five torpedoes causing major damage. At just about 1100 hours, aircrews from the *Yorktown* dove down on the blazing ship that now appeared to be dead in the water. With perfect aim, the *Yorktown* crews strike the wounded ship with eleven more 1,000-pound bombs and two more torpedoes. The stricken ship sinks at 1135 hours. Fearing the remaining ships would be attacked again, Admiral Goto withdraws his task force up to the north. However, he sends the destroyer *Sazanami* back at 1400 hours to see if there were any survivors in need of rescue. After such a long wait to be rescued, just 203 of the *Shoho's* 834-man crew were pulled from the sea. Two of *Lexington's* SBD's and one SBD from the *Yorktown* were lost in the attack. All but three of the *Shoho's* complement of aircraft were lost. Three of the fleet's covering planes managed to escape but were all ditched in the shallow surf near Deboyne Island. At 1210 hours, Lieutenant Robert E. Dixon*, pilot of a *Lexington* SBD, radios Admiral Fletcher that the attack was successful. His historic message simply said, "Scratch one flat top, signed Bob."

Afternoon operations May 7, 1941

By around 1338 hours, all surviving American aircraft had returned to the fleet where they were quickly fueled and rearmed for the next action sure to come. By 1420 hours, once again pilots sat in their fully armed aircraft on the flight deck, waiting for the order to attack. Fletcher had to make a big decision. Should he go after the Japanese invasion force preparing to land near Port Moresby, or should he hold off until he could get a confirmation as to the location of Goto's carrier force? Fletcher's concerns widened when he received an intelligence report from Pearl Harbor that it was possible there still might be four more large Japanese fleet carriers in the vicinity. With dark storm clouds beginning to cover the Coral Sea, Fletcher realized by the time any of his remaining search planes found the Japanese fleet, it would be too late in the day to launch an attack. He called it quits and ordered his task force to turn southwest into the large squall.

Japanese Admiral Inoue* was shocked when he heard about the loss of the *Shoho* and most of its crew. Knowing he no longer had the air cover he was planning to rely on, he canceled the invasion for the day and turned to the north. Angrily, he radioed Admiral Takagi, who was now 225 miles east of Task Force 17 to quickly destroy the American carriers at all costs.

As the invasion force was turning toward the north, it was attacked by eight U.S. Army B-17's, but once again the bombs from the large bombers missed their intended targets. Both Admiral Goto and Admiral Kajioka were ordered to regroup their task forces south of the Rossel Islands.*

Around 1240 hours, a sea plane from the Deboyne base reported seeing Crace's cruisers and destroyers on a bearing of 175 degrees about 90 miles from Deboyne. At about 1315 hours, a search plane from Rabaul also sighted Crace's ships, but once again sent wrong information. The pilot stated the task force contained two carriers and was located on a bearing of 205 degrees and 115 miles from Deboyne. Takagi is infuriated at the confusing reports, but realizes he needs to do something.

Although Takagi didn't yet have all his planes back on deck from the Neosho attack, he made the decision to turn his carriers due west at 1330 hours. At 1500 hours, Takagi informed Inoue that the American carrier task force was most likely 490 miles west of his current position, making it impossible to launch a strike against them any more today.

Still wanting to get the carriers as soon as possible, Admiral Inoue orders two groups of aircraft from Rabaul to go out after Crace's task force. The first group included 12 torpedo-armed bombers, while the second group had 19 Mitsubishi planes armed with bombs. It was nearly 1430 hours when the two flights found Crace's task force. The pilots were elated when they returned from the attack, claiming to have sunk a California type battleship and damaged a second battleship and a cruiser. It is hard to say why the pilots reported what they did because there were no hits on any of Crace's ships as they zigzagged in and out of a heavy storm squall. However, the American task force did shoot down four torpedo bombers during the attack. Sometime after the Japanese planes flew back to Rabaul, three U.S. B-17's attacked Crace's ships by accident, but thankfully missed every ship.

Fletcher received an urgent message from Admiral Crace about 1526 hours, that he could not finish his mission without some type of aerial support. After sending his message, Crace retired his task force toward the south, roughly 250 miles southeast of Port Moresby so he could increase the distance from any type of Japanese air attacks. His new position would allow him to observe any Japanese vessels moving past the Louisiades from the Jomard Passage or the China Strait.

In order to be ready for the fight the following day, it was imperative that Crace refuel his ships while out of attack range of Japanese aircraft. Meanwhile, as Fletcher believed the Japanese fleet was close by, he ordered his task force to maintain complete radio silence, so Crace no longer had any idea where Fletcher was, or what his attack plans were for the following day.

Around 1500 hours, the *Zuikaku* picked up a coded message from aircraft flying out of Deboyne, incorrectly reporting the location of a task force they were sure was that of Crace.

Takagi immediately figured the planes were wrong and that they had been shadowing Fletcher's carriers. He felt that if Fletcher held that course, he would be within striking range before darkness covered the Pacific. Both Takagi and Hara decided to set up an immediate attack with a hand-picked squadron without fighter cover. The problem was, the pilots would need to navigate back to the carriers in the dark after the attack.

At 1515 hours, Hara decided to send out 8 torpedo bombers to search the seas 200 miles toward the west to make sure the American fleet was where they predicted it would be. Just as that flight lifted off, dive bombers that had been involved in the attack on the *Neosho* set back down on the carriers.

Although the crews were very tired, six were ordered to be ready for another mission as soon as their planes could be checked over and reloaded.

With everything set, at 1615 hours, Hara launched 12 dive bombers and 15 torpedo bombers on a heading of 277 degrees out to a distance of 280 miles. As they were already on their way, the 8 torpedo bombers searching for the American carriers were turning back, reporting no sightings of Fletcher's task force.

At 1747 hours, planes from Task Force 17 flying under heavy clouds detected Takagi's task force on radar, 200 miles to the west. Using the radar positions sent in by the aircraft, Fletcher directed the 11 wildcats that were flying combat cover for the fleet to attack.

The Japanese were taken by total surprise. The pilots of the Wildcats went right to work shooting down 7 torpedo planes and one dive bomber, and seriously damaged a second torpedo bomber which crashed before making it to a carrier. Nevertheless, 3 Wildcats were lost in the scuffle.

After reviewing all their losses in the attack, and still being confused as to the accurate whereabouts of Fletcher and Crace, Japanese leaders contacted all their aircraft and told them to return to their ships. To rid themselves of excess weight so they had enough fuel to return to their carriers, the pilots dumped all their explosives into the ocean.

As the sun was setting at 1830 hours, several of the returning Japanese pilots observed American carriers in the gathering darkness. At 1900 hours, confused Japanese pilots thought the American ships were their own and prepared to land on the carriers. However, as they were met by heavy antiaircraft fire, they quickly turned away. Strangely, by 2000 hours, Task Force 17 and Takagi were roughly one hundred miles apart, but neither were aware of the other's presence. Realizing his pilots were lost in the darkness, Takagi took a desperate gamble, turning on all his spot lights hoping his pilots would home in on the fleet instead of crashing into the sea. By 2200 hours, eighteen surviving Japanese aircraft had safely returned to their carriers.

While this was all going on, between 1518 and 1718 hours, the crew of the *Neosho* had repaired their radio. They made two calls to Task Force 17, informing them they were drifting northwest with no mechanical power and beginning to sink. The radio operator making the call, once again gave the wrong coordinates, which made finding the stricken ship nearly impossible. When Admiral Fletcher was informed of the *Neosho's* situation, he became distraught, knowing the only ship to refuel them was now useless and sinking somewhere out in the Coral Sea.

As darkness enveloped the Coral Sea, Fletcher directed Task Force 17 to move west and be ready to launch a 360-degree search at daylight. At the same time, Crace turned west, hoping to stay within attack range of the Louisiades.

Upset with how the day had turned out, once again Admiral Inoue ordered Takagi to destroy all the U.S. carriers the following morning while delaying the Port Moresby landings until May 12. With those orders in hand, Takagi felt it was best to move his carriers 120 miles to the west. He was sure that a morning search to the west and south would still allow him to provide support to the invasion fleet. Admiral's Goto and Kajioka were not able to move their ships in time to attempt a night time attack on the U.S. fleet.

Both sides were expecting a massive battle the following day, and spent long hours during the night planning their strategies. Pilots and aircrews in both fleets attempted to get as much rest as they could, knowing they would be thrown back into combat in the morning.

After studying records from both sides, United States Vice Admiral H.S. Duckworth* wrote, "Without a doubt, 7 May 1942, vicinity of Coral Sea, was the most confused battle area in world history." Admiral Hara told Admiral Yamamoto that he was so infuriated with everything that had gone wrong on May 7, he gave serious consideration to resigning from the Imperial Navy.

With the battle of the Coral Sea being the first battle between fleets by use of air power, there was no doubt mistakes were going to be made, especially by anxious pilots, but the number of incorrectly coded messages, and messages giving false ship positions was a nightmare for both sides. The victor of this battle would be decided on who made the fewest mistakes the following day.

As darkness settled over the calm Coral Sea, the nervousness and fear that hung over the *Lexington* began to wane. The constant roar of planes screaming down the flight deck, and the rattle of the arresting cable had come to an end, as the last aircraft from the late afternoon patrol had set down on the dark flight deck.

Down below in the hangar deck there was a whirl wind of activity as mechanics and weapons specialists worked feverishly, checking over every aspect of the planes to make sure they were ready for the combat that was surely to come in the morning.

In the ammunition handling rooms near the magazines, bombs and rockets were set on pallets that would be taken up to the flight deck on special elevators to rearm returning planes once the Japanese convoy was spotted. Other ammunition in the magazines was being re-categorized, so in the morning, ammunition handlers would not have to guess or search for the appropriate explosives.

The cooks in the galley were especially busy stocking the serving line, as most of the men on board hadn't had much of a chance to catch a meal since breakfast. They were hungry and ate like a starving football team.

Up in the plotting room, the top brass circled around the main plotting table. Red lights illuminated the room and went out whenever a deck door was opened. They moved small ships that bore either small American or Japanese flags around on the plotting board, attempting to lay out the morning's battle with the amount of information they had, and what was coming in from the submarines that were attempting to track enemy movement. It wasn't much to go on, but it gave the task force commanders enough information to set up the carriers for the morning launch.

Cooper sat behind his 20mm cannon, staring out toward the horizon for any signs of Japanese aircraft determined to make a late afternoon attack on the *Lexington*. Scott had been standing behind Cooper most of the day, using large binoculars to search the skies, positive today was going to be his last.

Putting down the binoculars, Scott placed his hand on Cooper's shoulder. "Breathe, my friend, we have been given a reprieve by the war Gods. They have allowed us to live another day."

Slowly standing up, Cooper replied, "Yeah, but tomorrow the shit is going to hit the fan and you damn well know it. Like it or not, we'll be smack dab in the middle of it!"

Scott nodded his head as he looked down toward the deck for a moment. After looking over at Cooper, he said, "I hate to say it my friend, but I think this is what we signed up for when we enlisted. It's too late to take back that signature now."

Cooper smiled as he looked at Scott. "Yeah, I know all that for sure. But to be honest, I'm scared, just scared as hell. Pearl was one thing, but now we know the Japanese are out there somewhere over that damn horizon, and they are hunting us the same way we're hunting them. Their subs have got to be out there somewhere just waiting to pounce on us when we least expect it. I believe tomorrow we will either sail back to Pearl as victors, or end up at the bottom of the Coral Sea."

As Cooper stopped speaking, the evening relief crew stepped down on the gun deck next to the 20mm cannon. Gunners mate Harlow slapped Cooper on the back, "Go get some chow, Coop. It's not a bad meal tonight, and there's lots of it." Picking up the binoculars, he scanned the ocean out toward the horizon for a minute. "Subs, the damn subs have got to be out there hunting. I know the destroyers do a good job of keeping them in check, but they scare the hell out of me. Especially at night when you can't see a damn thing and then, BOOM, the whole ship is on fire."

As Cooper prepared to step up onto the flight deck, he turned to Scottie. "Yeah thanks, that will help me sleep a lot better tonight!"

Scott laughed as he put his arm around Cooper. "Don't worry, Coop. My bunk is right below yours. When I feel my toes getting wet, I'll make sure to wake you up." Both men laughed as they made their way down to the mess area to eat.

Throughout the long night, Cooper lay in his rack thinking about Lily and the baby they were going to have. The last thing he wanted was for Lily to end up like Sadie, having a child to raise with no father in its life. Cooper desperately wanted to see his baby be born and watch him or her grow into adulthood. That had been his dream as long as he could remember, and now the Gods of war were threatening to take it all away from him, and there was nothing he could do to change any of it. "Just stay alive, Cooper, just stay alive, that's all you have to do." He repeated that over and over before drifting off to a restless sleep.

Morning watch appeared to come way too early for Cooper. At 0530 hours, Cooper, Scott and a dozen more men left their berthing area, heading down for a quick breakfast before taking up their positions on the gun deck. Reaching the flight deck, the men could see the planes already sitting on the deck as flight crews swarmed over them like a bunch of drunken bees at a hive.

Before stepping down to the gun deck, Scott took a moment to look around the *Lexington* as sea spray washed over his face. That told him Admiral Fletcher had already turned the carriers into the wind in preparation for launching the aircraft. Looking over at Cooper, he said, "I think today will be our day of destiny. Be true to yourself, Coop, and you will survive."

Cooper thought over what Scott had just said but did not respond. Instead, he sat down behind the cannon and checked all the controls. Scott stepped up to the cannon, removed the ammunition drum to make sure the weapon would fire when Cooper pushed on the trigger. Seeing that everything was in order, he replaced the drum and picked up the binoculars. He sat down on an over-turned five-gallon bucket and took a deep breath. Looking left and looking right, Scott could see that every crew member was busy checking over their weapons one last time. The nervousness that had dissipated with the cover of darkness last night had reemerged as the sun broke on the horizon and the sound of warming aircraft engines broke the silence of the Coral Sea once more.

May 8, 1942 was now upon them. It was a day they would never forget.

Coral Sea Carrier Battle, Day Two, May 8, 1942

The Japanese were the first to launch planes on May 8, 1942. At 0615 hours, Admiral Hara had his fleet located 100 miles east of Rossel Island as the first planes roared into the air. The flight consisted of 7 torpedo bombers to search the area of 140-230 degrees, out to a turning point of 250 miles. Japanese planes from Tulagi and Rabaul joined in on the search.

At 0700 hours, Hara's force was joined by two cruisers from Goto's task force. Meanwhile, Goto and Kajioka sailed toward a meeting point 46 miles east of Woodlark Island,* with the invasion force. They were ordered to wait there to see what the outcome of the carrier battle would be.

The cloud cover that had been used by the American fleet overnight had now moved northeast, where it was covering the Japanese carriers, severely limiting their visibility, down to as little as two miles at times.

With Admiral Aubrey Fitch* taking over tactical command of Task Force 17, at 0635 hours, 18 SBD's were set off to a distance of 200 miles to make a 360-degree search. Skies over the carriers were well cleared off, allowing clear visibility out to 17 miles.

Pilot Joseph Smith*, flying an SBD off the *Lexington,* reported sighting the Japanese fleet through a break in the clouds at 0820 hours. Several minutes later a plane from the *Shokaku* sighted Task Force 17. The distance between the fleets was now only about 220 miles. Quickly, planes from both task forces were taking to the air, hoping to strike the first blow.

It was about 0915 hours, when a flight of 18 fighters, 33 dive bombers and 18 torpedo bombers took to the air from the Japanese carriers. At nearly the same time, American carriers each set off independent attacks. The *Yorktown* had 6 fighters, 24 dive bombers and 9 torpedo planes. Over on the *Lexington,* a launch of 15 dive bombers and 12 torpedo aircraft cleared the deck by 0925. In order to help their pilots have a shorter and safer flight after the attack, both fleets immediately began sailing toward each other at flank speed.

Dive bombers from the *Yorktown* arrived in sight of the Japanese carrier force at 1032 hours.

In order for the attacking force to have a coordinated attack, the dive bombers flew a wide circle over the Japanese fleet as the slower torpedo planes arrived. With all the planes lined up above the Japanese fleet, they found the *Shokaku* and the *Zuikaku* roughly 10,000 yards apart, with 16 fighters flying overhead. Also, the *Zuikaku* had sailed into a large rain squall comprised by many low hanging clouds.

At 1057 hours, the dive bombers from the *Yorktown* began their dive on the *Shokaku.* Although the skipper of the large fleet carrier was taking evasive action, two 1000-pound bombs struck on the forecastle of the vessel, creating serious damage and setting fires on the lower decks. It was questionable how much aircraft activity the *Shokaku* could participate in as the flight deck and hangar deck sustained major damage. Regrettably, all the torpedoes dropped by pilots from the *Yorktown* missed their mark. Each side shot down two aircraft during the quick battle.

At 1130 hours, flight crews from the *Lexington* made their appearance. Immediately, two dive bombers went after the wounded *Shokaku*, making one hit with another 1000-pound bomb, adding to the damage while panicking the crew as they attempted to fight the numerous fires that now blazed aboard the wounded ship. Two other *Lexington* dive bombers went after the *Zuikaku*, missing the twisting vessel with all their bombs. Unfortunately, the balance of *Lexington's* dive bombers could not identify the Japanese ships because of the gathering heavy clouds. Meanwhile, the eleven torpedo bombers from the *Lexington* missed the *Shokaku* with their torpedoes. In the air, 13 Japanese fighters were able to shoot down three Wildcats.

Things had gone from bad to worse for the carrier *Shokaku*. The flight deck was so badly damaged, repair crews lacked the materials necessary to make any part of it usable. The ship had lost 223 members of the crew, and much of the aviation gasoline on board had been lost in a major explosion. The engine repair shop was all but destroyed, along with all the equipment. After the skipper Takatsugu JoJima* reported all this information to Admiral Takagi and Admiral Hara, the ship was allowed to leave the task force at 1210 hours, along with two destroyers. JoJima immediately set a course to the northeast toward Japan.

All was quiet aboard the *Lexington* until 1055 hours. Crews in the combat information center found a blip on their radar scopes indicating there was a flight of Japanese planes approaching just 78 miles out. Within seconds, nine Wildcat fighters already stationed on deck for such a problem were ready to go. Believing there would be Japanese torpedo planes coming in at a lower altitude, six of the Wildcats were stationed too low, missing the enemy aircraft after they flew by overhead.

Due to the heavy loss of planes the evening before, it was impossible for the Japanese to mount a full torpedo attack on the *Lexington* and the *Yorktown*. So, they sent 14 torpedo bombers against the *Lexington* and just four to the *Yorktown*. Quickly, a Wildcat blew one torpedo bomber out of the sky, while 23 higher altitude patrolling SBD's from the *Lexington* and *Yorktown* took down three more as the torpedo bombers were descending. At the same time, Japanese Zeros were able to destroy four Yorktown SBD's.

Suddenly, at 1113 hours, the sky was alive with diving aircraft and heavy flak from the *Yorktown* and *Lexington* that were stationed 3,000 yards apart, along with their accompanying destroyers. A strange occurrence took place during the Japanese torpedo attack. All four pilots flying torpedo bombers toward the *Yorktown* missed the carrier completely. Japanese torpedo bomber pilots were considered the best in the world, and to have four misses all in a row was unheard of. The remaining 10 torpedo bombers broke into groups surrounding the *Lexington* as they bored in for an attack. Two type-91 torpedoes struck the *Lexington* at 1120 hours. No one noticed the first torpedo had buckled the bulkheads where the aviation gasoline storage tanks were mounted. Immediately, gasoline vapors began to escape into the ship. The port side water main was ruptured by the second torpedo, reducing water pressure into the forward firerooms. Consequently, the auxiliary boilers needed to be shut down, however. the *Lexington* was still able to make 24 knots with her other boilers. With accurate antiaircraft fire, four more of the torpedo bombers were knocked down.

Above the damaged carrier were 33 Japanese dive bombers, circling around like buzzards. They were ordered not to attack until after the torpedo bombers were finished. Slowly dropping down from an altitude of 18,000 feet, the planes didn't begin their dives until they reached 14,000 feet. Their attack began about four minutes after the remaining torpedo bombers had cleared the area. One after another, nineteen dive bombers from the *Shokaku* dropped down out of the sky, aiming for the *Lexington*. The remaining fourteen went after the *Yorktown*. Zeros worked closely with the dive bombers, attempting to stop the SBD pilots from getting involved.

Down on the gun deck, Scott pointed out the attacking torpedo planes, but most of them were too low for Cooper to fire at until after they finished their attacks, because the 20mm cannons did not traverse down that low. The Japanese pilots didn't make things easy as one pilot would climb to the right as the next would climb to the left, sending full power to their engine. Cooper chose the third torpedo bomber, figuring the pilot would turn right. With the pilot pulling up and turning right as Cooper suspected he would do, the 20mm cannon began to chatter. Cooper and Scott could see rounds striking the fuselage behind the engine, its left wing and the tail. Several pieces of metal were torn lose from the aircraft. As the pilot continued trying to gain altitude, it was clear the power to the engine was cutting out. Cooper stopped firing as he watched a Wildcat drop down from about 5,000 feet and rip the torpedo bomber to shreds. The plane skipped once across the water before exploding in a massive ball of flame.

Scott pounded his hands down on Coopers shoulders as he yelled, "We got the bastard, we got him!"

Cooper felt great, knowing he had damaged the plane, yet knew he could not take credit for the kill. A petty officer came running along the gun deck, yelling as he pointed to the sky above the ship. Cooper swallowed hard as he watched the dive bombers begin their dive above the *Lexington*. Never had he been so scared in his entire life. Scott had just placed a new drum on the 20mm as Cooper depressed the trigger. Once again, the weapon roared, sending out 750 rounds per minute at the diving aircraft. Now there would be no way to claim a victory with hundreds of guns in the task force firing into the brilliant blue sky. Black puffs from exploding shells pock-marked the sky as a steady stream of 20mm cannon rounds and .50 caliber machine gun fire roared into the heavens. The roar was deafening, making it nearly impossible to think. All he could see was Scotty throwing empty drums over board as he slammed another one in place. Cooper would reset the weapon and continue firing until another 750 rounds had been spent.

Suddenly, one of the dive bombers dropped his bomb from about 4,000 feet, allowing it to hit the ocean, wide of the Lexington. Quickly, the pilot struggled to pull out of the dive and escape the brutal anti-aircraft fire. As the plane neared 2,000 feet above the waves, Cooper could see smoke emanating from the engine bonnet. With a new drum of ammunition, he swung his weapon to the left and opened fire. As if in slow motion, Cooper could see his rounds tearing up the bonnet and cockpit, ripping pieces off the plane.

Seconds later, a ball of flame and a cloud of black smoke occupied the space in the sky where the plane had been. Cooper cheered as the report from the explosion echoed off the side of the carrier.

Not wasting time, Cooper spun his weapon skyward toward the menacing dive bombers as Scott prepared another drum.

During the ongoing attack, two Wildcats from the *Yorktown* were able to hit two dive bombers, dropping them into the Coral Sea. Several bombs that were aimed at the *Lexington* fell into the water alongside the massive ship. Water from the explosions covered Cooper and several other gunners along the port gun deck. Cooper did not mind the quick shower as it cooled him off somewhat as he continued working his gun. Two bombs struck the *Lexington,* starting several fires. Crews attacked the fires having them under control by 1233 hours.

While the *Lexington* crew was fighting for their lives, at 1127 hours, the *Yorktown* was struck in the center of its flight deck by a 550-pound bomb that penetrated down four decks before detonating. The massive explosion created dangerous structural damage to the aviation storage area, while killing or wounding 66 men. Quickly, the propulsion staff realized the super-heater boilers needed for power were no longer working. The hull of the *Yorktown* was also seriously damaged below the waterline by 12 near miss bombs. As the dive bombers attempted to fly off, two were shot down by Wildcat pilots.

American fighter pilots that were lined up on the perimeter of the attack went after the escaping Japanese aircraft creating a circus of whirling planes over the burning carriers. In the end, three Wildcats and three SBD's were shot down as well as three Japanese torpedo bombers, one dive bomber and one Zero. The morning battle had come to an end by 1200 hours. With the battle over for the time being, American and Japanese pilots began returning to their task forces. However, several American pilots that were lagging behind the rest of the air armada, caught the fleeing Japanese planes undetected. They managed to shoot down two more Japanese planes, killing the lead Japanese officer in charge of the attack force.

Repair crews on the American carriers worked like madmen, knowing the planes would have to ditch in the water if the decks were not repaired in time. By 1250 hours, planes began to land on both carriers. By 1430 hours, all planes had been received on the damaged carriers. Regrettably, while recovering the aircraft, five SBD's, two TBD's (Torpedo Bombers), and one Wildcat that had sustained battle damage crashed while landing.

The Japanese lost similar amounts of damaged aircraft during landings, including two Zeros, five dive bombers, and one torpedo bomber. A total of 46 of the 69 planes that were launched for the attack returned, all landing on the *Zuikaku*. After further inspection of the returning planes, three more Zeros, four dive bombers and five more torpedo planes were judged too badly damaged to be repaired and were rolled overboard.

Admiral Fletcher now needed to put together a summary of what the pilots were reporting from their attacks on the Japanese fleet. It appeared that one carrier was severely damaged while another was able to escape, probably undamaged. Consequently, he had to keep in mind that both his carriers had suffered significant damage and he had lost a good amount of aircraft. He also had to keep in mind that with the loss of the *Neosho*, there was no way to refuel any of his ships or get more aviation fuel.

While Fletcher was pondering his situation, Admiral Fitch's patrol planes reported the sighting of two undamaged enemy carriers. Fletcher now began to feel he was facing a stronger enemy than he had originally expected was in the Coral Sea.

Immediately, Fletcher gave orders to move Task Force 17 into safer waters, out of attacking distance from the Japanese. He also notified General MacArthur of the location of the enemy carriers, asking if he could attack them with his heavy bombers.

The Japanese were in a similar situation. At 1430 hours, Admiral Hara contacted Admiral Takagi, telling him that just 24 Zeros, 8 dive bombers and 4 torpedo planes could be relied upon for a further attack. Takagi was also very concerned regarding his fuel situation. It was reported that his cruisers were down to 50 percent fuel capacity, and that some of his destroyers were running as low as 20 percent. With the loss of so many aircraft, he could no longer offer proper air coverage for the planned invasion. This meant Admiral Inoue would need to withdraw the invasion force to Rabaul, postponing the entire operation until a further date. Inoue was then to take his task force to a spot northeast of the Solomon's.

However, Takagi was elated to hear that their pilots had erroneously sunk the *Yorktown* and one other carrier thought to be of the Saratoga class.

By now, damage control parties aboard the *Lexington* had extinguished all the fires and placed the ship back in operational condition. Nevertheless, some sparks from an unattended electric motor ignited escaping aviation gas fumes. At 1247 hours, an explosion near the *Lexington's* central control station killed 25 men and set off a major fire. While crews were working on the fire, a second explosion in the nearby fuel storage area started a massive fire just two hours later. More gas fumes ignited at 1525 hours, forcing the firefighting crews out of the area. At 1538 hours, the chief damage control officer reported the fires to be out of control and unmanageable.

As fires rapidly spread and fears of more explosions from unexploded ordnance was a real possibility, orders to abandon ship were issued at 1707 hours.

By now, smoke from the out-of-control fires had forced most of the men on the gun deck on the port side of the ship to abandon their positions. Most of them had assembled on the flight deck, waiting for additional orders. Some of the men were attempting to return to their berthing quarters to retrieve personal belongings they did not want to lose if the *Lexington* went down.

When the order came to abandon ship, Cooper and Scott walked over to the port side of the ship. Some men were attempting the slow process of climbing down cargo nets while others were jumping down into the sea and swimming toward destroyers that had come in close to rescue survivors. Cooper looked at Scott, "I'll probably break my damn neck crawling down those cargo nets, what do you think of just jumping?"

Scott shook his head, "What about sharks? You always say they scare you worse than anything."

Nodding his head, Cooper replied, "Yeah, but right now I don't see a shark fin anywhere nearby. I think all the explosions have scared them off for the time being. We should just jump and get the hell of off this thing before we get roasted alive!"

Before Scott could respond, an explosion blew open an ammunition elevator trap door about twenty feet away, sending a bright orange tongue of flame out across the gun deck. Before Scott could figure out what was happening, Cooper grabbed him by the wrist and pulled him over the side of the ship.

Cooper held his breath as he awaited the hard contact with the water that was coming up at them in a hurry. The next thing Cooper knew, he realized he was alright and several feet below the surface of the sea. With two large strokes, his head bobbed up to the surface about ten feet from the *Lexington*. As he spun around to find Scott, they were face to face just three feet apart. Scott was struggling to catch his breath as he shook his head.

"You could have given me some warning, Coop! One second, I'm on the deck, the next I'm crashing into the damn ocean. That really sucked!"

Cooper had to laugh as he was treading water. "Look at it this way, you didn't have to make a decision as to what the best way to get off the ship was going to be."

Scott laughed as he splashed water up into Cooper's face. "Yeah, I'll give you that. Let's get the hell away from this damn ship before it decides to kill us."

Nodding his head in agreement, the two men began swimming the roughly forty yards to the destroyer USS *Phelps** that had lowered cargo nets allowing survivors to climb aboard.

Grabbing hold of the rope net, Cooper and Scott pulled themselves out of the water and began climbing up toward the deck. The entire time they climbed, they could hear more explosions rocking the *Lexington*. Reaching the deck, several sailors grabbed onto them, pulling them up as quickly as they could, so sailors coming up behind them could be hauled aboard before they fell back into the ocean.

Cooper watched as life boats from the *Phelps* picked up Admiral Fitch, Captain Sherman and several other high-ranking officers from the cargo nets so they did not have to get their feet wet as they were carrying official documents, including the ships log.

As soon as the skippers of the destroyers were sure they had all the survivors out of the water, they slowly made a turn and sailed away from the burning hulk. The last thing they wanted was to have an ammunition locker explode and severely damage the destroyers, risking one or both of them going down with the carrier.

By now, the *Lexington* had begun to list hard to port as thick clouds of black smoke billowed from every opening on the ship. Understanding there was no way to salvage the Lexington, and since Admiral Nimitz did not want the ship to be taken by the Japanese, he ordered it scuttled. At 1915 hours, the destroyer *Phelps* launched five torpedoes into the side of the flaming *Lexington*. The ship shuddered as massive holes were torn into her already weakened hull. Quickly, the hull filled with sea water, causing large plumes of steam to rush out of the ship. As the Lexington began to settle, the survivors on the *Phelps* listened to the sickening moans of steel beams being stressed beyond their capabilities. Then at 1952 hours, the slow-motion death of the carrier ceased as the Lady Lex suddenly plunged to the bottom of the Coral Sea to a depth of 2,400 fathoms.

Sadly, 216 men from the 2,951-man crew went to the bottom with the ship, along with 36 aircraft. With the *Lexington* now gone, the *Phelps* led the other destroyers off to the west to join the *Yorktown* and the balance of Task Force 17, which had already sailed from the area at 1601 hours. Together once more, Fletcher ordered Task Force 17 to take up a southwesterly course. Later that evening, General MacArthur notified Fletcher that eight of his B-17's had attacked the Japanese fleet as it was moving off to the northwest, but had no estimate of damage.

Later that night, Admiral Crace ordered the destroyer *Hobart** that was seriously low on fuel, and the destroyer *Walke** that was having mechanical problems, to sail for Townsville in Queensland, Australia, where they could be serviced. Several times over the night, Admiral Crace had picked up radio messages making him believe the Japanese invasion fleet had turned back again, hoping to complete their mission. However, with Fletcher having withdrawn from the area, the only American task force available to meet the possible challenge was Task Force 17.3, belonging to Admiral Crace. So, instead of leaving the Coral Sea, Crace patrolled the area all night.

Low on fuel and aircraft, and not knowing exactly how many Japanese carriers were still in operational condition, on May 9, Task Force 17 changed course to due east, leaving the Coral Sea behind them. Fletcher intended to take his task force to New Caledonia for repair and replenishment. However, Admiral Nimitz ordered Fletcher to send the damaged *Yorktown* directly to Pearl ASAP after refueling at Tongatabu.*

Having no idea where Admiral Fletcher and Task Force 17 had gone, and not hearing any more reports regarding Japanese ships, on May 10, at 0100 hours, Admiral Crace turned his task force due south, heading for Cid Harbor in Australia, arriving there undamaged on May 11.

On May 10, allied bombers from Australia attacked Deboyne and the transport *Kamikawa Maru,* inflicting minor damage, thus ending the official battle of the Coral Sea. However, Admiral Yamamoto was angry that American carriers had slipped out of his hands. On May 8, he sent a strongly worded order to Admiral Inoue to reverse course to seek out and destroy the balance of the American fleet, and proceed immediately with the invasion of Port Moresby.

Inoue did not recall the invasion fleet, instead he demanded Takagi and Goto sail back into the Coral Sea, find the American fleet and destroy them.

Takagi could not follow through with those orders until his ships were refueled from the fleet oiler *Toho Maru.** With refueling finished late on May 9, Takagi and Goto turned southwest into the Coral Sea in search of the American ships. Usable aircraft out of Deboyne aided in the search for Fletcher's ships on May 10. After an exhaustive search of the Coral Sea environs, Admiral Takagi ordered the search be called off at 1500 hours, May 10, and let the fleet return to Rabaul.

After getting a complete run down of the search, Yamamoto agreed the Americans had slipped away and the search was fruitless. He ordered the *Zuikaku* to return to Japan for replenishment, and to pick up new air crews to bring the ships air wing back to full strength. Orders were also sent out for the *Kamikawa Maru* to break down the seaplane base at Deboyne as they felt it was no longer needed.

Around 1200 hours on May 11, as an American PBY was patrolling out of Noumea, New Caledonia, the crew observed the drifting hulk of the *Neo-*

sho. Seeing there were survivors on the deck, the plane called for a rescue attempt. The destroyer *Henley** sailed immediately to the wreck and rescued 109 crew members from the oiler and 14 from the *Sims*. The *Henley* then sank the gutted hull of the *Neosho* with five-inch gun fire.

With the battle of the Coral Sea in the rearview mirror, the Japanese high command ordered the invasion of Nauru* and Ocean Islands* on May 10. However, the invasion got off to a rocky start on May 12, as an American submarine sank the *Okinoshima*,* that was acting as the command ship for the operation. Immediately, Admiral Yamamoto delayed the landings until May 17.

Unknown to the Japanese, Admiral Halsey's Task Force 16 arrived in the South Pacific off the coast of Efate on May 13. His orders had been to turn north to stop the invasion of Ocean and Nauru islands. Nevertheless, on May 14, American intelligence people broke the code, giving them information on Japan's plan to invade Midway Island.

So, late in the day of May 14, Nimitz sent Halsey a message telling him to send out aircraft into Japanese controlled waters so they could be sighted by enemy patrol planes. However, Halsey was told to give his pilots strict orders not to engage. Once Halsey was sure his aircraft were sighted, he was to turn back toward Pearl Harbor and run at flank speed.

The plan worked well, as on May 15, a Japanese reconnaissance plane flying out of Tulagi sighted Halsey's entire task force at 1015 hours, 445 miles east of the Solomon Islands. Not only was Halsey's task force discovered, it unnerved Admiral Inoue. He felt Halsey's carriers would wreak havoc with his invasion force. Without delay, Inoue canceled the invasion, ordering his ships to flee to either Truk or Rabaul. After moving into safer waters, Halsey turned south, sailing back toward Efate where his ships could refuel. Once that was completed, Halsey sailed toward Pearl Harbor, dropping anchor on May 26. The damaged *Yorktown* and its escorting ships sailed into Pearl on May 27.

Like most survivors from the *Lexington*, Cooper and Scott were happy to be back in friendly waters. As the *Phelps* sailed into Pearl Harbor, Cooper stood on the foredeck, looking up the hill toward his home where Lily was probably still in bed. He knew everyone from the *Lexington* would be given shore leave, and he couldn't wait to see his beautiful wife again.

With the battle of the Coral Sea behind them, both sides needed to take a long look at the losses they had suffered. American commanders realized the loss of the heavy carrier *Lexington* equaled one fourth of their carrier strength in the Pacific, meaning they would need to cut back on some plans until a new carrier could arrive. They had also lost the fleet oiler *Neosho* and a destroyer, but both could be replaced in about ten days with ships from the west coast. The *Yorktown* was in dry dock getting repaired, but Nimitz was concerned on how long it would take crews to get her back in shape. Consequently, he ordered repair crews to work around the clock seven days a week. With the *Yorktown* out of commission, that meant he had just fifty percent of his carrier force intact.

The Japanese were celebrating the fact they had possibly taken out two of America's heavy carriers, while they simply lost a light carrier, the *Shoho*. Although they had one heavy carrier in dry dock for repairs, they knew the American fleet also had one carrier severely damaged. It had been an even trade on destroyers, but American pilots had sunk several small repair ships, while the Japanese sunk the *Neosho*, a greater prize. Overall, the Japanese command saw the battle as a major victory.

They felt it was now possible Nimitz only had one undamaged carrier left in his entire fleet. Excitement was running high among top naval officers as their dream of putting the American fleet out of operation forever may now be close at hand.

The Japanese government advertised the battle of the Coral Sea to the public as a major victory, while awarding medals to many of the officers and pilots. Although the United States considered it a military draw, they had actually gained much more, strategically. The battle forced Japan to call off the invasion of Port Moresby, along with the invasion of Ocean and Nauru Islands. It was the first time since Japan started their war in 1937, that anyone had forced them to retreat, although the Imperial High Command did not see it as a loss.

Nevertheless, the American press wrote scathing reports regarding the losses sustained in the battle of the Coral Sea, wondering if Roosevelt had the proper leadership in place. The single idea that the American press was now condemning the Coral Sea as a major defeat, while questioning America's leadership in the war, only emboldened Japan to make several large mistakes as they prepared for the invasion of Midway Island.

Before Cooper was able to get shore leave and see Lily, there was naval business to be taken care of. The second day in port, Cooper was called down to see a Captain Brenick. As Cooper sat down, the captain smiled. "Well Dodge, I see you were well liked aboard the *Lexington,* and had high marks for your gunnery skills. You even downed a plane during the Coral Sea affair. Nice shooting, Dodge."

Cooper did not want to speak for Scott, but he replied. "To be honest, Captain, my gunnery skills are only that good because I have an excellent loader that never misses a beat. He is ready with a fresh drum the moment I run out of ammunition."

Captain Brenick leaned back in his chair. "Let me have his name, and I'll see if he is in the group of men I am speaking to."

"Gunners Assistant Dowdle, Scott Dowdle, sir," Cooper replied nervously.

"Oh yes, here he is," the captain said, as he looked over Scott's paperwork. "He also comes with a great recommendation. I'm glad to see it."

Cooper leaned forward in his chair, asking, "What is it you're looking for, sir?"

"As you are aware, the *Yorktown* had casualties when she was hit. We are trying to find gun crews we can assign to the ship when she is finished being repaired that have experience, and you certainly fit the bill. We have several 20mm spots open we need to fill. Dodge, would you be interested in being assigned to the *Yorktown* with the same job?"

Smiling, Cooper replied, "Yes sir, I would love to be on the *Yorktown.* She is a good ship and I've met some of the crew already and they are good people. I think it would be a fine fit for me."

"Outstanding, Dodge. Consider yourself assigned to the *Yorktown.* You'll be getting your orders when you get your leave papers. Anything else I can do for you, Dodge?"

Nodding his head, Cooper replied. "Sir, all my belongings went down with the *Lexington*. To be honest, everything I'm wearing right now, and everything I've been using to shave has been borrowed from men on the *Phelps*. How do I go about being reassigned a complete set of navy issue?"

Laughing, the captain replied. "Everyone that survived the *Lexington* will be going ashore to Base Issue tomorrow to pick up everything you were originally issued. Then you can go to the Base Exchange to purchase your personal needs. It's standard practice after a ship is lost."

After shaking hands with the captain, Cooper left the office searching for Scott. He found his friend lying on the foredeck of the *Phelps* near the five-inch gun mount. Sitting down beside his friend, Cooper told him everything the captain had said. Nervously, he inquired. "Scott, would you consider going to the *Yorktown* to be my loader again? We made a good team, and I sure would like to serve with you again."

Scott sat up leaning against the gun casement. "I have given a lot of thought as to what I want next for an assignment. Part of me doesn't want to be back on a ship where I could end up in the ocean again. But I also don't want to be assigned to some backwater base where I will never see combat again. I joined the navy to see the world, and because I needed a job worse than anything else. I never counted on this damn war coming along. But now that it has come, I want to be part of fighting it. I don't want to bounce around on a damn destroyer, and I don't know if I want to be on a battleship. That kind of leaves carriers, and from what I saw in the Coral Sea, that's where all the action is going to be in this war. I think air power is going to be the end of battleships. So, I guess I can see myself going back to a carrier. But a lieutenant told me this morning there are three new carriers close to completion that the navy will need crews for. He told me I could go back to the United States and help train the new men and become part of the veteran nucleus, and that sounds damn good also."

Cooper felt deflated, thinking he was going to lose Scott to another ship. "Yeah, that all sounds good, I suppose, but Lily is here and we have a nice bungalow we are renting, so there is no way I'm going back to the mainland right now. So, I signed up for the *Yorktown*."

Nodding his head, Scott looked over at his friend. I think something big is in the offing. I mean, look at the work crews on the *Yorktown.* They are busting their humps to get her back in shape. If I go to the states, I'll miss whatever is going on now. And I think Nimitz is the kind of guy that wants to strike when the iron is hot, and so do I."

Cooper smiled as he looked into Scott's face. "Are you saying you will go to the *Yorktown*?"

Nodding his head, Scott replied. "On one condition. You said Lily is part Hawaiian. I want her to cook me a real Polynesian meal while we are on leave."

Laughing, Cooper replied. "Name the day, my friend, and it shall be yours."

The next day Scott was called in to see Captain Brenick. After a short conversation, Scott stated he would go to the *Yorktown*, just as long as he could be Cooper's loader. Smiling, the captain replied. "Son, the navy never wants to break up a team they can count on. The job is yours."

With his job assignment out of the way, Scott was feeling much better. He kind of knew all along that he wanted to go where ever Cooper went.

Three days later, with their new orders and shore leave papers in hand, Cooper and Scott went ashore to have all their naval clothing reissued. After leaving the Issue Building, Scott boarded a taxi bound for Kailua where his girlfriend was staying. Cooper walked over to a bank of phones and dropped in a nickel and dialed the phone. Seconds later, Lily picked up the phone and said, "This better be you, Cooper, or I'm going to go crazy!"

Cooper busted out laughing as tears rolled down his face. "Honey, I'll be at the gate in ten minutes. I can't wait to see you."

Pulling up at the gate, Lily jumped from the Studebaker and raced over to Cooper as fast as she could. She pulled him into her arms and kissed him as they both cried. "Looking into Coopers eyes, she said, "I have prayed to get you back here so often, God must be tired of hearing from me. But here you are, and I love you so much."

Cooper placed his hand over Lily's growing abdomen and said, "Boy or girl?"

Lily laughed, replying, "I think it's a girl, I really do."

Smiling, Cooper replied, "If she looks like you, she'll be an absolute keeper. Now please drive me home."

Lying in bed with Lily that evening was the happiest Cooper had been in a long time. For a moment everything in the universe appeared to be in the right place. He didn't want to think about the war, or all the death he had seen in the Coral Sea. It nearly made him sick that he would have to return to all of it in fifteen days, leaving Lily alone once again.

However, the next morning during breakfast, Lily continued asking question after question about the sinking of the *Lexington* and the battle. Cooper realized that she was not going to be put off, so he answered each question as best he could, leaving out some of the more sickening details he didn't want to talk about. The question he hated most was when she asked if he had killed anyone.

Once again, he could see the massive fire ball from the Japanese plane he had hit with his cannon. The explosion was like nothing he had seen before, as he had just witnessed two human lives being taken from this earth in a split second. Nodding his head, Cooper looked at Lily saying, "Yeah, probably. I fired a lot of rounds at the incoming planes, but there is so much flak out there it's impossible to know who hits what."

Smiling, Lily responded, "It's probably better that way so no one knows who killed the pilots. I'm glad for you that it happens that way."

It was the best answer Cooper could give his loving wife, so she would not dwell on what was really going on out in the war.

Over the next two weeks, Cooper and Lily spent time on several beaches enjoying the warm sun and gloriously warm water of the Pacific. However, when Cooper first entered the water, he came to a standstill. All of a sudden, he thought of all the men that had been killed during the Coral Sea battles that now called the Pacific Ocean their grave. For a moment, it felt like their hands were grabbing onto his legs, attempting to pull him out deeper to join them. If it hadn't been for Lily walking up behind him and pushing him down into the surf, he might just have walked back to shore and not returned to the water. But now, being with Lily and sharing the excitement of the baby, all the ugly thoughts of war once again disappeared from his mind. Still, Cooper knew they would return in the dark of night when he least wanted them to be there.

The fifth night he was home, Lily made the Hawaiian dinner Cooper had promised Scott. It paid dividends for Lily, as she found out Maria was a nurse at another clinic in Honolulu, not far from hers. Now she would have another good friend to spend time with when Cooper was back out at sea. The evening was full of laughter and good food and it made Lily happy that Cooper had found such a good friend after losing Paul.

While Lily and Maria cleaned up the kitchen, Cooper and Scott sat in the backyard with a cold beer. Scott looked intently at Cooper. "What do you think is going to happen next, once the *Yorktown* is ready for action."

After taking a large swallow of beer, Cooper shook his head. "After what all happened in the Coral Sea, I'm not sure I want to take a wild guess or even imagine what is still to come. We all know the Japs have a strong navy and several fleet carriers they can throw at us at any time. We have seen how devastating aerial war can be and that scares me more now than it did before. I don't know what to say, Scottie. I still see those Jap planes coming down out of the sky with machine guns blazing and bombs hitting the deck. It was totally different than at Pearl."

After looking up toward the sky for a moment, Scott replied. "I tried not to think too much about it before we sailed to the Coral Sea. But when you can't see an ounce of land for hundreds of miles, and you know the bottom of the ocean is miles down, it begins to wear on one's nerves. Then watching the Lex go to that bottom smoking and creaking, it really unnerved me, Coop. I've been having nightmares about it. I know we'll have to go back out there and meet the Japs in combat again, but I'm scared as hell. There's no place to go, and you can't run away from it and hide."

Finishing his beer, Cooper replied. "I'm glad I'm not alone with those fears. I try hide it from Lily, but I think she sees through it, and just doesn't want to bring it up. I know how she felt when Sadie left after Paul was killed.

No matter if she was heading back toward family, she was going to be alone with that baby forever, and that bothered Lily very much. Sometimes I wish we would have waited to have a baby, but Lily really wanted a child. Now that scares me, too."

As the men talked, just a few short miles away in the situation room in Cincpac Headquarters, Admiral Nimitz sat rereading the report from the Coral Sea and shaking his head. Sitting quietly across the large table from him drinking coffee was the rather reserved but ever thinking Admiral Raymond Spruance.*

After putting the report down, Nimitz looked across the table. "Ray, we think the Japs are going after Midway, but we aren't quite sure yet. I've got our best minds down in the intelligence office working on it. Commander Rochefort expects to have an answer very soon. I have a sick feeling Yamamoto will attack with the combined fleet in this battle, knowing we are down one carrier. Give me some perspective, Ray. Tell me what's been going around in that mind of yours?"

Admiral Spruance stood up, walking over toward the large map of the Pacific that covered most of the wall. After a moment of thought he pointed toward the Aleutian Islands. "Yamamoto has to know they are lightly defended and have very little naval strength in the area. There are several smaller islands where fighter bases could be established and many islands have some coves deep enough that submarines could work from. If they would land a sizable army up there, it wouldn't take them long to march all the way to Anchorage. We would have a devil of a time dislodging them. Defense of those islands is something we need to keep in mind, although I don't think Yamamoto wants them all that bad. But like you, I still think he wants Midway before moving on to the Hawaiian Islands and sending the American fleet back to the west coast. With the United States out of the central Pacific, that damn ocean becomes a swimming pond for the Japanese and then they will go after the Panama Canal. We best stop them before they get that far."

Walking over to the large map, Nimitz nodded his head. "I agree, Ray. We must defend Midway with all we have. With the *Lexington* gone and the *Yorktown* questionable, that just leaves us the *Enterprise* and *Hornet*. If we have to go there with only two carriers and the Japs bring four, we will lose them all, I'm afraid."

Spruance nodded his head. "This is the same conversation I had with Halsey last night. We need to have the *Yorktown* ready to go, so you've got to throw everything at it you can."

Nodding his head, Admiral Nimitz replied. "Ray, the ship is already like an ant mound. We've got every repair shop on the base invested in the project. We have hired all the ship fitters from around Oahu and the other islands that were available. I don't know what more we can do, but I'll run over there in the morning and give them a pep talk."

At Imperial Japanese Naval Headquarters, Admiral Yamamoto paced his office as several of his best fleet admirals sat listening to every word he said. "We must knock out the American carriers at all cost. Another attack on Pearl Harbor has been discussed. However, we know American submarines have been placed in strategic areas to watch for another such attack, which allows American war ships plenty of time to get in position, keeping us away from the harbor itself. Informants tell us the United States has added so many aircraft to the Hawaiian defense, they would wreak havoc with our fleet. That plan has been scrapped so we can concentrate on 'Operation MI' (Midway Island)."

Walking over to the large map on the wall, he pointed toward the Coral Sea. "We lost the *Shoho* and most of its well-trained crew. We cannot afford another such loss. We can be happy the *Shokaku* managed to sail away from the attack and return here for repairs. I have learned that the damage was less than we expected, and she will be ready when we launch operation MI against the American Fleet.

Midway Island now has fueling and resupply depots that can extend the range of American submarines by some 1,200 miles toward Japan. They have also constructed new longer airfields for long range bombers that can strike at Wake Island. All of these must be wiped out when we attack. In the meantime, I am working on a decoy plan for the attack." Pointing toward the Aleutian Islands he continued. "As of now there are no strong defensive positions covering the approaches to Alaska. We must use that situation to deflect a large part of the American fleet when we attack Midway.

I am positive Nimitz and many of his staff will see the decoy task force we are sending to the Aleutians as a serious threat. With their fleet divided, we should be able to take them apart in a piece meal attack. However, it is most important we draw out the complete American fleet and sink them in the deep waters around the Midway Atoll. It is imperative they do not escape the range of our aircraft. With just two carriers left in the American fleet, there is no doubt they will send some of their repaired battleships to try and attack our carriers. We will not let them get that close, and must send wave after wave of torpedo bombers to sink them. With Midway in our hands, I am sure the United States may want to withdraw from the Pacific and sue for peace. If they do not, we will force them to guard the Hawaiian Islands and the Panama Canal several thousand miles to the east. This they cannot do, and the war will come to an end. But the canal must be taken as well as Oahu, as we will need Pearl Harbor to maintain our eastern fleet. We also know that American commanders are having a hard time with the morale of their crews. Most of them have become demoralized by our victories over their fleet. They may not have the will to fight against our top pilots in a war so far away from their main base."

However strongly Yamamoto felt about his organized plan, not everything sat right with his army and top naval planners. A showdown was yet to come.

CHAPTER TWENTY-FIVE – BATTLE OF MIDWAY

Admiral Yamamoto wanted to spread the battle out over hundreds of miles of ocean, giving Japan the best advantage possible. He was satisfied they would be sending Vice Admiral Chuichi Nagumo with the combined First Carrier Division attack force containing four carriers. In the rear of the attack force would be Vice Admiral Nobutake Kondo's* invasion force, along with the battleships from the first fleet main force. As Yamamoto saw himself as a battleship Admiral, he decided he would lead the battleship task force himself. However, as the old battleships were much slower than the new carriers divisions, he was allowing them to sail several hundred miles behind the carrier fleet. The standing plan would be for the battleships to rush forward at flank speed and sink the balance of the American fleet after Nagumo's planes had already weakened them.

What Yamamoto did not know was that American code breakers had broken the newest Japanese code, JN25B. With the code broken, it was evident to American planners that the Japanese task forces were going to be so far apart, it would be impossible for them to offer aid to one another.

Yamamoto's plan stood, stating that Admiral Nagumo's force would pummel the island with dive bombers and level bombers, while Zero's swept the sky clean of any American fighters. The four carriers were to be screened by 12 destroyers, 2 heavy cruisers, 1 light cruiser and 2 Kongo class battleships, that would continue pummeling the island as Japanese ground troops rushed ashore. After all that, the island would fall and be in the hands of the Japanese empire.

However, the second fleet, operated by Admiral Yamamoto and Admiral Kondo, contained 2 light carriers, 5 battleships, 4 heavy cruisers, and 2 light cruisers. Here lies the problem for the Japanese. Still considering the battleship as the primary weapon of the Imperial Navy, Yamamoto had attached the 5 slow battleships to Kondo's assault force, not allowing it to keep up with Nagumo's main attack force. So, it was decided that Nagumo would sail in as close as possible to Midway without being detected, still having a chance for surprise. Plus, Nagumo would keep his task force in a tight secure battle group, and not let them be spread out over a large part of the Pacific, attracting attention from patrolling American planes or submarines.

However, this plan had two serious flaws. As Nagumo's fleet was concentrated over such a narrow section of ocean, his scout planes would also be searching a narrower band of ocean, allowing for the possibility of American attack planes to close in quickly without being observed. Secondly, with Yamamoto's cruisers and battleships several hundred miles to the rear, the main attack force would not have all the antiaircraft weapons those ships could provide in order to defend his task force.

Although the plan appeared to be sound on paper, it could not be approved unless the Imperial Army signed off on it, and Army commanders had a plan of their own. They wanted the decoy task force to be an actual invasion force instead, one that would land soldiers on Attu and Kiska Islands, allowing Japan to invade the United States from the north.

Japanese strategists felt American officials were aware of a possible invasion of the Aleutian Islands, but had not put any major plans into operation to stop it. If the army seized Kiska and Attu, that would give Japan bomber bases from which they could bomb the west coast of the United States. The War Ministers felt that once American strategists realized the Aleutians Islands was the major target, they would have no choice but to quickly send more ships north to stop the invasion, including the carriers from Pearl Harbor, leaving even less planes to cover Midway.

Yamamoto and the naval command reluctantly agreed to the overall plan, knowing it was the only way their Midway operation could get approval. With full agreement, the Aleutian operation was code named Operation AL.

However, to get everything the army needed loaded on ships, the sailing day for the Operation MI was backed up by one day.

Back in Hawaii, Admiral Nimitz was nervous about sending out his entire fleet to meet the massive threat that appeared to be coming over the horizon. Although his staff was attempting to persuade Nimitz to move ahead with a plan to defeat the Japanese task forces, Nimitz could not be pushed into a final answer just yet. Wanting positive proof that all the dispatches they were receiving in the new JN25B code were accurate, he called Commander Rochefort to his office.

During their give and take, Commander Rochefort tried to convince the Admiral they were reading the JN25B code perfectly. Seeing he was getting nowhere, Rochefort said he would have the radio operators at Midway send out a message on the operations channel the Japanese monitored constantly, stating that the water desalinization plant on the island was out of service and they needed fresh water. Rochefort told Nimitz he was positive Japan's response message to Yamamoto would be sent out over JN25B, and decoding station HYPO on Oahu would decode the message.

Nimitz agreed to the plan, still unsure it was going to work. The morning after radio operators on Midway sent out the message, station HYPO picked up the JN25B message regarding the failure of the desalination plant on Midway to Yamamoto.

Immediately, Commander Rochefort ran up to Nimitz's office to show him the dispatch regarding the water plant message. But even more importantly the message also contained the formalized dates for the Japanese attack, as June 4 and 5, 1942.

Firmly convinced now that everything Rochefort had been telling him from the beginning was accurate, Nimitz agreed with the entire plan to defend Midway.

But now, his steady as a rock fleet commander Admiral Bill (Bull) Halsey* had come down with a horrible case of dermatitis that left him scratching like a flea infested dog, landing him in the hospital and making it impossible for him to sleep. Going over to see him at the hospital, Nimitz asked Halsey who he would recommend to lead Task Force 16. Although Halsey and Ray Spruance were polar opposites in many instances, Halsey had come to respect the man, so he solidly recommended Admiral Raymond Spruance lead his task force until he could get out of the hospital.

After being informed of Halsey's decision, Spruance went immediately to the hospital to pick Halsey's brain on every aspect of the coming battle and the operations of his fleet.

Feeling confident after his meeting with Halsey, Spruance boarded the carrier *Enterprise* to get accustomed to his staff and crew. As Spruance had been appointed by Nimitz to command the *Enterprise,* Halsey's staff were somewhat apprehensive of their new commander. There was an air of tension as the ships officers took their places for the first Admiral's mess on the *Enterprise.* No one knew quite what to say, and many of the officers saw Spruance as an outsider, attempting to steal Halsey's command. A hush of whispers permeated the room, nearly as much as normal conversations would have, making things even more uncomfortable for everyone.

As coffee was about to be served to the officers, Spruance took a good look around the room. It was known throughout the navy that when Admiral Spruance was ready to speak with a well laid out plan, a natural sparkle emanated from his eyes. So now, with that typical sparkle gleaming from his eyes, Spruance raised the tone of his voice so everyone seated in the mess could hear him. "Gentlemen, I want you to know that I do not have the slightest concern about any of you. If you were not good enough, Bill Halsey would not have you." (Taken from the Ship's record.)

With that, the ice was finally broken and men began to smile and exhale enough to enjoy the evenings dessert. From that point forward, every officer accepted Spruance and fully cooperated.

Now Nimitz had to make an extremely bold decision. His intimates had told him to send the *Yorktown* to Puget Sound naval yard for repairs, but he had refused, keeping her in Pearl Harbor to be repaired. Workers at Pearl had the *Yorktown* sea worthy in 72 hours, with the flight deck completely ready for aircraft, and the elevators functioning properly. However, that did not include all the work that was needed to the interior of the carrier. Nevertheless, the

Yorktown was given permission to operate out at sea for two or three weeks of normal operations.

She left Pearl Harbor once again as part of the task force led by Admiral Frank Fletcher into the southwest Pacific for crew and flight operations training. During the training mission, the repair ship *Vestal* that had been damaged during the Pearl Harbor attack accompanied the *Yorktown*, so repair crews could continue working on the damage while at sea. Hearing all was well with the *Yorktown*, Fletcher's task force was recalled to Pearl to prepare for the upcoming Midway operation.

Yorktown had sailed from Pearl with only a partial complement of aircraft. When she returned to Pearl, her complement was filled with planes and pilots from where ever they could be begged, borrowed or stolen. Many of the planes came from the carrier *Saratoga* that was still on the west coast in San Diego. Since the *Saratoga* had been in the process of replenishing her flight crews after undergoing repair work in Puget Sound, many of the pilots were rookies and had never fired a shot in anger.

Preparing for the Japanese onslaught, the U.S. Navy had sent 31 PBY flying patrol boats to Midway for long range recon, along with 6 brand new Grumman TBF Avenger torpedo bombers. The marine flight wing sent 19 SBD Dauntless dive bombers, 7 Wildcat fighters, 17 SB2U Vindicators, an older model dive bomber the navy was in the process of phasing out, and 24 F2A Brewster Buffalo fighters, another aircraft that was beginning to be phased out. The U.S. Army added to the inventory by sending seventeen B17 heavy bombers and four Martin B-26 medium bombers equipped with torpedoes. It was a contingent of 126 aircraft the war department thought could surely hold off the Japanese invasion, or at least do serious damage to the Japanese carriers. Now with three carriers available and Midway armed to the teeth, Nimitz felt confident that the American force was up to the task at hand.

In Kure, Japan, the *Shokaku* was still being repaired while the *Zuikaku* sat in port being replenished with bombs, torpedoes, food and other needed supplies while it waited for aircrews, since she had lost nearly half of her well-trained, Pearl Harbor veteran compliment. The problem was, there were no crews readily available, as the replacement school did not have any graduates ready to fly. Training instructors from the Yokosuka Air Corp were pulled from training new pilots to fill out some of the squadrons. This would thoroughly dismantle the ability of Japan to continue supplying trained pilots to the carrier force for the rest of the war.

As pilots were arriving to the *Zuikaku* at varied intervals, they were not able to get the squadrons up to full operational capacity, so she would not be able to participate in Operation MI. Much to the regret of Admiral Nagumo, the two most advanced carriers in the Japanese navy, the *Shokaku* and *Zuikaku* would not be ready for service. This meant he would not be able to have six carriers at his disposal as he did at Pearl Harbor. Now he would only have four heavy carriers, the *Akagi, Kaga, Soryu* and *Hiryu.*

So, to make things work, the *Kaga* with 60 aircraft, and the *Akagi* with 72, were assigned to Carrier Division 1, under Nagumo's control, while the *Hiryu* with 57 aircraft and *Soryu* with another 57, made up Carrier Division 2 under the control of Admiral Kondo. A total of only 248 available aircraft would be divided up between the two fleets, hundreds of miles apart. Nevertheless, both Nagumo and Yamamoto still believed they were going up against just two American carriers, so four carriers should be all they would need to assure victory once more.

Going into the attack, the Japanese had a poor radar system that was erratic and often not in use as commanders desired sightings from actual pilots in scouting aircraft. The carriers they were taking into battle did not have associated antiaircraft batteries allowing them to mechanically direct fire at incoming aircraft. Gunners still replied on officers to point out attacking aircraft as they maneuvered their guns to take on the enemy. The two fleets also lacked enough fighters to cover their attacking planes, while continuing to fly cover over their own fleets to deter enemy aircraft. Japanese doctrine also demanded escort ships be used as scouting vessels in a ring around the main force at long ranges, making them unavailable for antiaircraft support when the fleet was under attack.

By the end of Cooper's leave, he was ready to report to the *Yorktown* and take his place in the antiaircraft section of the ship. On April 27, 1942, Cooper and Scott walked up the gangway to the ship and signed in. Most of the new men assigned to the *Yorktown* were survivors from the *Lexington*. Those that could not be assigned to the *Yorktown*, were sent back to the United States to become core crew members for new carriers coming out of production.

After being escorted to their berthing compartment, the men were given a quick tour of the ship as it was set up somewhat differently than the *Lexington*. Everyone on the tour was stunned to see how much of the ship had already been repaired. The flight deck was ready to launch and receive aircraft, and the massive elevators once more moved from deck to deck properly. The aircraft that would fill the hangar deck of the *Yorktown* were still parked on Ford Island waiting for the carrier to sail out to sea.

Over the next few days, gunners tore down their weapons to make sure everything was in working order before they sailed. Loaders ran extra heavy loads up and down the ammunition elevators to make sure nothing was hanging up. Late into the evening, gunnery crews added their muscle to moving pallets of new parts and steel beams around the ship, so repair crews could complete their jobs quicker.

Word came down from Admiral Fletcher that Task Force 17 must be ready to sortie from Pearl Harbor on the first of May. Admiral Nimitz wanted to make sure the *Yorktown* and her replacement crew members were ready and able to withstand the rigors of combat. When the *Yorktown* was roughly 50 miles outside of Pearl Harbor, all the planes that had been staged on Ford Island began returning to the carrier. As they were arriving by squadron, there were breaks in the landings, so aircraft handlers on the hangar deck could keep things properly sorted out. Consequently, the entire first day at sea was dedicated to getting all the air squadrons on board without incident.

Over the next few weeks, aircrews from the *Yorktown* flew attack missions against their own task force using methods Japanese aircrews had been known to use since the war began. A second group of aircraft responded to the enemy attacks, creating massive wild simulated dog fights that mesmerized every sailor below that had time to watch. At some point every day, gunners on the *Yorktown* were given opportunities to fire at target racks or towed targets, enabling them to sharpen their skills. Cooper enjoyed these sessions very much, although it kept Scott and his team very busy bringing up drums of ammunition from the magazines. Although it was only April, the warmth and humidity of the tropics had the men soaked with sweat in just a short time. Nevertheless, no one complained as they all remembered very well what happened to the *Lexington* in the Coral Sea battle.

However, not all the action took place during the day. At night, Admiral Fletcher ran submarine drills with real American subs attempting to break through the antisubmarine patrols that were spread around the *Yorktown*. Destroyer crews were allowed to roll depth charges against simulated targets while cruisers closed in tight around the carrier as a shield against torpedoes. It did not take long for Task Force 17 to become a cohesive fighting force once again.

Although no one on board the *Yorktown* knew the time or date, everyone was positive the next battle against the Japanese was not going to be far away. The *Yorktown* had passed every test she was given, and the work crews were getting close to finishing the balance of the interior work. There was not an officer on the *Yorktown* that would be sad to see the repair crews leave their vessel. No matter what was going on, it always appeared that special adjustments had to be made allowing repair work to continue.

While standing watch one dark night, Cooper, Scott, and several other sailors on the gun deck were discussing where the next battle would be fought. Everyone had their own ideas and arguments to back them up. Cooper thought the scuttlebutt and the, 'my friend that works on the bridge,' stories were always the greatest, because it proved that no one knew a damn thing.

However, it didn't take long for Cooper to realize Scott had begun to find ways to remove himself from the conversations. After their watch ended on May 14, Cooper walked up to Scott who was sitting alone near an ammunition ready box a short distance down the gun deck. Sitting down next to his friend, Cooper asked. "Are you alright, Scottie? I've noticed you've walked away from the peanut gallery early the last few nights. What's going on inside that head of yours?"

After taking another puff from his pipe, Scott replied. "This time we'll be sailing right into hell. The Japs are going to throw everything, including the kitchen sink at us, and it most certainly will not be pretty to say the least. I wasn't scared like you were in the Coral Sea, but this time we're going to be fighting for our lives from the start and I keep feeling a cold hand on my shoulder."

Cooper nodded his head. "Yeah, I know the feeling. I felt the same thing when orders came to abandon the Lex. I was sure I would drown or somehow be killed when I landed in the water, but I swam like I never had before, and well, here I am."

Scott smiled as he looked down at his pipe. "My dad smoked this pipe in World War One. He smoked it during the battle of the Somme and then Verdun. This old thing has seen a lot of war and death, yet here it is in my hand tonight. I guess I should look at it as a good luck charm, but still, my guts tell me another story. Make me a deal, Coop. If you see me going down, take this old pipe and send it back to my dad. Don't let it go to the bottom of the ocean."

Cooper nodded his head. "Yeah, I can do that, Scottie. But I'm going to keep you so busy loading my gun you'll be moving way too fast to be killed by any Japanese pilot. Mark my word, Scott, you and I are going to make a difference out there in the next battle."

Scott smiled as he looked at his best friend. "You're filled with an overflowing sense of confidence. I guess I need to let some of that rub off on me, and everything will be just fine."

Slapping Scott on the shoulder, Cooper replied, "There you go, Scottie. I knew I could bring you around to my way of thinking. You'll do just fine out there."

As Scott placed the pipe back in his mouth, Cooper leaned his head back against the bulkhead, wishing he believed everything he had just told his friend. In all honesty, Cooper was absolutely terrified about going back out to sea against the Japanese.

The following morning, Admiral Nimitz radioed Admiral Fletcher, ordering him to return to Pearl with the Yorktown immediately. As the ship sailed at flank speed toward the harbor, one of the aircraft mechanics became engaged in an argument with an officer, sharing his opinion as to how poorly everyone on the ship was performing their duties, leaving no doubt they were all going to die. Walking over to his tool box, he pulled out a live grenade, pulled the pin, then demanded Admiral Fletcher turn east, back toward the United States, not Pearl Harbor. Quickly, a marine security detachment arrived on the deck, surrounding the angry sailor. Everyone, including the Admiral, knew what would happen if that grenade detonated on the hangar deck. With the thousands of gallons of aviation fuel loaded in the tanks of the planes, the *Yorktown* would go up like a roman candle, and the possibility of anyone surviving was slim to none.

The marines could not shoot because the grenade would slip from the man's hand and blow the ship apart. No one would allow the admiral to be part of the on-site sight negotiations due to the danger involved.

Cooper had been down in the 20mm magazine, talking with several of the ammunition loaders. When he left, he took a short cut back to his weapon by climbing a ladder that led to the hangar deck. He arrived right in the middle of the deadly stand-off.

When the angry sailor saw Cooper, he yelled out. "Dodge, I want out of this damn ship, I just want to go back home and be with my family, just like you when we were in the Coral Sea."

Cooper held out both his arms, showing the man he had no weapons. "Sellman, right? Doug Sellman, isn't it?"

The man smiled, surprised that Cooper remembered his name. "Yeah, that's right, Dodge."

Nodding his head, Cooper responded. "Yeah, I was scared as hell and you're right. I almost felt like jumping over board and trying to swim back to San Diego. But that was about as dumb as it gets. Listen to me, Sellman, if you put the pin back in that grenade and hand it to one of the marines, this is over with. When we get back to Pearl, they'll take you off the *Yorktown* and nobody dies. What do you think about that?"

Sellman looked coldly at Cooper. "Who put you up to this? Tell me, who made you come up here to talk to me?"

Shaking his head, Cooper replied. "Nobody. I was just taking a short cut back to the gun deck like I have dozens of times before. No one sent me here, Doug. As my dumb luck usually goes, I just stumbled into this mess and I ain't one bit happy about it. Just put the pin in the grenade and let's all go back to work."

Sellman backed away from the nose of an SBD where he had been standing, until he was directly behind a large rolling tool cabinet. Slowly, Cooper walked out into the center of the hangar deck, where he once more could see the agitated mechanic.

Taking several steps toward Sellman Cooper said, "Come on now, Doug. Put the pin in that damn thing and give it to me. Let's end this now before anyone gets hurt. You told me the other day that you want to see your mother again and give her a big hug. Well, you can't do that if you're dead, Sellman. Just think of all the things you have left to do in your life. This ain't the way to end things."

One of the anxious marines grabbed hold of Coopers shirt, attempting to pull him away from Sellman. Angered by the marine's tactics, Cooper spun around, slugging the man in the side of the head. Pointing at the marine now on the deck, Cooper said. "You are about one stupid son-of-a-bitch. Touch me again and I'll throw your ass overboard first chance I get. Now get away from me!"

Trembling, the marine held up one hand, "Alright, alright, get your ass killed then, who cares!"

Cooper was about to reply, but instead spun around to look at Sellman. "Alright Sellman, you can see I'm on your side and don't want to see you hurt. Just put the pin back in and let's end this."

Slowly, Sellman began sliding the pin into the grenade, but then stopped. Reaching into the top drawer of the tool box, he pulled out a .45 semiautomatic pistol. "Looking around the hangar, he said, "You're all going to die out there, none of you are going to have a damn chance against the Japs. What the hell is wrong with you people?" That being said, Sellman carefully placed the grenade down on top of the tool box, then quickly slammed the pistol under his chin and pulled the trigger.

Cooper charged forward, grabbing the grenade and shoving the pin fully back into position. As he slid down to the floor with his back against the tool box, he bent the ends of the pin over so it could not fall back out by accident. Sweat poured from his face, as tears ran down his cheeks. His hands trembled more than ever before as he handed the grenade to a naval commander.

The commander knelt beside him, placing his hand on Cooper's shoulder. "Son, that is the bravest thing I have ever seen in all my years in the navy."

As tears continued rolling down Coopers face, he looked up at the commander. "I still failed, Sellman's dead. It shouldn't have happened this way."

As the commander helped him up from the deck, Cooper attempted to look back over at Sellman's body, now surrounded by marines with an empty tarp. "Nothing to see back there, Dodge, just keep walking. Just keep walking."

A marine lieutenant stepped in front of the commander, saying, "I'll take custody of the prisoner now, sir."

"Prisoner? What the hell are you talking about, Lieutenant?" The commander replied angrily.

"This man struck a United States Marine and he's going to the brig until his trial. He broke my soldiers nose and he'll pay for it. I'll see to it for damn sure, sir!"

Folding his arms across his chest, the commander stood eye to eye with the angry lieutenant. "I think we should take this case directly to Admiral Fletcher on the bridge and let him decide if Dodge should get a court martial or a decoration for bravery. Because I'll be putting him in for a decoration as soon as I get back to my office."

There was a moment of tense silence on the hangar deck as the lieutenant looked at the faces of all the angry mechanics and pilots that were now solidly glued on him. After hanging his head for a moment, he looked at the commander.

"No harm done, no foul, sir. Let's just forget the entire incident ever happened."

Cooper stepped forward, looking at the lieutenant. "Yeah, let's forget about Sellman, he just didn't measure up. Listen, he wasn't a coward or a maniac. The man was just plain scared, just like you, every one of your marines and the rest of us. He just reached his breaking point today. Maybe you'll hit yours during the upcoming battle. Have you given that any thought?"

Without saying a word, the lieutenant followed his men carrying the tarp down to sick bay.

The commander looked at Cooper. "Damn right, Dodge. We all have that breaking point, and we all pray to God asking him to help us get through the next battle, and then the one after that. There is nothing else any of us can do. And be assured Dodge, you will be receiving an award for what you did today. You just might have saved over four thousand men and a carrier we could not afford to lose."

Task Force 17 arrived back in Pearl Harbor on May 17. Immediately, every ship in the task force was refueled and resupplied in an around the clock operation. During mail call, Cooper had received a long letter from Lily. By reading it, he understood his beautiful and very pregnant wife was nervous regarding the next action of the fleet, but wasn't saying it in so many words. Folding up the letter, Cooper placed it in his locker, unsure of how to respond to all her questions and concerns.

At the naval base in Kure, Japan, Admiral Nagumo and his staff checked and rechecked everything on every ship, to make sure nothing was left undone. Although he still wished to take the *Zuikaku* with him, Admiral Yamamoto was satisfied with the fleet as it was. He did not wish to take a carrier that could not meet the recommendations of navy regulations. Understanding his commander, Nagumo reported that all three task forces were ready to sail.

During the early morning hours of May 27, 1942, Nagumo's task force quietly set sail from Kure under radio silence, as they did for the Pearl Harbor attack.

On May 28, the northern attack and invasion force set sail from Tokyo Bay. Now Carrier Division 5, the largest and most powerful fleet in the history of Japan was at sea. Admiral Nagumo was in command of Carrier Division 1, Admiral Kondo in command of Carrier Division 2, with Admiral Yamamoto in overall command, while also commanding the battleship task force.

At Pearl Harbor with Commander Rochefort's staff continuing to monitor JN25B, Admiral Fletcher informs Nimitz his fleet is ready to sail. Immediately, Nimitz names Fletcher as overall commander and gives his blessing to sail.

As Task Force 16 was preparing to sail the following day, Cooper sat down to write Lily what he thought might be his last letter. He sat there for several minutes, thinking about what to say.

My Dear Lily,

I'm sitting alone on the gun deck behind my cannon. The stars are so plentiful tonight, I wish you were here to enjoy them with me. I know we are heading out to sea over the next couple of days, but only the top brass knows where. There is quite a fleet boxed up here in Pearl at the moment, and nothing like I have ever seen before.

The Yorktown is mostly repaired, although some shop people will be going to sea with us to finish up the last work. These guys don't want to go at all, but Nimitz said they will either go to finish the last repairs or go to the naval brig. I guess he won the argument.

I'm glad your appointment with the doctor went well and that the baby is healthy and doing fine. Yes, I still believe it is going to be a girl and agree we should name her Sarah like we discussed, but if you have any other names you like, I'm alright with that. I just want you to know that I miss you more than anything in this world and wish we could be together one more time before we sail. You have made me a happy man since we have been together, and for that I thank you very much. But now we are going out to do battle with the Japanese, and we all know they want to sink our fleet in the worst way so they can rule the Pacific. There is no way to know right now what will happen when we meet in battle, but you can be assured I will be brave and do my duty to the best of my ability.

I pray to God that I return to you, but if I do not, please let our baby know I died doing my job for our country, and that I will always watch over her. Sweetheart, tonight my heart is ready to burst, and there is nothing I can do to stop it, and it hurts so bad.

Well, I have to be on watch in about an hour, so I must go.

Lily, I love you with all my heart and pray to God we shall see one another when this battle is over.

All my love, Coop

Sealing the letter, he went down to the berthing compartment and mailed it.

Late in the afternoon of May 28, Task Force 16 sortied from Pearl Harbor. Task Force 17, with Cooper and Scott, sortied on May 30, heading for what was hoped to be an ambush of the Japanese fleet already sailing toward them from the west.

However, right from the beginning problems arose with the Japanese plan. A group of submarines that were supposed to set up a picket line in front of the fleet failed to sail at the proper time, due to Yamamoto's last minute adjustments to the overall plan.

Since the Japanese subs failed to be in the proper position out ahead of their fleet, the American carriers were able to move undetected to their rendezvous point, code named, Point Luck.

Quickly, Admiral Nagumo and Admiral Kondo created a new plan to find the American task forces. They sent up large four-engine float planes, known as Emily's, to scout over Pearl Harbor to see if the American carriers were still in port.

Additionally, several Japanese submarines were deployed to French Frigate Shoals to refuel the float planes so they could return to their carriers. When they arrived near the Shoals, they found American war ships patrolling the area, since intelligence reported the Japanese had been using the Shoals to refuel float planes since the attack on Pearl Harbor and it had to be stopped. Having to find another refueling point farther off to the west, the float planes were not able to search the eastern approaches to Midway, where the American carriers were now situated.

As the Japanese attack force moved closer to Midway, they began picking up information on American submarine movements and coded radio messages from Tokyo. All this information was sent directly to Yamamoto, but he never gave any of it to Nagumo, for two reasons. First, he was sure Nagumo was getting the same information he was and secondly, he did not wish to break radio silence. Log books recovered after the war proved Nagumo was not getting the intercepts. Had the intercepts become available to Nagumo, it is most certain a battle-hardened admiral like him would have altered course during his approach to Midway.

Japanese Aleutian Attack, June 2-4

Admiral Yamamoto assigned Admiral Boshiro Hosogaya* to lead the attack on the Aleutian Islands, hoping to draw heavy American forces away from Midway. American forces in the Aleutians had already been alerted to a possible attack, so when weather permitted, air patrols were out searching the frontier seas for any signs of an attacking force. On the second of June, two small Japanese aircraft carriers were observed 400 miles due south of Kiska Island*. Immediately, planes from America's Eleventh Air Force were sent to advance bases at Cold Bay* and Fort Glenn.*

After three days of completely overcast skies that did not allow air operations to take place, on June 3, 1942, the skies dawned clear. As the attack on Midway was also beginning the same day, Japanese planes rolled down the carrier decks, heading for Dutch Harbor* and Fort Mears.*

Tied up to piers were the naval destroyers *King** and *Talbot,** a destroyer-seaplane tender *Gillis** and submarine *S-27**. The Coast Guard cutter *Onondaga** and the Army transports *President Fillmore** and *Morlen** were also sitting in the harbor. At approximately 0540 hours, the radar operator aboard the *Gillis* notified the local commander that a large wave of planes was coming in from the ocean. As all ships had boilers building steam, the order was given to every ship to go to general quarters and sail from the harbor at once. Every ship was able to clear the harbor before the attack force arrived.

Since the war had begun, standard operating procedure was for all units to automatically begin general quarters assignments at 0430 hours every day. With all stations fully manned, at 0545 hours, a group of 15 carrier-type planes appeared off the coast line.

The Japanese planes immediately dove on the bases, strafing them with machine gun and cannon fire. Their attack was met by a large salvo of antiaircraft fire. After making the original attack, the planes moved back out to sea, following a northern route.

With everyone now alerted, at 0550 hours, four Japanese bombers approached the coast line and swung in toward shore, dropping 16 bombs. Two bombs ended up in the water, while 14 struck the crowded area of Fort Mears. As all the buildings were of white framed wooden construction, they were an excellent target for the bombardiers. Several barracks, along with three Quonset Huts were completely demolished. Several other buildings were damaged by near misses, resulting in fires. As the planes departed, they left 25 men dead and 25 more wounded.

A short time later, a second bomber group that had become lost dropped their bombs without doing any damage. However, a third flight of bombers struck a few minutes later, severely damaging the radio station while destroying another Quonset Hut. It appeared that the last flight of bombers was attempting to destroy the large wooden oil tanks built near the hills, but while all the bombs missed the tanks, they did destroy an empty Army tanker truck, killing two men.

It was estimated that 15 fighters and 13 horizontal bombers took part in the attack from 9,000 feet. Regrettably, no fighter aircraft from Fort Glenn, just 65 miles away, responded to the attack, however, all the ships in the open ocean fired on the planes. The gunners on the *Gillis* proved to be the best as they brought down two enemy aircraft, while no American ships were damaged.

Air commanders at Fort Mears were positive the Japanese would return for another attack the following day. The morning of June 4 arrived with low hanging dark clouds and intermittent rain squalls, which greatly reduced visibility for any aircraft. Nevertheless, several Catalina flying boats were sent out to find the Japanese fleet and keep an eye on its movements. Due to the heavy overcast, the Catalina's were flying lower than they normally did, allowing the Japanese fleet to also track them. When one of the Catalina's came in too close to the fleet, it was shot down by antiaircraft fire. The second plane was immediately recalled as commanders on the ground now had a good idea as to where the fleet was headed.

Mid-afternoon, the heavy cloud cover broke up, allowing visibility to 3,000 feet. By 1740 hours, spotters at Fisherman's Point Observation Station observed three groups of enemy bombers flying in the direction of Dutch Harbor. At 1800 hours, ground observers reported the same flights near Mount Ballyhoo*. Just slightly after 1800 hours, ten Japanese Zero's dove on Dutch Harbor, using machine guns and 20mm. cannon fire. As the fighters cut off their attack, 11 dive bombers attacked, dropping down out of the remaining dark clouds in a steep dive. Each plane was armed with just 1 large bomb that was dropped when the aircraft reached approximately 1500 feet. Regrettably, during this attack, the pilots had better aim than the day before, as four brand new 6,666 gallon fuel oil tanks exploded in a massive fire ball. Sadly, the tanks had just been filled for the first time on the first of June, with 22,000 barrels of fuel. A nearby diesel fuel tank was also destroyed, however, bunkers built around the tanks kept the burning fuel from running into the balance of the tank farm. At the same time, Zero's attacked Fort Glenn on Umnak Island.*

Lieutenant Jonathon Fulbright and three other pilots were able to get their Wildcats into the air when the alarm came in signaling an air raid. Lieutenant Fulbright and his men poured fuel to their engines, racing skyward as quickly as their Wildcats could go. Reaching an altitude of about 4,000 feet, the pilots circled the base waiting for the Japanese that were somewhere out in the darkening sky. When the Zero's broke through the clouds to attack, Lieutenant Fulbright ordered his men to dive on the enemy formation. Quickly, a vicious dog fight broke out, but the Wildcats held their own against the more modern and better-armed Japanese fighters. Dropping down on top of a Zero, Lieutenant Fulbright cut loose with a short burst of machine gun fire. Seconds later the fuel tank on the left side of the fighter exploded, sending the plane into a death spiral over the bay. Moments later Lieutenant Stoneman came up behind a Zero that was attempting to break off his attack on the base. Pouring a long blast of machine gun fire into the bottom of the Zero paid dividends. The left wing broke off as fuel exploded, causing the plane to spin wildly before it also crashed into the bay. Several other Zero's were damaged by the four pilots before the 7 remaining enemy aircraft broke off their attack, heading south toward their carrier. The four Wildcats patrolled the skies around Dutch Harbor, looking for Japanese stragglers until low fuel and darkening skies forced them to land.

Near Dutch Harbor, The *Northwestern*,* a retired naval transport that had been beached and used as housing for contractors, was also set afire. However, crews worked valiantly to put out the fires and save the ship. Additionally, several warehouses and an empty aircraft hangar were destroyed.

At 1821 hours, three horizontal bombers dropped out of the darkening sky, dropping five large bombs, all of which failed to strike a target. At 1825 hours, from a much higher altitude, five more bombers approached from the northwest. It quickly became evident their targets were the ammunition magazines located near the south slope of Mount Ballyhoo. Thankfully, the first nine bombs missed the target completely, but the tenth killed four men in a 20mm gun emplacement.

No one will ever know for sure why Admiral Hosogaya ordered his carriers to turn south after sending off his planes to attack on June 4. However, Pacific Headquarters in Hawaii figured that due to the fact that American airbases on Umnak, Dutch Harbor and Fort Glenn were ready when the attack came, they could easily send out a large number of planes the Japanese carriers were not equipped to repel. Having the carriers turn south when they did, was still costly to the overall Japanese plan. Radio traffic picked up by ground stations in Dutch Harbor overheard several Japanese pilots pleading for the fleet to turn around as they were low on fuel and could not catch up with the retreating task force. Nevertheless, there was no response from the carriers that were maintaining radio silence in order to slip away, in case American bombers were coming out after them. Sadly, American officials at Dutch Harbor and Fort Glenn figured a large number of Japanese bombers and fighters went down when they ran out of fuel over the cold arctic waters, giving the pilots no chance of survival.

In the two days of attacks, Japanese air power killed 42 service men and 1 civilian, leaving 50 men wounded and a large amount of damage on the ground. The Japanese lost 4 planes in combat plus an unknown number due to water landings after the fleet abandoned them.

Slightly to the east, Admiral Theobald's* medium task force code named 'Tare,' consisting of 2 heavy cruisers, 3 light cruisers and 4 destroyers on station in the Gulf of Alaska roughly 400 nautical miles southeast of Kodiak Island, was ordered to stay in place and not attempt to chase down the retreating Japanese carriers. Fears still ran high that the Japanese may attempt to land a large invasion force on the south coast of Alaska, and Pacific Command did not want to be caught flat footed.

The following day, American search aircraft reported Japanese carriers roughly 200 miles southwest of Umnak, making a strike against them possible. However, because of inaccurate information and worsening weather conditions, planes that were sent out were unable to find the enemy carriers, but all returned to base.

Midway Attack

Approximately 0900 hours on June 3, 1942, Ensign Jack Reid,* flying a PBY from search squadron VP44, observed the Japanese invasion force roughly 500 miles west-southwest of Midway. However, he wrongly reported the ships he saw as the main attack force.

With everyone and everything on Midway Island prepared for the Japanese attack, within minutes, 9 B-17's rose into the afternoon sky at 1230 hours, making it the first assault against the attacking Japanese fleet. Some three hours later, they observed Admiral Tanaka's transport group, 570 miles to the west. While preparing to attack the task force, Japanese gunners put up a fierce amount of antiaircraft fire. While attempting to avoid the deadly fire, all the planes dropped their bombs, resulting in no hits against the enemy fleet that was practicing well-coordinated zigzag maneuvers.

With darkness still covering the Pacific Ocean, at 0100 hours, on June 4, 1942, a lone Catalina Flying Boat on patrol dropped its torpedo, striking the oiler *Akebono Maru*.* Remarkably, this was the only successful American aerial torpedo attack of the entire battle.

At 0430 hours, Admiral Nagumo began his first attack against Midway

Island. The flight of aircraft contained 36 dive bombers, 36 torpedo bombers and 36 Zero escort fighters. As soon as those aircraft cleared his decks, he immediately set off 7 search planes. Two from the carriers *Akagi* and *Kaga*, 4 from the heavy cruisers *Tone* and *Chikuma,* and one from the battleship *Haruna.* Due to mechanical difficulties, an eighth plane was launched by the heavy cruiser *Tone* a half hour later.

With the three fleets separated by such a wide expanse of ocean, as prescribed by Yamamoto's attack plan, there was no way eight patrol planes could cover the hundreds of miles of open ocean through the weather conditions that were poor and rapidly deteriorating toward the east.

As dawn broke over the Pacific, American commanders were also preparing for a massive battle against the Japanese forces. At 0430 hours, eleven PBY's were taking to the skies from Midway with well laid out search patterns. Quickly, at 0534 hours, one of the PBY pilots observed 2 Japanese carriers, while at 0544 hours, a second PBY observed the attacking Japanese air armada.

With ground crews on Midway glued to their air search radar screens, at 0556 hours, they sound the air raid sirens. The radar units picked up the attacking planes several miles out from the coast, enabling fighter pilots that had been waiting in their planes to take off and reach proper altitude for an attack. While the fighters were taking to the skies, un-escorted Army bombers left the island, hoping to inflict serious damage on the Japanese carriers. The aircraft that had been assigned to escort the bombers were kept on the island to defend their airspace from the attacking Japanese air armada.

It was just after 0620 hours, when Japanese dive bombers dropped their first bombs on Midway, creating heavy damage. Being prepared for the attack, Major Floyd Parks* took to the air, along with 6 F4F Hellcats and 20 F2A Brewster Buffalos. Slicing into the Japanese formation, the American pilots were able to shoot down 4 torpedo bombers and one Zero fighter before they were decimated by the balance of the Japanese fighters. Unable to defend against the massive onslaught, 2 Hellcats and 13 Brewster Buffalos were shot down. Breaking off from the dog fights, the American pilots dropped down toward the ocean south of Midway Island, hoping the Japanese fighters would stay over Midway instead of giving chase. As the Japanese attack on the island broke off, the surviving pilots worked incredibly hard to get their damaged aircraft back to the airstrip. The returning aircraft had been shot up to the point many of the mechanics were surprised the pilots had been able to keep them in the air long enough to bring them back. After doing a quick check over of the aircraft, only 2 were considered airworthy and able to get back into the air.

However, the new and upgraded American antiaircraft batteries that had been recently installed on the island put up an incredible amount of flak, shooting down two aircraft while damaging several more that broke of their attacks. Although Nagumo's attack force had caused severe damage on the island, out of the 108 planes he had put in the air that morning, 11 were destroyed by American weapons fire, while 3 more had to ditch in the ocean due to serious damage. Fourteen planes that made it back to the carriers were so badly chewed up from antiaircraft fire, they had to be pushed overboard. Another 29 were damaged but were thought to be repairable down on the hangar deck. The Japanese planes capable of returning were back with the fleet by 0641 hours.

The attack that was supposed to neutralize the land-based operations on Midway, had seriously failed. All the runways were still in good operational order, allowing American pilots to land to refuel and rearm their aircraft. Antiaircraft batteries and the coastal defense artillery were all still intact and ready for another attack. Returning pilots made it very clear to Admiral Nagumo that a heavy second strike against the island was going to be needed if he still intended to land the invasion force on June 7.

Although Admiral Nagumo was a crafty strategist, master of shrewd tactics, and a gifted ship handler, he was also somewhat of a Nervous Nelly when it came to losses in men and equipment. He had refused to launch a third strike against Pearl Harbor that would have been a fatal blow, as he was worried about the location of the American Carriers. Now realizing that most of the pilots and aircraft lost in the first attack on Midway were veterans from Pearl Harbor and the Coral Sea made his blood run cold. He understood without a doubt that the loss of so many aircraft in such a short time took away the potency of his carrier task force.

Nagumo loved the sea and loved commanding ships. He was his own man and often disagreed with Yamamoto's plans, and was not afraid to speak out against battle plans he thought were reckless or dangerous. Nevertheless, when he realized he was losing the argument, he quickly adopted the plan being presented and became a team member. For those reasons, Yamamoto respected Nagumo and saw him as a loyal and honest commander that would carry out his orders without hesitation.

A second flight of American heavy bombers that had taken off prior to the Japanese attack were now in position to attack Nagumo's carrier force. The flight consisted of 6 Grumman Avengers, 11 Marine SB2U-3s and 16 SBD dive bombers, along with 4 Air Force B-26 bombers armed with torpedoes, and 15 B-17 heavy bombers. The American air armada was met with stiff resistance by Zero fighters and heavy antiaircraft fire from the task force.

The American armada failed to incur any significant damage to the Japanese fleet while losing 5 TBF's, 2 SB2U and 8 SBD dive bombers and 2 B-26 bombers. During the battle, the Japanese lost 3 Zeros. From the beginning, Nimitz felt the Midway air force would probably not make a huge difference in the battle, but would keep the Japanese commanders nervous and engaged, and he was now accurate.

American Major Lofton R. Henderson* was the first Marine pilot killed in the action. The marines would later name the important airfield on Guadalcanal, Henderson Field in his honor.

One B-26 attempting to avoid additional damage from pursuing Zeros, dropped down to nearly sea level, actually flying the length of the *Akagi's* flight deck, while strafing the ship, killing two sailors. Another damaged B-26 nearly crashed into the bridge of the *Akagi* before cartwheeling into the ocean where it exploded.

During the American second attack, the submarine *Nautilus* fired a torpedo at 0820 hours on a battleship without success, and then had to dive to evade Japanese destroyers. Again, at 0910 hours, the skipper of the *Nautilus* fired another torpedo at a Japanese cruiser without success. Once again, the

Nautilus dove while taking evasive action for quite a long period of time as, the skipper of the destroyer *Arashi* continued to track the elusive sub while dropping depth charges.

Quickly, Murphy's Law of, 'Anything that can go wrong will go wrong,' came into play for Admiral Nagumo, resulting in tragedy. The following will provide context with each piece of the building disaster.

THE RESERVE PLANES: Following Yamamoto's plan for the battle, Nagumo had kept half of his air fleet in reserve. Those reserves consisted of two squadrons of dive bombers and torpedo bombers. It was customary to keep torpedo bombers armed in case any American ships were discovered nearby. Although Yamamoto had strictly prohibited Nagumo from making a second strike against Midway, the crafty old Admiral was still fuming over the near miss attacks against his flagship. So, despite orders, at 0715 hours, he ordered all torpedoes to be removed from the reserve torpedo bombers and be replaced with contact-fused general-purpose bombs, normally used for attacking land-based targets. Since the work was being completed at a frenzied rate on the hangar deck, all the torpedoes removed from those planes were not sent down to the magazines as was protocol. Instead, they were stacked in a corner of the hangar deck.

Meanwhile, the reserve dive bombers were taken up to the flight deck to be armed with their bombs. Arming aircraft on the flight deck takes time, as every bomb needs to be delivered to the flight deck by an elevator, then placed on carts for delivery to waiting aircraft to be mounted.

The chore of arming the planes had been in progress for about half an hour when at 0740 hours, a scout aircraft from the *Tone* sent a message stating it had sighted a large American naval task force to the east, but did not provide a description of what kind of ships were included. For some unknown reason, Nagumo did not receive the message until nearly 0800 hours.

Realizing he had made a terrible mistake out of haste, Nagumo quickly directed his crews to stop what they were doing, remove the general-purpose bombs, and replace them with heavy anti-ship bombs weighing anywhere from 500 to 1000 pounds.

Now the busy crews on the **HANGAR DECK** were removing the general-purpose bombs from the reserve planes and stacking them off to the side so the larger bombs could be installed.

On the **FLIGHT DECK** the general-purpose bombs needed to be sent back down to the magazines. However, down in the magazines, the general-purpose bombs were stacked off to the side, so the larger bombs could now be sent up to the flight deck.

ON THE BRIDGE: The message from the scout plane had not given Nagumo a good description of what ships were in the American carrier force. At about 0830 hours, Nagumo radios the scout plane asking for a description of the ships in the task force. Nearly another 40 minutes passed before the scout plane called back, stating there was one American carrier in the group of ships. The carrier he sighted was from Task Force 16. Because of clouds, he did not see the second carrier.

Nagumo now stood on the bridge, unsure of what his response should be. Quickly, Rear Admiral Tamon Yamaguchi,* who was leading Carrier Division 2 with the carriers *Hiryu* and *Soryu* insisted Nagumo attack immediately, using 16 Aichi dive bombers from the *Soryu* and 18 from the *Hiryu* while using half the cover patrol that were set to launch.

FIRST MIDWAY STRIKE FORCE: The possibility for Nagumo to launch a successful mission against the American fleet was now hampered, as the last planes from his strike force against Midway were beginning to return, and his deck was filled with the **RESERVE PLANES** that were being rearmed.

It was imperative that the **RESERVE PLANES** sitting on the flight deck be returned to the hangar deck with all due speed, so the returning planes being low on fuel would not have to crash land into the ocean. Additionally, all the Zeroes that had been flying cover for the fleet all morning were asking to land at the same time, as they were low on fuel as well. Nagumo decided the fighters should be given top priority as the American fleet was so close by. Now the flight deck was jammed with defensive and offensive planes, all awaiting service sitting in the open.

Down on the **HANGAR DECK**, plane handlers were demanding the **RESERVE PLANES** that were now armed be taken up to the flight deck so they could be launched against the American fleet, but there was no place to put them. It would take nearly half an hour to move the returning **MIDWAY BOMBERS** down to the hangar deck, to make room on the flight deck for the balance of the **RESERVE PLANES.** By now, massive confusion was the order of the day on both decks. Arming crews were scattered between the flight deck and the hangar deck, still attempting to change bombs, while several officers argued they stop arming planes for a carrier strike, and strictly rearm **THE MIDWAY PLANES** for a second attack. Nagumo was caught up in a situation where his immediate staff officers were arguing among themselves as to the proper course of action. He knew if he launched a strike against the carriers as many of his staff demanded, he would be committing some of his best reserves to battle, still armed with hundred pound all-purpose bombs and without the proper fighter cover. But now with his flight deck a tangle of reserve planes, Midway planes and fighter aircraft it was impossible to launch any planes.

Since Japanese naval doctrine clearly called for attacking the enemy forces that clearly represent the most serious threat to the fleet, it became obvious to Nagumo that at this point in time, Midway was the larger threat. He decided since his fleet had been attacked by such a large American land-based bomber group, and his returning pilots were telling him a second strike was needed, that would be the best course of action to follow. However, all of his aircraft that had returned from the first Midway strike were low on fuel and needed to be rearmed. Some were now on the Hangar Deck, others sat on the Flight Deck, while many of the **RESERVE PLANES** sat ready to go after the American carriers, but could not get off the crowded deck.

Nagumo quickly ordered deck crews to give priority to planes that returned from his first Midway strike, and get them all down to the hangar deck as soon as possible for refueling and rearming. He also felt this was a good time to remove bombs from the **RESERVE TORPEDO PLANES** still on the hangar deck and rearm them once again with torpedoes that would be needed in an attack against the American fleet. However, some of the **RESERVE BOMBERS** that had been hastily sent to the hangar deck still contained general purpose bombs and needed to be rearmed with anti-ship bombs, and no one was working on those planes. As quickly as possible those **RESERVE**

PLANES were rolled off to a separate area of the hangar deck, so more **MID-WAY PLANES** could be brought down from the flight deck to alleviate some of the congestion. It was a very confusing situation that threw the usually well-orchestrated Japanese attack system into total disarray, but that was not the end of it.

Watching time tick off the clock allowing the American fleet to move further away, Nagumo's hurried plan was now to hold off on the **MIDWAY PLANES** and get the **RESERVE TORPEDO PLANES** rearmed, moved up onto the flight deck, and into the air. This meant they would be flying off without proper air cover or bomber support. In order for torpedo bombers to attack successfully, it had to be a coordinated attack using high level bombers and fighters. But today, those planes were still sitting on either the hangar deck or on the flight deck and improperly armed. Nagumo and his staff hoped by the time the torpedo planes attacked the American fleet, the bombers would all be rearmed and ready to strike at the American carriers, hopefully already damaged by the torpedo planes. It was an extreme gamble, but it was all they had left. Finally, with all the planes involved in the carrier attack gone, they could once again turn their attention to the **MIDWAY PLANES** for their follow up attack.

What Nagumo did not know was that early morning air patrols from the *Yorktown* had sighted his fleet from a distance, and were able to give Admiral Fletcher a detailed account of what kind of ships were in the Japanese armada, and had provided their exact position. At 0700 hours, both the *Enterprise* and the *Hornet* began launching aircraft for an attack. Although the *Enterprise* and *Hornet* were finished sending off their plane by 0755 hours, Admiral Fletcher on the *Yorktown* didn't want to launch planes until he heard back from his own scout plane to confirm the location of the Japanese fleet. Once that information arrived, Fletcher ordered the planes from the *Yorktown* into the air at 0800 hours, but did not finish launch operations until nearly 0908 hours. Still, American pilots were going to have to fly an hour before reaching their targets, which meant they were going to have to burn a large quantity of fuel, leaving them with much less time over their target than was considered advantageous for a successful attack. Making matters worse was the fact that there was always the possibility that the enemy task force could change course, ever widening the distance attacking pilots would have to fly. It was clear at this point that the Japanese were much better at launching aircraft from carriers than the United States. The Japanese launched 108 aircraft in just seven minutes, while it took the Americans an hour to launch 117.

As the American planes closed in on the Japanese carriers, bedlam continued to reign. Bombs that had been removed from aircraft during the re-arming, were not sent back down to the magazines per directive. Instead, they were placed in piles around the hangar deck. Unused belts of machine gun ammunition were haphazardly strewn on the floor, as crews were attempting to refuel planes. It was reported by survivors that a strong odor of aviation fuel already drifted through the hangar deck as refueling precautions had been over looked.

Admiral Fletcher now became the soul American Admiral to ever launch a total offensive, well-coordinated attack against an opposing force, from the deck of a carrier. He and his staff had earned their bones during the battle of the Coral Sea, but had not had time to pass on all their information to other American commanders before sailing off to Midway, and it was evident. Due to the distance pilots were going to fly, Admiral Spruance ordered his pilots to head directly to the attack sight, without circling overhead to make sure the balance of the planes in the attack force were grouped up properly. His decision was based on the fact that destroying the enemy carriers was essential in preserving his own ships. He felt throwing anything at the enemy as soon as they could, was more important than the overall need for a coordinated attack.

Today, small individual groups of fighters, torpedo bombers, high level bombers and dive bombers were all flying toward the Japanese fleet to make piecemeal attacks. Spruance believed the lack of coordination could diminish the effect of the attack and most likely cost more casualties, but he felt it was better to keep the enemy busy for a longer period of time so they could not bring planes to the flight deck to launch attacks of their own.

Regrettably, American flight crews had problems locating the Japanese fleet, regardless of the position they had been given before flying off the carriers. In fact, Commander Stanhope C. Ring* was given a heading of 265 degrees, when in fact it should have been 240 degrees. Unfortunately, Air Group Eight's dive bombers never found the Japanese fleet at all. The fact that the course was wrong caused the fighters to fly farther than was planned, and before the day was over, 10 F4F fighters from the *Hornet* ran out of fuel and had to ditch their planes in the ocean.

In the operations room where pilots gather before missions, Commander John C. Waldron* had placed a message on the seat for each of his pilots from section Torpedo 8. It read, *"My greatest hope is that we encounter a favorable tactical situation, but if we don't, and the worst comes to worst, I want each of us to do his utmost to destroy our enemies. If there is only one plane left to make a final run-in, I want that man to go in and get a hit. May God be with us all. Good luck, happy landings and give 'em hell."*

Lieutenant Commander John C. Waldron's Torpedo 8, consisting of 15 Devastator torpedo bombers, took to the air on time following the course set by Commander Ring. After flying the course for quite some time and seeing nothing, a dispute raged over the radio between Ring and Waldron as to what the proper heading should be. Ring insisted 265 was the proper setting, while Waldron felt 240 appeared to be more accurate. Believing he was doing the proper thing, Waldron ordered Torpedo 8 to change course to 240, leaving them all alone.

Admiral Spruance paced the bridge of the *Enterprise* as he listened to the radio calls coming in from the air squadrons. After hearing more angry radio calls, he said out loud, "What the hell happened there, we're going to defeat ourselves the way this attack is unfolding. Have we heard from Commander Waldron's flight yet? Has anyone heard a damn thing or do we consider his attack another misdirected operation?"

As Admiral Spruance awaited an answer, Lieutenant Commander Waldron scanned the skies around him looking for any sign of American dive bombers or fighters from the *Hornet*. The six fighters from the *Enterprise* that had been providing air cover had already broken off and flown back to the carrier due to lack of fuel. Waldron knew making a full out torpedo attack without coordination from dive bombers and fighters was one step short of suicide. However, realizing his squadron was now all alone, had already flown unnecessary miles burning way too much precious fuel, and may never make it back to the *Hornet* if they did not attack, Waldron decided it was now or never.

Spruance smiled, but was also very concerned when he heard Waldron call out from 4,000 feet, "Directly below us boys, tallyho!"

Immediately, all 15 pilots from Torpedo 8 began their attack runs against the Japanese carriers. Since Japanese gunners did not have to concern themselves with dive bombers or fighters, every gun in the task force was directed at the slow-moving Devastators. One after another the torpedo bombers fell out of the sky or exploded in midair while attempting to launch their weapons.

Within minutes, every plane from Torpedo 8 was gone without damaging any Japanese ships. The only man to survive the attack was Ensign George H. Gay, Jr.* He had been able to complete his torpedo run against the Carrier *Shoho* before his plane went down. However, skillful ship handling by the commander of the *Shoho* had eliminated any chance for a direct hit.

At the same time, aircraft from the *Enterprise* were now in the battle, but were not fairing much better. Torpedo Squadron 6, commanded by Lieutenant Commander Eugene E. Lindsey,* went after the carrier *Hiryu*. In a wild melee, he lost 9 of his 14 Devastators.

Torpedo Squadron 3 from the *Yorktown* arrived at the Japanese fleet at 1010 hours. Ten out of twelve Devastators also went down into the ocean. Although many torpedoes launched by pilots from the *Enterprise* and the *Yorktown* slammed into Japanese ships, none exploded.

While the Japanese fighters were attempting to attack the planes from Torpedo Squadron 3, the skies were clear of fighters as three bomber groups arrived over the fleet. The problem was bomber squadrons VB-6 and VF-3, under the command of Air Group Commander Wade McClusky,* had been wasting precious time with Commander Ring before McClusky broke off and went in search of the fleet by himself, so they were getting seriously short on fuel. McClusky was about ready to tell his pilots to head back to the carriers, when he spotted the wake of the Japanese destroyer *Arashi*. The skipper of the

Arashi had broken off from the main fleet to chase down the *Nautilus* once again, but had been unable to sink her.

Although several of McClusky's planes were ditching due to lack of fuel, the commander felt following the *Arashi* would lead them directly to the fleet. It could not have been planned any better, as McClusky's VB-6 and VF-3 arrived over the fleet, by sheer luck VS-6 from the Enterprise also arrived over the target at nearly the same altitude.

Down below, plane handlers on the Japanese carriers were attempting to assemble their strike aircraft in the proper order on the flight decks. Fueling crews were still busy pumping fuel into waiting aircraft, and none of the bombs or torpedoes that had been stacked around the hangar decks had yet been moved back down to the magazines. As heavy fumes from loaded and spilled aviation fuel still hung heavy in the air of the hangar deck, the carriers were floating bombs just waiting to be detonated.

By 1020 hours, everything was in place for the American attack that would change the course of the war. Two squadrons from the *Enterprise* air group split with the intention of having one group attack the *Kaga* while the other half attack the *Akagi*. However, once again a mistake with communications sent both groups of planes after the carrier *Kaga*. Realizing too many planes were going after the *Kaga*, Lieutenant Richard H. Best,* along with his two wing men, quickly changed course and headed north, preparing to attack the *Akagi*.

From 1022 – 1024 hours, there just was not enough ocean for the ship handler of the *Kaga* to maneuver his ships as bombs from nearly two full squadrons of planes descended upon her. Within seconds, five direct hits by large bombs created massive damage while starting huge fires below decks. Another bomb struck directly in front of the bridge, killing Captain Jisaku Okada* and all the ship's top officers.

Lieutenant Clarence Dickenson* stated, *"We were coming down in all directions on the port-side of the carrier. I recognized her as the Kaga; and it was enormous. To say the least the target was utterly satisfying. I saw a bomb hit just behind where I was aiming. I watched the deck rippling and curling back in all directions exposing a great section of the hangar deck below. I watched my 500-*

pound bomb hit right abreast of the carriers island. The two 100-pound bombs struck in the forward area of the parked and readied planes."

As flames and smoke rose from the massive explosions now tearing the *Kaga* apart, Lieutenant Best and his wing men dove straight for the *Akagi*. Mitsuo Fuchida, the senior pilot that led the attack on Pearl Harbor, was once again on the *Akagi* during the Midway battle. Watching the attack unfold, he said, *"A look-out screamed, "Hell Divers!" I looked up to see three black enemy planes plummeting towards our ship. Some of our machine guns managed to fire a few frantic bursts at them, but it was too late. The plump silhouettes of the American Dauntless dive-bombers quickly grew larger, and then a number of black objects suddenly floated eerily from their wings.*"

Incredibly, at 1026 hours, as just one of those bombs struck the *Akagi*, the bomb landed at the edge of the mid-ship aircraft elevator, then plunged into the upper hangar deck, where it detonated. Parked near the spot where the bomb exploded, were several armed and fueled planes that added to the massive conflagration that could not be stopped. Explosion after explosion rocked the flagship, as piles of improperly stored bombs and torpedoes tore the ship apart.

Nagumo's Chief of Staff Ryunosuke Kusaka* stated, *"There was a terrific fire and there were bodies all over the place. Planes stood tail up as massive flames and thick black smoke made it impossible to bring the fires under control. Another bomb exploded underwater very close astern; the resulting geyser bent the flight deck upward in a grotesque configuration creating crucial rudder damage.*"

Observing the massive damage already inflicted on the *Kaga* and *Akagi*, Commander Max Leslie* of Yorktown's Squadron VB-3 decided to turn his squadrons attention on the *Soryu*. Three separate hits created a tremendous amount of damage. Once again, aviation gasoline and collected fumes exploded, setting off bombs and torpedoes that had been left out in the open on the hangar deck. Quickly, the ship became a roaring inferno. Several torpedo planes from the *Enterprise's* VT-3 attempted to make an attack on the carrier *Hiryu* that was surrounded by the burning carriers, but was not able to make a direct hit.

Officers on the *Akagi* claimed Nagumo was nearly in a state of shock as he looked out the windows of the bridge, watching his carriers burn. Although many officers on the *Akagi* told Nagumo he needed to abandon ship, he ignored their requests or stated it was not yet time. Admiral Kusaka was finally able to convince Nagumo to leave his beloved *Akagi*, as it was now impossible for crews to save the flag ship of the fleet. At 1046 hours, Nagumo and his staff transferred the Admiral and his flag to the light cruiser *Nagara*. At 1050 hours, Nagumo radioed Yamamoto that out-of-control fires raged on the *Kaga, Soryu* and *Akagi*, and the only operational carrier left was the *Hiryu.*

Amazingly, in merely six minutes, the *Soryu* and *Kaga* were blazing infernos from end to end, as roaring fires spread below decks with no possible way to extinguish them. After being struck by just a single bomb, the *Akagi* suffered much the same fate as the other carriers.

Realizing none of his carriers had received heavy damage below the water line, Nagumo hoped he could tow the *Akagi,* if not all the damaged ships back to Japan to be repaired. After receiving complete damage reports on all the carriers, the decision was made to scuttle them lest they fall into the hands of the American Navy and be taken back to the United States as trophies.

Although the bulk of the Japanese punch had been sent to the bottom of the Pacific, there was no way anyone could count out the possibility of an attack by the *Hiryu.* With vengeance on their mind, the crew of the *Hiryu* quickly began to line up aircraft for an attack against the American fleet. At 1058 hours, the first attack consisting of 18 dive bombers, along with 6 fighters, took to the air, staying far enough behind the retreating American planes so they would not be detected. A little over an hour later, the lead pilots observed the *Yorktown.*

As the alarm signaling an attack was sounded on the *Yorktown,* Cooper looked over at Scott who was scanning the sky with his binoculars. "We're in for it now, my friend. Get yourself ready, this is going to be a rough ride."

Putting down the binoculars, Scott nodded his head, "I'm afraid your right, Coop. These bastards are going to be out for blood. Just aim that damn thing straight and I'll keep you loaded."

At 1201 hours, the sky to the west became dotted with small black specs roaring in at about 5,000 feet. The closer they came, the bigger they became making, Cooper's heart beat faster and faster. Suddenly, the air above the *Yorktown* was filled with both attacking Japanese planes and American fighters, doing their best to repel the enemy aircraft.

Cooper was already hammering away at the multiple targets that were now in range of his cannon. He watched one dive bomber drop down out of formation after being hit by flak from the *Yorktown's* five-inch guns. Swinging his 20mm cannon toward the north, Cooper captured the wounded plane in his sights. Depressing the trigger, his sturdy weapon fired nonstop in the direction of the wounded plane. He could see pieces of metal being torn from the left wing, as the pilot attempted to climb higher to avoid more damage. Just as Cooper ran out of ammunition, the plane rolled over on its side and dove into the ocean. Scott cheered as he slammed a fresh drum onto the smoking weapon. Quickly, Cooper raised his weapon to its fullest azimuth and began firing at the diving aircraft above the *Yorktown*.

Suddenly, the *Yorktown* shuddered as a large bomb struck the flight deck, penetrating several decks below before exploding. Flames, smoke, and debris rolled skyward from the huge hole in the flight deck, but Cooper continued firing at the attacking planes. Moments later, another explosion rocked the *Yorktown*, as a second bomb struck the flight deck. This hit was much closer to the gun deck where Cooper's cannon was located. He could feel the heat of the explosion on the back of his neck, as shrapnel rained down on his steel helmet. Moments later, a third bomb struck the *Yorktown*, falling straight down through a hole in the deck of the carrier. Everyone on the gun deck could feel the bomb detonating somewhere deep inside the *Yorktown*, directly below their position. The explosion made the hair on the back of Cooper's neck stand up, as a chill rushed over his body. He knew instinctively that the *Yorktown* had taken some serious blows that could send her to the bottom, but as long as Scott could keep reloading, he would keep firing.

It was hard to believe with all the flak in the air that any enemy planes could penetrate the wall of steel and rampaging Wildcats, but several minutes later, a fourth bomb struck the flight deck. The massive bomb detonated immediately as it struck. Sections of the flight deck rose into the air, throwing huge shards of red-hot steel in every direction.

Cooper screamed, as he felt something extremely hot rip into his right shoulder. Taking his fingers off the trigger, Cooper leaned forward, attempting to catch his breath as he felt blood run down his back. Angry that he had been wounded, he yelled out. "Kiss my ass, you son-of-a-bitches!"

Re-cocking the gun, Cooper once more began firing at another dive bomber that was attempting to drop down alongside the ship. The pilot had dropped his bomb which ended up hitting the water, just a few feet short of the burning vessel. Now he was hoping to skim low along the water, in a risky attempt to escape the wall of flak. But Cooper had him set up perfectly in his sights. The plane was so close to the ship that Cooper and Scott could see the face of the nervous pilot looking back at them. Slamming his hands down on the trigger, the men were able to see the rounds rip the canopy of the bomber, killing the rear gunner instantly. Seconds later, a round from Cooper's cannon ripped a hole in the fuselage, directly behind the pilot, decapitating the bomb spotter. As rounds from the powerful weapon continued tearing into the plane, the body of the pilot slumped forward, nosing the plane over. The propeller shattered when it struck the water, throwing pieces skyward seconds before the plane exploded. The rear stabilizer assembly floated on the surface for several moments, before it joined the rest of the plane and crew on the bottom of the ocean.

By now, the *Yorktown* had lost power and was gliding slowly forward to a stop. The last bomb, hitting so far astern of the *Yorktown*, had done a tremendous amount of damage to the boilers. Crews were only able to keep one boiler going, but it was just not enough to propel the massive carrier.

As clouds of smoke billowed from the three holes in the flight deck, the *Yorktown* began to take on a serious list to port. That meant that shortly, it was going to make the port side antiaircraft guns unusable, as they would no longer be able to raise their barrels high enough to engage enemy planes. Realizing the port side guns were pretty much out of action, a dive bomber pilot dropped down low above the water, paralleling the massive burning ship. The rear gunner was strafing every gun position on the port gun deck. However, Cooper and one other 20mm battery were still able to bring their barrels up just enough to engage the attacking plane. A flurry of 20mm rounds tore into the plane as it was streaking by the ship. Pieces of the engine bonnet were ripped from the plane by the stream of nonstop cannon rounds.

After Scott placed a new drum of ammunition on Cooper's gun, he turned and ran back toward the ammunition hoist to retrieve another drum that was just coming up to the gun deck. As he bent over to pick it up, a machine gun round from the Japanese rear gunner struck Cooper's weapon. The fresh drum of ammunition exploded, ripping out the receiver of Cooper's cannon. The blast threw Scott to the floor, throwing him up against the short bulkhead. Although still shaken from the hard landing, Scott looked in horror over toward Cooper who was slumped forward on his weapon with blood covering his face, arms and chest as his clothes burned.

Staggering forward, Scott grabbed a chemical fire extinguisher and began spraying Cooper's clothing, as Cy Brewster the loader from the adjacent 20mm mount, attempted to pull Cooper away from the damaged, smoking cannon. With the fires extinguished, Scott and Cy pulled Cooper up to the damaged flight deck and laid him down. Scott looked in every direction, hoping to see a corpsman, but it appeared now that only the dead occupied the flight deck. Taking in a full breath of air, Scott yelled, "Corpsman! I need a corpsman over here, now!"

However, with all the continuing explosions and roaring fires, it would have been a miracle for anyone to have heard him. Turning back toward Cooper, he saw Cy placing his hand over Cooper's mouth checking for breathing. "He's still alive, Scott. Where the hell do we take him? He's in tough shape and lost a lot of blood already!"

Scott shook his head as he was trying to think of what to do next for his best friend. "Cy, I'll stay with Coop. Go see if you can make your way into the island and find someone who can help us."

Cy looked at the holes in the flight deck where huge walls of churning orange flames and thick black smoke were rolling skyward. After looking down at Cooper one more time, he yelled, "Keep him alive, I'll be right back!"

Without another moment of thought, Cy jumped up and ran across the ever-increasing tilt of the flight deck toward the island. Reaching the first water tight door, Cy realized it had been dogged down from the inside and there was no way he could open it. Running around to the rear of the island, Cy found that door closed but not dogged down. Entering the island, Cy ran up the ladder toward the bridge as quickly as he could. Half way there, he ran into a Lieutenant Commander that was headed down into the ship. The angry officer looked at Cy, yelling, "Don't you know where you're supposed to be sailor, because if you—"

Before he could finish, Cy cut him off, "I need a medic, sir, and I need one now. Do you know where I can find one!"

Shaking his head, the officer replied, "I don't know. The dispensary and hospital were destroyed by the second bomb, and I saw two of them get killed on the flight deck by the third bomb. Odds are good there isn't a damn one left alive. There are probably hundreds of wounded men all over this ship that need help, and no one left to help them. Do whatever you can do, because we're going to abandon ship shortly." That being said, the Lieutenant Commander brushed past Cy, disappearing down inside the smoking carrier.

As Cy turned to exit the bridge, he heard planes from the *Hiryu* circling back to strike again, strafing the *Yorktown*. Opening the door slightly to take a look, Cy could see the route back to Cooper was now in even worse shape than it was a few minutes earlier, but he wanted to let Scott know what was happening. Stepping out on the deck, Cy closed the door and began running back toward Scott when a bullet from a passing Zero struck him, shattering his pelvis and left hip.

Scott had seen the Zero dropping down from the sky at an incredible speed, preparing to strafe the *Yorktown* one more time. He knew he could not move Cooper, so he threw his body across his best friend, to avoid having him wounded again. He could hear the machine gun bullets ricocheting off the steel deck as the plane dropped down to about twenty feet above the burning carrier. Suddenly, Scott felt his right leg burn as shrapnel from the disintegrating shells tore into his flesh. As the plane flew off, Scott looked down at his pant leg and saw blood in several places.

Laying on the hot deck, Cy rolled in agony, as tears ran down his face. He never thought he would be the one to get hit, and now here he was, all alone without a medic to help him. But no matter how much he was hurting, he knew his injuries weren't life threatening, but Cooper's definitely were. With every bit of strength he could muster, he began crawling across the burning hot deck, past the gaping holes where super-heated air rolled sky ward. He choked on the thick acrid smoke as he continued sliding a few feet at a time until he could see Scott attempting to cover Cooper from the strafing enemy planes.

After what felt like an eternity, Cy crawled up to Scott, screaming when he attempted to take hold of Scott's arm. Looking at his hands, he was stunned. As he had used his hands to pull his way across the incredibly hot steel deck, they had been burned horribly, and now reassembled raw meet.

Scott took hold of Cy and cried out, "What the hell did you do? Oh God, Cy, what the hell happened?" Shaking his head in disbelief that all three of them were now wounded, he yelled at the top of his lungs. "Help! Need a medic over here! Help us for God's sake!"

Cy looked up at Scott with fearful eyes. "Sounds like the medics are all dead and, the hospital was blown up. There's nothing we can do for anyone, and now your hit, too. What the hell is going to happen to us, Scott? I don't want to die this way."

As Cy stopped speaking and laid down on the hot deck, a Chief Petty Officer came up from the gun deck. Looking down at the three wounded men, he yelled, "God damn it, what the hell am I supposed to do now? The call just came to abandon ship. Most of the rafts on the port side have been torn up by strafing. I've been telling everyone to get in the water and swim toward the destroyers coming along side. But I don't know what to do with you guys." After kneeling down by Cooper to assess the situation, the chief shook his head. Looking up at Scott, his pant leg pretty well soaked in blood, he said. "This guy is done, he'll never survive a transfer to a destroyer. Leave him here and we can help you and your other friend. Come on now, let's get moving in case this damn ship takes on any more water and decides to roll over and take us all down with it!"

Scott grabbed the petty officer by the arm. "I'm not leaving Cooper behind! I'll find a way to get him off the ship myself, and you can just get the hell out of the way!"

"Fine, the three of you will just end up dying, but I'm not going down with this damn ship!" In a second, he was back down on the gun deck, heading toward the stern of the *Yorktown*.

Scott looked at Cy who had now passed out beside Cooper, realizing he would need to decide which man to save, and which man would die today.

After Admiral Fletcher had ordered abandon ship at 1455 hours, he and his staff were transferred to the heavy cruiser *Astoria*, off the starboard side of the *Yorktown*.

Now, three destroyers were sailing close off the port side, taking on any crew members from the *Yorktown* that could make it. To Scott, the situation was incredibly painful. The destroyers were so close, he could hear the officers yelling out orders, but with Cooper and Cy unable to help in their rescues, those damn destroyers might just as well be sitting at the south pole.

Painfully standing up, Scott hobbled over to the gun deck, to see who might be left that could help him. A second later the petty officer, holding several blankets and a large first aid kit, grabbed Scott by the arm. "Sit down and let me bandage your leg as best we can before we get into the water. There's enough stuff here to bandage your friends burned hands before we put him in the blankets but I don't have much to help your other friend. We just have to get him to a destroyer and quick. I've got four more men on the way that will help get them off the ship if you still want my help?"

Scoot looked up at the chief, saying, "I didn't think God would let you go over the side and leave us here."

As the petty officer finished taping the bandages over Scott's injuries, he said. "Yeah, well don't tell the padre that when you see him. He'll get all gushy and crap, thinking he finally broke me."

No matter how bad the situation was, Scott had to laugh, as he carefully stood up once again. "I promise, chief, your secret is safe with me."

Seconds later, four men from a five-inch gun mount located near the stern of the *Yorktown,* arrived with several wooden poles. They quickly made two rather solid stretchers and laid them on the deck. Cy was drifting in and out of consciousness and was able to help the men move him onto the blanket before passing out again. On the other hand, Cooper completely woke up as the men attempted to move him. The pain was so intense he cried out loudly as he shook violently. Reaching into the first aid kit, the chief pulled out a morphine syrette jabbing it into Coopers thigh. As soon as he had settled down somewhat, the men began moving the homemade stretchers toward the side of the ship. Being extremely careful, the men lowered Cy and Cooper off the ship into the warm water of the south pacific. As soon as the salt water hit Cy' s hands, he screamed and fought his rescuers with every ounce of energy left in his body. The chief searched the bag, but he couldn't find another morphine syrette. Although the salt water made Scott's leg burn as if he were in an oven, he paddled over to Cy as best he could, grabbing onto him, "Cy, listen to me, listen! In just a few minutes you'll be on a destroyer and out of the water. But if you continue to struggle it will take a whole lot longer."

Cy turned to face Scott. "Oh God, my hands they hurt so much, and it feels like someone is poking a hot iron into my leg. Help me, Scottie, please!" Cy yelled and begged as tears rolled down his face.

Scott nodded his head, "Just a little more, Cy. Just a little more and we'll be home free. Just a little more, Cy, you can do this, I promise."

About a minute later, three sailors from the destroyer USS *Benham** dropped down into the water to help bring the injured men on board. Five minutes later, both Cy and Cooper lay on the mid-deck of the destroyer. One of the ships corpsmen knelt down with Cy. Quickly, he and an assistant placed an ointment on his badly burned hands, then wrapped them in gauze. Looking down at the twisted and shattered hip, he took a syrette of morphine from his kit and slammed it into Cy's thigh.

Looking at Scott, he said, "We'll let that work for a few minutes and see how he does." Kneeling down beside Cooper, he shook his head. "This man is in shock. He's lost a lot of blood and needs a surgeon. There isn't much we can do for him now. He needs to get to a carrier where they have a surgical team, but I'm not sure he'll survive that long. We can't transfer wounded until the attack ends."

After crew members took Cy and Cooper down to a lower deck, another corpsman took Scott off to the side, cut his pant leg off nearly up to his crotch, wiped off the water and poured sulfa into the wounds before applying new bandages. "Look, we've got a lot to do tonight, so come down to the dispensary in the morning and we can try and get some of the shrapnel out of your leg. Some of it will probably require surgery once we get you to a carrier, but you'll be alright.

After the corpsman left, Scott sat on the deck of the *Benham* and looked over toward the *Yorktown*. Unbelievably, some fire crews had refused to abandon ship staying on board. Through sheer tenacity they were beginning to get control of many of the fires. Repair crews that had stayed with the fire fighters were now attempting to patch the flight deck, so returning aircraft had a place to land, regardless of the list. By late afternoon, two more boilers were working at fifty percent power. Captain Buckmaster returned to the *Yorktown* with some of his staff and brought his ship back to an unbelievable 19 knots. No one would have guessed the *Yorktown* could have survived what she had gone through, but the real question was could she make it back to Pearl Harbor, as they were 1500 miles away.

Over the next half hour, several planes from the *Yorktown* cautiously set back down on their ship. There were no elevators to lower planes to the hangar deck, but the maintenance decks were pretty much gutted out anyway. Many of the survivors aboard the *Benham** stood and cheered as they watched the *Yorktown* begin to function as a warship, regardless of the severe beating she had taken.

But the worst was yet to come for the valiant carrier. About 90 minutes after the *Yorktown* had regained momentum, a second strike from the *Hiryu* descended upon her.

This attack squadron consisted of 10 torpedo bombers and 6 fighter aircraft. In short order, 2 Japanese long lance torpedoes had blown holes in the hull. The *Yorktown* took on a 23-degree list to port, with all her boilers put out of action by salt water.

With heavy antiaircraft fire from the destroyers that were still nearby, and fighters from the *Enterprise*, the second attack from the *Hiryu* cost the Japanese 5 torpedo planes and 2 fighters.

As the remaining planes returned to the *Hiryu*, a scout plane from the *Yorktown* that had been able to refuel on the *Enterprise* and get back in the air, followed the retreating planes back toward their carrier. As soon as he found the *Hiryu,* the pilot radioed back the exact location of the last Japanese carrier. That was just the information Spruance was looking for. Since he'd been hoping to find the last Japanese carrier before the end of the day, he already had armed and fueled planes on the decks of the *Enterprise* and *Hornet* so they were ready to go. Minutes later they were in the air.

On the *Hiryu,* elated pilots insisted they had attacked an undamaged carrier, putting it out of commission, but were not sure of the name of the ship. So now, Japanese officials were positive they had sunk two American carriers, and were sure only one more American carrier existed in the entire Pacific. It made sense to Yamamoto to put together whatever type of attack force they could to sink America's last carrier. As there had been some delay in waiting to hear back from Yamamoto, the planes sat on the flight deck of the carrier, waiting to be serviced and armed.

Once again, the Japanese were caught off guard during arming and fueling. Out of the northeast came the biggest American air armada of the day. It consisted of 24 dive bombers from the *Enterprise* and *Hornet,* and 14 from the *Yorktown* that had taken refuge on the *Enterprise.*

Flying SBD 1386 from the *Enterprise,* Lieutenant White, with his spotter Ensign Wesley Evans, were amazed at the air armada that was flying toward the *Hiryu.* It was bigger than anything they had seen before. Lieutenant White's adrenaline was pumping full speed as he hoped to be able to put his 500-pound bomb directly on the flight deck of the enemy carrier. He had lost several friends today, and now he wanted to repay the Japanese and their war Gods.

Looking down from the canopy, off in the distance they could see the Japanese carriers streaming thick black smoke before they made their final plunge to the bottom of the deep ocean.

Several minutes later, the flight leader gave the flight crews orders to line up for their attack. Quickly, Lieutenant White moved the 1386 into formation, being the fifth plane that would drop down on the elusive carrier. Moments later, Commander Grainger gave the order to attack. One by one, the dive bombers dropped out of formation, dropping down from 6,000 feet toward the surface of the ocean. Lieutenant White listened intently to every course change Ensign Evans gave him as they hurled down toward the *Hiryu* at an incredible speed. It was evident that at least one of the pilots in front of him had struck the carrier, as thick black smoke was already rolling skyward from a fire on board.

At 3,500 feet, the aircraft lined up on the deck of the *Hiryu* were easy to make out and made a perfect aiming sight for his bomb. However, the pilot of the SBD in front of Lieutenant White had the same idea. As his 500-pound bomb struck the aft section of the *Hiryu,* a massive explosion sent parts of planes flying off the deck, as fuel tanks and explosives detonated. Quickly, Lieutenant White told Ensign Evans to aim slightly in front of the burning planes where another group was parked and still untouched. Just as Lieutenant White released his bomb, shrapnel from an antiaircraft shell tore through the thin wall of his SBD, ripping into his left leg. Clenching his jaw shut tightly to help with the pain, the lieutenant threw his stick over to the right, to begin making his move to escape the gathering flak storm.

The SBD's engine sputtered once as he began leveling off at 300 feet, just as an explosion on the *Hiryu* sent a shock wave off in every direction. The SBD bounced as Ensign Evans screamed on the intercom. "Holy shit, sir, our bomb penetrated the flight deck before detonating. You need to get turned so you can see the flames rolling from that ship. It's incredible!"

Lieutenant White forced a smile as he attempted to wrap a tourniquet around his leg made from a long neck scarf he always kept in the cockpit. With the bleeding slowed, the lieutenant poured more fuel to his engine while pulling back on his stick, attempting to bring the damaged aircraft back to 3,000 feet.

Taking a deep breath, he said, "Evans, I'm hit. Flak tore open my left leg and I'm bleeding pretty good. I'm not waiting for the rest of the squadron, we're heading home right now. Call the *Enterprise* and let them know we're coming home a bit early and that I'm wounded."

Instantly, Ensign Evans sent the message to the *Enterprise* as sweat poured down his face. Looking down at the deep dark blue water below the damaged plane, Ensign Evans said to his lieutenant, "Damn, we're well out ahead of the rest of the attack force, if we go down there won't be anybody to mark our position for a rescue. We could die out in the middle of the Pacific and never be seen again."

Lieutenant White nodded his head, "You're right as rain on that thought, Evans. Now, start giving us some positive thoughts and get us home. Did you get that message sent?"

Nodding his head, the ensign replied, "Message sent, Lieutenant, they're going to be ready for us. How are you doing up there?"

After swallowing hard, Lieutenant White replied, "I'm okay right now, just keep talking to me, tell me your life story, or all about your mom's apple pie, or anything else that will keep my mind on what the hell I'm supposed to be doing up here."

Just as Ensign Evans prepared to speak, the engine on the 1386 coughed again and then sputtered several times before restarting. Shaking his head, Ensign Evans said, "Must be a Studebaker product, Lieutenant. Nothing to worry about, they can be a bit finicky at times. Did I ever tell you about the Studebaker I had right out of high school? Well, let me..."

Lieutenant White had to smile, as he'd had no idea what kind of a joker his spotter was. He knew the story was total nonsense, but was worth listening to for the humor. As the plane droned on with an intermittent cough, the ensign rambled on about cars and girlfriends, non-stop. Finally, the lieutenant could see the outline of two carriers cruising along the ocean about six miles to the northeast. Placing his hand on his radio mic, he said. "Gray Goose, this is 1386 coming in with battle damage and my left leg is in tough shape. Can I have the whole deck?"

Seconds later, the landing officer on the *Enterprise* responded, "The deck is yours, 1386, bring her in."

The problem was, every time Lieutenant White squared himself away to land, the engine would sputter, throwing him out of his approach lane. It was reassuring to hear the landing officer he knew so well giving him instructions and encouragement as he approached the carrier. When he pulled the lever to lower his landing gear, he knew he was in trouble as the lever appeared to be jammed.

Keying his mic, Lieutenant White said. "Hate to tell you this gray goose, but my landing gear handle doesn't work. I'm going to come in on my belly, nothing I can do about it."

The landing officer replied, "When I tell you to cut your engine, do it right away. I'd rather have a free-wheeling prop than a powered prop when you land."

Several seconds went by and the carrier was dead ahead of the crippled plane when the order came to kill his engine. With the power off, the 1386 dropped slightly, but not enough to foul up the landing. Lieutenant White held tightly to the stick as he counted: one thousand one, one thousand two, one thousand three, and the plane dropped down onto the carrier. Sparks flew as the prop tore itself to pieces. The sound of the skidding grinding plane scared the hell out of Lieutenant White and Ensign Evans. Moments later, the careening aircraft was stopped by the crash net.

Ensign Evans threw his canopy back and jumped from the cockpit. Grabbing hold of Lieutenant White's canopy, he pulled it back and removed the seat harness that held him in place. As he pulled him from the cockpit, medics arrived with a basket. After Lieutenant White was taken down to the hospital, a six-man crew tossed the 1386 overboard. After a quick sweeping of debris, the landing officer told the balance of the squadron that he had a ready deck for them.

Ensign Evans went down to the hangar deck, where he sat down on a stool near the rear corner of the shop. He sat quietly as he watched his hands shake like they never had before. Leaning back against the bulkhead, he slowly drifted off to sleep.

Although the *Hiryu* had launched 12 fighters to protect their last carrier, the American pilots pressed home their attack, undaunted by the Zeros. In a matter of minutes, five large bombs penetrated the flight deck of the *Hiryu*, while setting fire to every plane that was sitting on the flight deck and the hangar deck. The *Hiryu* quickly became a blazing wreck, incapable of any flight operations.

Admiral Fletcher was happy about the attack on the *Hiryu*, but desperately wanted to go after the balance of the Japanese surface fleet. After looking at the lateness of the afternoon combined with the gathering clouds, he decided against it and directed the task force to turn to the northeast and call it a day.

Midway Operations June 6, 1942

Approximately 0215 hours on the morning of the fifth, under heavy cloud cover and thick mist, the skipper of the submarine USS *Tambor** discovered ships 100 miles west of Midway Island, but couldn't be sure who's they were and didn't want to take a chance of moving closer. So, he radioed the message that he had found 'four large ships,' but couldn't identify what types of ships they were. The report went first to Admiral Robert English,* overall commander of the Pacific submarine force. He sent the message to Admiral Nimitz who was unhappy with the vagueness of the report, and sent it on to Spruance.

Spruance blew up when he received the message as it gave him no idea as to how he should respond. After much discussion with Admiral Fletcher, they felt what was reported by the *Tambor* was the main body of the Midway invasion force. So, the decision was made to block the invasion force, staying roughly 100 miles from Midway.

What the skipper of the *Tambor* had actually seen were the 4 cruisers and 2 destroyers Yamamoto decided to send to Midway to bombard it late on the fourth. However, at 0255 hours on the fifth, the task force received orders from Yamamoto to pull back.

Being in the middle of Japanese ship movements, the skipper of the *Tambor* continued looking for more of the Japanese fleet. It didn't take long for the submarine to be discovered by two Japanese cruisers, the *Mogami** and the *Mikuma** Focused on using protocols to avoid submarine attacks, the two ships accidentally ran into one another, creating serious damage to the bow of the *Mogami*. The skipper of the *Mikuma*, immediately slowed his vessel so he could stay with the *Mogami* in case they had an urgent need for assistance.

At approximately 0412 hours, the skipper of the *Tambor* rose to the surface to see if weather conditions had cleared up enough so he could now clearly identify every ship around him. Wanting to avoid further enemy contact, the *Tambor* once again went down to periscope depth as he trailed the two damaged ships. He fired torpedoes, but again, the Mark 13's failed to operate properly, so he broke off his attack and radioed the position of the damaged ships. Planes from Midway and the *Enterprise* sent off attacks to find the slow moving enemy vessels.

On the Enterprise Ensign Evans was assigned to the back seat of SBD 1897, flown by Lieutenant Winthrop. His spotter had been killed a week earlier by a bullet that had come through his canopy. Wanting to destroy more of the Japanese fleet, Admiral Fletcher quickly established an attack group to seek out any straggling ships. About 0600 hours, the attack group launched into the gray skies as rain squalls spread around much of the nearby ocean. About an hour later, the lead plane called out the position of the two cruisers, making only about twelve knots.

Several planes went after the damaged *Mogami,* while Lieutenant Winthrop chose the *Mikuma.* Clouds and increasing rain made lining up the cruiser a problem for Ensign Evans, but he set up his bomb aiming sight on the rear main deck battery that housed three 155mm guns. With the weather the way it was, Lieutenant Winthrop decided to do more of a glide bombing attack than an overall dive bombing. After making a second swing around the twisting cruiser, Lieutenant Winthrop began his dive from the stern of the ship. Ensign Evans was glued to his scope as the 1897 bore down on the cruiser, as antiaircraft fire raced up toward the attacking SBD. Just as Ensign Evans told the lieutenant to release his bombs at 1500 feet, several sharp pieces of shrapnel ripped through the side of the SBD, striking the ensign. After dropping his bomb that struck beside the 155-gun mount, Lieutenant Winthrop rolled hard to starboard and dropped down to about 300 feet, attempting to escape any more flack. Looking in his mirror, he said, "Ensign, how bad are you? We took some serious hits, but I'm not sure what condition we are in."

Attempting to hold a battle dressing against his shoulder, Ensign Evans responded. "Left shoulder and below the left knee, both hit. Get me back home, sir."

While the *Mikuma* was sunk by dive bombers, the skipper of the *Mogami* was able to duck in and out of storm squalls to save his ship. He brought her back to Japan where it was repaired. During aerial attacks on the *Mogami,* both the destroyers *Arashio** and the *Asahio** were attacked, receiving moderate damage requiring them to return to Japan's ship repair yards.

Keeping the damaged SBD at 3,000 feet, Lieutenant Winthrop prayed to find the *Enterprise*, knowing his spotter was seriously hurt and his aircraft had been damaged. The 1897 was handling poorly, with a tendency to pull toward the right, something his trusted plane had never done before. Looking back in the mirror, Lieutenant Winthrop could see his copilot had passed out and was bleeding badly. After breaking through two small rain squalls, the lieutenant forced a small smile as he saw the *Enterprise* task force off to his right. After making a quick course correction, he called out on the radio. "Gray goose, this is 1897 coming in with severe battle damage and a seriously wounded copilot. Request permission for a straight on approach and landing."

Seconds later, the air control officer from the *Enterprise* responded. "Rubber ducks, we have turned into the wind already to accept your landing, but are riding six-to-ten foot swells with a deck wind of twenty-five knots. Will that work for you, 1897, or do you want to ditch? Destroyers standing by."

Not happy with the conditions down at sea level, Lieutenant Winthrop had to make a serious decision in a matter of seconds. Taking one more look at his copilot, he answered back. "Gray Goose we're coming in as I'm not sure my copilot could survive a sea landing. He's currently unconscious and I might not be able to get him out before this crate sinks. Have fire crews standing by."

Immediately the landing officer replied, "Bring her in, Lieutenant, you're looking good, just remember we're rolling hard left to right, so don't try the deck when it's pitching up, it may toss you into the drink."

Shaking his head, Lieutenant Winthrop simply acknowledged, "Roger that."

Taking a deep breath, he pulled the handle releasing the landing gear, positive he had heard both wheels lock down in place. The light confirming the wheel lock was no longer working, as were several other instruments damaged when the port side of the plane had been struck by the blast that injured Ensign Evans.

Just three hundred yards from the *Enterprise*, Lieutenant Winthrop could feel his plane being sucked harder toward the right by whatever was damaged, and he knew it was going to be a real wrestling match to bring the 1897 down on that pitching deck. At two hundred yards, Lieutenant Winthrop observed the foredeck dropping down from a large swell and knew it was now or never. Pouring more fuel to the engine to close the gap before the bow rose up again, Lieutenant Winthrop cursed the wind that was attempting to slow his final approach, something he could normally easily adjust to.

With the landing officer signaling him to cut power, Lieutenant Winthrop swallowed hard as he closed his throttles and felt the plane drop like a rock before striking the deck with a major thud. The SBD skidded sideways for a second, aiming toward the gun deck where he could see men running for their lives. A moment later the left wheel dropped down into the gun deck as the prop slammed into the flight deck, bending the blades as if they were made of tin. The 1897 skidded for about ten feet before coming to a precarious stop, teetering on the edge of the flight deck.

As rescue crews moved toward the plane, one of the men yelled at Lieutenant Winthrop, "Sit still, Lieutenant, we don't need to be tipping this thing into the water just yet!"

In a matter of seconds, two rescue men pulled open the canopy and looked at the bleeding ensign. One of the men said, "Sir, if you can hear us, we need you to try and get up, slow and easy, and lean to your right. Any more weight to the left and we may all go for an unwanted swim with this plane."

Nodding his head, Ensign Evans carefully slid up toward the rescue team that was reaching down toward him. When he was half way out of his seat, the men literally pulled him out onto the right wing that was now pointing skyward. After sliding down to the deck, a corpsman grabbed him by his good arm and placed him in a basket before running toward the island. With Ensign Evans out of the plane, several deck handlers pulled down on the raised wing as two rescue workers helped Lieutenant Winthrop crawl out of his seat and jump down to the deck.

When the rescue workers carrying Ensign Evans reached the door to the island, the ensign called out for them to stop. Propping himself up in the basket with his good arm, he wanted to see what was going to happen with the aircraft. Ten deck handlers ran over to the SBD and gave it a good shove. The plane moved about a foot, but then stopped cold, refusing to leave the carrier. The crew members moved to the tail section of the plane and lifted it up from the deck, giving it a good push. As the men stood back, the plane slid over the edge of the flight deck, ripping apart several antiaircraft guns before disappearing into the rough seas. Watching the plane go over the side, Ensign Evans now understood why the plane was so hard to handle on the way back to the carrier. Nearly half of the starboard elevator was gone, and a large section of the stabilizer and rudder had been torn lose from antiaircraft explosions. It was a miracle the Lieutenant had brought the 1897 back as far as he did.

Lieutenant Winthrop walked over to the petty officer in charge of the deck crew. "She was a good plane, and losing her leaves me with an empty feeling in my stomach, yet watching the old gal get a proper burial makes things a bit easier. Now I just have to get another good plane... and keep my spotters from getting shot up."

With the 1897 off the deck, the debris was quickly cleared then one by one the rest of the flight landed without a problem.

Lieutenant Winthrop was taken down to the hospital to be checked over for any medical issues he might have incurred during the battle and hard landing. After getting a clean bill of health he was given permission to leave the hospital, but that was farthest thing from his mind. Walking up to the lead corpsman, he said, "I'm not leaving until I hear how Ensign Evans is doing."

Nodding his head, the corpsman replied. "No doubt he lost a lot of blood, but that is the worst of it. The doctor took a big piece of shrapnel out of his shoulder from an antiaircraft shell and put in ten stitches. His leg needed twenty-five stitches after we removed some small shrapnel, most likely from the plane. We have him on an IV right now with some morphine, so he should sleep for a while. Stop back later today and you can see him. He asked about you several times while we were working on him.

Walking out of the hospital, Lieutenant Winthrop had to smile. No matter how the 1897 had fought him, he had returned the ensign back to the ship where he could be treated, and now he was going to survive. He had put the plane down on the deck without starting any fires or killing any crew members, and he knew at least one of his bombs had struck the *Hiryu*. Taking everything into consideration, it had been a damn good day. Now, without a plane, the odds of him doing any more flying before they returned to Pearl Harbor were slim to none. But after everything he had been through during this battle, a few days at sea without having to fly combat patrols suited him just fine. Slowly, he walked over to the debriefing room where a hot cup of coffee awaited him as he explained everything that happened to the squadron commander.

Several hundred miles away, the heavily listing *Yorktown* was taken under tow by the Fleet Tug USS *Vireo*.* With emergency repairs completed to keep the *Yorktown* afloat, the *Vireo* began towing the *Yorktown* back to Pearl Harbor for repairs. No one can explain how the Japanese submarine I-168 was able to sneak its way through the protective ring of destroyers, however, the skipper was able to set up a good firing solution and send three torpedoes toward the damaged hulk. Two of the long lance torpedoes had slammed into the hull of the *Yorktown* doing tremendous damage. The third torpedo missed the *Yorktown*, but struck the destroyer USS *Hamman** which had been sailing close to the damaged carrier providing electrical power. The powerful torpedo tore a massive hole in the *Hamman*, snapping its keel. The ship broke in half sinking nearly immediately. Eighty crew members from the *Hamman* were either killed by the torpedo attack or by exploding depth charges on the stern of the destroyer that detonated below the surface.

The decision was made that the *Yorktown* could no longer be salvaged, and it was impossible to tow her back to Pearl Harbor now that she had taken on so much water. American vessels stayed nearby, not wanting the *Yorktown* to fall into the hands of the Japanese. The well-built carrier continued to list more throughout June 6, but stayed afloat. By the morning of June 7, the list had gotten much worse. At 0530 hours, the *Yorktown* groaned loudly as she rolled over onto her port side where she remained floating for several hours. About 0701 hours, the *Yorktown* rolled over one more time so her flight deck was now under water. Over the next few minutes, the *Yorktown* began to settle in the water, then sank going down by the stern.

About midday, the skipper of the destroyer *Benham* contacted the *Enterprise* regarding the number of wounded men on board that needed more care than they could provide. Admiral Spruance gave permission to bring the *Benham* alongside to transfer the wounded and other survivors she was carrying from the *Yorktown*. By 1330 hours, Cooper and Cy were aboard the Enterprise and were being attended to by the ships doctors. Scott argued with one of the corpsmen that he wanted to see Cooper one more time before he went into surgery, but the corpsmen refused, stating there was no time. Overhearing the argument, one of the doctors, Commander Quinton Sullivan, stepped in between the men, giving the corpsman a disapproving look.

Looking at Scott's bandaged leg, he said, "Son, we don't have much time as Dodge is in pretty bad shape, but go ahead and talk to him for a minute since he is conscious right now."

Bending down, Scott grabbed Cooper by the hand. "Hey Coop, you got to fight now, like you've never fought before. You have Lily and that baby to think about. Hang in there, Coop, you got to hang in there."

Cooper nodded his head slightly, as he forced a smile. "Scott, you tell Lily I never meant for this to happen. Tell her I love her and always will. Tell her..."

With that, Cooper's eyes closed and his head rolled slightly to the left. Jumping up, Scott yelled, "Doctor! Over here!"

Taking out his stethoscope, the doctor began listening to Coopers chest. Looking up toward the corpsmen he called out. "Room two, right now!"

As the doctor turned to follow Cooper, Scott grabbed him by the arm. "Is he still alive, is he going to make it? His wife is carrying their first baby, he can't die, doc."

Pulling Scott's hand free from his arm, the doctor replied. "He's alive, but barely. Will he make it? That is going to be up to your prayers and to God. He's lost a lot of blood and there are no guarantees."

Turning, the doctor ran down the long companionway, into the ships hospital.

Scott stood there quietly in the companionway for several minutes, thinking about Cooper and Cy before another corpsman walked up to him. "You must be gunners mate Dowdle. Come with me, we're going to get the rest of the steel out of your leg and stitch you up properly."

After looking down the companionway one more time, Scott followed the corpsman into a small surgical room.

Removing the metal from Scott's leg took about forty-five minutes. After a shower and a fresh uniform, Scott went down to the mess area, unable to remember the last time he had eaten. When he had finished, he went back to a small waiting room near the ships hospital. It was late in the evening when Doctor Sullivan walked over to Scott. "How is your leg doing? I heard they took a bunch of steel out of it."

Scott shook his head, "Don't worry about me, how the hell are Cooper and Cy?"

The doctor sat down beside him. "Dodge is in critical condition. We did all we could for him, but he had a lot of internal injuries. We removed his spleen and made the best repairs we could. If he survives, he'll need more surgery when we get back to Pearl. I can't guarantee you a darn thing. Just pray, gunners mate, just pray. As far as Brewster goes, his hands were horribly burned, and I can't be sure how that will turn out. Like Dodge, he will need ongoing surgery to get the best results possible. It will take a long time for his hands, not to mention his hip to heal. We did all we could manage here trying to put him back together, but it's a terrible mess. Brewster will be in hospitals for a long time to come. But to be honest, I don't know if either man will survive, but one thing I do know for sure is that this war is over for both men."

Tears rolled down Scott's face as he looked down at the floor. After a moment he looked up at Doctor Sullivan. "I appreciate all you could do for Cooper and Cy. Those guys are the best friends I've ever had. Somehow, they just have to come out of this."

As Doctor Sullivan stood up, he replied. "Prayers, my friend. Pray all you can."

With the battle over, the remainder of the battered Japanese fleet sailed back to Japan for repairs and replenishment of combat crews. The wounded were taken to a secured military hospital where they were classified as 'secret patients,' and placed in isolation wards away from other wounded men. This way the families did not know where they were and could not come to visit them. The Japanese government did not want people knowing the extent of the loss they had suffered. When the wounded were ready to return to action, they were dispersed among the fleet as a way to keep them from talking with other survivors. They were strongly admonished to never tell their families what happened at Midway. All of their mail was screened to make sure they were abiding by the rules.

The American task forces remained in the waters around Midway, continuing to search for any Japanese ships that still might be lingering in the area. On June 8, the carrier USS *Saratoga* once again joined the Pacific Fleet, giving Nimitz three heavy carriers to operate with. Admiral Fletcher moved his flag from the cruiser *Astoria* to the *Saratoga* on June 9, where he had more access to communications equipment. Late in the day on June 10, the decision was made to send the fleet back to Pearl Harbor.

With the battle officially over, Japan had lost 3,057 men, while the United States had 307 killed. Both sides had hundreds of wounded men, some that would never recover from their serious injuries.

However on June 7, 1942 the Alaska landing force did land 550 men on Kiska and Attu Islands in the Aleutian Islands. Although they built up a force of 5,640 combatants and 1,170 civilians, they were never able to launch a major attack. They withdrew from Attu on May 30, 1943 and from Attu on July 28, 1943.

Three U.S. Airmen were captured during the battle. They were all tortured aboard the enemy ships before being tossed into the ocean. Only two Japanese prisoners were rescued. After being treated for injuries at Pearl Harbor, they were sent back to the United States to sit out the remainder of the war in a POW camp.

After Midway, the Japanese never attempted to start another major offensive, as they now had to begin defending the islands they had already captured. The tremendous losses suffered by the Japanese forced Germany to cancel their long-range plans of joining Japan's forces in India, where they would celebrate complete control of nearly half the world.

For Admiral Nimitz and the naval planners in Washington, the battle of

Midway was an overwhelming success. Within days, ships that were supposed to be built as heavy cruisers were now designated as aircraft carriers. Funds to build newer and advanced carrier aircraft suddenly became available. Everyone now agreed that the war in the Pacific was going to be won by the carrier. The decision was made to finish the last of the four Iowa class battle ships, but the next larger Montana class were scrubbed.

CHAPTER TWENTY-SIX – THE RETURN

At 0215 hours on the morning of June 14, 1942, Task Force 16 and Task Force 17 sailed back into Pearl Harbor. Ambulances were waiting on the pier to transfer most of the wounded to the naval hospital, while the worst cases went to Tripler Army Hospital.

Scott was able to see Cooper and Cy loaded into the same ambulance for their transfer to Tripler. About a half hour later, Scott was taken to the naval hospital. After having x-rays to determine if there was any more metal that needed to be removed, Scott's leg was re-bandaged.

As soon as he was able, he found a pay phone and called Lily, whether the navy wanted him to do so or not. On the third ring, Lily picked up the phone. She knew the fleet had returned overnight and was waiting for Cooper to call, or to get a message that something bad had happened to him.

With a nervous voice, Lily answered, "Good morning, Dodge residence."

With tears rolling down his face, Scott fought to find the right words. After taking a deep breath, he said. "Good morning, Lily, this is Scott."

Immediately, Lily stepped backwards, grabbed the back of a kitchen chair and sat down. As tears began to flow, she said, "Don't sugar coat it, Scott, how bad is Cooper, or is he dead?"

"No, he's not dead, Lily, but he's in real bad shape. They have done a lot of surgeries on him already, but he's just not responding the way they want him to. That's about all I can tell you," Scott said, wishing he could be explaining all this face to face.

Feeling a small sense of relief that Cooper was still alive, Lily said, "Tell me, Scott, how did it happen? Were you with him when he was wounded?"

Scott explained how Cooper's cannon exploded, and how he had pulled him up to the flight deck. He went on to tell her about how Cy was injured attempting to find help for Cooper. Once again, Lily cried, knowing someone she didn't even know had put his life on the line to save her husband. Her heart ached after hearing what all had happened to the young sailor.

Finally, Lily said, "I have a feeling you are not telling me the entire story, Scott. What else happened? Are you alright?"

Scott explained about his leg, reassuring her several times that he was going to be fine.

After hearing everything Scott had to say, she said, "So, the navy is going to send you back to war after everything you've already been through? Scott, you have been on two ships that went down, and now you've been wounded. Don't you think you've done enough?"

Smiling, Scott replied. "Lily, I will gladly go back, just to make sure you and Cooper and Cy are safe back here at home. I can't think of anything else I would rather do."

Since Scott had given her all the information he had, she was able to deal well with the two officers that came to her door to give her the news about Cooper. The big question she had for the officers was when could she see him, and how could she get Scott released so he could go with her.

The next morning, Scott called Lily at about 1000 hours. He told her where she could pick him up so they could drive over to Tripler Hospital.

A doctor met Lily and Scott in a small waiting room, explaining everything they had done for Cooper. What he could not explain was why Cooper had lapsed into a coma. Lily sobbed as she grabbed onto Scott who was also crying. When Lily was ready, the doctor walked her into Cooper's room, while Scott stayed outside, allowing Lily to have time alone with her husband.

Even though Lily was a nurse, she was stunned to see all the tubes and wires hooked up to her husband. Walking up beside the bed, she shook her head. For the first time since she had known him, Cooper looked weak and frail, with an ashen gray complexion.

Reaching down, Lily took hold of Cooper's left hand. Bending over, she kissed it and struggled to fight back the ocean of tears building up inside her. Carefully, she took his hand and placed it upon her abdomen. "Can you feel your daughters heartbeat, sweetheart? She wants to have a big strong daddy when she is born, so you need to get better. Scott told me how brave you were and how you fought to the very last minute to save the *Yorktown*. That is exactly what I knew you would do, and you've always been my true hero. I know you won't be going back to the war when you are better, so I just want you to know I'll live anywhere you want to live. We can make a home here or in New York, or where ever you want to raise our children." After kissing Cooper on the cheek, she walked over toward the door, motioning Scott to join her.

Scott was not quite as prepared as Lily had been to see all the equipment hooked to his friend. Standing by the end of the bed, he said, "You need to wake up, Coop. You got a lot of living to do yet and a great family waiting for you. Come on buddy, we all need you back."

After a few more minutes, Lily brushed her hand over Cooper's cheek and said, "I'll be back tomorrow and every day after that until you wake up. I love you, Coop."

As Scott and Lily walked out into the corridor, Scott said, "I think I should check in on Cy to see how he's doing, he's just two doors down. Is that okay?"

"Of course, and I would like to meet the man that put his life on the line for my Cooper," Lily replied, as she started toward the room.

Quickly, Scott took hold of her hand. "Lily, it may be best if I go in alone. Why don't you get a cup of coffee and I'll meet you in the lounge in a few minutes."

Looking over at Scott, she replied. "Why Scott? Why would he not be alright with seeing me? After all, I want to thank him for his bravery and selflessness. He deserves that, and he is a hero in my book. Please explain yourself, Scott."

Shaking his head, Scott replied, "You are totally correct, Cy is a hero in every way. But the last time I saw him, he was angry over what happened to him, and I don't want him taking it out on you. He doesn't see things as you do."

Lily thought about what Scott had told her for a moment before answering. "Alright, you know and understand him, and he's been through a lot. I'll just wait in the lounge."

After Lily had walked down the corridor, Scott opened the door to see Cy laying alone in a dark room. As Scott approached the bed, Cy said angrily, "What the hell are you doing here, Dowdle? Haven't you done enough damage to my life already? I would prefer it if you just turned around and go back the way you came."

That was just the sort of reaction Scott was expecting when he was talking to Lily. Walking up to the side of Cy's bed, Scott looked down into the angry eyes of one of the funniest men he had ever known. "Look Cy, I feel—"

Cy cut off Scott instantly. "You feel what? You feel my pain? The hell you do. You feel bad about what happened to me, but I don't want your damn pity. You feel life is unfair, but I don't care about your sacred ideas. You feel that you should have gone to the island instead of me, yeah that one I would be alright with, because then it would be you laying here instead of me. I ran because you wanted help for Dodge, because I knew you were not going to leave him, even if it meant the ship rolling over on top of you. Yeah, I ran for help because I was a sucker, plain and simple. Now tell me Dowdle, what the hell am I supposed to do for the rest of my life? The doctors say my hip is so badly damaged I'll need to use a damn cane as long as I live. I was the best Packard mechanic in St. Louis before the war, and now I may never spin a wrench again. Yeah, I tried to do something good for a friend, and see what it got me? Sure you had shrapnel in your legs, but you're walking just fine. You make me sick, Dowdle! You want to be a good friend? Bring me a pistol so I can blow my damn brains out. But oh, that's right, I probably couldn't pull the damn trigger. You would have to do it for me, but I bet you're too big of a coward to do it. Get the hell out of my room and never come back. I never want to see you or Dodge ever again."

Without saying another word, Scott turned to walk out the door. Just before he turned the knob, he said, "I'll pray for you, Cy."

Laughing, Cy yelled, "Screw you and screw your prayers. Do you think your God actually gives a damn about me? Look what he allowed to happen, and you think he cares? Get out of here, Dowdle, before I find a way to get out of this bed and kick your ass out."

Scott turned and walked out the door, feeling totally sick. He knew Cy had suffered a tragedy unlike he had ever known and his life would never be the same, but there was no way Scott could set any of it right, no matter how much he wanted to.

Three days later, when Lily entered Cooper's room she gasped. Cooper held out his hand and said, "Where have you been, sweetheart?"

Lily cried as she ran across the room to take hold of Cooper's hand. She kissed it several times before placing it against her cheek. Wiping her tears away, she said, "I was here nearly all day yesterday. I read to you from the book I brought along and helped the nurses give you a sponge bath."

Cooper shook his head and smiled. "I woke up about two hours ago. I don't remember anything after my gun blew up. They tell me Scott had some leg injuries, but that Cy Brewster really was injured bad trying to get me help. I feel bad about that, it shouldn't have happened."

Just as Cooper finished talking, his doctor walked into the room. Looking at Lily, he said, "When are you due?"

Smiling, Lily replied, "Beginning of August. Will Cooper be home by that time?"

Nodding his head the doctor said, "If he continues to improve, he should be home in about two weeks, but he'll be on some serious restrictions for a while. I'm not sure what the navy has in store for him yet. They may discharge him or send him to a training base, but his combat days are definitely over."

Lily smiled. "I'll go anywhere the navy sends him, just as long as it's not on a ship out at sea."

Scott was overwhelmed when he walked into Cooper's room the following day. Lily had told him how good Cooper looked, but Scott couldn't quite bring himself to dare believe it. Walking over to Cooper's bed, Scott smiled. "Damn, it is great to see you looking so good. You really scared me last time

I saw you old friend. So, have you heard what the navy is going to do with you now?"

Shaking his head, Cooper replied. "There's supposed to be a commander coming to speak to me sometime today about what the navy has in store for me. The doctor says I can't return to combat, so that is one less possibility. How about you, Scott?"

Reaching into his pocket, Scott pulled out several sheets of folded paper. I have two more weeks of medical leave before I report to the destroyer USS *Jarvis* as a .40mm gunner. I'll probably be seasick half the time I'm on that bucket, but after the *Lexington* and *Yorktown,* I've had enough of carrier life. It's way too big of a target for the Japanese."

Cooper laughed a bit as he winced. "It still kind of hurts when I laugh, sneeze or cough. You'll do fine, Scott, and I think you'll like a .40mm cannon. Just make sure you have two good loaders to keep the beast firing."

Scott explained to Cooper that Cy had been sent to the naval hospital in San Diego aboard the hospital ship *Solace* several days earlier. Sadly, he explained that Cy's attitude had not changed much, and if anything, it may have deteriorated even lower.

After Scott had departed the hospital, a commander from the bureau of personnel arrived in Cooper's room. After exchanging some small talk, the commander said. "Well Dodge, your days of gunnery work on a combat ship have come to an end. We're sending you home for three weeks so you can work on regaining some of your strength. Then you will be sent to San Diego to teach gunnery school to new men joining the fleet. The additional surgeries you need will be coordinated over there, but to be honest, that is where you will probably stay until the end of the war."

Cooper nodded his head before replying. "What chance do I have to go out to sea to work with the new gunners?"

"Absolutely none, Dodge. You are a classroom and range instructor only. You can be promoted up the ladder when other trainers rotate out to sea, but the navy will not allow you to make a career of the service. Once the war ends, you will be considered dead wood and will be discharged within days. Nothing more that I can do for you, Dodge."

"I'm not sure Lily will be happy about moving to the mainland, but we will do what the navy needs me to do to help win the war," Cooper replied, feeling confident he still served a purpose.

Two weeks later, Scott reported to the *Jarvis* after it docked in Pearl Harbor. It had been on convoy detail from the United States and was in need of fuel and other necessary items as well as some minor repair. Scott was happy with the attitude of his loaders and knew they would get along just fine. With refueling completed, the Jarvis sailed south from Pearl Harbor, allowing the new crew members to train on their guns and begin working as a team.

In early August, the *Jarvis*, under command of Lieutenant Commander W.W. Graham,* sailed toward Guadalcanal* as part of Task Force 62.6. The ship, along with seven other destroyers, was used mainly for antiaircraft and screening duties as they guarded the invasion fleet. After the Savo Island naval battles of August 7-8, 1942, the *Jarvis* was assigned to escort troop ships into the landing zone for the invasion of Guadalcanal. During the mission, a Japanese torpedo plane struck the *Jarvis,* ripping a 50-foot long hole in the boiler room. The valiant repair crews on the *Jarvis* went to work sealing off the damaged compartments while quickly working to get one boiler up and running. With power being restored, Lieutenant Commander Graham was told to break off from the fleet and set a course for Brisbane, Australia for repairs. Making only eight knots, the *Jarvis* became a perfect target for Japanese dive bombers. Late in the day of August 9, 1942, the destroyer took several direct hits shattering its keel. The *Jarvis* broke in two, sinking within minutes, taking all 247 men from her crew to the bottom of the Solomon Sea.

Cooper was at home recovering from surgery when he received word Scott had gone down with the *Jarvis*. It was a terrible blow that haunted him for a long time. However, he knew the worst was to come. Since Scott and Maria were not married, he knew the navy would not be contacting her personally. That evening Cooper and Lily drove over to the house that Maria and Scott were renting together. As they approached the front door, Maria shook her head, "No, please don't tell me Scott is gone."

Maria covered her face and began to sob as Lily held her distraught friend in her arms. Slowly, Lily moved Maria over to a sofa so they could sit down together. After composing herself somewhat, Maria looked over at Cooper. "Tell me what happened, where is Scott right now?"

Marie screamed out in horror when Cooper explained what had happened to the *Jarvis*. Once again, she sobbed for a long time as she hung on to Lily. Looking over at Cooper, she said, "You mean he's gone, gone forever and I'll never see his face again?"

Nodding his head, Cooper replied. "There were no ships close by to try and save anyone, as they were a long way from the fleet. I'm so sorry, Maria."

Several minutes later, Maria stood up and walked across the room. I have nothing left to stay here for now. I guess I'll go home and live with my folks for a while until I decide what I want to do. All my dreams and wishes were tied up in Scott, and now that's all gone."

Several nights later as Cooper lay in bed half asleep, Lily walked into the bedroom and clicked the light on and off several times. As Cooper sat up, he looked strangely at Lily. Before he could ask what was going on, she said. "My water broke, we're going to have a baby!"

Quicker than Cooper thought he could move, he got dressed and helped Lily into the car. All the way to the hospital, he tried to comfort Lily as she was already going into labor. As Lily was taken upstairs into the delivery area, Cooper paced the waiting room, wishing he had Paul or Scott by his side to talk with. As he looked out over a darkened Pearl Harbor, he thought about everything that had happened to him since the morning of December 7. He looked over toward the West Loch where the *Tennessee* and several other victims of the December attack were still anchored, waiting to be taken back to the United States for repair and rebuilding. He was able to pick out the mast of his old battleship as she rode at anchor silently and empty. But like the birth of his new baby tonight, he knew the trusty old battleship would be reborn to help bring Japan to its knees.

As he was still deep in thought, a nurse walked into the room. "Congratulations, Gunners mate Dodge, you have a very pretty baby girl, and mother and daughter are both doing just fine."

Cooper ran over and hugged the nurse as he gave her a kiss on the cheek. "When can I see Lily? When can I see my daughter?"

The nurse smiled, "You can see Lily in about a half hour, and the baby in about an hour, after we bathe her and check her over."

Lily was smiling as Cooper walked into her room. "Did you see out little angel, Coop? She is absolutely perfect. I know we talked about names for a long time, but when I looked at her, all I could think of was Aolani. In Hawaiian it means heavenly cloud."

Cooper smiled and nodded his head. "Perfect, I love it. Aolani it shall be."

The young couple could not have been happier with their new baby, along with the fact that Cooper would not have to go back out to war again. Ten days later, the Dodge's walked up the gangway to the SS *Lurline* for the trip to San Diego.

After finding a place in base housing, Cooper went to work at the naval base. Before reporting to work, he went to the hospital to see Cy. Cooper found him sitting on a veranda overlooking the naval base. As he sat down, he looked over at Cy's blank stare. Without turning to face Cooper, he said, "What do you want, Dodge? Are you angry that I was unable to get you help?"

Cooper shook his head as a tear rolled down his cheek. "Cy, you did all you could, and you put yourself on the line for me. You are a true hero in my book."

Laughing, Cy turned to face Cooper. "Yeah, but you get to walk out of here and return to your family. What the hell am I supposed to do with the rest of my miserable life? Got any suggestions?"

"I haven't got a reason why God did what he did that day, and no one will ever know his reasoning. But Cy, your alive, and God gave you a chance to make something of all of this. I will do whatever I can to help you out," Cooper said, as he looked at the brave man that used to work on the gun deck, moving ammunition faster than most men were able to.

"You want to help, Cooper? Well, you and Dowdle just keep away from me and I'll be happy as hell. Now get the hell out of here," Cy yelled, as he went back to staring out over the base.

Cooper stood up to leave, then stopped. Turning back toward Cy, he said, "Just so you know, you won't have to worry about Scott Dowdle coming to visit you. He went down with the destroyer *Jarvis* in the battle of Savo Island. He won't be bothering anyone ever again."

Cy laughed slightly. "Glad to see he did something right."

Cooper wanted to backhand Cy more than he had ever wanted to hit anyone in his entire life. Instead, he turned and left the hospital, praying that someday Cy would find some sense of peace.

At first, Cooper wasn't sure he was going to like his job, but seeing how excited so many of the young men were to take their place in the fleet made Cooper's spirits rebound. He found there were very few goldbrickers that would need to be removed from gunnery school to become simple deck hands, or be drummed out of the navy altogether. He understood he was witnessing the resurgence of the United States Navy, and was proud to send these men off to battle knowing he had given them all the tools they needed to do their jobs well, and take the fight all the way back to Tokyo Bay, returning peace to the world.

With the war finally coming to an end, on September 30, 1945, Cooper was handed his discharge papers. Like every other G.I., he was excited and ready to return to a civilian life with Lily and Aolani. Walking into their small apartment, Cooper grabbed Lily, picked her up and spun her around. Showing her his discharge papers, he said, "I'm a free man, sweetheart. We can pack up and head back to Hawaii anytime you're ready."

After giving Cooper a big hug, she pulled him over to the worn used sofa they had purchased for thirty dollars and sat down. Taking hold of Cooper's hands, she said, "Is that truly what you want? Have you decided not to visit your sister before we leave?"

Cooper looked intently at Lily. "It has been a lot of years since Dierdra and I last spoke and I'm sure she no longer wants to see me. It's like I abandoned her, so why would she want to open her life back to me now?"

Lily smiled and shook her head. "Because you are her brother, her only sibling. I bet she has laid awake many nights since the war began, wondering if you were safe, if you were alive, and where you were. No Cooper, I believe Dierdra would want to see you. We must go to New York before we leave for Hawaii. It truly must be done."

After mulling the situation over and over for several days, Cooper finally decided a trip to New York should come first. Cooper and Lily enjoyed the four-day train trip to New York. It allowed them to see many sights neither of them had ever seen before.

Lily was taken back when she saw the skyline of New York. She had seen many photographs, but none of them did justice to what she was actually seeing now. Cooper continually smiled as the train rolled slowly throughout the five boroughs that comprised greater New York City. He sat quietly in his seat, reliving his childhood memories of the crowded, noisy streets where the real commerce of New York City took place. Finally, the train came to a stop at Manhattan's ornate Grand Central Station.

Lily was nearly overcome by the sheer number of people rushing from one train to another, or going down the constantly crowded escalators to the massive subway system. Outside the transportation hub, buses and hundreds of cabs fought for every inch of parking space available, as drivers blew their horns or yelled insults at one another. To Lily, it appeared to be an awkward way to live, with everyone piled on top of their neighbors, yet somehow it fascinated her.

Standing by a subway kiosk, Lily looked at Cooper. "This is what you grew up in? I can hardly understand what people are saying. It's like a foreign country."

Cooper laughed as he looked up at her from the subway map he was holding. "Sweetheart, there are people here from all over the world. Some speak poor English, some of them speak Bronx English and some of them are Jews that have adopted one of the New York dialects and made it their own. For better or worse, this is my New York and I forgot how wonderful it can be."

Gathering up Aolani and their luggage, Cooper led Lily to an elevator that took them down into the subway system where they looked for a train heading toward Fordham Station near the Little Italy neighborhood. Cooper smiled as the door to the subway car rolled shut, and the train took off through the tunnel at a tremendous speed. On the other hand, Lily closed her eyes as she was sure this was where she was going to die. She was relieved when she heard the conductors voice call out, "Fordham Station!"

With her knees still shaking, Lily walked off the subway car into an entirely new world called the Bronx. Everyone seemed to know everyone, and they talked with a strange accent while waving their hands to accentuate the conversation. She found the accent to be funny, yet somewhat pleasant to her ears. Many Jewish men with long beards wearing black Yamikas paid little attention to the bustle around them as they sat reading from prayer books as they awaited their train. Mothers dragged screaming children, and old men stood in circles reading newspapers and discussing each story as they smoked their pipes. Here and there, small boys knelt down with their shoeshine boxes, working incredibly hard to restore shines to very worn oxfords that could not be replaced because of the war. Although everyone appeared to moving at a fast pace, they must have taken time to eat as the station smelled of roasted peanuts, hot dogs, and strong coffee.

Climbing the escalator to the street above it was evident this was an old section of the city, with countless high rise tenement buildings, and shops and stores of all kinds occupying the street level floors. Once again, busy cabs with blaring horns raced through the streets, as many men still wearing military uniforms strolled with their girlfriends or wives, totally disregarding whatever was happening on the raucous streets.

Cooper smiled as he pointed toward a jewelry shop about a block away. Turning to Lily, he said, "Sweetheart, that's our first stop!"

A man of about seventy was sitting behind a wooden table working on a pocket watch when they walked through the door. Instantly, the man stood up calling out, "Carmine, the God of Israel has brought you back to your home, Shalom, my friend."

With a burst of energy, the man rushed over to hug Cooper and kiss him on both cheeks. Looking at Lily, he said, "And this is your wife and baby? I am blessed to have them in my shop this day. What can I do for you today, Carmine Santucci?"

Smiling, Cooper looked at Lily. "Sweetheart, this is Asher Cohen. He has been a family friend, as long as I can remember."

After Lily was hugged numerous times by Mr. Cohen, he turned to Cooper. "The walls have ears, Carmine. Your Dierdra says you have changed your name to Cooper with a last name like a car. Is that right?"

Cooper nodded his head. "It's a long story, Mr. Cohen. And yes, my name is now Dodge."

"Ah yes, Dodge. I looked at one when I bought my last car, but they wanted several hundred dollars more than a Plymouth. So, I went...."

As Cooper knew this would be a story that could go back all the way to the late 1930's, he cut him off. "Mr. Cohen, do you know where Dierdra is living now? I would really like to see her."

Actually, they live about two blocks from here in a new high rise where only the wealthier Italians can live. Her husband could not get in the service because of blood pressure problems. So, during the war he was able to take over jobs left vacant in the textile industry when men were called off to war. He has done well in the overseas textile markets and has many connections in Europe and the near east. His last name is Giracii. If you like I can drive you over there."

Carmine refused the ride as he wanted to look over the old neighborhood on the way to his sisters apartment. Lily enjoyed the walk as Cooper pointed out many interesting places from his childhood. Arriving at the new high-rise complex, Cooper looked at the mail boxes. On the fourteenth floor, he found Steven and Dierdra Giracii.

Suddenly, Cooper was not sure what to do as he stood in front of the door to their apartment. Lily shook her head in disbelief, saying, "Cooper, do you want me to knock? Your sister lives here, not some Italian executioner."

Smiling, Cooper raised his hand and knocked on the wooden door.

A moment later the door swung wide open and Cooper was face to face with Dierdra. Letting out a scream, she grabbed hold of her brother and pulled him tight into her arms. Then she scooped Aolani from Lily's arms and kissed her as she pulled Lily into the apartment. "This is a dream come true. I thought about you so much, but never thought we would see one another again. Steven will be so happy to meet you when he returns with the children from school.

After dinner that evening, the four of them drew up a list of all the places Cooper and Lily wanted to visit in New York City while they were there.

The visit with Dierdra and Steven had been a fabulous seven days that went by way too fast. Later that night, Lily looked at Cooper as they snuggled in bed. "Well Coop, have you made up your mind where you want to live. Remember, wherever you want to live, I'll be happy to be with you."

After kissing Lily, Cooper replied, "When we were in Hawaii, it was the first real home I had since leaving New York when I was just a kid. Sure, I was in the navy, but the house we had was our home and I loved it. With your blessing, I just want to go back to Hawaii and live out my life there with you."

Lily cried as she hugged Cooper tightly. "You have made me the happiest women in the world. We will need to tell Dierdra and Steven tomorrow, so they don't accept the deal on the vacant apartment they talked about. Then I'm ready to go back home whenever you are."

The following morning, Cooper told Dierdra and Steven they would always have a place to stay when they traveled to Hawaii. He and Lily thanked them for their hospitality, but made it clear that New York City just wasn't home for him anymore.

Two days later, after a very tearful good bye, Lily, Cooper and Aolani boarded a train in Grand Central Station bound for San Diego. They had booked passage once again on the SS Lurline, and were excited to return to Honolulu.

The trip was restful and exciting for both Lily and Cooper as they attempted to plan out their new lives. Arriving back in Honolulu, they soon found a nice bungalow that fit into their price range. Lily was able to get her job back at the clinic while Cooper went job hunting. After seeing an ad in the Honolulu newspaper regarding jobs at Pearl Harbor, Cooper checked to see what was available. He was excited to find out there were several jobs available in the weapons maintenance shop. He was hired several days later and began a job that would last over thirty years.

Cooper and Lily had one more daughter they named Pualani, which meant Heavenly Flower. The Dodge family lived well and enjoyed their life in Hawaii, but Cooper never forgot about the men he served with on that fateful

Sunday of December 7, 1941. Not a day went by that he didn't take time to stand on the 1010 dock and gaze out across the channel toward the Arizona. He was proud when the monument was built above the sunken battleship, allowing thousands of visitors to look down upon the resting place of 1177 young American sailors that died that fateful day.

In 1965, Dierdra traveled to St. Cloud, Minnesota to search for their father's grave. She met with Father Richards from the Bishop's office. He remembered the story of the bank robbery and recommended she not go to the police for help. After checking with a local historian, Father Richards drove Dierdra and Steven to the large Calvary Cemetery south of the city along with the historian. After a short walk, the historian pointed to a flat stone in the ground. Since Cooper had buried the license plates from the car along with the money, the police were never able to identify Frederico Santucci, so the grave simply said, 'Unknown only to God,' and the date he was buried. After Father Richards led the small group through a few prayers, Dierdra looked at the historian. "Please don't tell the police we were here. I don't want to have them disrupt Cooper's life."

Smiling the historian replied, "First off, the statute of limitations has long expired on the bank robbery, and did Cooper not tell you he paid the money back?"

Looking stunned, Dierdra replied, "No, he never told me anything about that."

The historian smiled. "The bank received an envelope with most of the money in it sometime in 1938. It was mailed from a post office in Idaho with no return address. It was short $100 dollars that a note said would be repaid in the future. They received the final payment from a post office in Los Angeles late in the war. As the bank received $500 dollars from the sale of your father's car to help cover their loss about six months after the robbery, in the end they were well satisfied. To find someone back in those days was next to impossible, so I don't think anyone ever looked for your brother. I'm sorry to hear about Paul, but I'm proud of him for being a war hero. What was a pretty sad story to begin with, had a fair ending. Tell Cooper he is always welcome back here if he decides to visit your father's grave."

Dierdra took several photos of the stone and sent one off to Cooper. About a year later, a new stone was placed in the ground that said, 'Frederico Santucci. Husband of Maria, father of Dierdra and Carmine. Born Florence, Italy. Died St. Cloud, Mn."

Cooper never traveled to St. Cloud to visit his father's grave, as the memories of what had all happened was still very painful for him. However the noisy crazy streets of the Bronx was where he was born and raised always resonated in his heart. It had been a painful experience to allow Carmine Santucci to fade into the past forever. Nevertheless the ranch in Montana and the attack on Pearl Harbor had cemented Cooper Dodge to Lily and Hawaii, and that was all he needed to complete his happiness and bring his life back full circle.

ADDENDA

ADDENDUM (A) SHAW EXPLOSION

*The photo of the USS *Shaw* exploding in the dry dock is an iconic photograph from the attack. The photo is one of the most widely published photos of the December 7 attack, next to that of the exploding USS *Arizona.*

*In fighting fires on every ship, it became evident the many generous layers of oil-based paint that had been applied over the years was a real problem. The burning paint created clouds of thick black smoke that penetrated throughout the ships, making many passage ways death traps. The extreme heat of fires on one side of a sealed bulkhead could ignite the paint on the other side, creating an entirely new situation. The navy changed the type of paint they were using and how it was applied shortly after the war.

ADDENDUM (B) TORPEDO PROBLEMS

*The Mark 13 torpedoes used by the American navy at the time the war broke out were worse than useless. Reports of unexploded torpedoes also came from submarines and PT boats. Regrettably, many senior staff at the bureau of ordnance blamed everyone but themselves for the weapons failure. Consequently, nothing was done to repair the problem until late 1943, when a new design of the weapon was created. It was labeled as Mark 13, Model 10, and was very efficient.

Needless to say, the failed American torpedo attacks were not an entire waste for many reasons. First off, while the torpedo attacks were taking place, Japanese ship handlers were kept quite busy taking evasive action against the many torpedoes being thrown at them. This made it impossible for them to set up operations to launch their aircraft. Secondly, the Japanese were not as good as the Americans at vectoring fighters to proper areas during an aerial assault. Consequently, more often than not, Japanese fighter pilots were caught totally off guard or out of proper position to attack incoming torpedo bombers.

*Although the Devastator had been a state of art torpedo bomber in the 1930's, its speed and range were not well suited for flying long distances from carriers across open ocean. The battle of Midway was the last time they were used for combat. Many of the planes continued service in search and rescue operations where speed was not essential.

*Largely due to the fact that Japanese pilots were vectored out of their assigned areas to help in other areas under attack, they burned a tremendous amount of fuel and fired off so much ammunition they needed to land to refuel and rearm more than should have been necessary. This meant if planes were running out of fuel, ship handlers had to stop evasive maneuvers making their vessels more vulnerable to bombing attacks in order to bring in their fighters so they were not ditched at sea.

*Prior to the battle of Midway, the Kate, the main Japanese torpedo bomber had been taken out of production and was in short supply. The Val, the main dive bomber used by Japanese carriers had been reduced to limited production, so replacements were few and far between. The Japanese carrier aircraft that was the backbone of the air fleet had all been designed and built during the 1930's. As war broke out, the Japanese war industry struggled to keep up with losses without having time to work on new designs. The United States on the other hand had plenty of older aircraft that came into production between 1938 and 1940. After the attack on Pearl Harbor, companies kept up with the needs of the military while producing many new types of planes that were in production by late 1942, right up to the end of the war making the Zero totally obsolete.

ADDENDUM (C)DAMAGED SHIPS

In all there were 130 vessels berthed in Pearl Harbor on December 7, 1941. Many of them were transports, tankers, mine layers, mine sweepers, repair ships and other types of naval vessels the Japanese did not consider essential targets. Only 28 ships were sunk or damaged during the attack. Below is a list of all the ships damaged or sunk at Pearl Harbor starting with the Battleships.

USS *Arizona*

On the morning of December 7, 1941, the *Arizona* was tied up facing the entrance to Pearl Harbor following Admiral Kimmel's orders after the November 27 war warning. She was tied up against the berthing quay on her starboard side, with the repair ship USS *Vestal* tied up on her port side, making it nearly impossible for the Japanese to hit her with torpedoes. Shortly after the attack began the *Arizona* was struck by two large bombs on her deck that did minor damage. However, about 0810 hours, a 1,760-pound bomb, reconfigured from a naval shell, struck the upper deck directly behind casement number two, penetrating five decks before exploding. The bomb detonated near the powder and ammunition magazines. The explosion broke open several of the massive oil bunkers on her port side. With millions of pounds of explosives and oil all exploding at the same time, the ship literally lifted out of the water several feet before dropping back down with the bow dropping down below the water. Fires roared through the unsealed compartments and companion ways in a matter of minutes. With the bottom of the ship nearly blown off, the *Arizona* sunk quickly. All though the *Arizona* was a raging inferno that had already sunk, the Japanese continued, dropping several large bombs on the ship. Only 334 crew members survived, leaving 1,177 crew members entombed on the ship.

USS *Tennessee*

The *Tennessee* was berthed directly in front of the *Arizona* between berthing quay Fox 6 and the *West Virginia*, so it was impossible for the ship to be torpedoed. Immediately after 0800 hours, a bomb struck on the forward deck without penetrating to lower decks. The blast damaged the center gun on turret number two and started several serious fires. A second bomb struck the top of main gun turret number three, putting the left gun out of service. Another bomb struck turret three and penetrated to the inside. It didn't explode but broke into pieces. After the attack, the pieces were identified as a 15" armor piercing shell that had been retrofitted as a bomb. The bomb weighed about 1500 pounds. Fires broke out on the stern of the ship in the catapult crane room but were quickly brought under control. Magazines 306, 310, and 312 were flooded as fires reached lower decks. Since the boilers on the ship had been fired up before the attack, she was prepared to get underway by 0930 hours, but could not move. However, the ships engineers set the prop speed to five knots in order to push burning oil from the *Arizona* away from the stern of the *Tennessee*. Due to the intensive heat from the *Arizona* fires, several fires broke out on lower decks of the *Tennessee* but were easily controlled. At 1800 hours, fires broke out in the aft crane room due to heat from the Arizona. By 1930 hours, the fires are knocked down.

There was also heavy damage to the forward machine gun platform and navigation bridge. The four float planes assigned to the ship were destroyed on Ford Island. Four men were listed as killed, twenty-two wounded and one missing.

At 2104 hours, antiaircraft batteries reportedly fired at enemy aircraft that flew over or near the ship. Firing ended at 2109 hours. They could not have been Japanese planes as their fleet had left Hawaiian waters after the planes from the second attack returned. Most likely those planes were from the *Enterprise.*

The ship fired 760 five-inch rounds, 180 rounds of three-inch rounds, and 4000 rounds of machine gun ammunition. Without any hull damage, the *Tennessee* sailed to the United States under her own power late in January, 1942, returning to service mid-1943. Since the *West Virginia* was going to be on the bottom of the harbor for a while, a month after the attack, docking quay Fox 6 was destroyed with dynamite so the *Tennessee* could be moved out of her position.

USS West Virginia

The battleship *West Virginia,* the third most damaged ship in the harbor, was berthed outside the *Tennessee.* She took six torpedo hits which basically shredded her port side, opening up most of the ship to extreme flooding. The ship almost immediately came to an eight-degree list. Repair crews immediately began counter flooding in the starboard holds as they were afraid the West Virginia would roll over. As the ship approached a twelve-degree list, the counter flooding began to take hold, bringing the ship back to only a slight list. With fires spreading so rapidly, the order was given to flood all the ammunition storage areas to prevent another explosion like the Arizona.

A five-hundred-pound bomb struck on the rear quarter deck of the ship, causing damage to the rear main turret and creating fires below on the second deck which were handled fairly quickly. A second five-hundred pound bomb landed on top of number two main turret, blowing out the majority of the main bridge structure of the ship. Captain Mervyn Sharp Bennion* was on the bridge when the bomb struck. Although being mortally wounded, he continued directing operations while using one hand to hold his massive abdominal wound closed. Although the crew tried desperately to remove the captain from the bridge, he refused to leave. He desperately continued monitoring the list of his ship, sending out counter-flood orders that saved the *West Virginia* from rolling over like the *Oklahoma.* Once the ship had firmly settled enough so it could not roll over, the captain died on the bridge. He received the Congressional Medal of Honor.

Over the next few months, crews worked unceasingly, welding new temporary plates to the side of the ship. Once all the panels were solidly welded, the inside panels were anchored in place with 650 tons of concrete. When the water was pumped out and she once again was floating, the engineers found that the main rudder had also been blown off by a torpedo. Cutting away the debris so a new rudder could be installed, workers found two all-purpose 100-pound unexploded Japanese bombs below the stern of the ship.

Many crew members were trapped below decks when the flooding started. Some died instantly, while others were trapped in water tight compartments and could not escape. Though they would continue to tap on the hull or pipes hoping to be rescued, none of them were. Several attempts were made to get to the men, but each time things went wrong nearly killing the rescuers. After the ship was raised, they found a compartment containing the bodies of three men. According to the marks on the wall, the last man died on December 23, 1941. They were Seaman Clifford Olds, Seaman Ronald Clifford and Seaman Louis Costin. A total of 106 men died on the *West Virginia.*

She was taken by tug to dry dock one on June 9, 1942. After extensive repairs were completed, the *West Virginia* sailed under her own power to Puget Sound, Washington in April of 1943. She returned to combat after a full reconstruction in July of 1944.

USS Maryland

Like the *Tennessee*, the *Maryland* was berthed between the mooring quay and the *Oklahoma*, on her port side so it could not be hit by torpedoes. However, she was struck by two large bombs that did a large amount of damage to the forecastle of the ship, destroying several antiaircraft weapons. A bomb falling in the water on the port side of the ship near frame ten created an 18" by 20" hole in the hull, about 22 feet below the water line, creating serious flooding. There were also some small holes near frame 9 and 20 that were easily sealed to stop additional flooding. The affected compartments were secured and pumps put in place to keep the water at a manageable level. There was a small hole in the hull near the bow caused by one of the bombs that struck the deck. There was minor flooding in a hold for machine gun ammunition and the anchor chain storage area, and the torpedo compressors were put out of action due to flooding. Quickly, most of the forward electrical circuits were knocked out by water. It was estimated that 1000 tons of water had flooded the forward compartments before it was stopped. Additionally, one of the forward five-inch guns was put out of action by flying shrapnel that damaged the guns piston.

The biggest threat to the ship was when the *Oklahoma* began to roll. Crews worked diligently with fire axes attempting to cut through the heavy mooring lines that tied the two ships together. They were able to get the lines cut before the *Maryland* rolled over on top of the *Oklahoma*. As there was no structural damage to the *Maryland*, she sailed to Puget Sound on December 30, 1941. After repairs were completed, she was back in action in June of 1942

USS *Oklahoma*

The *Oklahoma* was tied up on the outside of the *Maryland*. The first of nine torpedoes struck the port side of the ship at 0800 hours. The torpedoes tore hull plates completely off the ship while beginning the flooding process. Internal bulkheads that were supposed to be water tight no longer functioned, as they were bent, twisted, or blown completely away from where they had been located. The after-action report states the first three torpedoes were seen approaching by crew members. They struck near frames 25, 35-40 and 115. Immediately, the ship began to list to a 45-degree angle. The rest of the torpedoes were felt, but not identified at exact location. The ship began to roll to a 135-degree position within eight to ten minutes. Several antiaircraft guns did operate on the port side for several minutes, but only with ammunition from the ready boxes. The ammunition elevators and hoists were damaged or destroyed immediately making them unusable. Two antiaircraft weapons did get underway on the starboard side, but quickly became unusable as the ship rolled over.

As the ship began to roll, men inside raced for exits where ever they could find them. Every floor area quickly became slippery from bunker oil as the huge tanks were ruptured by explosions. As the ship finished its roll, what was up was now down and floors became ceilings. Gangways that once led to upper decks were now taking men down to compartments that were rapidly flooding. Within minutes, all the doors that led to freedom were under water, trapping everyone that was left inside.

Some of the heavy machinery in the engine room broke loose from where it had been mounted, crushing many sailors to death. Now the only possibility of escape was through the bottom of the ship, if men on the outside could cut through the heavy steel plates to create an opening. The steel plates on the bottom of the Oklahoma were made of six-inch armor which created problems for the rescuers. With all the deck hatches below water, there was no longer any fresh oxygen entering the ship. The survivors were now breathing oxygen contaminated with the smell of thick black engine oil and sewage that was escaping from punctured holding tanks. There were no longer any lights burning inside the ship, so the only light available came from battle lanterns located in strategic places throughout the ship. Some men began fires, burning dry paper and debris until they were told they were using up precious oxygen and fouling the air with smoke that had no exhaust paths out of the ship.

A civilian naval yard worker and resident Hawaiian named Julio DeCastro* led the rescue operation. At first, they attempted to use blow torches, but soon realized they were starting fires inside the ship and burning up much needed oxygen. Eventually, the heavy armor panels were broken lose using pneumatic chippers, crow bars and grinders. The navy flew in tons of equipment from California so they could put more crews on the job.

The ship was finally raised in 1943, using a cable system to right the hull. It was decided the ship was too badly damaged to repair. After cleaning out the ship, she was sold for scrap. In 1947 after making enough repairs to the hull, the ship was taken under tow by two ocean going tug boats. The tugs were about half way to Los Angeles when some of the repair panels broke lose during a severe storm. Unable to stop the flooding, the tugs cut the ship free. She quickly rolled over sinking to the bottom of the Pacific.

In the end, just 32 men were removed from the capsized ship. Another 429 died inside from either combat injuries or being trapped in unaccessible areas with no oxygen. Most of the bodies removed from the *Oklahoma* were unrecognizable. They were buried in common graves.

USS California

At 0805 hours, two torpedoes slammed into the port side creating a forty-foot hole. At 0820 hours, another torpedo struck at frame 47, creating a 27' by 32' hole six feet below the bottom of the armor belt rupturing fuel tanks. A large bomb struck near the radio room, flooding compartment A518. All internal electrical power to the ship ended and everything inside the ship went black. At 0840 hours, the ship was shaken by four large bombs that detonated in the water nearby.

At 0900 hours, the first bomb hit near frame 59 broke through the main deck, penetrating down to the second deck where it exploded. The blast ruptured the forward and aft bulkheads and overhead compartment A705. The armored watertight hatch to the machine shop was buckled and could no longer be closed to stop flooding or fires.

At 0905 hours, large fires were burning below decks and out of control.

By 0930 hours, the fires reached the main deck and by 1002 hours, oil fires in the water begin several fires along the hull, burning paint. At that point, the 'abandon ship' call goes out because of the massive fires in and around the ship.

At 1015 hours, several navy tugs arrived alongside to help fight the fires. The crew returned to the ship to help fight fires inside, but cannot get them under control.

Counter flooding is ordered to make sure the vessel does not capsize like the *Oklahoma*. However, as there is no way to stop flooding from the attack, the *California* continues slowly sinking. By December 10, she was sitting erect on the bottom of the harbor. Thanks to the counter flooding the ship does not roll over. She was raised in March of 1942. After repairs in dry dock, the *California* sailed back to the United States on her own power. She returned to service in 1944.

There were 125 killed, 100 wounded, 116 missing, and only 37 of the dead were identified.

USS Nevada

Ensign Joseph Tausig* was the morning officer in command of the ship. For a reason only known to the ensign, when he took command of the ship at 0730 hours, he ordered boiler number two to be brought on line. As the

Nevada had two boilers functioning, she had enough power to get underway if necessary.

At 0759 hours local time, the first torpedo struck port side, flooding several compartments. Immediately, crew members took fire axes and began chopping through the mooring lines securing the *Nevada* to the mooring posts. The *Nevada* shuddered as a five-hundred-pound bomb struck, sending a cloud of deadly debris across the forecastle. No one on the ship was aware that their skipper, Captain Francis W. Scanland* was not on board when the attack began. That left the officer of the deck, Ensign Joseph Taussig and Lieutenant Ruff* to be temporarily in charge. With two boilers operating at full steam and a third being fired, it was possible to get the behemoth up to speed and attempt to free her from the deadly onslaught, and get the ship out to sea. The way the ship was anchored along Ford Island, it was easy to maneuver her away from Battleship Row, while making a run down the main channel. With the acting skipper, Lieutenant Commander Francis Thomas* now at the helm, things began to happen quickly.

At 0832, the *Nevada* was underway, being steered hard to port to avoid the USS *Vestal* that was still moored aside of the *Arizona*. When the *Nevada* made the turn, engines were set to all ahead one third.

At 0900 hours, as the *Nevada* passed the 1010 dock with her forecastle on fire, Japanese planes converged on her. Between ten and fifteen bombs missed the ship, exploding all around her. At around 0950 hours, five 250-pound bombs strike creating holes in her forward deck in several places, while rupturing the forward hull in two locations.

By now there were eleven major fires burning on the ship. All available hands were called to fight the fires. Moments later, a bomb fell down the funnel of the ship. Exploding, it forced a deadly combination of smoke and gases through the entire ventilation system like a hurricane. Many men were severely burned or suffocated within minutes.

Realizing that sinking the *Nevada* in the channel would make Pearl Harbor useless for months to come, many planes in the second wave attack the ship with a vengeance. After having been hit by eight bombs and one torpedo, everyone on the bridge realizes the *Nevada* is too damaged to last out in the open sea. The decision is made to beach her on Hospital Point. With the bow now up on the beach, the strong outgoing current is attempting to pull the stern of the ship back out into the channel. A decision is made to drop the anchors on shore to prevent the ship from being pulled away. As this is being done, three one-hundred-pound bombs fall near the bow of the ship, killing everyone involved in securing the anchors.

While the ship is at Hospital Point, Captain Scanlon is finally able to catch up with his ship and take control. Even with the anchors down, the heavy current pushed the ship towards the rocks on the starboard side. Tugs arrive on scene and pull the *Nevada* off the beach and haul her over to Waipi'o Point, where her stern is shoved aground safely out of the current alongside Buoy 19 and directly opposite of Ford Islands seaplane ramp.

The ship burned for eleven more hours before crew members and tug boats extinguish the flames. The *Nevada* had 60 men killed and 109 wounded. The crew was credited with shooting down five Japanese aircraft. She was refloated late in December and taken to dry dock. She sailed back to the United States in April of 1942 under her own power, and reentered service in May of 1943.

She became a target ship in 1946 and was used at the Bikini Atoll atomic bomb tests in August of 1946. Being too radioactive to reuse, she was sunk by gunfire on July 31, 1948.

USS Pennsylvania

The *Pennsylvania* was the flag ship of the Pacific Fleet. She was in dry dock for repairs when the Japanese attacked. The destroyers *Cassin* and *Downes* were forward of the *Pennsylvania* undergoing extensive repairs. Since the base was on full alert because of the last war warning, the forward .50 machine guns were being manned around the clock. With the ship receiving electrical power and steam from the base, everything on board was working properly. When the first bomb fell on Ford Island, the machine gun crews opened up on the Japanese planes. They were considered the first gunners to return fire that Sunday morning.

Between 0802 and 0805 hours, they shot down one torpedo plane over

Battleship Row. Immediately, several bombers turned their attention on the Pennsylvania, but were quickly turned away due to the heavy flak.

At 0915 hours, several level bombers drop their bombs but they fall wide of the dry dock. During the second attack, one bomb strikes the *Pennsylvania* on the forward deck, and one bomb strikes the *Shaw* next door in another dry dock, penetrating the deck and starting fires. Moments later, two more bombs hit. One falls between the dry dock wall and the hull of the *Pennsylvania*, exploding on the dry dock floor sending fire and shrapnel all around the ship.

By 0906 hours, both the *Pennsylvania* and the *Downes* are hit by bombs, and the *Pennsylvania* is subjected to heavy strafing.

At that point, the decision is made to cut power to all ships in dry dock, forcing them to operate off their storage batteries.

By 0920 hours, the decision is made to flood the dry dock so the *Pennsylvania* can be floated out into the harbor to avoid damage from the burning destroyers.

Minutes later at 0930 hours, several more bombs strike the *Cassin* and *Downes*.

At 0941 hours, ammunition stored in the magazines of the *Cassin* and *Downes* exploded. A torpedo in one of the tubes on the *Cassin* ignited from the terrific heat, then slammed into the forward deck of the *Pennsylvania*, penetrating several decks where the war head exploded, causing a massive fire in a paint locker containing highly flammable aluminum paint.

At 1010 hours, the dock is flooded and the *Cassin* and the *Downes* were both completely covered in flames from bow to stern. Leaking oil from their ruptured fuel tanks ignited, burning the paint on the bow of the *Pennsylvania*. Fire hoses from the dock are trained on the *Cassin*, but there are no hoses to use on the *Downes*. Slowly, the *Cassin* rolled off her mooring blocks, crashing into the Downes.

While the Cassin is rolling over, a 500-pound bomb dropped from an altitude of about 12,000 feet slammed into the *Pennsylvania*, penetrating down two decks before exploding near the number seven five-inch gun. It created a 20" by 20" hole in the casement deck and the same size hole leading down into the next deck.

The number nine five-inch gun was put out of action by explosions in lower decks. Additional damage is done to the galley, where oil fires burned out of control. Ammunition service equipment for the number three .50 caliber machine gun on the quarter deck, and the 3" antiaircraft gun was also put out of commission.

Fires spread below decks to several foreword compartments, and it was noticed that the degaussing cable has several cuts due to bomb hits.

Another bomb strike near casement nine killing 26 sailors and 2 officers.

At 1030 hours, a motor launch was sent to west loch for ammunition. By 1800 hours, all ammunition for usable guns was replenished.

Crews worked feverishly, knocking down fires throughout the *Pennsylvania* in order to keep stored ammunition in threatened magazines, and full fuel bunkers from exploding.

Once the fires were controlled, the decision is made to leave *Pennsylvania* in dry dock so repairs could be made before moving her out into the harbor. All damage was repaired at Pearl Harbor and the *Pennsylvania* was fit for action by April of 1942.

During the attack, the *Pennsylvania's* guns fired 650 rounds of 5" shells, 350 rounds of 3" shells, and 60,000 rounds of .50 caliber machine gun ammunition.

USS Utah

The *Utah* was berthed on the south side of Ford Island among a group of heavy cruisers. She had been taken off battleship status in 1931 and then became a radio-controlled target ship for other battle ships and aircraft to use as a target. Her hull number was changed from BB-31 to AG-16. Most of her guns and other combat equipment had been removed to make the ship lighter and more maneuverable.

As the Japanese planes came over the harbor, Fuchida ordered his men to leave the *Utah* alone as it was no longer a combat ship. However, six torpedoes were fired at the ship, with two making contact. Since all the water tight doors had been removed, the ship flooded quickly. In just fifteen minutes she had rolled over. Her entire war lasted just fifteen minutes.

Over the next few days, crews began using cutting torches to attempt to rescue the men inside. Sadly, they were only able to pluck four men out of the wreck. Like the *Arizona,* there are still men entombed on the ship. Out of a crew of 471 men, 58 never made it out of the tangled wreck.

Destroyers Cassin and Downes in dry dock with the Pennsylvania

Japanese bombers attacked the destroyers with a vengeance. No one knows exactly how many bombs struck the two ships. However, massive fires were started on both ships that detonated ammunition magazines and torpedoes. The explosions ripped massive holes in the hulls while bending deck plates and bulkheads.

With all fires extinguished, engineers looked over the wrecks deciding the cost to rebuild the ships was more expensive than building two new vessels. All usable equipment including several gun turrets was removed and sent to Mare Island Naval Station in New York. After cleaning and maintenance work was completed, they were mounted on new destroyers under construction.

By February 5, 1942, the wreckage of the two ships had been pulled from the dry dock and sold for scrap, which would eventually be used to build new ships.

Destroyer USS Shaw in dry dock near the Pennsylvania

From 0755 to 0920 hours, the *Shaw* was the recipient of three bombs, ranging in size from 200 to 300 pounds. All three bombs penetrated several decks before exploding. Heavy damage was reported to the chart house, forecastle deck, ward room and crews mess. The explosions ruptured several fuel bunkers allowing oil fires to spread throughout the ship quickly.

At approximately 0930 hours, the forward magazine detonated, resulting in a catastrophic explosion that literally ripped the bow off the ship, from frames 35-65. Pieces of the ship actually came down on Battleship Row and areas north of the harbor. Many workers on the base were knocked off their feet by the massive shock wave.

The decision was made to cease fire fighting operations as it was determined that the ship would need to be scrapped.

With the fires finally out and the hull cooled, engineers entered the dry dock. They realized that the keel of the ship was still sound and straight. With the use of cranes and other heavy equipment, the bow was raised from the bottom of the dry dock, straightened, and set back in place. Through January of 1942, workers reattached the hull and made the forward section of the ship mostly water tight. On February 9, 1942, she sailed to San Francisco under her own power. August 31, 1942, the *Shaw* was back in service and went on to serve in several battles in the Pacific. She was taken out of service in 1945, shortly after the war ended. In 1946 she was sold for scrap.

USS Raleigh, light cruiser: Berthed on the south side of Ford Island. Between 0755 and 0800 hours, a torpedo smashes through the hull of the ship just below the armor plating. Fire rooms #2, #3 flooded along with the forward machinery room. Number three boiler had power up for sailing, but was killed by flooding. At 0900 hours, a 500-pound bomb dropped by a dive bomber penetrates the main deck down to deck three, then out through the side of the hull without exploding. However, one ammunition ready box is damaged along with the forward fuel bunker releasing oil into the harbor and inside the ship. The bomb explodes on the bottom of the harbor, damaging frame #13. Ship begins to heel over, so two nearby barges are brought alongside to keep the ship from rolling. Everything on the main deck that can be tossed overboard to reduce listing is tossed into the harbor. Captain Robert Simmons* orders counter-flooding of magazines and several holds, which helps stabilize the vessel. She is towed to dry dock on February 3, 1942. After repairs are made, she sails to Mare Island Naval Base in New York for refit and further repairs. She rejoins the fleet in early 1943.

USS Helena, heavy cruiser. Berthed near the Raleigh on south side of Ford Island. Torpedo strike about 0800 hours penetrated starboard side 18 feet below water line, near frame 75. Most damage to third deck, with six inches of water covering floor before flooded area sealed. Main power generator knocked out of service, but auxiliary unit on line quickly giving power to all guns. Deck plates on deck three buckled, along with several bulkheads. Fires below decks in plotting room and forward distribution room are extinguished quickly.

Four near miss bombs create no damage but sailors were hurt by flying shrapnel. Bomb hit on 1.1-inch gun near frames 39-49 puts gun out of action and kills one man. Most injuries on *Helena* were caused by flash burns when the torpedo exploded in the gang ways that were filled with sailors running toward their battle stations.

> *USS Sotoyomo, harbor tug. Berthed near dry dock YFD2 where the Shaw exploded. Shrapnel from the Shaw ruptures her hull and she sinks quickly. Engineers consider her a total loss, but after raising her, it is decided she can be rebuilt cost effectively.*
>
> *USS Sumner survey ship. Moored by the submarine base. Shrapnel from exploding bomb damages one antiaircraft gun, killing several sailors.*
>
> *USS Pyro, ammunition ship. Several near miss bombs damage hull and deck features. She was already berthed at buoy B-13 awaiting rebuild.*
>
> *USS Rigel destroyer tender. Berthed alone in west loch, had hull and deck damage from three near miss bombs.*
>
> *USS Tangier, sea plane tender. Berthed south side of Ford Island. Several close bomb hits buckle outer hull plates. Flooding quickly maintained.*
>
> *USS Henley, a destroyer. Berthed south side of Ford Island. Was strafed several times creating minor damage, especially to the lightly armored forecastle.*
>
> *USS Alwin, a destroyer. Damaged prop by near miss bomb. Berthed in east loch at buoy X-18.*
>
> *USS Cummings, a destroyer. Damage to hull and upper deck from near miss bomb. Berthed at buoy B-15, east loch.*
>
> *USS Bageley. a destroyer. Damage on the bow by near miss bomb. Berthed buoy 22 east loch.*
>
> *USS Huli, a destroyer. Moderate hull damage from near miss bomb. Tied up in east loch with four other destroyers side to side.*

USS Honolulu, light cruiser. Minor hull and upper deck damage from near miss bomb. Berthed in east loch at buoy 21, with cruiser USS St. Louis.

USS New Orleans, heavy cruiser. Berthed south side of Ford Island at buoy F-12. Damage from near miss bomb to hull, and shrapnel damage from bomb and torpedo attack on USS Raleigh.

USS Oglala, wooden mine layer. Although she was not hit by any weapons, a near miss bomb and a torpedo that struck close by, created several serious holes in her hull. She was raised and considered a total loss. But engineers decided she could be rebuilt cheaper than building a new vessel. After repairs, she sailed back to the United States for further work in December of 1942.

USS Curtiss, sea plane tender. The Curtiss was just one year old and berthed by herself at a buoy at the entrance to the middle loch, across from Ford Island. At 0845 hours, a damaged Japanese dive bomber slammed into her aft crane, tearing it off the deck and starting several fires. She was then attacked by several planes with machine gun fire and several near miss bombs. A bomb dropped on her superstructure penetrated down to the second deck, causing heavy damage and fires while damaging her aft engine room, several shops and her hanger deck. Fires were handled quickly. All damage was repaired by the end of December 1941, and she went back into service. Twenty men were killed.

USS Vestal, repair ship. The repair ship USS Vestal was berthed outside the Arizona, and had already taken two bomb hits that were meant for the battleship. The Vestal was struck on her starboard side by a bomb. It penetrated three decks, passing through the crew quarters and exploding below in the stores deck. Due to extreme fires forward, ammunition magazines needed to be flooded.

A second bomb on the starboard side passed through the carpenter shop and steamfitters shop before punching a five-foot hole on the bottom of the ship. The bomb never exploded.

When the *Arizona* exploded, every man on the deck of the Vestal was killed or thrown overboard, many with serious injuries. The skipper of the ship, Commander Cassin Young,* was one of those thrown overboard, along with many of his staff officers. When he heard his officers arguing about giving orders to abandon ship, Young said, "Hell no!" and began swimming back to the ship. After calling for a tug boat, the commander ordered full steam. Immediately, crew members began using fire axes to cut mooring lines to the *Arizona.*

When the tug arrived, the *Vestal* had created enough steam to back itself away from the *Arizona* inferno. Once the tug had the *Vestal* situated in the channel, it was determined the ship had two holes in the hull and would most likely sink. Commander Young sailed his ship to what is called Aiea Shoals in the southwest part of the harbor, off of McGrew's point where he beached his ship in 35 feet of water before it sank. Although the ship had sustained a tremendous amount of damage from the bombs and explosion of the *Arizona,* naval engineers decided to refit the ship and put her back in service.

ADDENDUM (D)

Takeo Yoshikawa / Bomb Plot Message

There was no way Japan could have arranged such a well laid out plan, without the help of a spy on the ground. Twenty-seven year old Takeo Yoshikawa,* a Japanese naval expert holding the rank of ensign, that worked in Japanese naval intelligence in Tokyo was picked to be that man.

While in the navy he had served time on battleships, submarines, and had been trained how to fly in the air wing. After much preparation, he sailed to Hawaii on the ocean liner *Nitta Maru,* under the alias of Tadashi Morimuru.* As the *Nitta Maru* docked at pier eight near the Aloha Tower on March

27, 1941, Vice Consul Otojiro Okuda* from the embassy stood by ready to greet him. Together, they drove to the consulate located at 1742 Nuuanu Avenue,* where Consul General Nagao Kita* greeted Yoshikawa, and conferred the title of chancellor upon him. At a welcoming party, he met most of the 234 employees that worked at the facility, and quickly began to decide which ones might be a help to him down the road. *(The Japanese Embassy is still at that address. Although there are some new buildings, the original security wall that surrounds the complex remains.)*

Being a senior member of the consulate, Yoshikawa was given a small cottage to live in behind the main building. However, within days, Yoshikawa went to work finding a second story apartment away from the consulate that over looked Pearl Harbor, so he could use it to spy on ship movement.

Knowing there was always a lot of information floating around the streets of a major naval base, he quickly became involved in the social life of Honolulu. He always carried a large roll of cash that he used to buy drinks and food, allowing him to make many friends. He spent countless hours getting local people and sailors intoxicated, in order to help him find out what bars, restaurants, and other social places that were favored by American sailors while they were on leave, and he also diligently studied ship schedules. Quickly he built the reputation as quite a ladies man, while building a small group of trusted Japanese men he could use to help gather information.

Although his supervisors in the embassy looked down on his behavior and felt he went too far, Yoshikawa was widely known to visit bath houses and Geisha houses of ill repute on a regular basis, where he collected volumes of information from intoxicated sailors and soldiers.

In the hills above Honolulu in Alewa Heights, he found a Japanese restaurant called Shunch-Ro on Makanani Drive,* that had large glass windows overlooking Pearl Harbor and Hickam Field. To make viewing better, the owner also rented out telescopes to her customers. The restaurant was built with small private dining rooms that could be rented for an evening, which was a custom in Japan. Since the establishment was owned by a woman that came from the same prefecture in Japan as Yoshikawa, she was always happy to save a room and a telescope for an up-and-coming diplomat that spent large amounts of money.

On many afternoons, he had John Mikami,* who owned a cab for hire, drive him around Oahu, especially close to the military bases. Not trusting cameras or note pads, everything he saw he committed to memory before sending it off to Japan. If he was not sure about something, he would go back a second time to make sure he had his information correct, but that did not happen often, as he had close to a photographic memory. If it was not possible to hire John for the afternoon, he would have Richard Kotoshirodo,* a consular finance clerk drive him around in the consulates 1937 Ford. Although Kotoshirodo was of Hawaiian /Japanese descent, he totally believed the Pacific should be for the Asian people, and the white people needed to leave. It also did not take long for Yoshikawa to find out that reading every newspaper written on Oahu was a must. Each paper would write daily articles as to which ships were sailing from the harbor, or what offsite training the army was taking part in, or what officers were promoted or were leaving the Pearl Harbor area.

Some days Yoshikawa would dress shabbily and hire himself out as a day laborer working in the Pineapple fields close to military bases in order to understand how each base operated.

Other days he would spend time on a hill slope south of Pearl Harbor where he could watch submarines and their tenders come and go. He also enjoyed going to Pearl City where they had a large civilian pier where he could observe the far side of Ford Island. It did not take long for Yoshikawa to know where the best spots were to watch what was happening at each base, and he returned often to note changes. He had learned that American Patrol planes seldom patrolled the north coast of Oahu, which was important information on Sunday, December 7.

As he had been trained in aviation in the Japanese navy, he quickly passed the test to obtain a certified pilots license. With license in hand, Yoshikawa went to the small John Rodger's Airport* that used to be located on Ke'ehi Lagoon in Honolulu. Renting small planes allowed him to see all the bases from the air, filling blanks in his information. He loved flying south out of

Honolulu where he could pass over the entrance to Pearl Harbor to get a birds eye view of how the gates worked, and how often they were closed. He had attempted many times to enter the gate areas on the ground, but was always turned away by sentries.

Yoshikawa was nothing short of stellar when it came to finding ways to check out the Harbor. Many times, he slipped into the water, only to swim under the surface breathing through a reed. He would only break the surface to get his directions straightened out so he could view whatever it was he was looking for on that particular day.

Not wanting to bring his group of spies into the actual consulate, many nights he would meet them at the gate to the grounds. They would stand there for hours, smoking cigarettes and trading information, while Yoshikawa would hand out their next assignments.

In 1936, German intelligence sent Bernard Julius Otto Kuehn* to Hawaii to seek out similar information that Yoshikawa was looking for. However, it was apparent that Kuehn did not have the skills possessed by Yoshikawa, as the information he sent to Berlin was generally less than helpful. However, Berlin felt it was important to have a spy on the ground with a European face, one that would be able to step up to the plate once Japan made their move, and Asian people would no longer be trusted.

Yoshikawa was not interested in working with Kuehn, as the Honolulu police and naval authorities were already aware of Kuehn's misguided intentions, though they never attempted to arrest him. However, under orders from Nagao Kita,* Yoshikawa met with Kuehn in mid-1941 to give him operational documents and $14,000 dollars in emergency operating money.

On September 24, 1941, Yoshikawa received the following message from Captain Ogawa* in Tokyo. It was marked, message 83, now known as the bomb plot message.

> *"Henceforth, please make your reports concerning vessels along the following lines.*
>
> 1. *The waters of Pearl Harbor are to be divided roughly into 5 sub areas. We have no objection to your abbreviating as much as you like. Area "A" waters between Ford Island and the arsenal, Area "B" waters adjacent to the island south and west of Ford Island. (This*

> *area is on the opposite side of the island from area "A")*
>
> 2. *Area "C" east loch. Area "D" middle loch, Area "E" west loch and the communicating water routes.*
> 3. *With regard to warships and aircraft carriers, we would like to have you report on those at anchor (these are not so important) tied up at wharves, buoys and the docks. (Designate types and classes briefly. If possible, we would like to have you make mention of the fact when there are two or more vessels along the same side of same wharf.)*

Yoshikawa agreed he would send them an updated map every two weeks, or more often if large movement of ships caused concern.

Kimmel and General Short were never made aware of the bomb plot message that had been decoded in early October. Kimmel argued at his court martial that a message of this type contained a very strong inference that an air attack was being planned and was probably imminent. As the Court Martial continued, the Chief of Naval War Plans in Washington persisted that it seemed proper to hold that type of intelligence in his own environment so it could not be leaked back to the Japanese that we were aware of what they were up to.

Mid November, 1941, Japanese Lieutenant Commander Suguru Suzuki* arrived in Hawaii on the *Taijo Maru*.* His diplomatic visa stated he was there for only a brief visit to discuss issues with the Consul General Nagao Kita.* Arriving at the Consulate, he handed Kita a crumpled up piece of rice paper he had hidden inside his clothing that was addressed to Yoshikawa. It contained a list of 97 very specific questions regarding operations at Pearl Harbor and several of the Air Bases on Oahu. The instructions told Yoshikawa that all the answers had to be sent to Tokyo within 24 hours. After delivering the message, Suzuki was taken back to the pier where he once again boarded the *Taijo Maru* for a return trip to Japan.

Many of the questions were easy for Yoshikawa to answer, but several of them were very specific questions that needed to be investigated in order to answer them. Exactly 24 hours later, Yoshikawa had coded and sent the answers back to Japan. He stated this was the first time he realized an attack against the United States was imminent.

Then on December 2, he received the following message:

Tokyo to

Honolulu

2 December1941

"In view of the present situation, the presence in port war-ships, airplanes carriers and cruisers is of utmost importance. Hereafter to the utmost of your ability. Let me know day by day. Wire me in each case whether or not there are any observation balloons above Pearl Harbor or if there are any indications that they will be sent up. Also advise whether or not the warships are provided with anti-mine (anti-torpedo) nets."

Although there have been many unanswered questions regarding what Washington knew or didn't know about the bomb plot plan, the above memo was found in Washington D.C. marked, *"Decoded and received Washington D.C. 23 December 1941."*

On the morning of December 6, 1941, Yoshikawa was instructed to send one more message to Japan regarding what was going on in Pearl Harbor by no later than 10:00pm local Hawaiian time.

Yoshikawa coded and sent the message at the time requested. When it arrived in Japan, it was immediately given to Adm. Yamamoto, and sent on to Adm Chuichi Nagumo aboard the aircraft carrier Akagi, leading the task force toward Hawaii.

The note arrived on the bridge of the Akagi at 0120 hours when the fleet was about 350 nautical miles northwest of Hawaii. It said;

"Vessels moored in harbor, 9 battleships, 3 class "B" cruisers, 3 seaplane tenders, 17 destroyers. Entering harbor are 4 class "B" cruisers, 3 destroyers. All aircraft carriers and heavy cruisers have departed harbor. No indication of any changes in U.S. Fleet activities. Relaxed air coverage, no barrage balloons, or aircraft carriers in sight."

By noon on December 7, 1941 everyone in the Japanese consulate was aware of the attack, and the Honolulu police department had sealed the building placing everyone on house arrest, allowing no one to enter or leave.

Yoshikawa and several of his men were arrested, but only Yoshikawa was considered to be a serious threat, so the others were released. For some reason he was booked under his alias of Tadashi Morimuru.

In mid-December he was taken to the Coast Guard Station where he was placed on a ship for San Diego. He was held there for several months of interrogation, but the investigators were never able to identify his real name of Ensign Yoshikawa. Had they found out he was a Japanese naval officer, he probably would have been sentenced to a prolonged period of incarceration or shot for being a military spy. Instead, he was sent to a Japanese internment camp in Arizona. In July of 1942, he was sent back to Japan in a swap for several high ranking American and British diplomats that were being detained in Tokyo. After the war he was shunned by the new Japanese government which refused to give him a pension. Unable to find employment, he opened up a candy store. However, people refused to buy his wares as they blamed him for the atomic bomb attack. He and his wife lived off the money she was able to make selling insurance. Yoshikawa spent his last years in a nursing home, penniless and very sick. He told a reporter, "I have been wiped clean from Japanese history. Five years ago, when I applied for a pension, they said, 'We never heard of you.' On February 20, 1993, at the age of eighty, Yoshikawa, Japan's only spy in World War Two, quietly passed away.

ADDENDUM (E) THE WINDS MESSAGE

For code purposes, Japan used what they called a PURPLE machine to encode all the top secret information they wanted to send to their embassies around the world. In the United States, all collected PURPLE intercepts were classified with the word MAGIC. The one mistake that was made with the MAGIC decryption plan, was that one of the cipher machines that was supposed to go to station HYPO in Pearl Harbor, ended up in England, and was never replaced. The Navy's code breaking group OP-20G, led by Commander Lawrence Safford,* was the primary collector of MAGIC intercepts in Washington D.C. Although Safford had collected the best analysts in the business, there were always disagreements among the team as to which information was pertinent and should be passed along the chain of command to what was called the Twelve Apostles.

The apostles were The President, Secretary of War Henry Stimson, Secretary of State Cordell Hull, Chief of Staff General George C. Marshall, Secretary of the Navy Frank Knox, Chief of Naval Operations Admiral Harold Stark, Secretary of the General Staff Colonel Walter Bedell Smith, Head of Arm War Plans General Leonard T. Gerow, Head of Navy War Plans Division Admiral Richmond Kelly Turner, Assistant Chief of Naval Operations Admiral Royal Ingersoll, Chief of Army Intelligence Division General Sherman Miles, and Head of Naval Intelligence Division Admiral Theodore S. Wilkinson.

What most people working in the cryptology office thought was strange, was that the list did not include General Hap Arnold, Chief of the Army Air Corp, or any of America's overseas commanders in Hawaii or the Philippines.

A few of the important intercepts the cryptologists thought of as a waste of time were as follows.

1. An intercept received on November 2 that stated if negotiations were not completed by November 29, things were automatically going to happen.

2. A message on November 5, 1941 from Tokyo to their embassy in Washington stated that a November 25, 1941 deadline had been set for the completion of negotiations with Washington. That was important because the Japanese Fleet was already set to sail for Pearl Harbor on November 27, 1941.

3. Another major message that was overlooked was on November 20, 1941. It informed all Japanese embassies with clear instructions on how they were to destroy their cipher machines.

The most controversial and misunderstood message that came through OP-20G before the war was on November 19, 1941. It was a message from Tokyo to their embassy in Washington D.C. setting out details for a "WINDS EXECUTE" message. The message was supposed to be added to the end of a Japanese news broadcast in case a state of war with the United States, England or Russia was impending. The message was to be read five times at the beginning and end of each transmission.

The November 19 message, Circular No. 2353, stated, *"Regarding to the broadcast of a special message in an emergency the following will be added in the middle of the daily Japanese language short wave news broadcast.*

In case of a Japan - U.S. Relations in danger Higashi No Kazeame (East Wind Rain)

Japan - USSR relations Kitanokaze Kumori (North Wind Cloudy)

Japan - British relations Nishi No Kaze Hare (West Wind Clear)

A second circular No. 2354 arrived somewhat later, it said:

"If it is Japan - U. S. relations: Higashi

Japan - Russia relations: Kita

Japan - British relations including Thai, Malaya and Netherlands East Indies, Nishi."

The intercept added, "The proper message will be repeated five times including at the beginning and end. Messages would be relayed to Rio de Janeiro, Mexico City and San Francisco."

The message was allegedly intercepted by many Allied listening stations around the world, but none of them had a complete message or stated it was garbled. The Singapore station sent the message to U.S. Asiatic Fleet Headquarters. The commander there, Admiral Thomas Hart,* resent the message to the fourteenth and sixteenth naval districts.

United States Consul General Walter Foote* in Batavia resent the message to the United States State Department, but added a footnote saying, *"I attach little or no importance and view it with some suspicion. Such has been common since 1936."*

Since the intercept was sent through the Japanese J-19 diplomatic code, and not the secure PURPLE code, the information was getting mixed reviews from many top state department and military officials. To be on the safe side, the navy notified all of its listening stations, including Commander Rochefort in Hawaii, to be watchful for any type of Japanese intercept having a phrase that included any part of the WINDS code. If anyone was to pick up the message, they were to contact Colonel Rufus Bratton, Commander of the Army Intelligence Far Eastern Section, immediately.

On December 4, 1941, at Station "M" at Cheltenham, Maryland, a radio operator stated he had picked up the words, *"East Wind Rain,"* in a weather broadcast from Japan. He stated he immediately sent his message to the appropriate agencies.

By 0900 hours on December 4, 1941, Lieutenant Commander Alvin Kramer, Commander of the Translation Section of the Navies Communication Unit, received a copy of the message from Cheltenham. Feeling this was the notice that an attack was imminent, he sent copies to all the proper command units, including the White House. As usual, no one contacted the overseas commanders in Hawaii or the Philippines.

Although there were disagreements over the message and what it actually inferred, during several investigations, George Linn,* a naval officer assigned to OP-20G, spent some time going through high security Japanese messages while searching for the alleged WIND message from Maryland. During several investigations he stated under oath, *"I found nothing, and therefore concluded that an execute had not been received prior to 2400 hours, 6 December 1941."*

In chasing down the possible WINDS message, things began to break down. The staff decoder in Maryland, a Mr. Ralph Briggs,* contradicted the date he alleged picked up the WINDS message. He said he intercepted it on the evening of December 4, while Safford claimed it arrived on the night of December 3. To make matters worse, the log book Briggs logged all his messages in states he received it on December 2, 1941.

Lieutenant Commander Alvin Kramer stated later that the WINDS execute intercept he had was actually dated December 5 and it only had three lines of text. He felt the WINDS message he looked over appeared to refer to a war between Japan and Britain. He added that, "It was a false alarm of the WINDS system. It was nevertheless, definitely my conception at the time, that it was an authentic broadcast of that nature."

In an investigative paper titled "East Wind Clear," written by Robert J. Hanyok* and David Mowry* in 2011 for the Center for Cryptologic History, they state there was in fact a WINDS message sent. But it was after the attack on Pearl Harbor on December 7, 1941. They state that the weight of the evidence indicates that one coded phrase "WEST WIND CLEAR" was broadcast according to previous instructions, some six to seven hours after the attack. They add that, "a British listening post might have picked up the broadcast one to two hours after the attack, but this only substantiates the anticlimactic nature of the actual broadcast."

In their closing statement they write, "There simply was not one shred of actionable intelligence in any of the messages or transmissions that pointed to the attack on Pearl Harbor."

Commander Safford argued to the day he died on May 15, 1973, that the WINDS message did in fact exist. However, there has never been any documentation discovered to back up his claims. He emphatically stated that the United States had a four-day warning of the attack and did nothing.

However, General George C. Marshall, Chief of Staff of the Army, and Commander Rochefort at Pearl Harbor, both stated under oath they had never seen any WINDS messages, and denied covering up the material.

After World War Two as American forces rounded up Japanese officials, Shinroku Tanomagi,* the Head of the Overseas Department of Japan's Broadcasting Corporation was brought in for questioning. He stated he never authorized such a message, and that he did not remember ever sending out any such coded message prior to December 7, 1941.

The cryptologists in Washington D.C. were kept busier than normal watching for the possibility of a WINDS message, while dealing with the fact that Japan changed its fleet code on November 1, 1941, and again on December 1, 1941. Intercepts piled up as cryptologists worked to break the new codes, and if there had been a WINDS message, it may simply have been over looked or misplaced or wrongly coded.

ADDENDUM (F) MEN OF COURAGE

Throughout all the rescue efforts, the top military officials on Oahu quickly heard stories of unbelievable acts of courage by both officers and enlisted men. It took time to sort out all the claims and interview the men and the witnesses that could verify the incidents to make sure the proper medals were handed out. It was not until February of 1942 that the first Congressional Medal of Honors were handed out. The process continued into 1943 before all the men deserving of the Medal of Honor received their awards.

Fifteen men were awarded the Congressional Medal of Honor for their outstanding heroism. Below are the words from their actual Medal of Honor awards.

Captain Mervyn S. Bennion:* For conspicuous devotion to duty, extraordinary courage and complete disregard of his own life, above and beyond the call of duty. During the attack of 7 December 1941 as commanding officer of the USS *West Virginia*, after being mortally wounded, Capt. Bennion evidenced apparent concern only in fighting and saving his ship, and strongly protested against being carried from the bridge. He remained on post guiding his crew to save the ship. He died at his post on the bridge, never attempting to leave his vessel or seek aid.

Lt. John W. Finn:* For conspicuous bravery during the attack by Japanese airplanes on the Naval Air Station, Kaneohe Bay on 7 December 1941, Lt. Finn promptly secured and manned a .50 caliber machine gun and mounted it on an instruction stand in a completely exposed section of the parking ramp, which was under enemy machine gun strafing fire. Although painfully wounded many times, he continued to man this gun and return the enemy's fire vigorously and with telling effect throughout the enemy strafing and bombing attacks and with complete disregard for his own personal safety for nearly two and a half hours. It was only by specific orders that he was persuaded to leave his post and seek medical attention. Following first aid treatment, although suffering much pain and moving with great difficulty, he returned to the squadron area and actively supervised the rearming of returning planes. His extraordinary heroism and conduct in this action were in keeping with the highest traditions of the U.S. Naval Service.

Ensign Francis Flaherty:* For conspicuous devotion to duty and extraordinary courage and complete disregard of his own life, above and beyond the call of duty, during the attack of the fleet in Pearl Harbor, by Japanese forces on 7 December 1941. When it was seen that the USS *Oklahoma* was going to capsize and the order was given to abandon ship, Ensign Flaherty remained in a turret, holding a flashlight so the remainder of the turret crew could see to escape, thereby sacrificing his own life.

Captain Samuel G. Fuqua:* For distinguished conduct in action, outstanding heroism, and utter disregard of his own safety above and beyond the call of duty during the attack on the fleet in Pearl Harbor, by Japanese forces on 7 December 1941. Upon Commencement of the attack, Lt. Commander Fuqua rushed to the quarterdeck of the USS *Arizona* to which he was attached where he was stunned and knocked down by the explosion of a large bomb which hit the quarterdeck, penetrated several decks, and started a severe fire. Upon regaining consciousness, he began to direct the fighting of the fire and rescue of wounded and injured personnel. Almost immediately there was a tremendous explosion forward, which made the ship appear to rise out of the water, shudder, and settle down by the bow rapidly. The whole forward part of the ship was enveloped in flames which were spreading rapidly. Wounded and burned men were pouring out of the ship to the quarterdeck. Despite these conditions, and while severe enemy bombing and strafing existed, Lt. Commander Fuqua continued to direct the fighting of fires in order to control them. He was instrumental in working out a process to get the wounded and burned removed from the ship. He continued to supervise the rescue of these men in such an amazingly calm and cool manner and with such excellent judgment, that it inspired everyone who saw him and undoubtedly resulted in the saving of many lives. After realizing the ship could not be saved and that he was the senior surviving officer aboard, he directed it to be abandoned, but continued to remain on the quarterdeck and directed abandoning ship and rescue of personnel until satisfied that all personnel that could be had been saved, after which he left the ship with a boat load of injured. The conduct of Lt. Commander Fuqua was not only in keeping with the highest traditions of the naval service but characterizes him as an outstanding leader of men.

Chief Boatswain Edwin J. Hill:* For distinguished conduct in the line of his profession, extraordinary courage, and disregard of his own safety during the attack on the fleet in Pearl Harbor by Japanese forces on 7 December 1941. During the height of the strafing and bombing, Chief Boatswain Hill led his men of the line handling details of the USS *Nevada* to the quays, cast off the lines and swam back to the ship. Later while on the forecastle, attempting to let go the anchors, he was blown overboard and killed by the explosion of several bombs.

Ensign Herbert C. Jones:* For conspicuous devotion to duty, extraordinary courage, and complete disregard of his own life, above and beyond the call of duty, during the attack on the fleet in Pearl Harbor, by the Japanese forces on 7 December 1941. Ensign Jones organized and led a party, which was supplying ammunition to the antiaircraft battery of the USS *California* after the mechanical hoists were put out of action when he was fatally wounded by a bomb explosion. When two men attempted to take him from the area that was on fire, he refused to let them do so, saying in words to the effect. "Leave me alone! I am done for. Get out of here before the magazines go off."

Rear Admiral Issac C. Kidd:* For conspicuous devotion to duty, extraordinary courage and complete disregard of his own life, during the attack on the fleet in Pearl Harbor, by Japanese forces on 7 December 1941, Rear Admiral Kidd immediately went to the bridge and, as commander Battleship Division One, courageously discharged his duties as Senior Officer present afloat until the USS *Arizona*, his flagship, blew up from magazine explosions and a direct bomb hit on the bridge that resulted on the loss of his life.

Lt. Jackson C. Pharris:* For conspicuous gallantry and intrepidity at the risk of his life above and beyond the call of duty while attached to the USS *California* during the surprise enemy Japanese attack on Pearl Harbor, Territory of Hawaii, 7 December 1941. In charge of the ordnance repair party on the third deck when the first Japanese torpedo struck almost directly under his station, Lieutenant (then Gunner) Pharris was stunned and severely injured by the concussion which hurled him to the overhead and back to the deck. Quickly recovering, he acted on his own initiative to set up a hand-supply ammunition train for the antiaircraft guns. With water and oil rushing in where the port bulkhead had been torn up from the deck, with many of the remaining crew members overcome by oil fumes, and the ship without power and listing heavily to port as a result of a second torpedo hit, Lieutenant Pharris ordered the shopfitters to counter flood. Twice rendered unconscious by the nauseous fumes and handicapped by his painful injuries, he persisted in his desperate efforts to speed up the supply of ammunition and at the same time repeatedly risked his life to enter flooding compartments and drag to safety unconscious shipmates who were gradually being submerged in oil. By his inspiring leadership, his valiant efforts and his extreme loyalty to his ship and her crew, he saved many of his shipmates from death and was largely responsible for keeping the California in action during the attack. His heroic conduct throughout this first event engagement of World War Two reflects the highest credit upon Lieutenant Pharris and cohances the finest traditions of the United States Naval Service.

Radio Electrician Thomas J. Reeves:* For distinguished conduct in the line of his profession, extraordinary courage, and disregard for his own safety during the attack on the fleet in Pearl Harbor, by Japanese forces on 7 December 1941. After the mechanized ammunition hoists were put out of action in the USS *California*, Reeves on his own initiative in a burning passageway, assisted in the maintenance of an ammunition supply by hand to the anti-aircraft guns until he was overcome by smoke and fire, which resulted in his death.

Machinist Donald K. Ross:* For distinguished conduct in the line of his profession, extraordinary courage, and disregard of his own life during the attack on the fleet in Pearl Harbor, Territory of Hawaii, by Japanese forces on 7 December 1941. When his station in the forward dynamo room of the USS *Nevada* became almost untenable due to smoke, steam, and heat. Machinist Ross forced his men to leave the station and performed all duties himself until blinded and unconscious. Upon being rescued and resuscitated, he returned and secured the forward dynamo room and proceeded to the after-dynamo room where he was later again rendered unconscious by exhaustion. Again, recovering consciousness, he returned to his station where he remained until directed to abandon it.

Machinist Mate First Class Robert R. Scott:* For conspicuous devotion to duty, extraordinary courage and complete disregard of his own life above and beyond the call of duty, during the attack on the fleet in Pearl Harbor by Japanese forces on 7 December 1941. The compartment, in the USS *California*, in which the air compressor, to which Scott was assigned as his battle station, was flooded as the result of a torpedo hit. The remainder of the personnel evacuated that compartment but Scott refused to leave, saying words to the effect, "This is my station and I will stay and give them air as long as the guns are going."

Chief Watertender Peter Tomich: For distinguished conduct in the line of his profession, and extraordinary courage and disregard of his own safety, during the attack on the fleet in Pearl Harbor by the Japanese forces on 7 December 1941. Although realizing that the ship was capsizing, as a result of enemy bombing and torpedoing, Tomich remained at his post in the engineering plant of the USS *Utah*, until he saw that all boilers were secured and all fire room personnel had left their stations, and by so doing lost his own life.

Captain Franklin Van Valkenburgh: For conspicuous devotion to duty, extraordinary courage and complete disregard of his own life, during the attack on the fleet in Pearl Harbor Territory of Hawaii by Japanese forces on 7 December 1941. As commanding officer of the USS *Arizona*, Capt. Van Valkenburgh gallantly fought his ship until the USS *Arizona* blew up from magazine explosions and a direct bomb hit on the bridge that resulted in the loss of his life.

Seaman First Class James R. Ward: For conspicuous devotion to duty, extraordinary courage and complete disregard of his life, above and beyond the call of duty, during the attack on the fleet in Pearl Harbor by Japanese forces on 7 December 1941. When it was seen that the USS *Oklahoma* was going to capsize and the order was given to abandon ship, Ward remained in a turret holding a flashlight so the remainder of the turret crew could see to escape, thereby sacrificing his own life.

Commander Cassin Young: For distinguished conduct in action, outstanding heroism and utter disregard of his own safety, above and beyond the call of duty, and commanding officer of the USS *Vestal*, during the attack on the fleet in Pearl Harbor, Territory of Hawaii, by enemy Japanese forces on 7 December 1941. Commander Young proceeded to the bridge and later took personal command of the 3-inch antiaircraft gun. When blown overboard by the blast of the forward magazine explosion of the USS *Arizona*, to which the USS *Vestal* was moored, he swam back to his ship. The entire forward part of the USS *Arizona* was a blazing inferno with oil afire on the water between the two ships; as a result of several bomb hits, the USS *Vestal* was afire in several places, was settling and taking on a list. Despite severe enemy bombing and strafing at the time, and his shocking experience of having been blown overboard, Commander Young, with extreme coolness and calmness, moved his ship to an anchorage distant from the USS. *Arizona*, and subsequently beached the USS *Vestal* upon determining that such action was required to save his ship.

ADDENDUM (G) – THE FOURTEEN PART MESSAGE

Note from the author: Below is the entire text of the message that was handed to Cordell Hull by the Japanese Ambassador. The message was sent in 14 parts beginning on Saturday morning. The fourteenth part which declares war, did not arrive in Hull's office until after the attack had begun.

Point 1. The government of Japan, prompted by a genuine desire to come to an amicable understanding with the Government of the United States in order that the two countries by their joint efforts may secure the peace of the Pacific Area and thereby contribute toward the realization of world peace, has continued negotiations with the utmost sincerity since April last with the Government of the United States regarding the adjustment and advancement of Japanese-American relations and the stabilization of the Pacific Area.

The Japanese Government has the honor to state frankly its views concerning the claims the American Government has persistently maintained as well as the measure the United States and Great Britain have taken toward Japan during these eight months.

Point 2. It is the immutable policy of the Japanese Government to insure the stability of East Asia and to promote world peace and thereby to enable all nations to find each its proper place in the world.

Ever since the China Affair broke out owing to the failure on the part of China to comprehend Japan's true intentions, the Japanese Government has striven for the restoration of peace and it has consistently exerted its best efforts to pre-

vent the extension of war-like disturbances. It was also to that end that in September last year Japan concluded the Tripartite Pace with Germany and Italy.

However, both the United States and Great Britain have resorted to every possible measure to assist the Chungking regime so as to obstruct the establishment of a general peace between Japan and China, interfering with Japan's constructive endeavors toward the stabilization of East Asia. Exerting pressure on the Netherlands East Indies, or menacing French Indo-China, they have attempted to frustrate Japan's aspiration to the ideal of common prosperity in cooperation with these regimes. Furthermore, when Japan in accordance with its protocol with France took measures of joint defense of French Indo-China, both American and British Governments, willfully misinterpreting it as a threat to their own possessions, and inducing the Netherlands Government to follow suit, they enforced the assets freezing order, thus severing economic relations with Japan. While manifesting thus an obviously hostile attitude, these countries have strengthened their military preparations perfecting an encirclement of Japan, and have brought about a situation which endangers the very existence of the Empire.

Nevertheless, to facilitate a speedy settlement, the Premier of Japan proposed, in August last, to meet the President of the United States for a discussion of important problems between the two countries covering the entire Pacific area. However, the American Government, while accepting in principle the Japanese proposal, insisted that the meeting should take place after an agreement of view had been reached on fundamental and essential questions.

Point 3. Subsequently, on September 25th the Japanese Government submitted a proposal based on the formula proposed by the American Government, taking fully into consideration past American claims and also incorporating Japanese views. Repeated discussions proved of no avail in producing readily an agreement of view. The present cabinet, therefore, submitted a revised proposal, moderating still further the Japanese claims regarding the principal points of difficulty in the negotiation and endeavored strenuously to reach a settlement. But the American Government, adhering steadfastly to its original assertions, failed to display in the slightest degree a spirit of conciliation. The negotiation made no progress.

Therefore, the Japanese Government, with a view to doing its utmost for averting a crisis in Japanese-American relations, submitted on November 20th still another proposal in order to arrive at an equitable solution of the more essential and urgent questions which, simplifying its previous proposal, stipulated the following points:

(1) The Government of Japan and the United States undertake not to dispatch armed forces into any of the regions, excepting French Indo-China, in the Southeastern Asia and the Southern Pacific area.

(2) Both Governments shall cooperate with the view to securing the acquisition in the Netherlands East Indies of those goods and commodities of which the two countries are in need.

(3) Both Governments mutually undertake to restore commercial relations to those prevailing prior to the freezing of assets.

The Government of the United States shall supply Japan the required quantity of oil.

(4) The Government of the United States undertakes not to resort to measures and actions prejudicial to the endeavors for the restoration of general peace between Japan and China.

(5) The Japanese Government undertakes to withdraw troops now stationed in French Indo-China upon either the restoration of peace between Japan and China or establishment of an equitable peace in the Pacific Area; and it is prepared to remove the Japanese troops in the southern part of French Indo-China to the northern part upon the conclusion of the present agreement.

As regards China, the Japanese Government, while expressing its readiness to accept the offer of the President of the United States to act as 'introducer' of peace between Japan and China as was previously suggested, asked for an undertaking on the part of the United States to do nothing prejudicial to the restoration of Sino-Japanese peace when the two parties have commenced direct negotiations.

The American Government not only rejected the above-mentioned new proposal, but made known its intention to continue its aid to Chiang Kai-shek; and in spite of its suggestion mentioned above, withdrew the offer of the President to act as so-called 'introducer' of peace between Japan and China, pleading that time was not yet ripe for it. Finally on November 26th, in an attitude to impose upon the Japanese Government those principles it has persistently maintained, the American Government made a proposal totally ignoring Japanese claims, which is a source of profound regret to the Japanese Government.

Point 4. From the beginning of the present negotiation the Japanese Govern-

ment has always maintained an attitude of fairness and moderation, and did its best to reach a settlement, for which it made all possible concessions often in spite of great difficulties. As for the China question which constitutes an important subject of the negotiation, the Japanese Government showed a most conciliatory attitude. As for the principle of non-discrimination in international commerce, advocated by the American Government, the Japanese Government expressed its desire to see the said principle applied throughout the world, and declared that along with the actual practice of this principle in the world, the Japanese Government would endeavor to apply the same in the Pacific area including China, and made it clear that Japan had no intention of excluding from China economic activities of third powers pursued on an equitable basis. Furthermore, as regards the question of withdrawing troops from French Indo-China, the Japanese Government even volunteered, as mentioned above, to carry out an immediate evacuation of troops from Southern French Indo-China as a measure of easing the situation.

It is presumed that the spirit of conciliation exhibited to the utmost degree by the Japanese Government in all these matters is fully appreciated by the American Government.

On the other hand, the American Government, always holding fast to theories in disregard of realities, and refusing to yield an inch on its impractical principles, cause undue delay in the negotiation. It is difficult to understand this attitude of the American Government and the Japanese Government desires to call the attention of the American Government especially to the following points:

1. The American Government advocates in the name of world peace those principles favorable to it and urges upon the Japanese Government the acceptance thereof. The peace of the world may be brought about only by discovering a mutually acceptable formula through recognition of the reality of the situation and mutual appreciation of one another's position. An attitude such as ignores realities and impose (sic) one's selfish views upon others will scarcely serve the purpose of facilitating the consummation of negotiations.

Of the various principles put forward by the American Government as a basis of the Japanese-American Agreement, there are some which the Japanese Government is ready to accept in principle, but in view of the world's actual condition it seems only a Utopian ideal on the part of the American Government to attempt to force their immediate adoption.

Again, the proposal to conclude a multilateral non-aggression pact between Ja-

pan, United States, Great Britain, China, the Soviet Union, the Netherlands and Thailand, which is patterned after the old concept of collective security, is far removed from the realities of East Asia.

2. The American proposal contained a stipulation which states - 'Both Governments will agree that no agreement, which either has concluded with any third power or powers, shall be interpreted by it in such a way as to conflict with the fundamental purpose of this agreement, the establishment and preservation of peace throughout the Pacific area.' It is presumed that the above provision has been proposed with a view to restrain Japan from fulfilling its obligations under the Tripartite Pact when the United States participates in the war in Europe, and, as such, it cannot be accepted by the Japanese Government.

The American Government, obsessed with its own views and opinions, may be said to be scheming for the extension of the war. While it seeks, on the one hand, to secure its rear by stabilizing the Pacific Area, it is engaged, on the other hand, in aiding Great Britain and preparing to attack, in the name of self-defense, Germany and Italy, two Powers that are striving to establish a new order in Europe. Such a policy is totally at variance with the many principles upon which the American Government proposes to found the stability of the Pacific Area through peaceful means.

3. Whereas the American Government, under the principles it rigidly upholds, objects to settle international issues through military pressure, it is exercising in conjunction with Great Britain and other nations pressure by economic power. Recourse to such pressure as a means of dealing with international relations should be condemned as it is at times more inhumane than military pressure.

4. It is impossible not to reach the conclusion that the American Government desires to maintain and strengthen, in coalition with Great Britain and other Powers, its dominant position in has hitherto occupied not only in China but in other areas of East Asia. It is a fact of history that the countries of East Asia have for the past two hundred years or more have been compelled to observe the status quo under the Anglo- American policy of imperialistic exploitation and to sacrifice themselves to the prosperity of the two nations. The Japanese Government cannot tolerate the perpetuation of such a situation since it directly runs counter to Japan's fundamental policy to enable all nations to enjoy each its proper place in the world.

BELOW IS PART FOURTEEN THAT WAS HELD

UNTIL SUNDAY MORNING

The stipulation proposed by the American Government relative to French In-do-China is a good exemplification of the above- mentioned American policy. Thus, the six countries, - Japan, the United States, Great Britain, the Netherlands, China, and Thailand, - excepting France, should undertake among themselves to respect the territorial integrity and sovereignty of French In-do-China and equality of treatment in trade and commerce would be tantamount to placing that territory under the joint guarantee of the Governments of those six countries. Apart from the fact that such a proposal totally ignores the position of France, it is unacceptable to the Japanese Government in that such an arrangement cannot but be considered as an extension to French In-do-China of a system similar to the Nine Power Treaty structure which is the chief factor responsible for the present predicament of East Asia.

5. All the items demanded of Japan by the American Government regarding China such as wholesale evacuation of troops or unconditional application of the principle of non-discrimination in international commerce ignored the actual conditions of China, and are calculated to destroy Japan's position as the stabilizing factor of East Asia. The attitude of the American Government in demanding Japan not to support militarily, politically or economically any regime other than the regime at Chungking, disregarding thereby the existence of the Nanking Government, shatters the very basis of the present negotiations. This demand of the American Government falling, as it does, in line with its above-mentioned refusal to cease from aiding the Chungking regime, demonstrates clearly the intention of the American Government to obstruct the restoration of normal relations between Japan and China and the return of peace to East Asia.

Point 5. (sic) In brief, the American proposal contains certain acceptable items such as those concerning commerce, including the conclusion of a trade agreement, mutual removal of the freezing restrictions, and stabilization of yen and dollar exchange, or the abolition of extra-territorial rights in China. On the other hand, however, the proposal in question ignores Japan's sacrifices in the four years of the China Affair, menaces the Empire's existence itself and disparages its honor and prestige. Therefore, viewed in its entirety, the Japanese Government regrets it cannot accept the proposal as a basis of negotiation.

Point 6. The Japanese Government, in its desire for an early conclusion of the negotiation, proposed simultaneously with the conclusion of the Japanese-American negotiation, agreements to be signed with Great Britain and other interested countries. The proposal was accepted by the American Government. However, since the American Government has made the proposal of November 26th as a result of frequent consultation with Great Britain, Australia, the Netherlands and Chungking, and presumably by catering to the wishes of the Chungking regime in the questions of China, it must be concluded that all these countries are at one with the United States in ignoring Japan's position.

Point 7. Obviously, it is the intention of the American Government to conspire with Great Britain and other countries to obstruct Japan's effort toward the establishment of peace through the creation of a new order in East Asia, and especially to preserve Anglo-American rights and interest by keeping Japan and China at war. This intention has been revealed clearly during the course of the present negotiation.

Thus, the earnest hope of the Japanese Government to adjust Japanese-American relations and to preserve and promote the peace of the Pacific through cooperation with the American Government has finally been lost.

The Japanese Government regrets to have to notify hereby the American Government that in view of the attitude of the American Government it cannot but consider that it is impossible to reach an agreement through further negotiations. December 7, 1941

EPILOGUE – AMERICA

*Sadie Merchant (Darnell), wife of Paul Darnell, returned to Montana where she lived with her parents for several years. She delivered a healthy baby boy that she named Paul Darnell, Junior. She married an insurance broker in 1946, and had two more children. She was never able to bring herself to visit Pearl Harbor, although Paul Junior visited several times. Sadie passed away at the age of 87 in 2009.

*Chief Petty Officer Herman Keppers who directed Cooper to help fight fires in the vents on the Tennessee served on several ships during the war. He retired from the Navy in 1955. He then worked on Fire Fighting Boats in the Port of Seattle for fifteen years until retiring in 1970. He died in a car accident in 1997.

*Chief Petty Officer Alfred Morrow, who enlisted Cooper and Paul, was seriously injured when a plane he was flying in was shot down in the Solomon Islands in 1943. After recuperating from his injuries, he went back to being a recruiter. After retiring in 1961, he and his wife retired to Dallas Texas, to be near to her parents. He witnessed the assassination of President Kennedy on November 22, 1963. The Chief passed away from cancer in 1976.

*Ed Wilkinson owner of the Double D Ranch died of a heart attack in 1952.

*John Winslow, foreman of the Double D Ranch, took over the operation of the ranch for Ed's widow until 1965, when he retired. He passed away quietly in his sleep, in March 1980.

*Lieutenant George Welch moved on with his naval career after Pearl

Harbor, shooting down twelve more enemy aircraft during the war. His combat tour ended after catching a bad case of Malaria in 1943. He went on to be a test pilot for the Air Force and was killed ejecting during a test flight of a F-100 Super Sabre fighter in 1951 when the plane began to disintegrate in mid-flight.

*Lieutenant Kenneth Taylor returned to fighter status when his wounds healed. He shot down one more enemy plane near Guadalcanal. His war ended after his leg was severely broken during an air raid on Henderson Field. He later returned to war duty training pilots in the United States. He served a total of 27 years in the army, rising to the rank of Brigadier General, commanding the Alaskan Air National Guard until his retirement in 1985. He passed away in Tucson, Arizona in 1986.

*Father Henry McCloud continued working at the Pearl Harbor Hospital until June of 1943. He then took an assignment with the Second Marine Division. He was with them when they invaded Tarawa in November of 1943. He was last seen crawling forward to help several wounded marines. After pulling the first man back to safety, he crawled forward a second time, but was never heard from again.

* Lieutenant Norman, Hospital Point, December 7, 1941. The Lieutenant survived the invasion at Guadalcanal and Tarawa, but was seriously wounded during the invasion of Peleliu in 1944. He remained in the marines, climbing to the rank of Colonel in 1966 when he retired. He and his wife and two children lived in Seattle, Washington, where he worked for the city government for ten years. He passed away in 1997 from cancer.

*Petty Officer John Finn was awarded the Medal of Honor at Kaneohe and lived to be 100 years old.

*Lieutenant Kermit Tyler, who told the men at Opana Point to ignore the radar screen, was never implicated for dereliction of duty. He spent four years in the marines and twenty-two in the air force, retiring from the military as a lieutenant colonel in 1961, then becoming a very successful Realtor. He testified before several Boards of Inquiry and believed his participation kept him from getting a higher rank. He passed away January 23, 2010 at the age of 96.

*Scott Dowdle, from Irving Texas, went down with the destroyer USS *Jarvis* after it had been badly damaged in the battle of Savo Island.

*Cy Brewster was in naval hospitals until January, 1944. He lost several fingers on both hands due to infection and neither hand ever worked properly after being burned so badly. Surgeons did the best they could do for his shattered hip, but he was left with a painful limp. Several months after returning home, he walked out into his parents back yard with his father's pistol and committed suicide.

*Lieutenant Landon White was shot down twice more during the war, but survived both crashes. With his left leg shattered after his last crash, he went on to teach air combat maneuvers in Pensacola, Florida until after the war. He married a nurse he met while in the hospital, and settled down in her home town of Wheeling, West Virginia. He became a vice president for Eastern Airlines. He died of a heart attack in 1991.

*Ensign Wesley Evans recuperated from his injuries and was assigned his own SBD Avenger. He was killed during a bombing raid over New Britain in 1944.

*Ensign George Gay flew off the U.S.S. *Hornet* during the battle of Midway. He attacked the carrier Soryu under tremendous antiaircraft fire. As the ship was zigzagging his torpedo missed. He attempted to fly away but his plane was being struck by heavy enemy fire. While skimming just above the water a Zero shot him down killing his rear machine gunner. As the plane began to sink, he pulled out the cushion he was sitting on, and used it to cover his head in the water to avoid being strafed by enemy planes. He spends thirty hours in the water and is rescued the next day. He is the only witness to the sinking of three of the Japanese carriers. After the war he flew for TWA Airlines for thirty years. He gave many speeches about his ordeal and helped in putting together the movie "Midway."He died of a heart attack on 10-21-1994. After his body was cremated, his ashes were spread in the Pacific over the coordinate the *Hornet* had been at when they launched the Midway attack.

*Griffin Westberry from the *Arizona*, went back to the United States where he became part of the crew on the new carrier *Essex*. He served on the ship until late 1944, when he was assigned to the new carrier USS *Valley*

Forge. He retired from the navy in 1972 after 32 years of service. With his wife Pat and their three children, he lived in Galveston, Texas where he worked for Pat's father in a textile mill. He died from natural causes in 2002. His ashes were interred on the *Arizona.*

* Maria Schoenburg, Scott's girlfriend, moved to Phoenix, Arizona to live with her parents after Scott was killed. She went back to school and received a degree in nursing, working at Banner University Medical Center in Phoenix for 28 years. She married a doctor at the hospital and had three children. She died of kidney failure in 2001.

*Admiral Nimitz had a splendid naval career throughout World War One and Two. He was promoted to five-star admiral in World War Two and was never taken off active-duty status. After leaving command of the Pacific Fleet, he took the job of Chief of Naval Operations until 1947. He spent much of his retired life attempting to build better relations with Japan and raised millions of dollars for their reconstruction. Nimitz wrote numerous letters to the Nuremberg war crimes tribunal, testifying as to why German naval officers should not be prosecuted for the use of unrestricted submarine warfare, as the United States also used it in both oceans during the war. In late 1947, he was appointed as ambassador to Pakistan, but they refused to have him. While the Nimitz family lived in Berkeley, California, he served as regent for the University of California from 1948-1956. He then served in several charity organizations until suffering a serious fall in 1964. They then took up residence at the Yerba Island Naval Officers quarters. The Admiral passed away at home on February 2, 1966. He was buried on February 24, the day of his eighty-first birthday. He was buried in the Golden Gate National Cemetery in San Bruno, California. By prior arrangement, Nimitz and his wife Catherine are buried next to Admiral Raymond Spruance, Admiral Richmond Kelly Turner, and Admiral Charles Lockwood.

* Admiral Halsey served in many billets during World War One and Two. Although being a sailor, many marines were stunned when Halsey was given overall command of the South Pacific. They found him to be very fair as he listened to marine commanders in every battle. He served in command of the fifth fleet during the battle of Leyte Gulf, the largest naval battle in the history

of the world. He also served with distinction in several other major naval actions during World War Two. When preparing for the surrender ceremony in Tokyo Bay, he still mistrusted and had great disdain for the Japanese military. He was worried some Japanese pilots might attempt to crash their planes into the Missouri during the ceremony. He told the pilots that were flying cover over the bay, "If any Japanese airplanes appear, shoot them down in a friendly way." Halsey retired in March of 1947, with the rank of five-star admiral. He was never taken off active-duty status. After retirement, Halsey made a 28,000-mile good will trip through South and Central America. In 1946, he joined the Sons of the American Revolution. In 1951, he was hired by ITT and American Cable and Radio Corp. until 1957. He died of a major heart attack in Fishers Island New York on August 18, 1959, at the age of 76. He was buried on August 20 in Arlington National Cemetery. His wife Francis is also buried there.

*Admiral Raymond Spruance is considered the best admiral that has ever served in the history of the United States Navy. He was highly decorated in World War One, and became one of the best overall planners and fleet commanders of World War Two. He and Admiral Halsey took turns commanding the main Pacific Fleet throughout the war. He replaced Admiral Nimitz as Commander of U.S. Pacific Forces when Admiral Nimitz stepped down after the war ended. He retired from the Navy on July 1, 1948. He then became president of the U.S. War College. In 1952, President Truman assigned him as Ambassador to the Philippines. He stayed there until 1955 when he resigned. He filled many positions in the government and private sector throughout the rest of his life. He passed away on December 13, 1969 at the age of eighty-three at his home in Pebble Beach, California. He and his wife are buried near Admiral Nimitz in the Golden Gate National Cemetery in San Bruno, California.

*Admiral Fletcher was awarded the Congressional Medal of Honor in 1914 during World War One during the battle of Veracruz. He served in nearly every large naval battle of World War Two, retiring from the navy in 1947. As most of his personal papers were destroyed during the war, he refused to reconstruct them or to be interviewed by Admiral Samuel Elliot Morrison, who wrote the history of the United States Navy in World War Two. In his later life, he felt he was cheated out of the recognition he should have received in Morrison's writings. He passed away four days short of his eighty-eighth birthday at the family estate near Araby, Maryland. He and his wife Martha (Richards) Fletcher are buried in Arlington Cemetery.

*Commander Rochefort, code breaker at Station Hypo Pearl Harbor. The work of Station Hypo was so accurate that Nimitz trusted it more than the intelligence operations in Washington. This angered Admiral King, Chief of Naval Operations, so much that he removed the commander from anything to do with intelligence, transferring him to the command of dry dock ABSD-2 in San Francisco. When Admiral Nimitz put Rochefort in for the Navy Distinguished Service Cross, King refused, saying, "Rochefort was one of the most unmilitary-looking officers he ever encountered." Rochefort retired from the Navy in 1953 at the rank of Captain. He led a quiet life after the war, doing some writing, but he never bad-mouthed Admiral King for how he had been treated. He passed away on July 20, 1976, in Torrance California. He is buried in Inglewood Cemetery in Inglewood, California. On May 30, 1986, a ceremony took place in the Roosevelt Room of the White House, where President Ronald Reagan presented the Distinguished Service Medal posthumously to Rochefort's son, Joseph Junior and his daughter, Janet, an honor that was well overdue.

*Cooper Dodge. Cooper and Lily had two daughters, Aolani and Pualani. Cooper worked in the U.S. Navy weapons department at Pearl Harbor until retiring in 1975. He then worked part time at the Pearl Harbor Historical Museum until 1990. After suffering a major heart attack, Cooper decided to permanently retire. After recovering from the heart attack, he settled into working in his beloved rose gardens behind their house, and became part time baby sitter for his four grandchildren. On November 20, 2005 Cooper, laid down to take a nap after working in the rose gardens and never woke up. He is buried along with Lily in the National Cemetery of the Pacific, commonly known as the Punch Bowl. Cooper was 83.

*Lily Dodge took a full time job as a nurse at the St. Francis Medical Center in Honolulu, which she loved very much. She retired from the hospital in 1980. She then worked part time in a senior retirement center not far from their home. She enjoyed helping Cooper in the rose gardens and looking after their grandchildren. Lily made sure that Cooper and Dierdra visited each other at least every three years, most often in Hawaii. Lily passed away in 2010, at the age of 87. She is also buried in the National Cemetery of the Pacific with Cooper.

*Aolani (Cooper) Kapuli. Aolani married a full-blooded Polynesian man named Tai Kapuli, who taught language skills at the University of Hawaii, where Aolani worked as a teacher's assistant. They had two girls and loved hiking the many nature trails of Oahu and the other islands in the Hawaiian chain. Aolani and her husband are still alive as of this writing and live in Honolulu.

*Pualani (Cooper) Lawrence. Pualani and her husband Chad Lawrence live on the island of Maui where Chad and his brother own a Toyota Dealership in Lahaina. Pualani graduated from college with a degree in education, and teaches fifth grade at a grade school nearby. They had one daughter and one son. Pualani and Chad are both alive and living in Lahaina as of this writing.

EPILOGUE – JAPANESE

*Admiral Isoroko Yamamoto was the overall commander of the Combined Japanese Fleet. He planned the attacks on Pearl Harbor and the Battle of Midway in 1942. By that point, the United States had broken Japan's purple code and knew every step they were making, which led to Japan's defeat at Midway. Commander Joseph Rochefort in Station Hypo informed Admiral Nimitz of an upcoming base inspection planned by Yamamoto. A very secret Operation named Vengeance was put into action. On April 18, 1943, American P-38 lightning fighters out of Kukum Field in Guadalcanal ambushed the naval transport plane Yamamoto was flying in. The plane crashed and exploded on the Island of Bougainville in the Solomon Islands. His ashes were flown back to Tokyo for burial.

*Prime Minister Hideki Tojo, also known as the Razor for his anger and sharp tongue, was also a general in the Imperial Army. Although he worked well with the navy, he had contempt for its top leaders, throughout the entire war. He was a ruthless man who fully authorized much of the brutality in the Pacific. General MacArthur put out a warrant for his arrest immediately as the war ended. He was captured at his home giving no resistance, and accepted guilt for all the charges against him. He was found guilty of war crimes and was hung on December 23, 1948.

*Prince Kanin Kotohito retired from the Army in 1940. However, he came back to be part of the Imperial War Council. He died in Odawara, Kanagawa, Japan at his summer home on May 5, 1945, from a massive infection.

*Fuimaro Konoye was prime minister as the war broke out with China. He worked hard to bring about peace, but was unable to work with Tojo and the other militarists. He resigned his position on October 18, 1941, allowing Tojo to become Prime Minister. Konoye continued being a chief aide to the emperor throughout the war. He committed suicide on December 16, 1945.

*Admiral Osami Nagano was one of the chief planners of the Pearl Harbor attack. He was promoted to Naval Chief of Staff on April 4, 1941. In 1943, he was sent to sea to become a fleet commander. After terrible defeats, he was demoted to shore duty in 1944. He was arrested and charged with war crimes, but had a major heart attack while on trial. He died on January 5, 1947.

*Yosuke Matsuoka was a high-ranking Japanese diplomat. He wrote and signed the Tri Partite Act with Germany and Italy. He signed several nonaggression pacts with Russia, but refused to attack German assets when Russia went to war with Germany. He was arrested in 1945 and held at Sugamo Prison to await trial. He died of natural causes June 26, 1946, before his trial began. In 1979, he was enshrined in the Yasukuni Shrine with twelve other Japanese war criminals.

*General Hoime Sugiyama was an ardent supporter of the war in the west against China, and heavily advocated for the war against the United States and England. He held many commands in China and Tokyo during the war. He was given the job of disbanding the army in 1945, as commanded by MacArthur and the Emperor. When he had finished sending out all the final orders of surrender to commanders, he sat down behind his desk and shot himself in the chest four times before dying. His wife committed the same ritual at their home at the same time. They are buried in Tama Cemetery in Tokyo, Japan.

*Admiral Chuichi Nagumo was a favorite officer of Admiral Yamamoto. Because of his extreme loyalty, he was placed in charge of the fleet that attacked Pearl Harbor and Midway in 1942. After Japanese naval forces were defeated in battles around Guadalcanal, Nagumo was demoted and placed in charge of a small task force of ships in the Marianas. After Admiral Ozawa was horribly defeated in the Philippine Sea battle on June 15, 1944, Nagumo took charge of ground forces on Saipan. After the invasion of Saipan by American forces on July 6, 1944, Nagumo committed ritual suicide in a cave. His remains were discovered in the cave by U.S. marines.

*General Takuma Nishimura was one of the top Japanese officials involved in the capture of Singapore. He was charged with crimes against humanity for the Sook Ching Massacre. He was sentenced to life in prison. After serving four years in Singapore, he was repatriated to Japan to serve out the rest of his sentence. While his ship was in Hong Kong, Australian military police took him from the ship and transferred him to Manus Island, where he was tried for war crimes in the Perit Sulong Massacre. He was found guilty and hanged on June 11, 1951. There have been several investigations as to whether he was actually involved in the Perit Shillong Massacre or if he was used for political reasons to close the case.

*Admiral Fukudome was a career naval officer before the war began. He was involved in high level discussions regarding Pearl Harbor and other Japanese war plans. When the war ended, he was arrested and questioned in Tokyo December 9-12, 1945, by American Rear Admiral Ofstie. After the interrogation was completed, Ofstie said that Fukudome was intelligent and spoke freely of Japanese plans. He shared his vast knowledge of the inner workings of the war ministry. He was charged with war crimes, but finally released. He became a major advisor to the emperor in setting up Japan's new self-defense force after the war. He passed away January 1, 1971.

*General Tsuji Masanobu was an ardent supporter of Japan going to war with China, Britain and the United States. He was considered one of Japan's most aggressive and influential militarists. He led many of the army forces in the war against China, and was wanted for many war crimes. He avoided prosecution by escaping to the mountains in Japan. However, he returned in 1949, and was easily elected to the ruling Diet. After people began bringing up his war crimes, he escaped to Laos in 1961. Rumor had it that he worked with both the Laotian and North Vietnamese Armies in their war against the United States. There is no record of his death. The rumor that he worked with the North Vietnamese army against the United States is true.

*Emperor Hirohito. General Douglas MacArthur understood full well that if the Allied governments either removed Hirohito from power, or found him guilty of war crimes, the surrender document would become null and void, and a new war would begin. Although many American politicians disagreed, the decision to leave him in power was final. After the new civilian government was established, he renounced his divinity and signed the new constitution. His position as emperor became just a figurehead after that. Hirohito died from cancer on January 7, 1989, at the age of 87.

GOVERNMENT INQUIRIES

Changes came quickly after the attack on December 7, 1941. President Roosevelt fired Admiral Kimmel, replacing him with Admiral Nimitz, who was not able to take over the position until December 31, 1941, due to issues with the job he had at the time. Lieutenant General Delos C. Emmons* was ordered to replace General Short. Emmons arrived in Oahu on December 17, 1941.

However, that did not absolve President Roosevelt of his anger regarding the events of the Japanese attack. He felt the lack of preparedness throughout the command structure on Oahu needed to be addressed at the highest level, and he wanted the guilty parties held accountable. He ordered an immediate inquiry into the attack led by Supreme Court Chief Justice Owen J. Roberts.*

Along with Roberts, were Admiral William H. Standley,* Admiral Joseph M. Reeves,* General Frank R. McCoy,* and General Joseph T. McNarney.* They began their investigation in Washington, D.C. on December 22, 1941. When they were finished interviewing witnesses there, the panel moved to Hawaii, where they concluded their investigation on January 10, 1942. During the investigation they interviewed 127 witnesses, including Admiral Husband E. Kimmel and General Walter C. Short, the commanders at Pearl Harbor on December 7, 1941.

After deliberation, the panel voted unanimously to find both Kimmel and Short guilty of dereliction of duty. Both men were forced to retire immediately.

Since many politicians of the day felt the Robert's Commission was nothing short of a kangaroo court, there were nine more inquires held between 1941 and 1946, and a tenth inquiry, named the Dorn Report in 1995.

All the investigations found fault with other officers, but none of them were subjected to charges, as Kimmel and Short had been.

The Army Pearl Harbor Board of Inquiry of 1944 found the following;

"The chief of staff of the Army George C. Marshall, failed in his relations with the Hawaiian Department in the following particulars:

A. To keep the Commanding General of the Hawaiian Department fully advised of the growing tenseness of the Japanese situation which indicated an increasing necessity for better preparation for war, of which information he had in abundance and Short had little.

B. To send additional instructions to the Commanding General of the Hawaiian Department on 28 November 1941, when evidently, he failed to realize the import of General Short's reply of 27 November which showed clearly that General Short had misunderstood and misconstrued the message of 27 November and had not adequately alerted his command for war.

C. To get to General Short on the evening of 6 December and the early morning of 7 December 1941 the critical information indicating an almost imminent break with Japan, though there was ample time to have accomplished this. Chief of War Plans D, War Department General Staff, Major General Leonard T. Gerow, failed in his duties in the following respects.

a. To send to the commanding General of the Hawaiian Department on 27 November 1941, a clear, concise directive; on the contrary, he approved the message of 27 November 1941, which contained the confusing statements.

b. To realize that the state of readiness reported in Short's reply to the 27 November message was not a state of war readiness, and he failed to take corrective action."

The Naval Court of Inquiry on Pearl Harbor in 1944 found the following;

"It is the prime obligation of Command to keep subordinate commanders, particularly those in distant areas, constantly supplied with information. To fail to meet this obligation is to commit a military error.

It is a fact that Admiral Stark, as Chief of Naval Operations and responsible for the operation of the Pacific Fleet, and having important information in his possession during this critical period, especially on the morning of 7 December 1941, failed to transmit this information to Admiral Kimmel, this depriving him the latter of a clear picture of the existing Japanese situation as seen in Washington.

The court is of the opinion that Admiral Kimmel's decision, made after the dispatch of 24 November 1941, to continue preparations of the Pacific Fleet for war, was sound in light of the information then available to him.

The court is of the opinion that Admiral Harold R. Stark, U.S.N., Chief of Naval Operations failed to display the sound judgment expected of him in that he did not transmit to Admiral Kimmel during the critical period 26 November through 7 December 1941, important information which he had regarding the Japanese situation, and especially on the morning of 7 December 1941, he did not transmit immediately the fact that a message had been received which appeared to indicate that a break in diplomatic relations was imminent, and that an attack in the Hawaiian area might be expected soon."

The Joint Congressional Committee report of 1946 found the following

The errors made by the Hawaiian commanders were errors of judgment and not dereliction of duty. The War Plans Divisions of the War and Navy Departments failed.

a. To give careful and thoughtful consideration to the intercepted messages from Tokyo to Honolulu of 24 September, 14 November, and 28 November (the Harbor bomb plot dispatches) and to raise a question as to their significance. Since they indicated a particular interest in the Pacific Fleet's base, this intelligence should have been appreciated and supplied to the Hawaiian Commanders for their assistance, along with other information available to them, in making their estimate of the situation.

b. To be properly on the qui vive (alert or lookout) to receive the one o'clock intercept and to recognize in the message that the fact that some Japanese military action would very possibly occur somewhere at 1 pm. 7 December. If properly appreciated this intelligence should have suggested a dispatch to all Pacific outpost commanders supplying this information, as General Marshall attempted to do immediately upon seeing it."

The Army Board for the Correction of Military Records (1991)

"The Army Pearl Harbor Board (of 1944), held that General Marshall and the Chief of War Plans Division of the War department shared in the responsibility for the disaster. The applicant in this case must show that the FSM (in this case General Short) was unjustly treated by the Army. The majority found evidence of injustice. In this regard, the majority was of the opinion that the FSM, singularly or with the Naval commander, was unjustly held responsible for the Pearl Harbor disaster.

Considering the passage of time as well as the burden and stigma carried until his untimely death in 1949, it would be equitable and just to restore the FSM to his former rank of lieutenant general on the retired list.

Recommendation, that all of the Department of the Army records, related to this case be corrected by advancing the individual concerned to the rank of lieutenant general on the retired list."

The Dorn Report (1995)

Responsibility for the Pearl Harbor disaster should not fall solely on the shoulders of Admiral Kimmel and General Short; it should be broadly shared.

It is clear today, as it should have been since 1946 to any serious reader of the JCC (Joint Congressional Committee) hearing record, that Admiral Kimmel and General Short were not solely responsible for the defeat at Pearl Harbor, the evidence of the handling of these (intelligence) messages in Washington reveals some ineptitude, some unwarranted assumptions and misestimates, limited coordination, ambiguous language, and lack of clarifications and follow-up at higher levels.

The fourteen-point message and the one o'clock message on the evening of December six point to war at dawn (Hawaiian Time) on the seventh, not to an attack on Hawaii, but officials in Washington were neither energetic nor effective in getting that warning to the Hawaiian Commanders.

In sum, I cannot conclude that Admiral Kimmel and General Short were victims of unfair official actions and thus I cannot conclude that the official remedy of advancement on the retired list is in order. Admiral Kimmel and General Short did not have all the resources they felt necessary. Had they been provided more intelligence and clearer guidance, they might have understood their situation more clearly and behaved differently. Thus, responsibility for the magnitude of the Pearl Harbor disaster must be shared. But this is not a basis for contradicting the conclusion, drawn consistently over several investigations, that Admiral Kimmel and General Short committed errors of judgment. As commanders they were accountable.

Senate Joint Resolution 2000

In 2000 Senate Joint Resolution 19 was passed requesting the president to give Admiral Kimmel and General Short the senior ranks they held before the attack on Pearl Harbor. Below is the resolution, but no president to this date has ever signed the resolution.

"S.J. Res. 19 – A joint resolution requesting the President to advance the late Rear Admiral Husband E. Kimmel on the retired list of the Navy to the highest grade held as Commander in chief, United States Fleet, during world War Two, and to advance the late Major General Walter S. Short on the retired list of the Army to the highest grade held as Commanding General, Hawaiian Department, during world War Two, as was done under the Officer Personnel Act of 1947 for all the senior officers who served in positions of command during World War Two, and for other purposes."

FINAL COMMENT

There is little doubt that historians will argue over who was at fault for the disaster at Pearl Harbor until the very end of time. Clearly there were mistakes made in the Hawaiian Command Structure, but there were most definitely egregious errors made by many officers and politicians in Washington D.C. as well. There is little doubt that Kimmel and Short should have been supplied with the information gleaned from the purple code Washington was translating on a daily basis, including the full fourteen-part message. As Admiral Kimmel stated early in December, "Why can't Washington send us all the pertinent information so we can get the entire picture for ourselves?"

What angers many people was that Kimmel and Short were demoted and forced into retirement to live in disgrace for the balance of their lives, when General Douglas MacArthur's Air Force was caught on the ground and destroyed, seven hours after learning about the attack on Pearl Harbor. MacArthur was neither forced to retire or demoted, in fact he was promoted upward to become a five-star general.

Additionally, Lieutenant Kermit Tyler was working the Information Center at Fort Shafter when the call came from Opana Point at 0715 hours regarding a large flight of planes coming in from the north. His response was, "Yeah, well don't worry about it." Had he alerted the command structure immediately, the attack on Pearl Harbor could have been totally avoided or greatly minimized. He survived all the inquires and retired a Lieutenant Colonel in 1961.

In the same vein, had Captain John Earl taken Lieutenant Kaminsky's information regarding the USS *Ward's* attack on a Japanese submarine early on the morning of December 7 seriously, the navy would have been alerted and ready to repel an attack. Earl continued in service, holding several important positions throughout the war. His record was never blemished for his failures.

Of the 2,341 service members that died on December 7, 1941, nearly half perished on the USS Arizona, a total of 1,177. There were 38 sets of brothers on board the *Arizona* including three sets of three brothers. The second largest loss of life came from the USS *Oklahoma* with 429 lost. From December, 1941 until June of 1942, the navy worked tremendously hard to recover remains from inside the *Oklahoma*. There were 394 sets of remains that were left unidentifiable after initial efforts were unsuccessful. They were buried in the National Cemetery of the Pacific in Honolulu. As of this writing, 361 sets of remains from the *Oklahoma* have now been identified through DNA testing at the Dover Air Force Base Mortuary Affairs Operation. Regrettably, there are still 33 sets of remains that are considered to be unidentifiable. Once remains were identified, they were returned to family members for final interment.

Today, too many young Americans have no idea what the attack on Pearl Harbor was all about. Consequently, they will never come to grips with the horrific cost in human lives sacrificed to bring peace back across the Pacific basin.

Regrettably, currently there is a large group of historians attempting to rewrite the history of World War Two in the Pacific, placing blame squarely on the shoulders of the United States, and many young people are believing their lies and disinformation. Yes, it is a fact that many high-ranking politicians and military officers made dreadful mistakes, but they all had to work with the information they had in front of them at the time. There was no satellite communications, no 24-hour news channels bringing them minute by minute updates from across the globe, and no satellite photographs they could use to make informed decisions. One must realize that in 1941, it could take hours or sometimes even days to get a message from Washington to Hawaii if weather conditions were favorable, and there was always that five-hour time difference that no one could ever overcome.

Eighty-two years ago, life stopped across the United States as news of the attack struck the American public like a sledge hammer. Most of the men and women who survived that attack are gone from this earth. Many of them took their stories with them, never allowing us to have their firsthand knowledge and insight into the attack to study. There are many questions about that fateful day that may never be answered, regardless of how much we search for those elusive bits and pieces of information. Pearl Harbor is a giant piece of history with a legacy all of its own that changed the world in countless ways.

I hope this book will help you keep the memory of Pearl Harbor alive throughout your lifetime and beyond. It is a story that should be passed on to future generations. We must never forget!

Gerry Feld

"There are no Great men, just great challenges which ordinary men, out of necessity, are forced by circumstances to meet."

~ Admiral William Halsey,
after the battle of Savo Island, 1943.